The Gifts of Man

The Gifts of Man

❡

S. M. McElligott

ISBN-13: 9781534732179
ISBN-10: 1534732179
Library of Congress Control Number: 2016910208
CreateSpace Independent Publishing Platform
North Charleston, South Carolina

Dedicated to my husband Jack
Who can always make me smile

Table of Contents

Map Illustrations

The Ancient Middle East

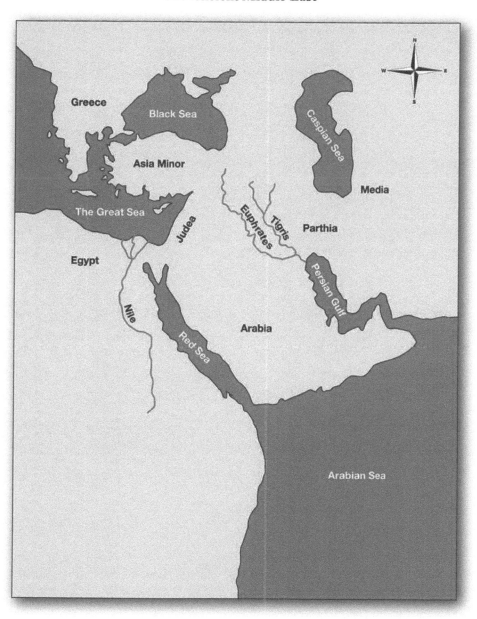

Acknowledgments

§

As a practicing Catholic, every year I would attend Mass on the Feast of the Epiphany and hear the Gospel relating the Visit of the Magi. Matthew Chapter 2:1-12 is the only place in the bible that mentions them. I was always intrigued by their story and would leave church often remarking to my husband: Those are three mysterious men! They come from nowhere in seek of the Messiah and return again to nowhere. What became of them? Did they care what happened to the baby they travelled so far to see? My husband would nod his head silently before hopping in the car. Finally one year after I retired, my husband said in response to my queries: You have the time now. Write their story.

There are many traditions concerning 'the wise men' and their countries of origins but nothing definitive. Their story as I imagined it includes not only their famous journey to Bethlehem, but the details of their lives before and after, including some very personal reasons for their journey. And yes, these characters bear the first Christmas gifts of gold, frankincense and myrrh to the Christ child, but they also bear gifts to each other, which in their way hold value beyond compare.

I am a firm believer that the greatest gifts of men are not the store bought packages under the tree but true gifts of the heart, a sharing of self that often involves sacrifice. I have been the grateful recipient of many such gifts in my life and especially while writing this story. Thus I would be remiss not to thank my family and the friends who encouraged me so steadily. I am particularly grateful to my mentor, Tom

Monteleone. His Borderlands Boot Camp was invaluable, and I highly recommend it to new and aspiring writers. Thanks also to my friend and writing buddy, Gail Tanzer, who helped critique my work, and who was the first to read my manuscript in its entirety. A big thank you to Kelly Carlson, the lovely young lady who designed the maps, and to Ashley Hoffman. And last but not least, my thanks to Elliot and Peggy Spiegel, Kathy Eschbach, Dorothy Gaines and Carol Showalter. Your friendship means so much.

Prologue

§

My name is Inaran. It means "ray of light". I didn't know at the time that my name had anything to do with my selection to watch over Melchior, but looking back, I understand. I am a Guardian, you see. What you humans often call angels. Don't look so surprised. Surely you have suspected we exist? No? Then perhaps you're one of the many who see only on the surface of life. You will never discover us that way.

Like you, we were created to share love, but we do it in the most challenging way: by watching over you, one on one, birth to grave. The before birth and after grave work is reserved, as you humans are fond of saying, for a higher pay grade than mine.

As you may suspect, I have interesting tales to tell. After many millennia of looking after The Holy One's most challenging creations, how could I not? Which reminds me of Melchior. He turned out to be one of my most interesting assignments. The tale I will recount is his, and that of his friends, Balthazar, Gaspar and Alima. We four Guardians who watched over them had our hands full. No wonder we shared the details of their lives, for our assignments were as inter-twined as their lives.

Book One

CHAPTER 1

Melchior

§

5 BC in Seleucia - a City in the Empire of Parthia

Not again! Thought Melchior. For the third time in a fortnight, wind-whipped sand pelted the house and flew through the un-shuttered window above his bed. Instinctively, he pulled the blanket over his face. After thirty-odd years, he knew to protect himself from the fine dust storms that blew from the eastern sky. How many had he known who had not done so only to suffer later? He'd seen them groping their way through Seleucia, short of breath, eyes swollen and red. In time, many went blind. Of course he couldn't be certain the haboobs caused their maladies, but it seemed a likely cause. His scholar's mind sought the threads of logic in nature, the connections between earth, sky, and man, and cursed the ignorance of those who ignored its truths.

As he waited for the storm to pass, he sat on his woven palm bed, pondering the day ahead. For weeks he and his friend, Gaspar, had poured over their charts, trying to reconcile what he had learned of the Messiah prophecies with their knowledge of Jewish astrology. Would today be the day when their work was finally recognized? Would they get their leader's approval for further study and help from their fellow astrologers? His mind whirled in anxious anticipation.

The storm had hardly abated when Bina entered his room. The old slave woman had served him since his birth, but slave or not, he took as much pleasure in her company as with an old friend. "Good morning, Bina. Quite a storm, was it not?"

"Yes, master. It left a covering on everything, including me. I'll be washing all day to be rid of it."

"But that is the way with haboobs. Like our kings, they leave an untidy trail behind."

"How well you know!" She set a crockery bowl before him, poured water into it from a glazed pitcher, and commenced to scrub the grit from his neck, face, and feet.

"This feels good," he said as she finished up. "See that you make time to wash when you leave me."

"Have I a choice? Your brother and his wife will never let me to serve them like this." A fine film clung to her clothing and her blotchy, sand-streaked skin resembled tree limbs bleached too long by the sun.

"They are unusually particular, aren't they?"

Bina raised her brows in what he knew was understated agreement.

"Can you have a bath ready for me later?"

"I can."

"And perhaps some duck for supper? You make it better than anyone."

Bina nodded. "I will search the market, if Dahab allows me to leave the house after my cleaning."

"That woman!" barked Melchior suddenly. "You are my servant, not hers. She will not dictate what you may and may not do. Tell her I commanded you!"

"I will do so gladly," said Bina with a slight smile.

"Good. Now help me dress quickly. I cannot be late for this meeting." Melchior dried his face and examined the clothes she placed out for him. "I like those," he said, pointing to a pair of loose-fitting ginger colored trousers and a short V-shaped tunic of blue silk.

Bina was accustomed to his routine, and followed it with the same precision every day. On his cue, she turned her back as he donned his clothes and when he announced "Ready," she stooped to tie his sandals, as he fastened a fine leather belt around his waist. Then she ran an ivory comb through his short curly hair and beard, attempting to remove any remnants of sand. "Will you wear your kulaf today?"

"Yes, but I'll put it on later."

"As you wish. Can I bring you breakfast? I made a stew of lentils and pine nuts."

"No, I haven't the time. I'll enjoy your duck all the more later."

"Then I'll try to find a fat one," said Bina as she bowed. Then she picked up the pitcher and bowl of dirty water, and preceded him out of the room.

As Melchior approached the entry courtyard he heard the raised voices of his mother and his brother's wife, Dahab. Hating the delay but with no desire to become embroiled in another of their quarrels, he waited in the adjoining hall where he could see them both.

"Really, mother-in-law, I don't understand the way you cling to these old ways!" said Dahab. "Our religion teaches good words, thoughts and deeds, just like yours. We even worship a single god like you Jews. But my children must be raised in the religion of our empire! Our faithfulness to the prophet Zarathustra will help ensure their advancement. I will not have them worshiping this foreign god of yours!"

He saw his mother's jaw tighten. "Jews are hardly foreigners in Parthia! It's true my ancestors came in bondage, but we have lived here over five hundred years! And you know that my husband allowed me to raise my sons in our Jewish tradition. It's our God, the God of Abraham and Moses, who has showered us with so many blessings." Dodi swept her arms out widely. "All of this is due to him!"

Dahab snickered. "My, you are a simple-minded old woman. Have you forgotten how this god of yours allowed your people to be massacred when you were a bride? Many thousands were killed, including some in your family! As I understand it, if you hadn't been away with your husband, you too would have fallen! What kind of blessing was that, I ask you? Our wealth is due to the hard work of our husbands! Your God had no part in it!"

Melchior shook his head, knowing his mother would not to be put off so easily. "But don't you see?" Said Dodi. "After that massacre our synagogues closed and our rabbis fled! Since then we've worshipped

5

only in secret. It's more important than ever to teach our young what our rabbis cannot."

Dahab drew closer to his mother and spoke with a vehemence Melchior had never heard. "Don't preach to me, old woman. Listen well! You have no say in this. My children are not Jews! You'd best keep your covenant and traditions to yourself." She raised a finger to Dodi's face. "Do not defy me. Mered and I alone, shall decide how our children will be schooled and it will not include your Jewish god."

"But . . ."

"There is nothing more to be said! If I hear a word that you're ignoring us, I'll see to it that you never see your grand-children again!" Dahab marched from the courtyard, brushing past Melchior in the hall as she left.

He wasted no time joining his mother in the courtyard where she sat on a stone bench staring at the fountain. "You're trembling, Mother. Are you all right?"

Dodi interlaced her shaking fingers. "In truth, I do not know. I never imagined Mered would thwart me on such a thing. And to have Dahab threaten me like that!"

"They are his children, Mother."

"Yes. But it's not right that they should be denied knowledge of the true God. You know how important it is. How your father allowed me to tutor you through childhood at great risk! If the king had known of my ancestry, your father would have lost his position as satrap."

Melchior took his mother's hand. "Father loved you, but he is dead two years. Mered rules the household now."

Dodi closed her eyes for a moment. "I know. But does what I taught him mean nothing? How can he turn his back on me and his ancestry? He won't allow me to teach the children, nor to make offerings. It's a sad day, my son."

"I know, mother, but try to think of it as Mered does. He's proud of father's accomplishments, but now that he's gone, Mered seeks new sources of pride and wealth. He wants to be recognized in his own right.

And he won't be seen taking orders from a woman, whether you be his mother or not."

"I understand his pride. And I know well enough how my womanhood binds my hands. But why should his wealth make a difference? This is not a question of wealth or influence."

"Mered and Dahab think it is. Mered has ambitions."

"Ambitions? He inherited your father's wealth as well as Dahab's father's lands. He's the wealthiest trader in Seleucia! What more can he want?"

"Father's old post. He wants the Seleucia satrapy."

"But doesn't he know that your father came to regret his appointment? That his friends avoided him and he never had a peaceful day in his life? Why would he seek such a thing?"

"Mered knows father's regrets, but he wants the power that comes with the post. And he worries that if the king finds out you are a Jewess, the satrapy will never be his."

"I see," said Dodi pressing her hands to her temples.

"Don't worry, Mother. I know how important the children are to you...so we must think of a way to convince Mered. Arguing with Dahab will achieve nothing." Melchior pulled her closer and gave her a gentle hug. "What will you do now? I know you don't give up easily."

"You're right, I won't give up. I will do what I've always done when life presented a challenge, I shall pray."

"Be careful, will you? I heard enough of your quarrel to know that Dahab won't tolerate any challenge to her authority."

"I'll try not to upset her, but I have a responsibility to my grandchildren. No threat can dissuade me."

Dodi kissed Melchior on the cheek, and together they walked out the courtyard gate. She headed uphill toward the estate's gardens, and he down toward Seleucia and the School of Astrology.

He walked with purpose, anxious to make up for lost time. The estate was soon far behind him as he trod on trying to ignore the pull of the glistening Tigris to his left. That winding serpent of a river displayed docks full of boats and playful children on its banks. Oh, to be a boy again splashing there! But the sweet memory had hardly receded when Seleucia loomed large before him. Plaster lions and dragons glared down from its high, thick walls. They were designed as symbols of Parthian power, but he was not convinced. Depending on his line of sight, the fiery dragons could wear a smile, and the lions' paws appear more apt to play than pounce. He thought them a strange mix of mirth and might; not unlike the confusing spectacle of Parthian politics itself.

Trudging past some large drifts left by the morning's storm, he arrived at one of Seleucia's seven gates. I've made good progress, he thought as he mounted the cobbled processional street. But he was only a few paces up the grand walkway when he was forced to stop as a large crowd loomed before him.

"You idiot..." He swore at himself. How could he forget the festival? Two by two, scores of chanting Zoroastrian priests strode before him, snaking their way from the fire temple at the city's center to the festival site outside the city. Nothing but delays today, he thought trying to calm himself. It would never do to let frustration show at his school.

Thirsty from his walk, he skirted the edges of the crowd making his way to a public fountain. There he drank his fill and refilled his leather water bladder. The timeworn troughs that brought river water to the fountains still worked well, and Melchior was glad of it, especially on a hot day like today.

He made his way down two wide avenues where the wealthy citizens lived, then veered off into an area of narrow streets inhabited by commoners. Though the houses were much smaller here, most still had courtyards and some even had palm plantings and terra cotta sculptures. It was congested, but not an unpleasant place to live. The school where he taught was situated not far from the city market and as usual, he could see the arcade packed with goods and shoppers eager to spend their drachmas. As he emerged from the crowded market, he increased his pace and rounding a corner, was suddenly doused by a huge splash of water.

"Throw yourself to the crows, you pissing...!" Melchior swore the rest under his breath as a young woman walked by, scolding him with her eyes. He plucked his wet kulaf from his head and looked up as he moved away from the wall of the house he was passing. Sure enough, his old friend Gaspar stood on the rooftop garden holding a bucket and smiling down at him.

"You old swine. Why so glum? I thought you would welcome a little morning bath! Surely you didn't have time to bathe after that mother of a sand storm this morning? Perhaps you are not clean enough? Would you like a little more refreshment?" And tossing over yet another bucketful, he roared with laughter as Melchior raised his arms in mock defeat.

CHAPTER 2

Gaspar

§

GASPAR RAN DOWN THE OUTSIDE steps from his roof, and joined his friend in the street with a broad hug. "Here's a cloth to dry yourself."

Melchior pressed it to his hair. "Truly you are not to be trusted, always surprising me as you do. You make life very unpredictable!"

"Would you have it any other way? Life can be so routine! We are getting older every day, and neither of us with women to spice up our nights! Surely you must welcome an occasional surprise? Some little disruption from the monotony – that is my specialty, old friend!" Gaspar smirked. "Indeed, I'm sure that without me, your life would be quite boring."

Melchior smiled back, "Maybe true, but I should like to try it just the same. If only for a week or two?" Melchior stared at Gaspar's tall frame as he shook the excess water from his tunic. "I see you have donned your most favored attire once again!"

"Would you expect the son of a Magi to dress without distinction?" Gaspar twirled around, alternately kicking out his legs under his long pleated white silk tunic embroidered with gold and silver threads. "Besides, my long legs can stride easily in these garments. If I were a short fellow like you, trousers might be a better choice."

"Hah! First water, now words! You must be feeling hardy, indeed, to assail me twice in one day!"

"Yes, my friend! I haven't much to complain of."

"If only I could say as much. My morning was quite sour 'til I saw you."

Gaspar frowned. "I thought you looked a bit troubled."

The two men walked on as Melchior explained. "Dahab, and my mother argued again, and it was more intense than usual. Dahab threatened to remove mother from the house unless she stops teaching the children about our Jewish God."

"Why would she do that?"

"She doesn't understand my mother's devotion to her ancestral ways or why she would want to pass it on to her grandchildren."

"But Dahab accepted it while your father was alive, didn't she?"

"Yes. My father was the satrap. She had to accede to his wishes, but it didn't keep her from complaining to my brother even then."

"And now?"

"My father's death changed everything. Now when Dahab complains, Mered listens."

"Is the man tethered to her like a mule?"

"No, but he hates to be badgered. And she does a good job of it."

"A good reason not to marry, I think."

Melchior laughed. "Maybe. Mered wants his children to be raised as Zoroastrians, not Jews. He views our ancestry as a stain that can blemish their futures ... and his."

Gaspar raised his brows. "Is that surprising? You're not especially anxious to have your heritage known either. Other than me and Seleucus, I doubt that anyone in our school knows you're a Jew."

"Because of King Phraates! You know he doesn't trust Jews. I want to be able to advance based on my intellect and knowledge of astrology, not be held back by my ancestry."

"Which is not so different from Mered, is it?"

Melchior scowled. "I'm nothing like Mered! He denigrates our God and traditions in our own house where he has no one to fear. I may not express my faith in public but I still believe, and uphold my mother's right to pass on her traditions if only in the privacy of her dwelling!"

"But they are Mered's children. Doesn't he have the right to raise them as he chooses?"

"I said as much to my mother, but she feels a responsibility to them. I'm worried about her, Gaspar. I'm worried about what will happen if Dahab follows through on her threat."

Gaspar frowned. "Where would your mother go if she must leave?"

"A good question. I could buy her a house here in the city and get her a servant of her own. But it would kill her to leave the family."

"Are you sure Dahab has Mered's backing in this?"

Melchior shrugged. "I doubt she'd have spoken as she did without knowing his mind. But it's possible she's trying to frighten mother, or assuming Mered's support when she shouldn't. Either way, I should find out."

"Let me know if I can help."

"I will."

Gaspar looked up to see the School of Astrology ahead of them. "It should be an interesting meeting today. Do you think Seleucus will announce what you've been hoping for?"

Melchior's eyes widened. "You mean about the Messiah prophecies? I don't know. He's of Babylonian descent, so his loyalties are divided when it comes to Judaic astrology."

"I know it doesn't interest him," said Gaspar. "The bulk of his time lies in keeping the king happy so he continues to support our school."

"That's true," agreed Melchior. "It's remarkable he's allowed us to study as much Judaic astrology as he has. But I can't believe he'd ignore the positions of Jupiter and Saturn."

"Nor I. It's clear that their positions indicate something momentous, a new kingship somewhere, but whether it's a portent for Judea or another kingdom is hard to know. It needs more study and it would help if others could work with us. "

"I've been urging Seleucus to allow it. We'll know soon enough if he agrees."

The men bowed to their fellow astrologers as they hurried into the building. There were no students at the school today, only teachers like themselves, gathered to discuss new findings and predictions for the coming months. Gaspar and Melchior sat with their twenty-three peers and waited for Seleucus to begin. Many of their colleagues were coughing, and the sounds echoed through the large stone amphitheater, rimmed with columns and marble busts of astrologers long dead. These meetings were usually lively and engaging, but that was not his sense today. The hall felt unusually somber.

Seleucus entered the room, raised his arms and bowed. All talking ceased. "Good day, my friends." He began in tones so low, Gaspar strained to hear him. "I bid welcome to our new teachers. Please stand so we may acknowledge you." Five young men rose in unison at the front of the hall. They bowed and were roundly applauded before resuming their seats.

Seleucus stood, Gaspar thought unsteadily, next to a low marble column. "Before I review our findings and predictions..." He stopped in mid-sentence to wipe some sweat from his brow and appeared to be shaking.

"What's wrong with him?" asked Gaspar in a low voice. "I can hardly hear him. And do you see the tremors?" Many others were whispering as well.

"He's so pale," said Melchior. "The sweat is pouring off him."

Gaspar watched as Seleucus began again in a shallow voice. "I have news of enormous import. We follow in the footsteps of great men." He raised a feeble hand to the busts encircling the great hall. "They hailed from Mesopotamia, Babylon, Egypt and Greece. These men identified the stars, planets and constellations. They understood the connections between heavenly bodies and the affairs of men. Because of them we know all nature is affected by the heavens...." He paused, coughing loudly for some time, then sipped water from a cup atop the nearby column.

Gaspar could see many in the audience exchanging worried glances. His own arms felt like gooseflesh. "Do you think he's well enough to continue?" He asked Melchior.

"I don't know. He looks very sick."

The audience strained to hear Seleucus as he struggled to go on. "Since our studies began, we've based our predictions on the movement of the planets in relation to earth, the unmoving center of the world."

"Where's he going with this?" asked Gaspar, not expecting an answer.

"But today, I tell you . . . based on my studies of the moon and tides, that the earth is not the center of the firmament! Like the great Greek astronomer, Aristarchus, I believe that the sun is the center of ..." Seleucus stopped speaking. Suddenly his face turned blue and he fell to the floor where his body twitched for some time then lay still.

A huge collective gasp echoed across the chamber. Several young men ran to him, forming an impenetrable curtain around his body. The remaining spectators rose quickly and rushed to join the melee' of astrologers congregating in the center of the hall. Shouts and questions rang from floor to ceiling as men jostled and pushed to get a look at their fallen leader. "Make way, man! How is he? Is he alive? Tell us! Don't shove me, you cretin! Does he breathe? Can he speak?" Exclamations, insults and shows of concern came from every quarter. Louder and louder the cacophony rose until finally someone near Seleucus yelled out with authority. "Quiet everyone! Listen to me. He's breathing faintly. Make way! Open a path!"

"Move aside, please!" Someone else shouted out. "We must carry him to his rooms!"

Finally, after several loud curses, the crowd parted. Several men took hold of his arms and legs and carried the unconscious man from the hall. Though many followed Seleucus and his attendants from the chamber, the eruption of sound persisted. Gaspar touched his hand to his ear as he shook his head, and beckoned Melchior to follow him. They were forced to walk beyond the courtyard walls before they could hear each other.

"This is bad!" exclaimed Gaspar shaking his head. "Very bad."

"Yes," said Melchior as his eyes darted from place to place. "Did you see how he struggled to stay on his feet? He was clearly very sick yet he persisted. Why didn't he cancel the meeting? Was his announcement so important that he couldn't put it off?"

Gaspar put his hands to his forehead, shifting his weight from foot to foot. His insides felt jumpy, as if he himself might be sick. He took a deep breath. "Seleucus wasn't a foolish man. He's cancelled meetings before. Something must have been different this time. Maybe he didn't think he would recover."

Melchior looked astounded. "You mean he knew he was dying?"

Gaspar shrugged. "I don't know. It's possible he thought he was so sick that if he didn't announce his findings now, he never would. You know his work was everything to him. Like your Messiah prophecies are to you."

Melchior frowned but said nothing.

Gaspar looked at Melchior more intently. "Did you have any idea he was planning this announcement about the sun?"

Melchior blinked several times and shook his head. "No. I remember him talking about Aristarchus, but I had no idea he was convinced of the man's conclusions."

"Look around," said Gaspar gesturing to those around them. "Everyone is stunned. Even his confidantes look confounded by it."

Melchior sighed. "It means re-evaluating everything. All our predictions! And just when I hoped he might support our study of . . ."

"The prophecies. I hoped for that too. But Seleucus may be dying. The prophecies are the last thing we should be thinking about!"

"I know it's selfish of me. But it's hard to imagine someone other than Seleucus leading us. Cooperating with us." said Melchior in a somber voice.

"We've a lot to discuss and I have a thunderous thirst! Will you join me for some refreshment in a quieter place?" asked Gaspar.

Melchior clapped Gaspar on the shoulder. "Lead the way, friend. This place has turned into a mad house."

CHAPTER 3

Melchior

§

MELCHIOR RETURNED HOME THAT EVENING after spending the day with Gaspar. He'd consumed several mugs of beer as they talked, but the long walk home and the prospect of speaking with his brother, had thoroughly sobered him.

He headed straight for Mered's workroom, where he could be found most evenings, planning his trades and counting his money. And since it was Mered's chamber, they wouldn't be disturbed by Dahab. He must speak to his brother alone if he wanted to accomplish anything.

As expected, Mered sat at a desk with several sheets of papyrus spread before him. Some bags of silver lay clustered nearby. The desk always brought back memories for Melchior because it had belonged to their father. He remembered how as children, he and Mered would sneak into the room to see their father, who often set his work aside to play, pretending the desk was a tree in the wild. They would chase each other under the desk and between the wide pink terra cotta columns that were sculpted like tree trunks to support the desk top. If Mered had ever played with his own sons that way, Melchior had never noticed it.

Mered looked up to acknowledge him but continued counting his drachmas as Melchior waited. He rose when he was done. "Well, well. How nice of you to visit! What brings you back at such an hour? You missed one of Bina's better meals tonight. Duck is one of her best!"

"Yes, I know," said Melchior, feeling a little guilty to have missed the meal he requested. "But I had other business. I hope I'm not disturbing you?"

Mered waved his right hand in the air as if swatting a fly. "Not really. I've been wanting to speak with you, too." He came from behind the desk, spread his long legs wide and folded his arms across his skinny chest. "Dahab told me she and mother had another disagreement. This can't go on! You must talk some sense into her. She's over-stepping to insist my children be taught as we were. My children must be raised as Parthians!"

Melchior looked at his brother, trying to assess his disposition. Mered's moods could change with the phases of the moon and it was full tonight. He decided to press on. "Yes, I happened to overhear their quarrel. I'm sure it was distressing for them both. But you must know it's been difficult for mother since father's death. I'm the only one she can discuss the old ways with, and unfortunately, I haven't been very attentive. My studies of the Messiah prophecies have been taking all my time."

"Messiah prophecies! What a waste! You should concentrate on prophecies for the satrap. At least those might be to our advantage. How can the prophecies of a Judean kingship help us? What happens there has nothing to do with us."

Melchior took a deep breath to calm himself in the face of his brother's usual obtuseness. "Judea may be far away, but what happens there could well affect us. There are many like us, descendants of the Jewish exiles, living here and in other places outside Judea. What if the Messiah tries to reunite them? The prophecies say his kingdom will be a powerful one. It would alter the balance of power in the whole region, and affect all neighboring kingdoms, including Parthia."

Mered's eyes opened wide. "People like us? Don't put me in the same basket with you and mother. I don't follow the old ways anymore. And even if such a messiah comes, and attempts what you suggest, he'd have to overthrow the Romans to succeed. You'd be a fool to think it possible!"

Melchior tilted his head from side to side. "It would be difficult, but not impossible. There have been rebellions in the past. Herod fled to Rome years ago because of one. It could happen again."

Mered snorted. "You are so naïve. I've been to Judea. The Romans have a strangle-hold. They crucify men and woman alike when they get even a sniff of insurrection. Again I say, we're Parthians, not Judeans. It has nothing to do with us!"

Melchior raised his hands in frustration. "Yes, we're Parthians, but of Jewish heritage! I may not observe the rituals or offer sacrifices, but our traditions, the commandments, our shared faith . . . these things are still important. Does our ancestry mean nothing to you?"

Mered rolled his eyes. "Don't take that superior tone with me, brother. Outside this house, you have no more desire to be known a Jew than I do." He sneered. "Do your astrologer friends know you're a Jew? And why haven't you taken mother to Judea? She has asked you countless times, but I don't see you packing for that journey." Mered pursed his lips. "No! We're not so different you and me."

Melchior swallowed hard and turned away as Mered returned to sit as his desk. *First Gaspar and now Mered! It's absurd. He's just trying to bait me, and I am not a fish to be caught so easily.* He turned to face his brother and began again in a more level tone. "Maybe I haven't made myself clear. You know as well as I do that the prophecies, should they come to pass, have the potential to benefit one of us astrologers in a very personal way. There is no king in this region so secure in his reign that he doesn't fear an insurrection. Our King Phraates is no exception. He spends much of every astrological consultation quizzing us about such possibilities. And believe me when I say, that he cares not whether the threat comes from within his family or from reunified Jews. Wouldn't you like to be the brother of the astrologer who first brings news of a Messiah to our king? I imagine he would be very grateful for it,"

Mered raised his brows. "I can understand him wanting to be warned. And yes! I would very much enjoy being recognized by the king as the brother of the astrologer who imparts such news. Assuming it is welcome."

"That's always our purpose in consulting with the king. We astrologers aim to prepare him for all eventualities."

"I would hope so, or the cost of your school would hardly be worth it."

Melchior nodded. "Then you won't want to be known as the wealthy trader who allowed his wife to stand in the way of my progress." This statement brought him Mered's undivided attention, and he was glad. Mered had been underestimating his political astuteness for years, and he was tired of it.

"What do you mean? I've never allowed Dahab to dictate what I do, though I sometimes find it convenient to let her think so. How is she getting in the way of your progress?"

"Because if she forces mother to leave this house, I won't have mother's counsel interpreting the prophecies! Since the rabbis left Parthia, there are none to advise me, and mother is getting frail. Time may be of the essence for my work. I cannot emphasize how important my success may be to the continued influence of our family!"

Melchior watched Mered's expression change, and the look of disquiet that betrayed his feelings brought him a deep sense of satisfaction.

"For once you are right," replied Mered after a long pause. "There is nothing more important than my, or should I say, our family's influence! Mother may stay and help you, but why must she teach the children?"

Melchior had anticipated this. "I asked mother about that, but she took it as an insult. She said I was showing disrespect. That if I want her help, she must be allowed at least to tell the children her stories."

Mered scowled. "That old crone." He stood and drummed his fingers on the desk top. Melchior waited patiently until Mered spoke again. "For the time being I will tell Dahab that mother may tell her stories. Dahab won't like it but she will obey. But no sacrifices, do you hear? And I warn you, Melchior, this is not open-ended. If you haven't finished your work on the prophecies in six months, I will personally tell mother to stop and arrange her living arrangements elsewhere if she doesn't comply! Do we understand each other?"

"We do."

CHAPTER 4
Balthazar

§

5 BC – IN THE VILLAGE OF KHALAN, THE HADRAMAUT KINGDOM (NOW YEMEN)

BALTHAZAR WAS ALMOST FINISHED.

Tears streamed down his face as he went through the motions. Sprinkling myrrh on their bodies and placing a small coin in each of their palms. He had no fine linen, so he wrapped them in a blanket. The dirt came next. After he'd heaped it as best he could, he sat on the mound itself. His hands caressed the soil as if they had minds of their own. Back and forth, again and again they moved over the rough graveled soil of the grave. Rubbing. Caressing. Smoothing it out. Wanting to make their final place better, more acceptable. As if such a thing could be done. His parents and sister lay under him, killed by Himyarite raiders and he didn't want to leave. But the sun was lower in the sky. The cold air cut through his robes.

One final pat of his hands on the mound, and he rose to walk away. But leaving the grave did not put death behind him. Everywhere he looked he saw death, smelt death. Men, women, children. All of Khalan dead! Anger boiled inside him like a hot cauldron.

At the edge of town he found his camel, Melwah, head bent low, gorging himself on the fresh flowing water of the wadi. Weary and spent as he'd ever been, Balthazar sat down on a nearby rock. Unbidden sighs came loudly from his mouth, a tumble of breaths he could not control. Then the sighs became sobs.

Sometime later he looked up to see Melwah still slurping water from the stream. How long had he been here? He looked around trying to determine the time of day. The tall palms were already casting long shadows. He felt so tired. And limp. Like an old robe his mother might have beat against a rock when she was washing. He wiped his eyes on his blood-stained sleeve and looked at his camel. "You are so aptly named, my friend. You never miss a chance to drink, do you?" The thought creased his façade of sadness. For years Melwah had carried him over caravan routes with his parents as they bought and sold spices in southern Arabia. From Qana on the Gulf, across the edge of the desert to Timna, Marib and Ma'in, the camel had been his constant companion. Then he remembered the day his father had given him Melwah so many years ago and the tears flowed anew.

"We will miss them, won't we, Melwah?" The camel lifted his head and snorted. "That's how I feel, too. But I need a plan. I don't know what to do. Do you have any ideas?" This time the camel ignored him, lowered his head and went on drinking. "No? I'm not surprised. I'm pretty confused myself."

Still settled on the rock, Balthazar spread his legs, picked up a stick and scribbled randomly in the dirt. What now? His life here in Khalan was over. The Himyarites had scavenged what they could and left, but he knew they'd be back. Arable land near a wadi like this was highly prized. They would probably wait long enough for the fires to die down and return to stake claim. He hoped they had missed the cave where his parents hid their valuables. If he could get there safely, he'd re-provision and rest before heading back to Qana. Perhaps he could connect with a caravan, and sell spices like his parents. But was that what he really wanted?

Confusion and questions swirled through his mind like dancing girls round a fire. His dirt scribbles grew wider, more insistent as he pressed harder on the stick. If he'd returned sooner, he might have helped in the fight. He knew it wouldn't have affected the outcome, but he wished it just the same. Suddenly, the stick snapped. He threw it hard away from him as he looked skyward. 'Why have I been spared, Oh Great One? What do you have in store for me?' He divined no answers, and knew only one thing for certain: If he wanted to stay alive, he must leave before the raiding party returned.

Balthazar stood. His sharp whistle brought Melwah's head up from the stream. A second whistle and the camel plodded over to nudge his chest. "We've another trek ahead, Melwah. But I'll give you a night to rest. Come along, my friend."

As Balthazar led his camel toward his parent's cave he heard someone crying. Had somebody actually survived this carnage? His ears guided him in the deepening gloom back toward his father's land. Could it be one of their servants? The cook's daughter? No. The sounds were coming from the neighbor's land. Was it a child or a woman? A few more paces and he could see her. The neighbor woman, Alima, sat under a tree next to her husband's body.

He approached slowly calling her name, but she did not respond. "Alima!" He said again more forcefully, and touched her chin. "It's not safe here. The raiding party will be back soon, and they'll finish us, too. Come. I have food and money. We can rest 'til daybreak in my family's cave, then leave for Qana."

She looked at him but said nothing.

"Alima, come." This time he waited for no response, but pulled her up with his arms. She didn't resist. With his camel trailing behind, he escorted her like a child, across the village, along a stream and up into the rocks to the hidden cave.

Three myrrh trees grew in front of the entrance. Balthazar was glad to see it looked undisturbed. He brought Melwah some yards past the entrance to a grazing area and tied him to a small tree. Then taking Alima by the hand led her into the cave. He lit two small torches with a flint he always carried and led her to a back room where a wide, flat stone was covered with hay as a bed. To be alone with an unmarried woman was forbidden but what choice did he have? He couldn't leave her knowing the raiding tribe might return.

"Sleep here tonight," he said pointing to the slab bed. "There's a blanket. We can't chance making a fire, but I'll leave you this torch." She picked up the blanket, tucked it beneath her feet and hugged it to her chest as she sat on the hay. He kept one torch for himself, and placed the other in a holder on the wall. The light flickered, casting shadows around Alima's slim form. She looked so vulnerable. He had only ever thought of her as his neighbor, Sahl's wife. Now and for the next few days she was his responsibility. And she was beautiful. How had he never noticed that? He looked down briefly, chiding himself, then back at her. "I'm sorry about your husband."

"Thank you." said Alima, looking surprised. They were the first words she had spoken. "I grieve for your family, too. They were good people."

"Yes, they were." Balthazar shifted his weight from foot to foot, anxious to leave, but Alima looked as if she would say more.

"When I helped my husband deliver our spice, your mother told me of this cave. It has everything a person could need."

He frowned. "Yes. I helped my parents set it up when I was small. I wish they could have made it here today. Maybe they would still be alive. But my mother was proud of it." He pointed to the array of tin plates and bowls, leather storage bags, the pottery cisterns and pitchers for water and wine, as if they were new. "She was always looking for well made, beautiful things. Those rugs and terra cotta statues were for my sister's betrothal."

"I think she would have liked them," said Alima. "Your memories must be good."

Balthazar nodded. He drew a leather pouch filled with dried figs from inside his tunic and handed it to her. "Try to eat a little. We may not have time in the morning. I'll keep watch and wake you before sunup." He started to leave.

"Balthazar?"

"Yes?"

"Thank you for sheltering me tonight. You're a kind man, just like your father."

"You're welcome," he said, bowing slightly. "My father was a good man. I don't know if I'll ever be as good."

Leaving her alone with her thoughts and her tears, Balthazar moved toward the entrance and collapsed onto the floor. He massaged his aching calves and shoulders, and poured himself a cup of wine from a vat they always kept full. It tasted so good. He quickly downed three cups, then chewed some berries savoring their pungent flavor. Hunger gnawed at his belly but his thoughts were of Alima. He sipped more wine as his mind wandered. How had she survived the attack? Had the Himyarites spared her or had she merely done a good job of hiding? The questions nagged at him.

Then he remembered that his parents had liked her. His father had even held her up as an example. "That, my son, is what you should look for in a wife. Like your mother, a cooperative woman who can keep you well fed during the day and smiling at night."

He hoped his father had been right, for the trek to Qana would take many days, and nothing could be worse than traveling with an uncooperative woman. At least she had come willingly into the cave. And he couldn't deny, she was beautiful. Thoughts of her hovered in his mind like an enchantress, drawing him near. Her slim, enticing figure, her shining hair, those brown eyes that glinted with gold. He rebuked himself again. There's much to do and no time for thoughts like that.

The wine called to him again. How he wanted to drown himself in it! To destroy the memory of death and what his village had become, but not of his family. Alima was right that those memories were good. Those he wanted to remember.

"Balthazar, move yourself, boy! This is no time for playing!" His father, Fatin, chided him. "Help your sister shovel this hole."

"But why father? Why must we dig at the top of this hill?"

"Because our cave is just below. While you and your sister are digging up here, I'll dig underneath. If we do well, our holes will meet and we'll have a clear

path from the cave to the surface. Then any smoke from our fires won't choke us to death in the cave."

It had been a difficult task for the boy, and his sister hadn't been much help. But he'd kept at it in the heat with his small tool 'til his arms ached, and eventually heard his father's voice echoing up from below.

"Good job! You've done it. Come down to see!" He and Chana raced to beat each other to the cave's entrance, then inside to find father.

"Look up! Can you see the light?" Fatin asked. They strained their eyes to see the thin funnel of light coming from above. He'd craned his neck for a long time, mesmerized by what they had achieved. "You did well, children! Now it will be your job every day to walk up that hill and make sure the hole remains open." How seriously he'd taken that responsibility, and every job his father gave him since.

Balthazar gazed up at the hole above the fire pit. He remembered a night not long ago when the starlight shone so brightly it seemed heaven itself shone down on him. But tonight there was nothing. No moonlight, nor the starlight he loved so much. There was only darkness and he wondered if the light would ever shine on him again.

Shaking off the wine's lethargy, Balthazar entered the adjoining cavern used as a storage room. Ceramic amphorae lined one wall and hundreds of spice-filled burlap bags another. The room was a mélange of exotic aromas but to Balthazar it smelled like home. Transporting amphorae with only one camel wasn't an option, so he selected only small burlap bags. He laid aside the best quality frankincense knowing it had many uses and would bring a good price. He could tout its medicinal qualities and its aroma to priests for sacred offerings. And everyone knew it was a great way to fumigate homes from the odors of poor sanitation. Next he set aside the best myrrh. He chewed it after meals to improve his breath, and heard it could heal exposed bones when rubbed on the skin with the flesh of a snail. Could it also cure dysentery and kill worms? He wasn't sure, but he would mention any quality he could if it helped him sell for a good price.

He added some cinnabar and a small bag of cassia, then secured several bags of gold nuggets and gemstones his parents had been saving for his sister's dowry. Finally, he searched for as much food as he could, and prepared it to pack on Melwah before dawn.

With weariness returning, he stretched out just inside the cave entrance behind a low rock. He closed his lids but kept alert for the sounds and smells of human and animal prowlers. His bow and knife lay next to him, but he hoped he wouldn't need to use them.

CHAPTER 5
Alima

§

ALIMA WOKE TO PITCH BLACK dampness. Her hands were invisible before her. Where was she? She felt hay and rock beneath her. A cave? Yes, she remembered. The torch on the wall must have burnt itself out. She rose and began to feel her way along the cold rock wall hoping she moved toward the entrance. When she detected a faint glow ahead, she breathed a sigh of relief. Balthazar lay sleeping on the floor.

What a protector he is! She couldn't resist kicking him in the ribs. The young man jumped up suddenly pointing his knife in her direction. She drew back, raising her hands in mock defense. "It's only me. I thought you were going to wake me before sunrise."

A woodpecker outside the cave announced the coming dawn as Balthazar yawned. "I'm sorry," he said scratching his head. "I must have fallen asleep." He stretched and yawned again.

"It would seem so." Alima smirked, enjoying his obvious discomfort.

"We must go. I gathered our provisions last night." He pointed to the pile of spices and supplies on the floor. "I'll fetch Melwah so we can pack."

"Do you think it's safe? What if the raiders returned?"

He shook his head. "The night was quiet except for the wind."

"How can you know? You fell asleep!"

"Achh! I was awake almost all night! Anyway, if Melwah isn't where I left him we'll know soon enough. I tied him up and untying himself is a trick I haven't taught him yet. But it doesn't matter. We can't hide in here forever."

"I know. Is there something I can do to help?" Alima asked, feeling only slightly reassured.

"Not until I retrieve Melwah. There's some water in that jug if you want to wash. And some food over there if you're hungry."

"Thank you." Alima washed dirt and her husband's blood from her face and hands, and brushed her long brown hair. She wanted to burn her dress, but it was the only one she had. She braided her hair and tied it into a knot to keep it off her neck, then fixed her headscarf. Through the many difficult days of her marriage, a morning wash helped her face the day. Even if she churned inside, she could look composed. It might seem a little thing but it was the one thing she could control.

She drank some water from the jug and walked out of the cave. She felt a little better when she saw Balthazar with his camel.

"You found Melwah with no problem?"

"Right where I left him. We must hurry to be away before sun up. Can you carry the provisions out to me?"

"I will," said Alima hurrying back to the cave. She made several trips back and forth while Balthazar packed Melwah. She could tell he'd done this many times for soon the camel was packed high with provisions, with only a little space open at the front of the saddle.

"Come on then," said Balthazar offering to help her into it.

"You don't want me to walk?" she asked in surprise. "Sahl always made me walk when we traveled."

Balthazar raised his brows. "Really? My father never made my mother walk if he could help it. I mean no offense, Alima, but your husband had some strange ideas about how to treat his woman."

Alima said nothing. She was sorry that her father had married her to the man, but it had seemed a good match at the time. "I shall happily ride if you're sure Melwah can handle me."

28

"That should be no problem. He's handled many heavier loads and much bigger women!" He blushed. "I mean, you aren't a big woman ... you're not the load ... I mean..." he stammered.

"Don't worry," said Alima raising her hand to stop his apology. "I know what you mean, and thank you. Can I ask you to lend me your sling? I'm a good shot. I might be able to help out if we come upon bandits."

Balthazar handed her his sling and a bag of sharpened stones. Then he helped her into the saddle. "Ready?"

"Almost."

"What else do you want?" He asked with irritation.

"I'm wondering what your plan is. What route will we take? Do you know the way to where my family lives?"

Balthazar looked up and shook his head. He doesn't like to be questioned, she thought. "Don't you trust me?" He smacked Melwah's rein against his palm.

Alima did not reply, preferring to wait for his answer.

"Oh blazes, woman! We'll head south on the same route I took yesterday. I know it pretty well by now. We shouldn't encounter any Himyarites. Their stronghold is to the west. But we'll stay clear of the village as we leave and keep to ourselves. I know some sheltered areas where we can camp off the road at night. And if anyone bothers us, I'll say you're my sister. My father told me your family lives near the gulf in Qana. You can direct me when we get closer. Will that suit you, Princess Alima?"

"Yes. That will suit. And Balthazar, thank you for watching over me last night. I may not be your traveling companion of choice, but I promise not to cause trouble."

Balthazar rolled his eyes and raised his brows.

Alima frowned. "Why do you make faces? I'm putting my trust in you. You might at least take me at my word. I'm very capable of doing whatever is needed."

Balthazar nodded. "I'm sure you are. My father spoke well of you. It's just that you pick the oddest times to ask questions. We must hurry! As for your trust, I'm not sure you have much choice. It would be foolish to stay in Khalan."

"There's always a choice, Balthazar. Some are just better than others."

He shook his head. "Ready now?"

"Ready."

It was almost sunrise. She could see the sky flirting with her, showing its first pink and golden rays of the new day. A clear sky would be welcomed, but even the stormiest day would be better than yesterday. It might wash the village clean, and disguise the stains of her bloody dress, but it would be a long time before her memory was washed clean. Maybe never.

Alima held Melwah's reins in her right hand and the sling in her left. Her saddle high view of the road made it easy to watch for approaching travelers and bandits. Balthazar walked several paces ahead with his staff, a small pack on his back and weapons over his shoulder. Once or twice every hour he would break into a short run when the road was wide and flat, and Melwah would briefly outpace him. It broke the monotony, and Alima was glad of the breeze when the camel ran.

With the rainy season months away, the air was hot and dry. The land around Khalan was encircled by rugged low rock ridges, flat-topped hills and desert plain. She remembered the last time she'd made this journey. When she'd been a new bride, filled with hope for a family with her much older husband. It was only three years ago but it seemed longer, and her hopes had never been fulfilled. There had been no children. Now there was no husband. As they got closer to Qana, the land would level off toward the coastal plain and the air would become more humid, but already the air was oppressive as widowhood bore down on her. She removed her headscarf and fanned herself. What would the future hold?

When evening came Balthazar chose a place to camp and started a fire in a well-used pit. Alima tended it, and prepared some tea and roasted lentils. She felt safe knowing that Khalan was well behind them, their first long day of travel over. After serving Balthazar, she prepared her own plate and reclined to eat by the fire. Balthazar had finished and sat staring at the starry sky. It was peaceful and strangely comforting, and she hated to disturb the moment. "Forgive me for intruding on your thoughts, but I'd like to ask you something. May I speak?"

Balthazar laughed. "You needn't ask, Alima. I don't hold much with the old customs. Neither did my father. Please speak whenever you wish. Except if we're in a hurry."

Alima smiled recalling the morning's conversation. "I've been thinking about your father and wondering what he thought of my husband. Sahl wasn't an easy man to live with, but your father always seemed to get along with him. How did he do it?"

Balthazar gazed at her across the fire. "They did business together, Alima, so I suppose you could say they had an understanding of sorts. But it wasn't an easy one. Sahl was a difficult man. I don't think it mattered who you were. Man or woman, adult or child, slave or free man, he could deride everyone in equal measure."

"I know well enough how he treated me, but I always thought he was better with the villagers."

"No. Surely you could see people didn't want to be around him?"

Alima shook her head. "I suspected so, but it was hard to judge. He never wanted to attend festivals, or visit with neighbors. He wouldn't let me visit either; he always wanted me by his side."

"It wasn't natural. He kept you away from everyone! How could you abide it?"

"He was my husband. I had to obey, and I wanted to please him. But I knew it was unusual that your parents were the only ones he ever would share meals with."

"I think my mother invited you to spite him. She didn't like his possessive ways and knew he couldn't refuse her invitation."

"Your mother was a kind woman," said Alima nodding. "She introduced me to many women in the village, and most of them were good to me. But how was I to know they disliked Sahl, when they never spoke of him?"

Balthazar pursed his lips as if deciding what to say. "Your husband always sold my father high quality spice, and he was a tough negotiator. My father respected that. But Sahl was moody, and angered easily. We never knew day to day whether we would deal with the agreeable Sahl or the angry one. And we learned to double-check the weight of everything he sold us because my father often discovered errors."

"I never knew! I wondered why he never let me weigh the spice. I asked him often, but he always said no."

"I'm not surprised," said Balthazar. "My father never openly questioned Sahl's honesty. Partly because of your husband's temper; mostly because my father liked doing business with a local harvester. But my father was like that. He never demeaned people, even when he had good reason. When he found an error he would say, "Sahl, you must have had a sleepless night! You made a mistake weighing today. Can you fix it?"

"And did he?"

"Yes. Sahl would laugh and shrug it off, but he fixed it every time. My father said he was like a little boy caught in a lie. He tried to cheat but he knew losing our trade would ruin him. My father stayed watchful and never trusted him."

Alima knelt in front of Balthazar, touching her head to the ground. "It may be too late, but I must apologize for my husband." She was greatly embarrassed and wanted Balthazar to know she'd had no part in Sahl's deceptions.

Balthazar raised his hand up. "There's no need. My father knew you weren't like him."

She smiled and rose, grateful to be understood as separate from Sahl. Many would not be so kind.

Balthazar helped himself to another cup of tea. "Did you know how to harvest spice before you married Sahl?"

"No. When Sahl brought me to Khalan I worked as any wife. Washing clothes in the wadi, tending our garden, cooking. He was good to me then. But when the first year ended and no child came, things changed. He would lose his temper. Sometimes he would strike me." She looked away. "Then his knees started to hurt, so he brought me to help harvest the spice. Of course I still had all my woman's work to do. But he stopped hurting me, and I loved riding out to find the frankincense trees. Sahl made the first cuts for the resin while I mapped the trees' positions on scrolls. We'd go back a few weeks later to scrape the hardened resin into baskets and bring it home for me to grind. It was something we could do together that didn't make him angry, and I was glad of that."

"Were you careful of the snakes? My mother never got used to them when she helped my father harvest years ago."

"Oh Yes! All those different colored winged snakes! They surprised me at first. I didn't expect to see so many clustered round the trees like that, but Sahl taught me how to keep from being bitten. We burned the gum of storax bushes and the fumes drove them away. It worked like magic! And I took extra care. I made leather leggings to protect myself. They saved me more than once from bites when we had no gum to burn."

"Who would think Sahl could be a good teacher?" Balthazar looked astonished.

"Why are you surprised? The more I worked the less Sahl had to. And the more I learned the better I liked it. I kept asking. What's next? I suppose I badgered him a little."

"You? Badger a man? I can hardly believe it!"

Alima blushed. "My father always said I was a determined girl. But I worked hard and we harvested much spice. I was proud when Sahl told me how much your father paid for it. That's when I finally realized I had value to Sahl even if I never bore him a child."

"You should be proud of your skills. My father praised you. He said Sahl's spice was better after you helped him. That you had patience and knew how to get the prized spice from the yellow teardrops of the third cutting."

"I confess I grew to like the work, but Sahl complained no matter how well we did."

"That was his nature, Alima." Balthazar yawned. "I'm tired, and we must rise early. Good night."

"Good night." She sighed, sorry that their talk was ending. She laid out her blanket next to a rock wall, rolled herself in it and closed her eyes. But she felt restive. She was used to sleeping on a soft hay bed and the ground was hard. I must get used to this, she thought, wiggling to find a comfortable place. She breathed deeply, hoping for sleep, but her mind moved on like a swift flowing stream. Tomorrow I'll be one day closer to my family. She'd not seen or heard from them since her marriage three years ago. Would they welcome her back or view her as a burden?

If any of her brothers had married she would be another mouth to feed in a house that might already have too many. What if they don't want me, will they force me to marry my cousin? She had two male cousins on her father's side and either one could insist on his tribal right to her now that she was widowed. She turned again restless, unable to sleep. All her life she had done the bidding of men. Would that go on or could she find another way? An idea came to her but she would need Balthazar's help to make it happen. He had said he didn't hold much with tradition. Would she be brave enough to ask him? She tossed for hours until sleep finally came.

The next two days of their journey were tranquil ones. They encountered few travelers and no threats to their safety. On the afternoon of the fourth day Alima prodded Melwah forward with the whip until she was near Balthazar. "Could we rest a little, please? I must relieve myself and there's something I'd like to ask you."

He nodded. "Very well. I'd like to speak with you, too."

Except for a few words about the heat, they had hardly spoken since their fireside talk, and she wondered if something was troubling him. Balthazar led Melwah to a shady tree on the side of the trail where Alima dismounted. She found some privacy and when she returned Balthazar offered her some water and figs.

"Thank you," she said, looking around uneasily. "How may I ease your mind?"

He sat down, leaned his back against a tree trunk and stretched his long legs out in front of him. Alima settled herself under some of the low hanging branches a few feet away.

"A question nags at me. How did you survive the attack? You were the only one left alive in the whole village. Why?"

Alima's eyes welled with tears. "I hoped never to speak of it."

"It was a bitter day for me, too. But I think you owe me an answer. I would know the truth of it."

"Why? It has nothing to do with the attack or your family."

Balthazar stared at her, waiting for his answer.

"Ah! So it comes to that. I'm in your debt, so I must answer." She bit her lip and turned away briefly before looking him full in the face. "I'm so ashamed," she said wiping her tears away.

Balthazar remained still, his gaze steady on her face.

Alima sighed. "Early that morning, Sahl told me he'd made a decision. It was something I'd feared for a long time. He said he needed a son to continue his line, and that he'd arranged to bring another wife into our house." She closed her eyes. "He said the bride price was decided and the new wife would come within days." Her tears streamed silently. "I know it was my duty to give him a child, but I tried potions, prayers, talismans, and other things ..." She continued in a whisper. "It was humiliating. Children come so easily to most. I always tried to be a good wife, but the harder I tried to please him, the less pleasure he took in my company. And that morning, when I knew I might have to take orders from this young girl. . . "

Balthazar handed her a cloth for her tears and after a few moments she continued.

"I begged Sahl. I pleaded with him to give me more time, but he said nothing. He wouldn't even look at me. So I left. I walked into the mountains outside of town to offer a sacrifice. I didn't know what else to do. I fell asleep after the offering, and when I woke up I heard screams. I made my way along the ridge to see what was happening. By then, it was too late to help anyone. So I hid, and waited."

Balthazar nodded. "So you never saw how the attack started?"

"No. I wanted to help them but I was afraid. I was a coward."

Balthazar sat quietly for some time then moved closer and picked up her hand. "You're not a coward. If you had gone into town you would have been killed like the rest."

"But we live Balthazar! You and I live and breathe and I feel guilty for it. Why do we live?"

"I don't know. And I don't know why The Great One chose that you and Sahl should have no children. Those questions have no answers. Our fates are written in the stars. We are fools to fight it. The best we can do is to discover what they portend, and make the best of it."

"But I don't know how to read the stars. I failed as a wife and I failed our village. How can I make the best of that?"

Balthazar shrugged. "I've heard there are learned men who study the stars. Some say they can even predict the future. Someday I'd like to study with them and see if it's true. But until then I only have my thoughts to share. I haven't known you well, but from what you've said you tried to do your best. Don't punish yourself for what was beyond your power. You're a good woman, with many years ahead of you. The stars may yet hold surprises."

She clasped her hands together. "You're a young man yet you speak with such wisdom and hope. I want you to be right, Balthazar! I want the stars to hold surprises. I do."

He pulled a flask from his robe, took a swig and offered it to Alima. "Would you like some wine?"

She raised the flask to her mouth. "That's good." She took another sip. "Must I give it back?" She grinned mischievously.

"What do you think?" He held out his hand, but instead of returning it she hid it behind her back.

He laughed loudly at her attempt to tease. "Do you really think I would come with only one flask?"

Alima smiled sheepishly. "Here you are then. It's not nearly so amusing if you have another."

Balthazar grabbed the flask and quickly drained its contents. "I hope your father has wine to refill it!"

"He loves good wine," said Alima. "I'm sure he'll be happy to . . . Wait. . . .Is that?"

"My only wine flask? Yes!" He shrugged, a wide grin on his face. "You're not the only one who can tease. I look forward to meeting your father. We should be there in another day or so. Where in Qana does your family live?"

"On the gulf. My father built our house next to his shipyard. He's a master boat builder. I'm sure he'll welcome you to stay with us." She'd never known her father to deny hospitality to anyone, except for her cousin Seif when he was drunk. The thought of him made her frown.

"Why do you scowl? Is there a problem with your family?" asked Balthazar.

"There could be. Do you remember how you said your father didn't always follow the old customs? Well, my family does. And according to our custom, my male cousins on my father's side have first rights to marry me now that I'm widowed. I have two of them and I pray my family won't have me marry either one."

"Are they that bad?"

"They used to be. The younger one, Umar, was a trouble-maker. He cheated, stole, and lied when it suited him. But it's Umar's older brother, Seif, I'm most worried about. He was brutal, used to getting his way. There was a girl I knew in Qana that he took against her will, then denounced as a whore. When the girl's family deserted her, she was stoned and left for dead in the street."

"But surely your father wouldn't force you to marry a man like that!"

"I hope not. But I come back to him with nothing! What is he to do if my cousins assert their rights?"

"They may already be married, and have no wish for another wife." Alima could see Balthazar's concern in his face. Was he actually one of those rare men who could understand her feelings?

"I hope for that, but what if they're not?"

"Perhaps they can find you someone else. Someone trustworthy and good. You're a beautiful woman, Alima, and Qana's a big city. I'm sure another man can be found who would be more suitable if you can't live with your family."

Alima considered his remark and made up her mind. "I have no right to ask this, Balthazar, but I have an idea. And since we're getting closer to Qana, I think this a good time to ask you."

"This sounds interesting. What kind of idea?"

"I will tell you." She was quiet for a few moments as she steeled herself to say what she had in mind. "It is our custom that another man may buy a cousin's bride right. My idea has to do with this custom."

"Go on. I'm listening," urged Balthazar.

"If my cousin Seif should claim his right to me, I would like you to offer him a price for me. He may not accept at first, but he's selfish. I'm sure he'll consider a bride price preferable to taking care of a barren widow. In return, I will work as your servant until I repay you. I can help in your spice trade or do whatever household work you need. I'm a good cook and cleaner, and will serve you well."

Balthazar wrinkled his brow. "It's an interesting idea. And I'd like to help you, but I'm not sure it can work. I have no idea where I'll go when I leave Qana. I may head out with a caravan or I may travel north. I've heard of schools where a man can study the stars with learned men. I'd like to do that. But I need to do it alone. I'm not ready for a wife."

Alima bent forward. "But I don't want to be your wife! I may not want to wed ever again!" She gripped her hands together, closed her eyes and looked down. "I'm sorry. I don't mean to offend you, but marriage is not what I'm suggesting."

"Then I'm confused," said Balthazar raising his brows. "Because if I pay your cousin for the right to marry you, I will be considered your betrothed."

"Yes. But it would only be an arrangement, a trick, so Seif would believe it. I want to buy my freedom, indirectly of course. I don't want to marry Sief, but my father may have no choice except to allow it. Seif would be a hundred times worse than Sahl ever was."

"If that's true, I can understand why you worry."

"I tell you, it is. Please help me! I would be a good servant to you. And if it shouldn't work out, perhaps you could find someone to assume my indenture. Whoever I will serve, shall surely deal more kindly with me than Seif."

Balthazar frowned. "That may not be true. But I will ponder it. Perhaps by the stars, we'll find Seif and Umar are gone, or don't want you. Then you can live with you family in peace."

Alima nodded and accepted that once again her fate might hinge on the decision of a man.

CHAPTER 6
Balthazar

§

FOR THE NEXT TWO DAYS, they followed the path south to Qana, up and down through the jagged volcanic ridge that bordered the sandy coastal plain.

Finally, late on the morning of the fifth day, they rounded a bend to see a sparkling expanse of blue-grey water. "Look, Alima! We're almost there."

Alima saw the gulf and breathed deeply. "It's a wondrous sight! I had almost forgotten how beautiful it is." She dismounted, gazing toward the water as Balthazar held the reins.

"So tell me about your family," said Balthazar. "What are they like?"

Alima smiled. "Well, as I said, my father, Mehir, builds boats; and he builds all sizes, from small fishing boats to the large vessels that sail to the Great Sea. He's devoted to my mother, Jun. She loves to cook, and delights in getting compliments for her food, so remember that if you want to stay well fed!"

"I will. Do you have any brothers or sisters?"

"Yes. I have three brothers: Waled, Akram, and Sameer; they all work with my father. And I've a younger sister, Baysan. I've missed her greatly."

"A sister? Is she as pleasing as you?"

Alima ignored the compliment. "Much more so," she said promptly.

"And as bold?"

"What do you mean by that? I'm not bold!"

Balthazar laughed.

"You think me wrong?" asked Alima.

"You are wrong! You suggested I fake our betrothal. If that's not bold, I don't know what is."

"Perhaps. But I'm a widow now, and I saw what happened to widows in Khalan. If I can control even a little of my life I mean to do it. Besides, if I don't try to protect myself, who will?"

"Your father and brothers. You're their responsibility now."

"I know. But if we follow my plan, my father won't have to confront his brother Nibal, nor make enemies of my cousins. I'm sure he'd rather keep peace in our family if he can."

"But what if I don't agree to your suggestion? Will your father arrange for you to wed your cousin if he knows you won't be happy?" Alima didn't answer and Balthazar could only guess why.

They journeyed on, and as they got closer to Qana, other trails joined theirs until the road became crowded. Balthazar labored to guide Melwah between the many travelers, ox-drawn carts, camels and occasional horses. When they reached the last promontory overlooking the city, they stopped for Alima to dismount so she could walk the remaining way to her father's house. They stood together, inhaling the sea air before descending the winding, narrow cliff road to the city.

Qana wasn't a big city, but compared to Khalan, it seemed so. It stretched almost a league, from the flat-topped rocky cliff where they stood to the sandy shore of the bay and gulf beyond. Looking to his right, Balthazar noticed many nomad families camped on the plateau that stretched to the western horizon. To his left and east, a long fortified stone wall skirted the edge of the rocky cliff. Interspersed along it were many tall cistern towers that collected and held rainwater for Qana's citizens. And toward the shore, scores of caravan tents covered the city's sandy outskirts.

As they descended the escarpment, Balthazar looked back toward the black cliff face and grimaced.

"Is something wrong?" Asked Alima.

"I was just remembering how much my father hated that large warehouse building there."

"You mean the one built into the hillside?" asked Alima.

"Yes."

"I remember it was being built when I married Sahl. Why did your father hate it?"

"Because by order of the king all frankincense moving through Qana must be stored there before it's sold or shipped. It's the way he controls the trade and gets his share of the profits."

"And cuts into yours?"

Balthazar nodded.

They continued in silence down the narrow, uneven path and soon the city crowded in on them, and the smells of human habitation replaced the clean air of the gulf. Mud and stucco dwellings of every size surrounded them. A few had tiled roofs but most were built with mud roofs, supported by wooden posts and columns. The windows were small and high. Many of the larger houses were enhanced with stone and colored tile, but most were simply-built baked clay houses the color of desert sand. Palms, pomegranates, olive, and sidr trees dotted the landscape and populated the edges of the narrow, winding streets.

"Do you see those sidr trees?" asked Alima pointing. "My sister, Baysan, and I used to help our mother collect honey from the hives that are near them. We made good money selling it as an aphrodisiac in the market."

"Did it work?" Balthazar asked grinning.

"How would I know? I was just a child. But the people we sold to, always wanted more!"

"Does the city look as you remember?" asked Balthazar.

"Mostly. Though the docks look bigger."

"That may be," said Balthazar. "I met a ship captain last week who said more docks were added to make room for the larger ships. The merchants are hoping to encourage more trade with the Romans."

"That must have been after I left. I never saw many Roman ships when I lived at home."

Balthazar observed many vessels in the harbor but none with Roman flags.

They came to a large clearing midway through the city and Alima pointed toward the shore. "My father's house is located near that dock on the west side."

Balthazar looked where she pointed, then pulled on Melwah's reins, cajoling him away from some shrubs he was nibbling. "Come Melwah! Only a little further and you'll have plenty to eat and drink." The animal picked his head up and moved on. "He's hungry and thirsty just like me," said Balthazar. "I'm glad this journey's almost done."

When they were within a stone's throw of her father's house Alima touched Balthazar's arm. "Could we wait a little before we go in?"

"Has the sun affected your judgement? We've been walking for days!"

"Please," begged Alima. "Just a few moments."

Balthazar felt as if he'd been walking all his life and the lure of food and sleep was strong. But what difference could a few moments make?

CHAPTER 7

Gaspar

§

In Seleucia, Kingdom of Parthia

Gaspar greeted the new day in his customary manner, by exercising in his garden. It had been his ritual for over twenty years. It relaxed him, and enhanced his mental concentration and stamina. Now in his mid-forties, he was at ease with his aging body, and felt no shame in the little sags of skin now on full display as he exercised in the nude, in conscious imitation of the Greeks. Nudity was more comfortable in the heat, and he could stretch and contort his body more easily than if he was clothed. Now he watched his calves and thighs stretch as he bent to hold his ankles, and liked that his buttocks were still hard when he tightened them. Oddly, today's regimen seemed more strenuous than usual. Only half his routine was complete when he became short of breath and decided to stop and wash.

As he donned his traditional attire, he continued to inspect and admire the contours of his body. He might not have a wife to hold each night but he knew he could attract a woman if he wanted to. Unlike Melchior who was too obsessed with astrology to make time for a woman, Gaspar had searched but never found a woman of high station who suited him intellectually.

Too fatigued to cook for himself, he decided to break his fast at a local inn. On the outskirts of the market, the inn was usually quiet, and Gaspar liked the simple, delicious food he found there. He greeted the owner upon entering and seated himself on a small cushion near a low table. A servant stood nearby waving a large palm leaf and though the heat wasn't great, the breeze felt extraordinarily good. It took him no time to decide on a helping of his favorite chicken, beer and biscuits.

He paid for his food and took his time eating, enjoying the aromas coming from the cooking pit behind him, and listening for the accents and languages of other visitors. Seleucia was near the Silk Road and it wasn't uncommon to see many eastern travelers in his adopted city. He'd traveled widely before settling in Seleucia and spoke many languages, but loved to listen for people from the other Median tribes of his homeland: the Busae, the Paraetaceni, the Strukhat, the Arizanti, and the Budii.

There were no echoes of those languages today; only the cries of babies in the courtyard, and the virulent coughing of a couple near the door. He'd heard a lot of that lately. Not only Seleucus but some teachers at his school and a few of his neighbors as well. As soon as he finished, he thanked the cook by name and walked slowly through the city and up the hill toward Melchior's house.

By the time he reached the hilltop estate, he was sweating profusely, so he was happy to be greeted by Melchior's servant, Bina. "Good day, Master Gaspar! You look hot. Allow me to wash your feet."

"I would be most grateful," replied Gaspar as Bina removed his sandals. Melchior arrived to greet him as Bina dried his feet. "That felt very good," said Gaspar.

"I must make you comfortable, so you keep returning." replied his friend. "I'm so thankful that you're acting as mother's scribe. These writing sessions always lift her spirits."

"I enjoy it! You know I'm way too selfish to do anything that doesn't give me some satisfaction."

"What can it be? Scribing Mosaic stories for an old lady on a hot day? You could be cooling off in the river."

"I could, but I understand the pride she takes in her ancestry. I have a little of that myself, you know."

Melchior laughed, "You? The man who always dresses in his ancestral garb? I would never have guessed!"

"I like that she wants to hand down the stories for younger generations. Sharing knowledge is important. But the biggest reason I do it is because I like your mother. I feel good when I'm with her."

Melchior patted Gaspar's shoulder, then escorted him to his mother's large, bright room.

"Gaspar's here to scribe for you, Mother."

"Good! I just want to say a prayer before we start," said Dodi.

She looked frailer to Gaspar than the last time he'd seen her. Though she moved with difficulty, she got down on her hands and knees, looked toward the high window, closed her eyes, and raised her arms up toward the roof. "Oh Lord, look down upon your servant and incline your ear. Let me know your wishes as in the day of Moses when you guided his hands and feet, and brought your people out of Egypt. Now we labor to serve you in a foreign land. Many of our people struggle to remember you. Forget not your promises, oh Lord. Help me to find the words to remind your people of our covenant and your loving ways." Then she sat on a raised cushion and said, "Let us begin."

She spoke slowly, with inflection, stopping at the end of each phrase to be sure that Gaspar understood as he wrote.

The loving deeds of the Lord I will recall,
The glorious acts of the Lord
Because of all the Lord has done for us,
The immense goodness to the house of Israel,
Which he has granted according to his mercy
And his many loving deeds.
He said: "They are indeed my people,
Children who are not disloyal.
So he became their savior
In their every affliction.
It was not an envoy or a messenger,

But his presence that saved them.
Because of his love and pity the Lord redeemed them,
*Lifting them up and carrying them all the days of old.**
(* Isaiah 63:7-9 – Prayer for the Return of God's Favor)

Dodi stopped speaking and looked at Gaspar. "Have you gotten it all? Would you like me to repeat anything?"

"There's no need to repeat. I'm almost done." He finished the last few lines with one of the flourishes he liked so much. The physical process of making the words look beautiful on the papyrus gave him great satisfaction. Then he sat back. "I can understand why you like those verses. That poem would remind you that God is always present, that you're not alone, even in your disagreements with family."

"That's right," said Dodi. "Strange isn't it . . . how our minds work? I learned those verses as a child, but I only remembered them when I needed to have them in my heart. They comfort me greatly." She took a sip of water from a wooden cup, drew a deep breath and continued. "I've heard from my friends who visited Jerusalem, that the temple has many scrolls recording our ancient stories and laws. They are used to teach the young. But we don't have anything like that for the Jews here in Parthia. When our rabbis left us, they took all our sacred writings with them. I want my grandchildren to be able to read the words of our prophets on the scrolls you're penning so they'll know how much God cares for them."

"It will be a wonderful inheritance for them," said Gaspar.

"There are a few more things I'd like you to write today. Do you have the time?"

"Of course! I'm at your command."

Dodi laughed. "These words were also handed down from the prophet Isaiah. I remembered this because Melchior has been asking me about the Messiah prophecies. There have been many sayings through the years about a great king who will come to save us. Someone stronger even than Moses and David, who will lead our nation. Our people have been praying for this king to come, and this prophecy offers us hope." She stopped speaking and indicated with her hand that he should begin.

> *Therefore the Lord will give you a sign,*
> *The young woman pregnant, and about to bear a son,*
> *Shall name him Emmanuel.*

"Emmanuel. That's a Hebrew word isn't it? What does it mean?" Gaspar asked.

"Yes, it's Hebrew. It means: God with us. It's a wonderful name because we Jews have always wanted to have God with us. We urge God to listen to us through our sacrifices. Our ancestors built a golden ark to hold the covenant tablets, and our temple in Jerusalem to hold it. It was our way of keeping God with us. This prophecy hints that maybe God isn't found in a temple or an ark or even in our sacrifices. Maybe this woman will bring us a child who is from God. Maybe God will be with us in a new way."

"You don't mean an incarnation, do you? The Greeks have believed in those for thousands of years, but they are just stories. You're an intelligent woman, Dodi, why would you believe it possible?"

"I'm not a learned woman. I attended no schools like you and Melchior. So I'm not sure if it hints at an incarnation. I just believe in my God. That one day he will be with us in a new way. There's another prophecy about a child, you know. Write this down, too."

> *The people who walked in darkness have seen a great light;*
> *Upon those who lived in a land of gloom a light has shown.*
> *You have brought them abundant joy and great rejoicing;*

"I've forgotten a few words," said Dodi, "but the rest I remember well."

> *For a child is born to us, a son is given to us;*
> *Upon his shoulder dominion rests.*
> *They name him order-Counselor,*

God-Hero, Father-Forever, Prince of Peace.
His dominion is vast and forever peaceful,
Upon David's throne, and over his kingdom
Which he confirms and sustains by judgment and justice
Both now and forever. The Seal of the Lord of Hosts will do this!

"That's interesting," said Gaspar stroking his beard. "Those first words about seeing a great light … and a light has shown … do you think that could mean a star?"

"What do you think? After all, you interpret prophecies, or at least your people, the Magi, do."

"My father did that, but I've always interpreted the stars, not dreams or prophecies."

"But you may have some of his power. Perhaps, you are capable of interpreting other things too? But since we speak of stars, it reminds me of one more saying:

A star shall rise out of Isaac, and a scepter shall spring up from Israel.

"Ah, now that's very interesting. Has Melchior heard that?" asked Gaspar as he finished writing and wiped some sweat from his brow.

"Yes, many times. It's the reason he's convinced a star will announce the birth of a Jewish king. Of course, you astrologers are very used to stars coming at the birth, even at the death of kings. Melchior told me that a comet blazed when the Roman Julius Caesar died. I'm sure there have been others, so why not a star for a Jewish king as well?"

"Yes, why not?"

"Thank you so for coming, Gaspar. For helping me express my gratitude to the Lord! I don't know what I'd do without you."

"Let's hope you won't need to find out. Is there anything else you would like me to scribe for you today?"

"No. We've done enough and I'm very tired … I haven't been feeling myself lately."

"I'll be on my way then. I'm not feeling well either. Perhaps it was something I ate. I'll see you again soon."

Dodi nodded as Gaspar bowed in farewell. He rushed out of the house into the hot afternoon sun, and walked quickly past Melchior in the garden, waving his goodbye. He'd intended to ask how Melchior's talk with Mered had gone, but wasn't up to lingering.

His head began to pound as he walked downhill, and then a buzzing began in his ears. What a strange sensation, he thought. He started running hoping to get home sooner, but he'd only run a few paces when dizziness overwhelmed him. *What's happening to me?* He couldn't remember much of what he'd been doing just moments before. He struggled to calm himself and then recalled he'd been with Dodi and Melchior. I should return, he thought, and turned around, determined to make it back to Melchior's house. He felt foolish but knew something was very wrong. His vision was blurring. Just a little further, he thought. He was just outside the garden wall when he collapsed.

CHAPTER 8

Melchior

MELCHIOR WATCHED GASPAR DEPART THROUGH the garden gate. *It's not like him to leave without speaking to me.* He walked into the house looking for his mother, and found her in the kitchen with Bina.

"Mother, may I speak with you? I have some good news to share."

Dodi raised her head. "Of course, my son. I just came for some fresh water."

Bina poured from a large jug and handed the cup to Dodi. "Tell your momma to rest, Master Melchior. She looks exceeding pale today."

Melchior took his mother's arm, walked her to her room and helped her to a seat on a large floor cushion where he sat down beside her. Bina was right. She didn't look well. "How are you feeling Mother?"

"I'm tired and have a cough, but I'll be fine. What's your good news?"

"I spoke with Mered about the children."

"Oh? And what did he have to say?"

"He's agreed to let you continue teaching the children for six more months."

"The Lord be praised! Tell me how you accomplished this, and why for only six months?"

"It's complicated, but I told Mered I need you to help me interpret the Messiah prophecies. I convinced him that our family can gain influence with the king, if I can be the astrologer who predicts when the Messiah will be born."

"So he's willing to let me live here and teach the children as long I help you with the prophecies? Sometimes I find it hard to believe he's my son. To bargain with his own family like this!"

"Don't blame him. It was *my* suggestion he agreed to."

"Mmm. But he liked your appeal because it may bring what he craves: gold and power." Dodi shook her head. "Why couldn't he be more like your father? He liked wealth and influence, but valued family more. As satrap he worked hard to better the lives of the people in Seleucia. Your brother never seems to think of anyone but himself."

"That may be, but I'm glad he agreed, because you'll have six more months to teach your grandchildren, and I'll have your assistance with my work!"

"And I shall give it gladly if you keep bringing that handsome friend Gaspar to help me!" She laughed, and the laughter triggered a coughing fit. Melchior could tell she was struggling to catch her breath.

"Maybe you should rest a while, mother."

Melchior retrieved a pitcher of fresh water from Bina and brought it back to her. "Have a drink. I'll leave this for you in case you want more."

After he got her settled, he resumed his work in his room, reviewing old charts and scrolls to see if any of his predictions were impacted by Seleucus's startling announcement about the sun. Several hours later when his work was done, he decided to stroll before his evening meal. He called for Bina and asked if she could again prepare roast duck.

"I predicted your desire, master!" Bina replied. "I bought a duck at the market this morning and was preparing it when you came in. Truly our stars must be in alignment!" she grinned and he laughed at her joke. He knew she had little knowledge of the stars but was glad they had both been thinking about duck.

"Wonderful! I'm so hungry I could eat a horse, but a duck will be much better. Do you know if Dahab and Mered are home? I haven't seen them or the children all day."

"They left early this morning to attend the wedding of Dahab's cousin. They won't be back for a week or two."

"I see. Then perhaps you can serve dinner for my mother and me on the terrace near the garden? She likes the view of the river from there."

"Most gladly."

Melchior left the house for his evening walk. He took a regular route, always exiting the house by a back door and walking north to the crest of the hill through an area heavy with date palms. Though the land between the two rivers, as this area was often called, was mostly flat, there were a few hills, and this one afforded some beautiful views. He could see fields and plains stretched out in a patchwork as far as the eye could see. Some were covered with barley, others with the yellow and white tubular flowers of sesame plants, and still others with herds of sheep and goats.

Though his mother often spoke of her ancestral country near Jerusalem, he felt blessed to have been born in Parthia. He looked down into the valley where the rushing river flowed and couldn't imagine living anywhere else.

As he walked, he reviewed his conversation with Mered. Like a rotten piece of fruit, his brother's words had left a bad taste. Was Mered right? Was he afraid to acknowledge himself a Jew? His parents had kept it secret for fear of how it might affect his father's career. It had never seemed wrong in those years, so why should the notion of secrecy bother him now? Was it just that he didn't like being compared to Mered? Did his own discretion for ambition's sake mark him a coward, or was there more to it? The whole question felt like a thorn in his foot. Could he find a way to dig it out?

He traversed the entire date farm tract as the sun sank lower before turning toward home. As he approached the garden wall, he saw what appeared to be a bright white rock reflecting the rays of the setting sun. *It's odd I've never noticed that before.* He sped up and soon realized it was no rock. Running now, he called to anyone within the sound of his voice.

"Help! Help! Please! Come quickly! It's Gaspar!" He shouted as loudly as he could. Bina came running, followed by Amro, the gardener. "We must get him inside. Quickly! He's been here all afternoon!"

"Let me fetch the litter, Master." No sooner had Amro returned with the litter than they moved Gaspar onto it and carried him to Melchior's room where they laid him on the bed.

Melchior turned to Amro. "Why didn't you notice him this afternoon? Surely you must have passed outside the garden wall as you worked?"

"I was working on the other side of the property," replied Amro. "Your brother asked me to tend the vegetable patch there. I surely would have told you if I'd seen Master Gaspar in such a state!"

"I'm sure . . . it's just . . . I can't believe he was there all afternoon, and none of us saw him! Bina, please fetch a water basin, a cup and some cloths. Fast as you can!"

Melchior knelt down next to Gaspar, lifted up his hand to feel for his life blood and bent over his face to detect for breath. He could tell Gaspar still lived, but barely. His skin felt like hot tinder, his normally tanned complexion was blotchy and red. His eyes swelled beneath purple lids.

Bina came with water, and watched as Melchior attended to his friend. He pulled off Gaspar's tunic, and covering only his private parts, wiped down Gaspar's body from head to toe. He repeated this twice more and when he was almost done Gaspar began to moan. Melchior couldn't make sense of the words and swore at himself. "What a cursed friend I am! If only I had walked out with you. What's the matter with me?"

"Don't berate yourself, master. Some things are in the stars and can't be changed," said Bina.

"That may be, but this wasn't one of them."

"What else can we do?" She inquired.

"We must keep him cool. Amro, bring me a palm branch so I can fan him. Bina, please bring more water, then tell my mother what's happened, and wait on her for dinner. I must stay with him. I fear I shall be missing your duck dinner once again!"

He remained at Gaspar's side for the rest of the night and the day after. Throughout that time, Gaspar took only a few sips of water.

He seemed oblivious to where he was, almost delirious at times, and Melchior wondered how he had become so sick. The third morning Bina interrupted Melchior's ministrations to give him some news.

"Master Melchior, I went to the market this morning and found many sick people in Seleucia. There are warning flags on many doors because so many are dying. Some say it is a plague sent by the gods because King Phraates has elevated his Roman concubine to be first wife. They say we will all die unless he sends her away."

"I don't like the king's Roman wife, but I'm not convinced of that. I think other forces may be at work here. Unfortunately, there's no way to know if Gaspar has the sickness that's spreading in Seleucia, or if he was stricken from the heat. In any case, we best stay away from the city. What else are the people saying?"

"The butcher said that some merchants from China visited the satrap last month and many were sick when they arrived. Several of them died here."

"Do you know what the sick are complaining of?"

"The butcher said they cough, and retch, and that many have terrible blisters before a painful death."

Melchior shook his head. "Gaspar and I heard many coughing at our school the day Seleucus collapsed. Maybe he had the sickness too. I hope you came back quickly!"

"As soon as I paid the butcher. Most of the market stalls were closed anyway. I tell you master, it's good that we raise our own animals because it may be awhile before I can buy anything at the market again."

"I fear you may be right. It's good that Mered and his family are away. Maybe they can be protected from this. Do you know how my mother is? I haven't seen her since I started looking after Gaspar. Is she all right?"

"I worry for her. She's been unusually tired and didn't want any food today. Her coughing is worse, too. Maybe I should check on her."

"Yes please, and let me know at once if she show signs of sickness."

"I will, master."

Melchior looked at Gaspar with new concern. Until now, he thought his friend might be suffering from sun sickness. He had seen it before with similar signs, but what Bina reported was entirely different. A spreading sickness could take the lives of half the city. He should warn his brother, Mered, but how?

Soon Bina returned looking upset. "Master, your mother is very ill. I'm sure she has a fever. She's shivering, and sweating and . . ." her voice trailed off.

"And what?"

"She's has blisters on her body, such as I have never seen. What can we do?"

"We must send for a doctor, if there's one to be found."

Bina frowned and shook her head. "We cannot. There are only two in the city, and the butcher said they both went to attend the satrap. His whole family's been stricken."

"Then we'll take care her ourselves. I'll prepare her a dose of wild ginger. I have some stored in my chest. Could you tend to Gaspar for a few minutes while I get it for her?"

Bina bowed and moved next to Gaspar's bed while Melchior went to retrieve the ginger in the small store-room where he kept his herbs. He knew it could help nausea, and had used it successfully in the past but this sickness was worse than anything he'd seen. He also picked up some henbane, an herb he used for its pain killing properties. If Bina's information was correct, Gaspar and his mother would need it.

Melchior mixed the ginger and henbane into potions in separate cups, then entered Dodi's room. Though Bina had cleaned up well, the odor of vomit remained. Dodi's eyes look glazed and many large blisters had erupted on her arms, hands, and neck.

"Mother, I'm here. Can you see me?" He bent over Dodi's still form and took her hand.

"Yes. I don't know . . . what's wrong. I feel worse than the king's horse after a long ride." She made a feeble attempt at a smile.

"The king's a fat man, but I don't think even he can make a horse feel this bad."

Dodi's feeble attempt to laugh brought on a spasm of coughing. When it subsided, she took a deep breath. "You're right. I feel terrible."

Melchior gripped her hand. "I know Bina told you about Gaspar. But I have other news. A deadly pestilence is killing many in the city. Do you understand what I'm saying mother?"

"Yes . . . It means this is a spreading sickness. The kind that kills quickly." She squeezed his hand and sighed. "If this is the way the Lord has chosen to take me, so be it. I wanted more time with my grandchildren." She coughed. "But maybe my work is done."

He shook his head. "I hope not. . . Gaspar is gravely ill. He hasn't spoken since we found him outside the garden three days ago. And you may grow sicker, too, before you recover. I have some potions for you, one for your stomach and one for the pain of your blisters." Melchior lifted her head so she could drink from the cups he held, then he laid her down gently. "I can give you more as you need it, Is there anything else I can do for you?"

"Yes, there are important things . . . only you can do." She stopped to cough again and he saw she was having trouble catching her breath. "Please put the scrolls Gaspar scribed . . . in a safe place. I . . . don't want them destroyed . . . want the children . . . to read one day."

"I will. I'll find someone who can keep them safe. Is there something else?" He could tell his mother was tiring, and her swollen tongue made speech difficult.

"Please offer . . . sacrifice to Yahweh for me. I taught you ... when you were small. I want Yahweh to know . . . I'm faithful."

Melchior drew his brows together. "I'm sure Yahweh knows it, Mother. You have always been faithful." He sighed. "But I can do as you wish."

"One more thing ..." Dodi hesitated and motioned to her mouth. "I am . . . so thirsty." Melchior raised a cup of water to her lips and let her drink. "If I die, bury me . . . near Jerusalem."

Melchior shook his head and looked away. He didn't want to hear this.

"Look at me, son. Please."

He knew of Dodi's lifelong desire to visit the home of her ancestors, and that she would want a Jewish burial, but he never expected this. How could he answer her? Jewish law required the shrouded body be interred within a day of death, preferably before sundown. But he'd heard stories of famous Jews being re-interred. His mother taught him that Moses had brought the bones of Joseph, the one known for his many colored cloak, out of Egypt to rebury him in the land of his ancestors. His mother must be asking him to do the same. He looked at her but he knew she sensed his hesitation.

"Please, Melchior. I tried to be a . . . good mother, and you've always been … a good son. This is a big request, but . . . important. I know . . . the Lord wants this . . . Please tell me you will do it." Her swollen red-rimmed eyes watched his.

Melchior's eyes welled up as his mother's words touched his heart. How could he say no to the woman who had inspired his work with the stars, who had taught him the prophesies, and who had a smile on her face whenever he was near her?

"Yes. If this is what you want, I will do it."

"Thank you. Please find a good place . . . holy place."

"I will. I promise. Now rest. I'll send Bina to stay with you, but I'll check on you soon." He tenderly ran his hand over her brow and rose from her bedside. Lest he forget, he went at once to retrieve the parchment scrolls his mother had narrated to Gaspar in the past year. He was so proud of their work. It didn't seem right that they should both be stricken in such a painful way.

It took him several trips to move the scrolls from his mother's room. For the time being he would keep them in a corner of his room covered by an old blanket. Who can I ask to hold these? He wondered. Gaspar would have been the best person, but would he survive? He would do whatever was needed to protect the scrolls even if he had to hide them himself.

"Is there any improvement, Bina?" Melchior asked when he returned to Gaspar's bedside.

"None, Master. He appears like your mother, except he has no blisters."

"I guess that's some consolation. I've been thinking about Mered and his family. When did you say they will return?"

"When the moon is high again."

"That's the end of next week. I've been trying to think how we can warn them of the sickness, but we are needed here. Can you think of anyone to send who wasn't with you in the city?"

"I'm sorry master, but I cannot."

Melchior nodded. "Perhaps Amro will know someone. Please send him to me."

Soon after, Amro stood outside the doorway of Melchior's room, too timid to venture closer. Melchior respected his concern, and spoke to him from several paces away. "I'm worried about my brother and his family. You've served us well for many years, and I trust you. Do you know anyone we can send to warn them of the sickness? I don't want them to come back with the children until it has run its course."

"I fear that may be some time yet, Master Melchior."

"I know. But can you think of anyone?"

"Only one person. My youngest son, Asher, works as a shepherd in the lands to the south. He's always out in the fields and never comes to the city. I can try to find him if you'd like."

"Yes, I would!"

"But it will take him away from his flock for many days and he may lose sheep, if they go untended."

"He won't go unrewarded." Melchior untied a small pouch of coins from his belt. He pulled out five large gold ones and flipped them across the tiled floor to Amro, who picked them up one by one and whistled. Melchior could tell it had probably been a long time since Amro had seen so much money.

"Please, take one for your trouble, and give the rest to your son. That should be enough to pay him, for his travel and any lost sheep. Find out from Bina where Mered is. When you find Asher, keep your distance, but tell him to deliver my message to Mered. They must not return until they hear from Asher again that the sickness is over. If Asher is successful, there will be more gold for him, and you, when he goes back the second time." Melchior could see from his expression that Amro was satisfied with the arrangement. "One last thing. Please report to me when you return."

Amro bowed. "I will, master."

Melchior felt some measure of relief. Whatever might become of those in his house, at least he'd done what he could to protect his nieces and nephews.

For the next seven days, Melchior continued to care for Gaspar and Bina for Dodi. His mother worsened day by day. Chills and coughs tormented her slight frame, but the worst was the daily increase in blisters. No part of her body remained untouched, and no position seemed better than another for comfort. Bina sat by her day and night, turning her from side to side, keeping cold cloths on her head and neck, and giving her water when she could, but Dodi only got worse.

Gaspar however began to show improvement. He had never coughed much, had never developed blisters, and the swelling of his eyes and tongue subsided. He wasn't eating but was drinking more, and Melchior was encouraged that he was showing the first signs of recovery. He continued to give herb potions to them both, but he knew that they were small comfort to his mother. She had stopped vomiting but only because she had eaten nothing for two weeks. She was hovering near death.

One morning, Gaspar asked for something to eat. Melchior was overjoyed and ran to the pantry where he found some mushy rice and returned with it quickly. He helped Gaspar to sit up and spoon-fed him while his friend did his best to swallow. The men were silent but the smile on Melchior's face said everything.

Now that Gaspar was improving, Melchior considered his mother's request to offer a sacrifice. He had wanted to do it sooner, but had been too afraid to leave Gaspar's bedside. Now he knew a few hours away would be good for them both.

He left the house and went up to the palm grove on the hill. He searched for something to use as an altar, a large rock or fallen tree but nothing seemed suitable. Then it occurred to him that the right thing was waiting back in Mered's counting room. The wooden desk that had been his father's was easily movable and just the right size. He returned to the house, dismantled the desk and pulled it on a wagon to the summit of the hill. Then he reassembled it under the shade of the largest date palm he could find.

Finally, he returned to the house, washed and dressed in his finest robes and took a sharp dagger from his room. His next stop was the fenced pen on the west side of the house where the sheep and chickens were kept. He found what he judged to be the youngest, choicest lamb, tied a rope around its neck and led it toward the summit where he'd set up the desk as an altar.

He didn't remember many of the prayers his mother had taught him as a child but there was one saying that he thought would be fitting. It was actually part of the song the Israelites sang after they passed through the sea to escape the Egyptians. Though he remembered only parts of it, he thought it might suffice as he offered up the sacrificial lamb.

He covered the top of the altar with the largest palm leaves he could find and layered it many times, so the lamb's blood wouldn't seep into the fine wood of the desk. Then he bound the lamb's limbs, held it down on the altar and above its bleating cries recited the words of the song loudly as he looked to the evening sky.

I will sing to the Lord for he is gloriously triumphant;
Horse and chariot he has cast into the sea.
My strength and my refuge is the Lord,
And he has become my savior.

This is my God, I praise him.
The God of my father, I extol him.
The Lord is a warrior,
Lord is his name!

Then he added:

My mother is your faithful servant, Oh Lord.
Remember her now in her time of need. Be merciful to her,
Oh God.

He slit the lamb's throat with one powerful motion and allowed its blood
to seep briefly onto the palm leaves below. Then he wrapped the dead
lamb in the leaves, and put it in a pit he dug some yards away. There he
lit a fire, and as it began to burn in earnest, he sat down to keep vigil for
his mother, his friend, and all the people of Seleucia.

At dawn, he roused himself. Only the charred bones of the lamb
remained in the pit. He'd watched it burn all night, hoping his supplica-
tions rose with its smoke. Satisfied that he'd done what his mother asked,
he walked home. He was cold and hungry, but his first thoughts were
for her and Gaspar. He would relieve Bina as soon as he could, but went
first to wash and change clothes, and to see Gaspar. He was gladdened to
see his friend sitting up, eating a piece of bread left from the day before.

Gaspar looked up. "You're a sight for my sore eyes, and I mean what
I say, for my eyes have never been so sore!"

"They were pretty swollen. In fact, they were almost as bad as
your worst night of drinking! As was your tongue, I might add," joked
Melchior.

Gaspar smiled. "If only I could have enjoyed this half as much! What
happened to me? The last thing I remember was scribing some passages
for Dodi."

"You've been very sick. For well over two weeks, so I'm not surprised
you don't remember."

"What was wrong with me?" Gaspar asked in an unusually quiet way.

"It's a spreading sickness. My mother got sick too, and lingers on death's door."

"What of Mered's family? Are they . . . ?"

"Safe, I hope. They left to attend a wedding in another village. But I fear many have died in Seleucia and the nearby countryside. I'm so glad to see you better, my friend!" Melchior grasped Gaspar's shoulders and kissed him on the top of his head. "Welcome back to the land of the living."

"Glad to be back."

"Will you forgive me if I leave you for a while? I must see to my mother."

"Let me come with you," said Gaspar. "If she is failing, I must come."

"Are you strong enough?

"I think so. This old body may look haggard, but on the inside I'm strong as an ox!" but he wobbled as he tried to stand.

"Yes, sure, strong as an ox!" Melchior chided as he grabbed at Gaspar's arm. "But come if you insist. I'll help you." Melchior held Gaspar around the big man's waist as they walked ever so slowly to Dodi's room.

As they entered, the men could smell the stale odor of sickness. Dodi had been confined to her bed for almost two weeks, and though Bina did her best to keep her clean, it was obvious that her failing organs had affected her bowels and bladder. They looked at each other acknowledging their unspoken dread. Was she already dead?

Her face was pale and Melchior couldn't see her chest rise. He looked to Bina for confirmation.

"She lives, Master, but death is near."

Her cheeks were sunken and the blisters which covered her body looked like one continuous sea of purple and red. As Bina moved away, Melchior knelt down next to his mother, hoping she might at least feel his presence. He held her hand lightly in his.

"Mother," he said quietly. "I'm here. I offered up the sacrifice you wanted. I burned the choicest lamb, just as you taught me, and stayed until it was consumed." He swallowed, tears streaming down his cheeks. "I know Yahweh will accept our offering. I know he will be merciful."

Dodi stirred the slightest bit. Did she hear him? Her eyes fluttered and she began to whisper. "Melchior? You look ... older. Only yesterday I played with you. Remember?"

"I remember mother." He wiped away a tear.

She pulled slightly on his hand, urging him closer. "Don't cry, boy. I know ... I'm sick."

Melchior nodded.

She moved her head and opened her eyes a little wider. "Gaspar? Is that you?" Gaspar moved closer to hear her better. "Melchior said he'll take me . . . Jerusalem. Help him . . . He'll need you. . . Together you'll find the way. . . God will show ...."

With an astonished look on his face, Gaspar opened his mouth to reply. But before he could utter a word her hand went limp in Melchior's grip and her head sagged in a final gesture of departure. Gaspar closed his eyes. Melchior bent his head and sobbed.

CHAPTER 9

Gaspar

WHILE MELCHIOR WEPT AT HIS mother's bedside, Gaspar considered her final words. Had he heard correctly? That Melchior would take her to Jerusalem? He knew she had always wanted to go there. She must have been imagining things. It happened sometimes. The dying imagined things, saw strange places or ancestors that had gone before them. He would have done almost anything for the old lady, but now it was too late for earthly journeys.

Soon Melchior rose and left the room. Gaspar followed him out slowly steadying himself on the wall as he walked. They returned to Melchior's room, now become Gaspar's. Tired from his first small exertion he was happy to lie down.

"I must leave you for a while," said Melchior.

Gaspar nodded, as Melchior left the room.

Gaspar stared at the ceiling, trying to gather his thoughts. There was no denying he was weak, and after seeing Dodi's body, he realized how lucky he was. But to lose Dodi! He was almost ashamed to admit how much she had meant to him, how jealous he'd been of Melchior.

He thought back to his childhood, to the mother he'd never known and the father who raised him alone. Women had never been a part of their household. Even their servants had been men. Not until his teenage years, when his father took him to a brothel, did women come into his world. But they weren't women like Dodi. He'd often imagined that his mother might have looked like her; not beautiful but intelligent, strong, loving, and determined. Was that why he enjoyed visiting Melchior so often? Not entirely. The man was his friend after all. But he felt like family when he was with them, that Dodi looked on him as a son. It was a pleasure he had never known. And now she was gone.

After several hours, Melchior returned to sit with him and for a long time, neither spoke. Then Melchior broke the silence. "Gaspar, in her last moments did you hear my mother speak of Jerusalem?"

"Yes. I thought she imagined she was going on the journey she always wanted."

"It was more than that. In her last days she made a final request. She asked me to bring her bones to Jerusalem. She wants to rest there with her ancestors."

"By my stars! That trip that will take you hundreds of miles and many months!"

Melchior frowned. "I know, but how could I refuse her?"

"You couldn't. But when would you go?"

"Not for some time. I'll bury her tomorrow. And when the time seems right I'll make the trip to Jerusalem with her bones."

"Do you have any idea where her ancestors are buried?"

"No. But I think as long as I bury her near a holy place, in a Jewish burial site, she will rest happy. The main thing is, I'd like you to come with me. That's what she asked for."

"I haven't taken a journey of that distance in years!"

"Does that mean you won't come?"

"Of course not. I would do almost anything for you my friend, including this long and hazardous journey."

"I hoped you'd say that. Did you hear what she said about the Lord showing us the way? What do you make of it?"

"I'm not sure. She knew we use the stars to guide our journeys. What else could she have meant?"

"I don't know. Nothing is making sense right now."

"You must give it time," said Gaspar.

"Yes. It was hard losing my father, but her. . ." his voice trailed off.

"She was an extraordinary person. What a memory for all those stories!"

"Yes." Melchior smiled. "But enough of this. Now you must rest. I want you to stay here 'til you're stronger and we know the sickness in Seleucia has abated."

"Thank you. I'd like that," said Gaspar.

"If you're up to it, will you come to the burial tomorrow?"

"I'll make sure I'm up to it."

CHAPTER 10

Melchior

§

MELCHIOR FOUND BINA PREPARING DODI's body for burial. "Since Gaspar is still so weak, you and I are the watchers for my mother. She deserved many mourners but so be it. Though there are only two of us, we'll observe the customs as far as we can."

"I've done the best I could, Master."

"You may be a Samaritan, but no Jew could have done better."

Bina smiled. She had closed Dodi's eyes and was already performing a ritual cleansing. It was difficult because the body was so covered by blisters. Melchior picked up a cloth to help her. They worked solemnly and when they were done, sprinkled drops of olive oil over the body. Then they unrolled a long swath of white cloth, and beginning with the feet, began to wrap it around her, sprinkling in frankincense, myrrh and cypress.

Next they covered her head with a second, smaller cloth, wrapped the full body cloth over the head cloth and tucked it up tightly. When they finished, they moved Dodi's shrouded body onto the bier he had prepared in the main hall. He had retrieved his father's desk back from the site of his sacrifice on the hill, set it up in the main hall and covered it with the choicest fabric he could find in his sister-in-law's closet. He thought his mother would be pleased that one of Dahab's purchases had finally been worth the cost.

Bina and Melchior sat near the body through the night. Just after sunrise Melchior dug a shallow grave outside the garden, thinking that it would suffice until his mother's reburial. When he was done, he washed, dressed and went to waken Gaspar.

"It's time, my friend. Are you strong enough?"

"Yes. Just give me a moment." Melchior watched as Gaspar sat up, rubbed the sleep from his eyes and rose to his feet. He seemed quite a bit stronger than the day before, and moved more steadily.

Since Amro had not yet returned from his journey, Melchior and Bina used the litter to carry Dodi's body to the grave site, with Gaspar following close behind. After setting down the litter, Melchior jumped into the grave, and guided Bina as she gently nudged his mother's shrouded body into his waiting arms. Carefully, he positioned it on the floor of the grave, climbed out and used one of Amro's shovels to fill in the dirt. Then he bid Bina and Gaspar to sit down before he began to recite one of the prayers he'd heard his mother say many times before:

> *I bless the Lord who counsels me;*
> *Even at night my heart exhorts me.*
> *I keep the Lord always before me;*
> *With him at my right hand, I shall never be shaken.*
> *Therefore my heart is glad and my soul rejoices;*
> *My body also dwells secure,*
> *For you will not abandon my soul to Sheol,*
> *Nor let your devout one see the pit.*
> *You will show me the path of life,*
> *Abounding joy in your presence,*
> *The delights at your right hand forever.* *
> **Psalms 16:7-11**

Then he offered a prayer of his own:

Oh, Lord, please remember my mother, your devoted one.
She strove always to do what is right and true.
I don't understand why she was taken as she was

But she always said your ways are not our ways, Oh God.
And my mother was wise.
Now I place my trust in you as she did.
Guide me as you guided her.
And let that be her legacy,
That I will follow your pathways all my life.

Gaspar and Bina rose. They gathered some soil in their hands, threw it on the grave and followed him back to the quiet house.

CHAPTER 11

Back in Qana

ALIMA STOOD WITH BALTHAZAR BEHIND a large palm near her father's house. Her three bare chested brothers were hammering planks onto the skeleton of a new boat in the yard.

The eldest, Waled, shouted out directions while Akram, the best looking middle brother, followed along in his gentle, efficient manner. Her youngest brother, Sameer, always the good humored one, still enjoyed teasing the others. The banter between them reminded her of days gone by.

She drew closer, looked up into their raised work area, and waved. It took a moment, before Waled jumped down from his perch. She could tell he was surprised, not only to see her but because she stood with an unfamiliar man.

"Alima? Is that really you?" asked Waled.

"Your eyes do not deceive you. Have you missed me?" She held out her arms for the hug she hoped would come.

Waled responded with a huge enveloping embrace. "It's so good to see you! What good fortune brings you home?"

Alima took a deep breath. "I only wish it was good." She swallowed. "Our village was attacked six days ago. Everyone was killed except for me and my neighbor Balthazar here."

"Your husband Sahl?" Waled asked.

"Dead."

Waled's face became grave. "This is great misfortune indeed. I am sorry. But I praise The Great One that you live!"

She watched as Waled looked Balthazar over and waved for Sameer and Akram to join him. "Balthazar is it? Thank you for bringing our sister home." He paused. "But why did you travel alone with her? You know it is not permitted."

"Yes, I know. But I trust you'll understand when you hear my explanation." He bowed formally to the brothers, who now stood facing him shoulder to shoulder, an impenetrable wall of muscle.

"I am Balthazar, son of Fatin. My family is well known in the region, and have been traders for generations. Khalan was attacked and all were slaughtered including all of my family and household. We live only because we were out of the village when the Himyarites attacked. By the code of my fathers, I couldn't leave Alima there to die. I had no choice but to travel alone with her. Your sister will attest that I respected her privacy during our journey."

"Yes, brothers. That is true!" exclaimed Alima.

"She hasn't been compromised, I promise you," said Balthazar in a serious tone.

Waled placed his hands upon Balthazar's shoulders. "I understand, and on behalf of my family, I thank you. Alima is precious to us and you were right to act as you did. Let's go in. You must be hungry, and our mother will want to welcome you."

Alima preceded the men into the house. It was as she remembered, not big, but sturdily built of mud brick and stone with pleasing proportions. The plain interior revealed several woven hangings, some threadbare floor coverings, and a few decorative urns, all cracked. The house looked old and worn compared to Sahl's house in Khalan, but it mattered not at all. She was home.

"Mother!" Sameer burst out before Waled could speak, "Look, who's home!"

Her mother, Jun, came rushing into the room. "Alima! Oh! I can hardly believe my eyes!" Jun began to shower her with kisses, on her cheeks, on her hair, ears, and hands. Tears flowed freely as Jun held her hands and studied her, looking for any changes wrought by the intervening years. Similarly overcome, Alima hugged her mother tightly, weeping as she did so.

It was some time before the women were able to sit next to each other without one or the other tearing up. "I am so grateful to be home!" said Alima when she was finally composed. "These last few days, I longed to see your faces. And now I am rewarded for you all look well. But where are father and Baysan? Are they at the market? I know how she coaxes him to take her." She looked around expectantly, but her eagerness was met by frowns from her brothers and tears again from her mother. No-one spoke.

"What's wrong?" asked Alima, her voice shaking. "Where are they?"

Balthazar rose to leave, but Alima caught his eye and shook her head. He remained, leaning against the wall at the back of the room.

Akram knelt down before Alima. "About six months after you left with Sahl, a Roman merchant vessel entered the harbor. We figured they came to buy spice. Father was surprised, since it had been over a year since they'd come. We'd sometimes spot them out at sea, but they rarely sailed into the bay. So it was a rare opportunity for us to see one of their ships up close. The four of us took regular walks to where it was docked." He paused to sip some water before continuing.

"One evening, well after sunset, we saw flames coming from the vessel's forward deck. We watched as the fire grew, and a short time later noticed someone swimming toward us from that direction. The night was dark with clouds, so only when the man ran from the water did we recognize him as our cousin."

Alima gasped. "Was it Umar or Seif?"

"It was Seif. And we knew right away he was in trouble. His tunic was torn, and blackened with soot. One of his hands was bleeding. Father wanted no part of him and told him to leave, but before he could, two squads of Roman soldiers came running up the shore. They seized Seif, searched him and found stolen coins from the ship in his belt. In his panic, Seif blamed father, saying he had planned the theft. Why he did so we'll never know. We protested. Vowed father had nothing to do with it! But they ignored us. They arrested them both, and marched them away. They beheaded Seif the next day."

Tears ran down her face. "Father, too?" asked Alima with a look of dread.

Akram shook his head. "No. When they found out who he was, they decided to enslave him instead. "

Sameer cut in. "They put him to work, repairing the ship, and soon after sailed away taking Father with them. The merchants who dealt with the Romans said they wanted him to help build boats at one of their northern ports. We never got a chance to say goodbye."

"No. This cannot be!" Said Alima angrily. "I always knew Seif was a troubled man, but this! Father arrested and enslaved for a crime committed by that fool! But where is Baysan?" She looked at Sameer trying to keep her voice steady. "Has something befallen her as well?"

Alima's mother spoke in a low voice. "It was an accident. Two days after the Romans sailed, Baysan took a small skiff into the gulf. She said she needed to be on the water. That she would feel closer to your father. It was a sunny day when she set out, but a storm came up suddenly. When the storm settled, your brothers sailed out to look for her. They found only the capsized skiff."

Her mother wept as Alima held her. In one terrible week, her sister and father both gone. Alima felt the loss of Sahl a mere trifle in comparison. How foolish she had been to worry about a possible betrothal to Seif. He was dead and she wasn't sorry. Looking at her family, she realized how the retelling of those days had made the sting fresh again.

She kissed her mother. "I hate to add to your grief, but I, too, have bad news." She took her mother's hand. "My husband, Sahl, was killed in a raid on our village. In fact, all the villagers were killed except for myself and my neighbor, Balthazar, who was on the road when the Himyarites attacked." She looked in his direction. "I don't understand why we were spared, but I thank The Great One that we were. Sadly, I return a poor widow. Everything of value was taken or destroyed. I hope I won't be a burden to you." She looked at her family in uncertainty.

Jun did not hesitate. "Do not even think such a thing! Your valuables are as nothing compared to you. I lost Baysan, and your father. Praise to the Great one, I have not lost you!"

Alima squeezed her mother's hands, relishing her warmth and caring. "My husband was at least a good teacher. He taught me about the spice trade. I feel certain I can bring value to our household in some way. I pray you'll let me live with you."

"How can you doubt it?" asked Jun.

Alima smiled widely, then approached each of her brothers in turn, hugging and kissing them in consolation for their common losses. When she was done, she stood near Balthazar and addressed her family.

"Mother, I want you to meet Balthazar. Sahl and I were his neighbors. He protected me on our journey from Khalan. I ask you to offer him our hospitality, for I would be dead if not for him."

Jun walked over to Balthazar. "Young man, thank you for bringing Alima home to us. Our house is yours for as long as you wish. It's not grand, but it's clean. And I'm proud to say our food is tasty. Maybe it's time we shared some?" She motioned for them all to join her around the low serving table.

Alima took comfort watching her mother scurry around. Despite her advancing age Jun moved gracefully with purpose and energy. Alima set out wooden cups for wine while her mother hung a pot of soup above the fire. She could feel the pulse of the room gradually return to normal. The men sat around the table talking. Sameer teased Waled about a woman he was pursuing but apparently scaring away instead, while Akram spoke with Balthazar of shipping and spice.

How thankful she was to be home at last.

CHAPTER 12

Balthazar's Plan

§

"IT APPEARS YOU HAVE MUCH work. Was it hard to get jobs after your father was taken?" Balthazar asked Akram as he took his first taste of Jun's soup.

"We worried about that at first." Akram replied. "Qana's fishermen are our best customers, and we wondered if they would give their business to other builders. But they continued to come to us. They knew father had trained us well, and that he was unjustly arrested. If anything, we probably got more business than we could handle the first year he was gone."

"I don't ever remember having so much work," added Sameer.

"Indeed." Waled rejoined. "We spent every waking hour working that year, but we stayed afloat." He chuckled at his own joke. "Of course, things gradually returned to normal. We still build dhows and other small fishing boats, but once in a while, we get a commission to build a large ship for one of the wealthy merchants or sea captains. Like the one we're working on now. If piloted by an able seaman, a ship like that can deliver goods much quicker than a caravan."

Balthazar saw Waled's pride shining on his face. "I didn't know your father, but I'm sure he'd be proud of your success. My father was also successful. He was starting to let me make decisions for our spice business when Khalan was attacked. In fact, I was in Qana ten days ago to accept a delivery of cinnabar from Socotra. It's stored in a nearby warehouse. I planned to suggest to my father that we move it by sea. I even met with a sea captain when I was here."

"Who did you meet with?" asked Waled.

"A Captain Ghali. Do you know him?"

"Yes, yes. We know all of the seamen in the city. Ghali is true to the meaning of his name. Dealing with him is always expensive." The three brothers laughed heartily at what Balthazar considered a personal joke.

"I see. Then perhaps you can direct me to someone else? The cinnabar is my decision now, and I want to move it quickly to take my profit."

Waled raised his eyebrows in thought. "I may know someone. The man who gave us our current job has another ship that will be sailing soon. I'm not sure if he has room for more cargo, but I can arrange for you to meet him."

"I'd like that," said Balthazar.

"Normally, I'd advise you to sell your spice here." Waled continued. "Money in hand is usually better than risking the loss of your cargo at sea. But only two Roman ships have come to Qana since our father was taken, so your chance of selling to them here isn't good. In spite of what they've done to our family, they pay well for spice. Their people are spoiled, you know! They can't do without their spice."

"I know that well enough. And I know the risk of storms and shipwreck. But if I can save money and time, I'll be willing to accept the risk. Can you arrange a meeting with this captain as soon as possible?"

Waled laughed "You're an eager one aren't you? Yes, Yes. I'll send word to him today."

"Thank you." Balthazar bowed his head, and resumed his meal. He spent the rest of the day eating, drinking, and getting acquainted with Alima's brothers. By late afternoon, he was overcome with fatigue. Ten continuous days of grueling travel had taken its toll, and he could hardly keep his eyes open.

"Come, Balthazar," said Jun. "You may stay in this room with Akram." He lay down on the straw bed she pointed to, and surrendered quickly to sleep. When he awakened the next day, he was embarrassed to see the sun high and hot.

"Good afternoon, young man," said Jun when he emerged. "I hope you slept well. Alima has gone to the market. Are you hungry?"

"I am indeed." All he'd eaten the day before had not vanquished his hunger. Within moments, Jun served him a dish of chickpea fatteh, one of his favorite foods. He savored each bite, and drank generously when Jun served him a hot cup of red tea. Alima's family had welcomed him, but watching them together sharpened his own feelings of loss.

"Do you not like the fatteh young man?" asked Jun as she joined him at the table.

Balthazar realized he had stopped eating. "It's very good. I was just thinking of my mother. She was a good cook too."

Jun smiled. "As is Alima. What do you think of my girl? She is a beautiful, no?"

Balthazar almost spit out his tea. He could understand Jun's interest in finding Alima a new match, but so soon? Then he smiled, thinking his mother hadn't been much different. She had often teased him about finding a nice girl to have babies with.

"Yes, Jun. Alima is beautiful. But you must understand … I never thought of her in that way. She was married to my neighbor, and I respected their marriage."

"As you should have. But she is widowed now."

"Yes. But she may not be ready to marry again. She told me Sahl wasn't an easy man to live with."

"I have heard a little of that," said Jun rocking her head from side to side.

Balthazar sipped his tea before continuing. "Still, good husband or not, she'll want to mourn him properly."

Jun eyed Balthazar directly. "Young man, you don't need to remind me about mourning. We observe our traditions. Our family mourned Baysan, and we felt as if we should mourn my husband too, though we knew he wasn't dead."

"I mean no disrespect. But Alima and I are only starting to know each other."

"That's good! And of course, you're right. Mehir and I brought Alima up to respect our customs, and I will see that she mourns properly. But I'm a practical woman. In four months, when her mourning is over, she'll need a husband. A woman without a husband has no status and I will not let that happen to her. I do only what my husband would have done; I'm looking after her future. I will not apologize for that no matter what our customs are!"

Balthazar considered her explanation. Practical indeed. Still, her suggestion stirred new feelings. He couldn't deny he was attracted to Alima, but what he might do about it he could not guess.

"Jun, I can only imagine how much you miss your husband. I told Waled that I may ship some cinnabar to a Roman port on the Great Sea. If I accompany my cargo, the voyage might give me a chance to ask about Mehir. Perhaps I can discover where he is working. Maybe even get a message to him. Would you like me to do that?"

Jun's face sparked. "Oh, yes! To let him know he's not forgotten would mean everything. . . But the Romans wield the power of life and death. I wouldn't want any harm to come to you!"

"I know the Romans can be dangerous. But please understand, I don't propose to rescue him. Only to find him. And to give him your message, if I can. After I sell my spice, I plan to head east. I want to study the stars, and I've heard there's a school in Parthia where I can do that."

Jun looked at him in confusion. "You mean you won't be returning to Qana?"

"That's right. So if you must know the result of my search, you should send one of your sons along with me."

"I see," she said, rubbing her forehead. "I'll need to think on this. I'm not sure the small chance of getting a message to Mehir is worth the risk of losing another child. I can't answer you now." She rose somberly from her cushion and left the room.

As Balthazar finished the last of his meal, he heard raised voices coming from the boatyard. Curious to discover the cause of the commotion, he walked to the doorway. A large muscled man with a scraggly red beard stood nose to nose with Sameer. "You've all been holding out on me! I saw Alima at the market but she ignored me. Why didn't you tell me she's back in town and widowed? I'm your family! But no…I had to hear it from a fishmonger!" The man paused then spoke slowly with exaggerated emphasis as he looked toward Waled and Akram. "She's even more beautiful than I remembered and we always did get along … so, very, well." Balthazar's hackles rose.

Before the brothers could respond, the man added, "And you know my rights to her as your cousin." He spat on the ground just short of Sameer's sandaled feet.

Sameer's facial muscles tensed. Akram descended from his scaffold to join his brother as Waled watched from above. Tension hung heavy in the air, and Balthazar waited for the fight he knew would follow. Instead, Akram clapped his hand on the man's left shoulder.

"Umar, why must you assume the worst! We had every intention of telling you, but Alima only arrived yesterday! Be reasonable, cousin. Would you have us lose a whole day's work to walk the city streets and announce it aloud? For truly, we have no idea where you live these days. You must tell us where you rest your head so we may negotiate with you appropriately in the days to come!"

Balthazar laughed at Akram's masterful back-handed swipe at Umar's uncertain living arrangements, and caught the not quite silent chuckle of Sameer. He had not spat back, but the veiled insinuation at Umar's reduced circumstances was almost as good.

Balthazar could tell Umar had been caught off guard for he began to stammer. "Well yes, it's true." Said Umar. "I've had to change my dwelling lately. There were people I was trying to avoid you see. But that's not your business, is it?"

At this remark, Waled joined his brothers, his hammer prominent in his right hand. The three strapping men stood shoulder to shoulder in front of their cousin as they had with Balthazar the day before. They were a formidable sight.

"That's not exactly true, Umar," said Waled. "If you mean to assert your right to Alima, then we must know and approve your living arrangements. Do you think we're anxious to lose yet another sister? Regardless of your "rights" you should take care where Alima is concerned. If she is to be wed again it will be to the right man. Although, I must say it may not be an easy task."

Umar raised his head, a questioning look on his dissipated face. "And why is that? Surely the bride price for a beauty like Alima will be high."

"Because cousin, though she may be beautiful, she is barren. She was married to Sahl for over three years and bore no children. Are you so anxious to take her into your home, knowing that she will produce no heirs? Do you wish to feed, clothe, and shelter such a woman for the rest of your days?" Waled let his words sink in, and Balthazar saw Umar's consternation as he realized he'd approached his cousins without knowing all the facts. His stammering became more pronounced as he turned away from the brothers.

"S-so sad, s-so s-sad! I, I did, didn't know. What a curse on your family! B-b-but then, Alima never was as friendly as Baysan! Th-th-that one was a t-t-true loss to your house. N-n-not like Alima who always has airs. She understood a woman's place. Perhaps, I m-must reconsider. B-but I'll be back. Alima may have *skills* to make up for her b-barrenness. Her b-beauty may still find value for me." Umar paused, spun around and spoke close to Waled's face. "Yes, yes, the more I think on it, her barrenness is s-s-sad, but it may make other p-p-pleasurable pastimes more rewarding."

The brothers and Balthazar gasped in unison as they realized what Umar had in mind. Before Balthazar could move, the three brothers pressed forward as one. Sameer, the youngest and most agile, grabbed Umar from behind and spun him around as Waled punched him in the stomach and Akram took a poke at his head. Umar's slurs had gone past the point of ignoring, and Balthazar was glad to see them take a stand for Alima's honor. It was something he would have done, if he still had a sister to protect.

The pummeling went on long enough to subdue Umar, who tried to fight back but had little chance against the angry threesome. When the punches stopped, they dragged him off their property and dropped him in the sandy road. "We're finished cousin!" Waled spoke to the half-conscious man. "Kinship like yours is a curse. Don't come back unless you want to lose your manhood."

As the brothers walked into the house for water, Balthazar laughed in admiration. "Well done, very well done! How you held off for so long against that louse of a man I don't know. I might have thrown a punch as soon as his spittle neared my sandals!"

Sameer nodded as he gulped some water. "I thought about it. He's been a thorn in our family's side for years. His brother, Seif, caused us to lose father and Baysan. Umar's not much better. We can't let him assert his right to Alima. He clearly intends to sell her for sex. How can we stop him?"

Waled and Akram exchanged troubled glances, but neither offered a plan. Balthazar took the silence as an opportunity to speak.

"I may have a way to help," he said.

"Please…" said Waled.

"I respect Alima and would hate to see her wed to that man. If it would suit your purpose, tell him I have offered a bride price for her. He seems like the kind of man who can be bought."

The brothers raised their eyebrows in surprise.

"Please don't misunderstand," continued Balthazar. "I'm not ready to take a wife. But if we can make Umar believe it, I will play along." Balthazar could see his suggestion was unexpected, but one by one the brothers agreed to the concept of a possible deception and discussed how it might work.

A few hours later, Balthazar yelled out: "She's coming!" The brothers put down their tools and came inside. Alima arrived soon after, set down her basket and poured herself a cup of water, as the men hovered nearby.

"What? I can tell that something's happened," she said turning to face them. "Are you going to tell me or must I coerce you? Maybe with some wonderful sweet cakes?" She smiled so radiantly that Balthazar briefly forgot his next thought.

"Sit down, please," he said finally, angry to have appeared flustered. "We must talk."

Alima sat on a nearby cushion and the men clustered around her. Akram took the lead, explaining the confrontation with Umar, leaving out only a few of Umar's ugly remarks. She remained silent, nodding now and then, and frowned as Akram described the fight that ended the encounter.

Sameer cut in impatiently. "You know it would be the accepted thing to marry him when your mourning is done, but we can't allow it. Umar's a dog!"

Alima's eyes welled up. "Since leaving Khalan I have worried about nothing else. I was actually relieved to hear of Seif's death."

"Losing him was no loss!" said Akram. "I curse him still for our father's bondage."

"So do I." said Alima. "And now to hear this about Umar! I tell you I'd rather drown like Baysan than submit to such a man!" Her brothers fell silent. "I know it's a bitter thought, but I just can't be with him, no matter what our traditions say."

"You won't have to," said Waled.

"But what can we do? What if Umar goes to his father? Won't Uncle Nibal insist on me as Umar's right?"

"I've come up with a plan," said Balthazar. "Do you remember what you suggested on the road from Khalan?"

Alima's hands flew to her face. "You told them?"

"Don't be embarrassed." Waled interposed. "Balthazar told us you had an idea to protect yourself from our cousins. We understand. We were surprised, but we understand."

"You're ... you're not angry with me?" she asked searching their faces.

"Why should we be?" asked Akram.

"Because! Because women ..." her voice trailed off.

"Are not supposed to have ideas?" Balthazar finished her sentence for her.

"Maybe not most women," said Akram. "But our family has always been a little different, don't you think?" He smiled.

"Besides," said Waled. "You're our only sister and we would protect you with our lives. If a good idea happens to be yours, what of it?"

"Do you think that too?" Alima asked Sameer.

Sameer looked at her directly "I can't deny I was shocked to hear it was your suggestion. It was a bold thing to do."

"That word again!" Said Alima. "Don't you see ..."

Sameer raised his hand. "Alima, please! I haven't finished. Bold or not, I would agree with almost any idea that protects you from that scum cousin. It doesn't matter that it was your idea. It matters only that it succeeds."

"That's right," said Balthazar. "I'm willing to offer a bride price to convince Umar to release his right to you."

"It's really Uncle Nibal we need to convince," said Waled. "And he must accept as long as Balthazar makes a fair offer."

"I plan to give him my family's land in Khalan," said Balthazar. "And I'll toss in a little gold and spice to seal the agreement."

"Balthazar says he doesn't plan to return to Khalan, so there's no loss to him," added Waled.

"But what of the Himyarites?" Alima asked.

"What of them? We don't know for sure that they took over the village, but if they did, it'll be Umar's problem," said Balthazar.

Alima looked at him in amazement. "You would do this for me? I never expected you to give away your land!" She hesitated. "How can you be sure you won't want to return some day? I'm not sure I can let you to do this."

"But the plan is your idea!" said Balthazar.

"I know, but perhaps you're being hasty. You may change your mind someday."

Balthazar couldn't keep from laughing as he considered her reaction. Wasn't it just like a woman to object based on how he might feel years from now!

"No, Alima," he replied. "I'm not being hasty. I'm being honest. My family's spice business was all I knew, but it will never be the same now that they're gone. Giving it away is no sacrifice. And I'll get great satisfaction from helping you."

"I am still willing to work as your servant. To repay the bride price."

"There is no need. I am doing this to help you and for that reason only."

Tears brimmed in Alima's eyes. "Are you sure?"

"Yes!"

"Then so be it." Her smile returned only briefly. "But . . . Umar must think your offer is serious; that we're really getting betrothed. How can we make it seem so?"

"It'll be hard to deceive him if we stay in Qana," said Balthazar. "But if we leave, your uncle and Umar will never know if we actually marry."

"Are you planning to join a caravan so soon? We only just got here!"

"Not exactly."

"Tell me then," said Alima.

"I've got some cinnabar stored in a nearby warehouse. I'd like to sell it at a port on the Great Sea, and am thinking to move it by ship instead of caravan if I can negotiate a good fee. Waled knows a captain who'll be sailing soon, and if you agree, I'll pay for the two of us to go. The sail may also give us the chance to ask about your father, because we'll be stopping in several Roman ports."

"You think we can find my father?" asked Alima in surprise.

"I don't know, but we can inquire as we go. Your brothers think there can't be many places where the Romans build big ships outside of Rome. If we can find one, we might have a chance of finding him."

"Do you really think so? It would be such a blessing!" Alima exclaimed. Then her bright face turned suddenly gloomy. "How long will we stay at the Great Sea once you sell your spice? We can't stay away from Qana forever."

"You're right. That's why I hope one of your brothers along with us."

"I . . . I don't understand," stammered Alima.

"I have two reasons for this. First, we can't be alone during your time of mourning so your brother can be your travel companion. And second, you'll need someone to come home with."

"Won't you come back to Qana after you sell your spice?"

"No. I plan to move on. Remember I told you? I want to study the stars. You need to make a new life for yourself too."

Alima looked away. Balthazar could tell she looked troubled but he had to get this settled. "You'll need a way to get home. Even if we find your father it's unlikely we can free him. If one of your brothers comes along, he can accompany you so that everything is done properly, both on your journey north and back again."

Balthazar looked at her eldest brother. "What do you think, Waled?"

Sameer spoke up before Waled could reply. "You know I do my best each day to follow your directions, brother, but I ache to see new places. If I go with them, I could help find father and accompany Alima home."

"If that's what you want, Sameer, I will agree," said Waled.

"As will I," said Akram. "It's worth your absence for a chance to find father."

"And you, Alima?" asked Sameer. "Do you agree? It will mean a long voyage, but I promise to watch out for you."

She hesitated. "I guess it could work . . . but what about mother? What do we tell her?" asked Alima. "She will be losing two more of us."

"Only for a time. We'll return, and she'll take comfort knowing we're together." said Sameer. "What's more, she likes Balthazar and will be happy thinking you'll be wed."

"I dread having to mislead her," said Alima shaking her head.

"We have no choice." Balthazar cut in. "If our plan is to work, we must convince her we are betrothed."

Sameer bobbed his head. "He's right, Alima. If mother doesn't believe it, neither will Umar or Uncle Nibal."

"We are all agreed, Alima," said Waled.

"It will be so hard to leave without telling her the truth." said Alima. Balthazar heard reluctance in her voice.

"It must be done," said Waled.

"Yes, I know." Said Alima with a sigh.

Akram patted Sameer on the shoulder. "We will miss you, little brother. Make sure you come back safely. And if you find yourself a wife, make sure she has some pretty sisters for us!"

"As if you need any help finding pretty women! You're pretty hard to compete with, you know."

Akram smirked. Waled slapped Akram on the shoulder as he nodded his head toward Sameer. "Just think how much more work we'll get done, now that we won't have to fix his mistakes!"

Sameer pulled his head back in surprise. "Is that so? Well, I won't miss your body odor! And a few of your other nasty . . ." The three brothers began talking all at once, and Balthazar enjoyed their good-hearted teasing.

"It's decided then," said Waled when the kidding subsided. "I'll send word to Uncle Nibal that we want to meet. He can tell Umar, if he can find him. Today we'll meet with Captain Musa."

"Will you come along, Sameer?" asked Balthazar.

"We're almost there." Waled announced as they approached Captain Musa's shipyard. "The man's a gifted pilot. He's never lost a ship."

"Never?" asked Balthazar sounding surprised.

"Not one," said Waled. "There he is now."

Waled pointed to the captain, who stood on the dock near the gangplank to his new ship. "Hey, Musa! I've brought you some business," shouted Waled.

"It's about time!" said Musa smiling widely.

"This is our friend, Balthazar," said Waled. "He's a spice trader from Khalan."

"Welcome," said Musa bowing. "What business do you bring?"

"I'm considering shipping some cinnabar to a port on the Great Sea, and Waled tells me you plan to sail that way soon."

"Yes. This ship heads north in ten days."

"Have you room for more cargo?"

"As luck would have it, I do. My ships are large and the best in the kingdom! Waled and his brothers built this one, you know."

"So I'm told."

"And did they tell you that I do all I can to safeguard my cargo?"

Waled interrupted. "What he says is true. Before the Romans took him, my father came up with a new design for hulls. We build an inner and outer layer, and place wool that we soak in wax between the two layers to make it extra watertight. We also use new iron fastenings that are a great improvement over the old wooden ones."

"That they are!" said Musa. "Come aboard so you can see what a beauty they built for me!" The four men boarded and walked the deck, inspecting the fine craftsmanship, and after some minutes gathered at the bow. Balthazar noticed the sky was darkening off shore.

"Doesn't she look grand?" asked Musa. "Your father's hull design is well worth the cost because my ships can survive the worst gales!"

"What have you named her?" asked Sameer.

"You mean you don't know? She's called *The Baysan* in honor of your sister who was lost."

Sameer and Waled stared at Musa as if struck dumb.

"I hope you're pleased?' Musa asked after several moments of silence.

"Very much so!" exclaimed Waled. "May we bring our mother to see her? It's a wonderful thing you've done to remember Baysan this way."

"I hoped you'd think so. And yes, your mother's welcome to come by. Now we should get down to business. You must have questions, Balthazar?"

"I do. This would be my first voyage, and I hear it will be a long one."

"It will take many months," agreed Musa. "But it's actually two voyages, not one."

Balthazar raised his brows. "Waled never mentioned that."

"I figured you'd know," said Waled.

Balthazar looked sheepish as he shrugged his shoulders.

"Let me explain," said Musa. "The first voyage takes us west along the gulf coast to Eudaemon then north through the strait into the Red Sea. There the journey gets more interesting. We sail within sight of land as much as possible."

"Why is that?"

"Because the weather can be so changeable. When the winds are good we can make good time, but we can also meet some fearsome gales. We must also watch for pirates. I can promise, it's not boring!"

"What ports do we stop at in the Red Sea?" asked Balthazar?

"Just Two. Berenike on the Egyptian coast. It's a busy port, a little past half way on the western shore. We'll probably stay a week to rest and replenish supplies. Then we continue north and disembark at Arsinoe where we'll transfer our cargo to camels. A caravan can always be found there. We'll pay as we go for that part of the journey."

"I used to travel with my parents on some caravans to Ma'in. How do they charge in Egypt?" asked Balthazar.

"We pay a fee to join plus the cost of food, water, camel fodder, and government duties. All together in addition to what you pay me for the shipping, it'll cost you several hundred denarii per camel for the overland trek. Will you be taking your own camel along?"

"I will. Waled told me you have a special hold in the ship for animals."

"That's right."

"But I'll need many more camels to carry my amphorae."

"That's never a problem for the caravan. The more camels you need the better they like it."

"Good. How long is the overland journey?"

"About a week from Arsinoe to Pelusium on the Great Sea, if sandstorms don't slow us down."

"And then?"

"Then we board another of my ships in Pelusium. *The Serafina* will take us east to Caesarea Maritima."

"You own another ship? How many do you have?"

"Three ply the waves of the Great Sea, and this one in the gulf. From Berenike north we must be wary of those Roman buggers. Their taxes are the scourge of my existence! But I manage a profit despite them, so I keep sailing. These journeys keep my belly full and my wife happy ... I always bring her nice gifts when I return!"

"My father used to surprise my mother with gifts after his caravan journeys. And that reminds me ... Can you suggest where I should sell my cinnabar? Where can I command the best price?"

"A good question," said Musa. "The closer you are to Rome the higher price you can ask, so the best places to sell are the ports on the Great Sea: Alexandria, Pelusium or Caesarea."

"How do you charge for the cargo?" asked Balthazar.

"Two denari per amphorae. How many do you have?"

"A thousand."

"This ship can carry three thousand and I've booked only half that, so I have plenty of room for yours."

"How about passengers?" Balthazar asked. "How do you charge?"

Musa scratched his head. "I don't usually take passengers, but seeing as you're a friend to Waled I can take you for 400 denarii, unless of course you can help with the ship, then maybe I can do it for 300."

"I'll be happy to help. Will the 300 include food and water for all of us?"

"Yes, of course. But what do you mean 'all of us'?"

"There will be three of us: Myself, Sameer and his sister, Alima."

"A woman! No, no, no! It's impossible!" said Musa shaking his head forcefully.

"But my sister is no ordinary woman, Musa. Surely, you remember her?" asked Waled.

"I do. But you know it's bad luck to sail with a woman, even if she is your sister. And I have no way to provide the privacy she would need."

"I have an idea to help with that," said Waled.

"And the money should not be a problem," added Balthazar.

Musa looked at Balthazar and made a face. "But why pay extra to take a woman along, when you can find them easily in every port?"

"We're talking about my *sister*, Musa!" said Waled with a hint of anger. "Not some evening's entertainment. She knows her way around boats. My father taught her well!"

"I'm sure that's true, but she can't help with the work, and she'll be a distraction to my crew!"

Sameer spoke up. "She'll keep to herself, I promise you. Anyway, your crew should know better than to mess with our sister. And I'll be watching over her."

"As will I," added Balthazar.

Musa scowled as he stroked his long beard. "I don't like it! But . . ." he paused. "if I make an exception, it will cost you! Five hundred denari for your sister's passage."

Suddenly a gust of wind whipped a line toward Musa's head and he ducked swiftly to keep from being hit. The dark clouds unleashed a torrent of rain and the men followed Musa into one of the cargo holds to finish their negotiation.

"That squall came up quickly," said Balthazar.

Musa scowled. "You see! The woman is not yet aboard and already the bad luck is starting. I tell you it's a bad idea."

Waled interrupted. "Listen, Musa. What if my brothers and I build something special for you? I have a new design for a special captain's room. It would give you a place to sleep and to keep your charts safe and dry. It would also provide privacy for passengers like Alima and others you take aboard in the future. We could build it amidships or near the bow as you see fit. Just think how jealous those Romans will be when they hear you have something they don't. We could barter our work in return for free passage for Alima. What do you think?"

Musa screwed up his face and squinted. "I don't know. What I really need is to have one of my old ships fitted with a new hull. Then I can use it again for voyages to Socotra. I'd like it rebuilt using those new iron fasteners of yours. If you agree, and can also build the quarters you speak of, maybe we have a deal."

Waled laughed. "Musa, you old sea serpent! Refitting an old hull will take us six months! That's not a problem but if you want it, we'll need more than free passage for Alima. We can build the captain's quarters so you're ready to sail on time, and begin the new hull on the old boat when we're done. But in return we expect all three to sail for free, plus return trips for at least two of them!"

Musa shook his head. "Not a chance."

Waled continued. "You said yourself our work is the best. And no one else in Qana knows our new hull technique or uses our iron fasteners. Think of the profit you'll make on those sails to India."

"Hmmph. You drive a hard bargain! I'll agree to free passage for the men, but you must pay for your sister. Balthazar must pay for his cargo plus you all bear the cost of the caravan trek. Agreed?"

Waled looked at Balthazar. Balthazar had never expected anything else, and the fact that he could make the voyage for free was an unexpected boon. He put both his hands out toward Musa as a sign of agreement, and bowed. "Agreed."

"Excellent," said Musa looking to Waled. "You and your brothers can begin your work tomorrow. I'll make sure my men know you're coming. Where is your spice stored, Balthazar?"

"At the king's warehouse near the escarpment."

"What size amphorae?"

"The small ones, about 18 fingers high. How do you stack them?"

"We stagger them on their sides with reeds for cushioning. We usually see little breakage even in the strongest gales."

"That's good. I'll hire some laborers to deliver them when you're ready."

"Let's give Waled time to do his work, then my men can help load your cargo. It will take two days to load. Barring bad weather we'll set sail in ten days."

The men walked slowly as they left Musa's dock in the pouring rain. Balthazar noticed Waled's self-satisfied expression. He was evidently pleased, but Balthazar wasn't sure why. When the rain let up, Balthazar approached him. "I haven't bargained like you did with Musa, so I've got to ask: Aren't you concerned that you gave away six months of income? I planned to pay for my passage and don't want your family to suffer on my account."

Waled shrugged. "We won't. Ever since we finished *The Baysan* we've wanted to get more work from Musa. Now with his agreement for a new hull, we're getting that. And the job won't take us six months … more likely three."

"All right. But won't you work more slowly without Sameer?"

"Not likely. I'll hire two men to replace him, but combined they'll cost less than Sameer, and I can work them longer. If they work out, we can take on more jobs, so Musa's will not be our only work. We've been making a name for ourselves ever since the word spread about sea worthy vessels. I'm hopeful that by the time Sameer returns, we'll have more work than we can handle."

When the three men got home, Waled yelled to Akram. "We've had a good day, brother! Only one thing more to do to make this day complete."

"What's that?" asked Akram.

"Meet with Uncle Nibal."

"Already? Should I come with you?" Balthazar queried.

"By all means, he must meet you. Now that my father's gone, Nibal can allow or deny the offer of any outsider who may want Alima."

"Do you think he'll give us trouble?"

"I hope not. I'm sure he knows Umar is a scoundrel, but he's a proud man and I don't want to embarrass him. We'll say nothing about Umar's insults and hope that we can conclude things in a friendly way. Agreed?"

"You'll get no argument from me!" said Balthazar.

"We've got to convince him to permit an early betrothal." added Waled.

"How will you do that?"

"By saying that your union will bring the family influence."

"And suggest that Nibal has something to gain?"

"Suggest nothing! He has much to gain. Come, let's eat. I'll tell the women we'll leave when we're done."

A short time later, Balthazar followed the brothers through the streets he'd trod only a few days before. They walked through a steady drizzle until their pace slowed and Waled pointed to a small hut on the edge of a date palm grove. "Nibal lives there."

"Is this his grove?" asked Balthazar.

"No. He's the caretaker, but the owner lets him live here. He has little money of his own."

"Can I come in with you? I'd like to listen in on things."

"If you wish, but remember not to speak until we're finished! And we won't accept anything to eat or drink until we reach agreement. Understand?"

"Yes. We did things that way in my village too."

When they came to Nibal's door Waled exclaimed loudly, "Peace be upon you, Uncle!"

After a few minutes Nibal came to the entrance to return the greeting. "And also on you."

"How are you?" asked Waled.

Nibal raised his arms up and held his hands together. "I am good, thanks be to The Great One. Come in. Come in."

"May he grant you rest." said Waled as he entered the hut.

"And you as well," said Nibal as he took Waled's arm. Balthazar and the brothers removed their sandals just inside the doorway. It was a dirty little place, in need of cleaning, and a little spice. Too bad I didn't bring any, thought Balthazar.

"Please, sit down." Said Nibal. "Tell me why you've come. I know you're too busy for friendly visits!"

Following Nibal's example, they dropped onto the reed mat and sat cross legged in a circle. "You're right uncle," answered Waled. "We are busy, but it's always good to visit with family. First, let me make introductions. Surely you remember Akram who looks so like our father? And Sameer, my youngest brother?"

"Sure, sure! I remember. I haven't lost all my memories yet, nephew. You're most welcome. Both of you. And who is this young man?" Nibal looked in Balthazar's direction.

"He's a friend. Uncle, I'm proud to present Balthazar of Khalan. He's the reason for our visit!"

"What? . . . What was that?"

"I said Balthazar is the reason for our visit!" Waled fairly yelled out his words.

The old man patted the side of his head. "I'm sorry, my ears are not so good. Sometimes I can't hear all the words."

"Don't worry," said Waled. "I'll speak louder . . . Balthazar, we're pleased for you to meet our Uncle Nibal, the patriarch of our family."

Balthazar raised both his hands in an outward sign of respect and bowed at the waist so his head almost touched the mat.

"We're here on Balthazar's behalf," said Waled loudly. "We seek your permission for his betrothal to Alima."

Nibal blinked. "Alima! Betrothal? She's already married! How can we speak betrothal?"

"She's widowed, uncle. Didn't Umar tell you? Her husband died some weeks ago."

"Umar! Huh! . . . No, he told me nothing. I hardly see him ... but we'll talk of that later. How did this happen?"

"An untimely death ... in a Himyarite attack," said Waled.

Nibal threw up his hands. "Himyarites! An ugly people!" He mumbled something unintelligible under his breath.

"But Balthazar kept Alima safe, and brought her home to us. Our family is most grateful."

"As you should be! Thank you for watching over my kin, young man." Nibal bowed.

Balthazar did likewise, smiling broadly.

Waled continued, "So when Balthazar showed an interest in her, we asked him to consider a betrothal."

"I see, I see. So you want to talk betrothal … if I'd … if I'd known." he stammered, "I would have worn a cleaner robe … ahh! Such is life." He paused. "Please tell your sister I'm sorry, but it's too soon to talk betrothal. When did you say her husband died?"

"A few weeks ago," answered Waled.

"Then she has only begun to mourn! No offers are proper until the lamenting time is over." Nibal stood up. "There's nothing we can do now. I'll make some tea." He shuffled to the back of the hut and returned a little while later with a wooden tray. It held five cups of steaming tea and some dates. "Please help yourselves." He set the tray down on the reed mat.

Akram spoke up. "It's kind of you to offer refreshment, uncle. Such fragrant tea and plump, enticing dates. You tend the orchard well. I hope your master appreciates you!"

"Eh! I'm not sure any master values a good hand. But come, partake! This is for your pleasure." Nibal held out the dates for the others.

"You are most gracious, but our mother has charged us to speak on Alima's behalf. We do so with some urgency, so, we must not eat until we can celebrate together." Waled stated with finality.

Nibal stuck a date in his mouth and sat back down with a stony face. "Acch! So like young men! Always in a hurry. What is this urgency? Your sister has months of mourning ahead. Why can't you return with him then?"

"Because Balthazar's a wealthy spice merchant. And men like him don't stay long in one place lest their business suffer. He's sailing soon to trade along the Great Sea. He may not return for a long time."

"But your sister is a true gem! Worth waiting for! In just a few months this can be done properly. Doesn't your friend care about proprieties?" Nibal looked at Balthazar as if he were an ant crawling on the mat. Balthazar struggled to keep smiling.

"He does, uncle. He is a most traditional man! But his trip cannot be put off. There are only certain months of the year when the winds are good for sailing. Alima may never have a better chance at such a marriage. And as her Ibn 'Amm you must provide for her future. This is a very good match, uncle."

"He's a wealthy merchant?" Nibal eyed Balthazar from head to toe. "He looks very young…"

"He is, uncle. But he inherited his family business and all their valuable spice growing land."

"But what of your cousin, Umar?" Nibal countered. "As my son, it's his right to marry Alima. He must be consulted."

Waled rose to his feet and began to pace. "If you can find him, by all means consult him. But Balthazar is leaving town soon, and this must be decided quickly. Alima has value to him beyond that of wife and companion. She worked for Balthazar's father and is quite skilled in spotting and pruning spice trees."

Nibal nodded. "But what of her other qualities? She is still a great beauty! That alone is a reason for Umar to want her, let alone the children she can bless him with. How many does she have from Sahl?"

"None. She is beautiful, but barren." Waled emphasized this last word so loudly that his words had the finality of a death sentence.

"I see … that does make a difference!" Nibal stated plainly.

Waled nodded. "Unfortunately, she'll not fetch a great bride price again. Balthazar is willing because she can help his business. Should he desire children, he has the wealth to consider a second wife, not something Umar would be able to do."

Nibal shrugged. "Sadly, you are right. Umar hasn't been the same since his brother's death. He doesn't work, always moves from place to place. He used to help me with the palms, but not anymore. I don't even know where to find him to tell him of this offer!" Tears glistened in the old man's eyes. Umar might be a louse of a man, but Balthazar could see his father still loved him.

"What do you think, uncle? This is a good match!" Waled urged him to agreement.

Nibal wore a pained expression. "I don't know. Can Balthazar offer anything to Umar's benefit?"

Balthazar felt like smiling but kept a straight face. He knew they had reached a point in the talks that could mean success.

"He can. I too have heard that Umar was affected by Seif's death. Perhaps a journey to take possession of new land would give him a fresh start. Balthazar is prepared to deed his land in Khalan along with a generous purse. But you must approve today, so that he can arrange for Alima to sail with him. Sameer will go with them and they will marry only when her mourning is done. My mother has approved the arrangements."

Nibal frowned but Balthazar could sense an underlying interest. "How many acres are offered, and how much is the purse?" asked Nibal.

"Forty acres. And the purse is generous: one thousand denari! It will be given half in gold and half in spice stored here in Qana. You will be free to sell or barter it as you see fit."

Balthazar watched Nibal's face for any trace of discontent, but saw none. The old man closed his eyes. Balthazar looked around the hut and considered the offer as if he was Nibal. He's old, getting lame, almost deaf and will work until he dies. The gold and spice will give him something to rely on.

After several moments of silence, Nibal opened his eyes and looked to Waled. "You say the mourning period will be observed?"

"Yes, uncle."

Nibal bobbed his head. "Then I consent. It will be a good alliance for our family, and if he was here, your father would think so too. Umar should find it agreeable. Now I can give him a purse to travel as has wanted. Let us celebrate. Please enjoy some dates while I go make more tea."

Nibal retreated to the rear of the hut with the tea tray. Balthazar and the brothers leaned into the center of the circle and clapped each other's palms.

Sameer grinned from ear to ear. "Good news!" he said in quiet tones. "I could see he wanted to speak to Umar, but big brother was too persuasive!"

Waled held his finger up. "Shh! Here he comes." An hour later, after the tea was drunk and the figs eaten, a betrothal contract was scrawled on papyrus and Nibal congratulated Balthazar.

Balthazar put his hands together and bowed. "Thank you, Nibal! I promise I will always watch over Alima."

Nibal bowed in turn. "See that you do!"

The young men bid Nibal farewell and took their leave.

When they were well away from the hut Balthazar clapped Waled on the shoulder. "Well done! I hope that when I'm actually ready for a bride my negotiations will go so well."

Waled beamed at the compliment as he looked to his brothers. "It did go well, didn't it? I doubt either of you could have done better."

"I agree for once," said Sameer. "You were at your best today, brother ... in all of your bargaining!"

Waled went on. "What a day! Alima will be relieved, and now we can concentrate on getting Musa's ship ready for your voyage."

Balthazar felt relieved, too. And proud of how he'd helped Alima. She was safe from Umar, and their voyage was planned. For the first time since Khalan, everything had gone well. Was he being superstitious to think: *Almost too well?*

That night he drank his share of wine, and joined in the gaiety as Alima's family celebrated their good day. Would their journey to the Great Sea go well or end in disappointment? He looked at the stars and wished he could read them. More than ever he yearned for the day when he would know how.

CHAPTER 13

Farewells

§

A FEW DAYS LATER, ALIMA was surprised when Balthazar and Sameer asked her to go with them to the market.

"Do you really need me? I have a lot of sewing to do before we sail."

"Yes." said Sameer. "Waled gave me the day off to shop with Balthazar and we'd like you to help us."

"Very well," said Alima. Before the sun was overhead, they arrived in the crowded marketplace. Sameer nudged Balthazar and pointed to a small house on the edge of the market. "That's the place you asked about."

Balthazar nodded. "Come along," he said to Alima.

"But that hut sells only fabric."

"I know," said Balthazar. "I want to buy some."

When the hut's owner approached Balthazar, Alima was astonished to hear him say, "I'd like to have some robes made for my betrothed. I think four robes and a shawl."

"It will be my pleasure!" said the owner. "I have many fine fabrics for your lady to choose from."

"I can see that. But I'd like them finished within five days. Can you do that?"

"If you are willing to pay a little extra," said the man.

"I am," said Balthazar. "Alima, please select the cloth you like. This man will gauge your size and make up robes for you."

It took her only a few minutes. She chose light sturdy fabrics that would be comfortable in the heat. The material she chose for her shawl was edged with beautiful embroidery.

"Thank you," she said to Balthazar when they left the hut. "You didn't need to do that."

"Yes, I did. You lost everything you had in Khalan so you need new clothes just as I do. And a betrothal gift is traditional, isn't it? I want everything to look as real as possible to people who know your family. I hope you will like the clothes when they're done."

"I know I will," she said with delight. "Now I won't have to do so much sewing!"

"Can you stay to help us select our things? Your woman's eye will help us choose well."

"With pleasure!" said Alima. They spent the rest of the afternoon looking for items the men needed. They bought tunics, belts, sandals and head scarves as well as canteens and a new saddle for Balthazar's camel.

"I think we're done," said Balthazar as he paid for his last purchase: a pair of new sandals for Alima.

"I should hope so," said Alima. "I've never seen anyone spend so much in one day!"

"We didn't buy anything we didn't need. And now you can enjoy your mother's company instead of sewing until we leave."

"It was kind of you, Balthazar. Thank you," said Alima smiling broadly. "Thank you so much." When she got home, Alima rested for a while then took her mother for a long walk along the shore.

The next day they reminisced in the garden as they planted seeds. She looked forward to her journey with a combination of excitement and anxiety. She knew long voyages could be dangerous, but wanted to find her father. For that she would brave any danger.

Several days later, when her brothers had completed their work on Musa's ship, and her own preparations were complete, she watched from the dock as Balthazar oversaw the loading of his spice. All morning, laborers carted the spice-filled amphorae to the ship and stacked them carefully on the dock. Musa's men laid out large, heavy nets on the dock. The nets were attached to lines and pulleys on the ship's rigging. They transferred the amphorae a dozen at a time onto the netting, carefully laying long sheaths of palm and grass under and between them as cushioning. Then the nets were hoisted over the rails, and into the ship's hold where they were stacked with the palms onto specially built racks. It took two days to complete the transfer.

"Do you think they'll be safe in the hold?" she asked as they walked home together that evening.

"As safe as they can be, barring a wreck." said Balthazar. "Are you ready to leave? We sail in two days."

"I know. The days have gone so fast. I'll be saying my farewells soon, and the thought is filling me with sadness."

"It will be hard," said Balthazar. "But at least you have family to bid farewell to." The dust from his new sandals rose into the air as he suddenly walked quickly ahead of her.

Tears stung her eyes. I didn't mean to hurt him, she thought. But she couldn't deny that she dreaded the parting. She had no idea when she would return, but what was worse, she hated the deception. She was used to sharing her thoughts with her mother, but the ruse of the betrothal prevented it.

She wiped her tears on her head scarf and walked slowly, as Balthazar's figure dimmed in the fading light. It occurred to her that she was seeing a vision of the future. One day our journey will be over and Balthazar will walk away to study his stars. The thought made her feel empty. As much as she hated it, she knew she enjoyed the pretending, and the way he attended to her wishes when her mother was around. He'd said he had no wish to marry, but she wondered if he liked it, too. Yes, it was all make-believe, but she would savor it for as long as it lasted.

Book Two

CHAPTER 14

After the Great Death

LATE ONE AFTERNOON, TWO WEEKS after Dodi's death Melchior took a break from his work in the garden and looked up to see Amro. "You're back!" Melchior rose from his haunches and moved to embrace the gardener. "And looking quite healthy, I see."

"I never got sick," said Amro. "And what's this? You toil at the earth? Have you taken over my job, Master Melchior?"

Melchior laughed. "Only temporarily. I'm not very good at it. But tell me ... how was your journey? Did you find your son, Asher?"

"My journey went well. After some searching I found Asher in the hills where he usually tends a flock and I spoke to him from a distance. None of the pestilence has reached there, so I sent him to find Mered, and followed at a distance to be sure he got there unhindered."

"Excellent! And what can you tell me about my brother and his family?"

"They are well, Master. Asher told Mered of the sickness and bade them stay until you send word again. He was more than willing to comply when he heard of all the deaths."

"Very good! You've done well, Amro."

"Thank you, Master. May I ask, how are your mother and Master Gaspar?"

Melchior frowned. "My mother died soon after you left."

"I'm sorry, Master. She was a good woman. She always treated me well."

"Yes. We're all missing her."

"And Gaspar?"

"Recovered! And resting in my mother's old room. I dare say he'll be helping with this planting when his strength is back. We'll need to work together until we can go again to the market or draw water from the river."

"I was thinking the same," said Amro. "Without Master Mered's servants, Bina and I alone must work the whole estate, and we're not young anymore."

"It wouldn't be right or sensible. That's why Gaspar and I will help in the gardens and with the animals, and collect rain water as best we can. We'll do what we must to survive."

"Thank you, Master," said Amro.

"I hope it will be enough. Do you see there's almost no boat traffic on the river?" He pointed toward the Tigris. "All the boats look abandoned."

"There are few travelers on the roads and those I saw were all heading *away* from Seleucia. I fear they may spread the sickness far and wide."

"You may be right, but there's nothing we can do about it. We must bide our time and watch for signs of improvement. Perhaps the river will be our best signal. When river traffic returns to normal, you can go again to find Asher."

Several months passed with Melchior, Gaspar, Bina and Amro cooperating as best they could. They ate meat only on rare occasions subsisting mainly on grains, beans, nuts and fruits. When they did slaughter an animal, they salted the meat to keep it longer. Blessedly, they received more than the usual amount of rain, so there was plenty of drinking water, and the crops grew well. They wondered how the people fared in Seleucia. The months dragged on with little change until finally, one morning Gaspar yelled out, "Melchior! Come look! There are five new boats on the river today! Surely that must mean things are improving in the city."

"I see the boats, and they look busy. I'll send Bina to make inquiries at the market."

Bina returned a few hours later to find both men awaiting her in the courtyard. "What did you find?" Melchior asked anxiously, as Gaspar looked on..

"The city is in a terrible state. There are many bodies in the streets, but some vendors are reopening their stalls. There is very little for sale, but the butcher told me that things are getting better. He said those who have survived are coming out of their houses."

"Do you think it safe for Mered and his family to return?" asked Melchior.

"I think so," said Bina. "I saw children wading at the river, so things must be better if their parents are letting them out."

So once again, Amro left to seek out Asher. This time the message to Mered said it was safe to return.

One morning, soon after Amro departed, Gaspar approached Melchior to express his thanks. "What can I say? I'll never be able to thank you for your care while I was sick."

"There's no need," said Melchior. "I don't know why things happened as they did, but I know we were meant to help each other through this. I'm so grateful you were here to help me grieve my mother's death. It was a true gift, my friend."

Gaspar shook his head in denial. "But I did nothing! You were the giving one. I would have died if not for you."

"I couldn't very well leave you there, Gaspar! A big man like you? Your carcass would have stunk up my garden for years! The important thing is we survived. Now we'll find out what remains of Seleucia and our school. Things may not be what they were."

Gaspar departed, wearing the same, now almost threadbare robes he'd worn on his arrival five months earlier. But this time he held a large cloth bag filled with the scrolls he'd scribed for Dodi. He knew a cool place in his house where they would be safe.

As he walked through the city gates, he saw it as if for the first time, for it appeared a different city. There were few people were about, and those who were, moved as in a fog. Many looked emaciated. He realized how lucky he'd been, for if he'd fallen ill, alone in his house, no-one would have helped him. There was little for sale in the market which still looked deserted. Had many farmers died? Without food, many more would die of starvation in the months to come. The stench of the city brought tears to his eyes. Why hasn't the satrap sent soldiers to collect the bodies? He grew angrier with each step. Are they still so afraid?

When he got to his house, he set the scrolls down, and inspected the area where he planned to hide them. There was a small under-ground food cellar not far from his cooking pit where earth had been removed and mud bricks laid as a floor. It wasn't a huge space, but it was cool and except for a few small lizards and spiders, mostly empty. Gaspar thought it would be an excellent enclosure to store the scrolls in safety.

He removed the few remnants of rotted food, swiped a knife to scare away the lizards, and wiped the floor clean of webs. Then he laid a cloth on the floor and set the bag of scrolls on top. Satisfied with his work, he closed the wooden door to the space, drew out his water pouch and drank deeply. His strength was back, but he was always thirsty. No matter, he thought. It was a small price to pay for his recovery.

He headed off to the astrology school and was startled to see it looked deserted. "Hello! Is anyone about? Anyone here?" he yelled out. Finally, after searching for some time, a small man with a dark beard popped his head up from behind a stone bench in the grand hall.

"Ah! You're Seleucus' servant, are you not?"

"That's right, sir. At least I was," corrected the man.

"Is he dead then?" asked Gaspar.

"Yes, sir. Dead these past five months. The satrap called on him for a prediction, wanting to know when the sickness would end. I went with Seleucus, so I heard all that was said." The man paused and sniffled.

"And?"

"Seleucus told him the Romans had brought the sickness, though in truth he thought it was the Chinese. We heard from other travelers that many on the Silk Road have gotten sick these past six months. Then, only two days later he collapsed in the great hall. He died the next day!"

"Such bad news … though I feared as much. What of the satrap?"

"Very sick, sir. I hear he's alive but his mind is gone. No-one has seen him in months. Some say he's fled into the hills."

"I see." Gaspar said quietly, trying to take it all in. "And how were you? Were you sick also?"

The man looked surprised. "Me sir? I thought surely I would die after my master but I never got sick. Don't understand why, for I saw many die." The servant looked away as if ashamed.

Gaspar sat down on a bench near him. "Look here! It's not your fault Seleucus died! It was in the stars. You're a free man now that your master is dead, but you may serve him still by helping me clean and revive this school. Before you go your way, will you help me? I will pay you well."

The man looked up at Gaspar and responded eagerly, "I served Master Seleucus since I was a boy and have no-where to go. Gratefully will I help you, for these last months I felt myself a lost man. I may be free, but with no work and no money, there is no life. May I ask, how did you survive when so many other teachers died?"

"Like you, I was one of the lucky ones." Gaspar replied, "When I got sick at Melchior's, he cared for me. Will you go to him now? His house is on the hill just below the date palm orchard. Tell him what you've told me, and ask him to come to my house, soon as he can. And ask him to bring food. Can you do that?"

"Yes! I know the house. I'll go now."

"Thank you. I'm sorry but I've forgotten your name."

"Matthias."

"Thank you, Matthias. We'll share some food when you return. Do you know where I live?"

"Yes, sir – just past the market. And thank you sir."

Gaspar walked back to his house slowly, pondering what to do next. Seleucus dead and the satrap maybe good as; it was no wonder there were so many rotting bodies in the streets. Someone must go to the satrap's palace to determine the situation, and inform the king. Until someone took charge, a group of citizens must guard the city, collect bodies and make sure there were adequate supplies of water and food. And as for the school, he would call together the surviving teachers to elect a new leader. If the king lived, he would want new readings soon enough.

Melchior arrived later that afternoon with Matthias. Just one look at Melchior's face confirmed his own concerns. Unless you saw the death with your own eyes, it was hard to fathom.

"Welcome, Matthias. And thank you."

"You're welcome, sir."

"My friend and I have things to discuss. Make yourself at home in my courtyard, and please eat what you want from the food Melchior has brought. I'll join you soon."

"Thank you," said Matthias with a wide smile.

"Well, what do you think?" asked Gaspar when Matthias had seen himself out. "We can't leave the city as it is, without government, without leadership!"

Melchior sat down on the floor. "I agree, but we must act carefully. These many years we've worked and studied without becoming embroiled in the politics of the satrapy. We must keep it that way."

"Your old cautious self, I see." said Gaspar looking glum.

Melchior shrugged. "I'm as anxious to avoid chaos as you are, but . . ."

"I know. I know. You're more familiar with the affairs of state than I, but something must be done! I thought of sending a messenger to the king. What do you think?"

"Yes. We should send someone. Perhaps Mered? He returned late yesterday. I know he's self-interested but he knows how a city should be run. He saw my father do it well and it's been his goal for years to be chosen satrap. He'd be in our debt if we can steer him ahead of any rivals."

"I don't know," said Gaspar shaking his head. "Mered isn't my choice for a new satrap, but then you know him better than I. Do you think he would drag his feet on this?"

"Are you joking? He'll be more eager than a hawk for a hare."

"Then I suppose … You're right about one thing, old friend. Our talents are best used at our school."

"We're agreed then. I'll speak with Mered. We should find out how many of our fellows are still alive, and hold a vote for new leadership soon. I'll return early tomorrow."

Gaspar was tired but his hunger and thirst outweighed his fatigue. After Melchior left, he got two cups and a large carafe of wine from his cupboard and went out to join Matthias. There would be plenty of time in the morning to summon his strength for the work ahead.

CHAPTER 15
News of the Satrap

§

MELCHIOR WENT HOME AND PROMPTLY told Mered his concerns. "There's no time to waste. We must leave right away," said Melchior. He could see the spark of interest in his brother's eyes.

"We? Isn't this a little out of your realm brother?"

"Perhaps. But if we do find the satrap, I can at least offer him a reading, something positive about the future. It will give us a reason to be there, besides the obvious one of checking on his health. I assume you don't want him to know you're after his position?"

"True. . . But let me doing the talking."

Though it was late afternoon, the brothers rode immediately for the satrap's palace. Melchior could see the look of shock on Mered's face at the number of dead along the road. 'The Great Death', as the populace was now calling it, had been indiscriminate in choosing its victims. Travelers, nobles, beggars, merchants had all fallen prey to it.

Since Zoroastrian funeral practices varied throughout Parthia, Melchior wasn't surprised to see corpses left for the birds to pick, especially in the countryside. He knew many wealthy families would eventually collect the bones of their loved ones to inter in ossuaries, or bury in special tombs. But in heavily populated Seleucia, bodies must be collected and moved outside its gates to avoid the stench and sights that lingered for months while nature did its work. If the satrap couldn't be found, civic minded men would have to act.

They found the satrap's palace abandoned except for a few servants. As was his way, Mered ignored them, walking through the place as if he owned it. They scanned the faces of the dead, but the satrap was not among them. Melchior listened as Mered finally started questioning the servants. "Where is the satrap? Did you see him? Do you know where he is? Come now man! You must have seen something!"

"Damn then all!" yelled Mered loudly when the last servant shook his head in silence. "Can they all be this ignorant? The satrap is no ghost!"

Melchior almost laughed at his brother's impatience. "They were all scared, Mered, and had families of their own to worry about. The satrap's comings and goings may not have been their first worry."

"Hmmph! It was their job to serve him. When I'm satrap there will be no more of this. Their duty to me will come first or they will pay the price!"

"When you are satrap? Unless you know for sure the man is dead, you'd best not approach the king for an appointment," said Melchior.

"Do I look simple minded, brother? That much I can figure out on my own!"

"But you've never been a patient man, and now your success with the king may depend upon it."

Mered was still scowling when he led Melchior into his counting room sometime later, and began pounding his fists into his desk.

"Calm down! I know you're frustrated," said Melchior. "But things will work themselves out. The satrap isn't in his palace, so he must be dead or as good as. It's only a question of time before you can approach the king to replace him."

"You're always so blasted sure of yourself! Shut up will you? And leave me in peace!"

"In a while. We have matters to discuss first."

"Taking over are you? Always the big brother! I may have been gone for months, but this is still my space . and I will thank you to let me use it."

"If that's what you want." Melchior said pleasantly. "I envy you that desk. Since mother's passing I've come in here often. It brings back many good memories."

"My, my. So sentimental. Maybe you should have been born a woman. Don't you realize what father paid for this? That he brought it all the way from China?"

Melchior frowned. "I know, but that's not why I like it. By the way, I should tell you that it has recently borne a great honor. It served as the bier for mother's body before her burial."

Mered's face grew red. "How could you use such an irreplaceable item to hold her diseased body? Have you no respect for our possessions?"

Melchior's ire finally rose to the fore. "You ought not to lecture me. I cherish the old desk, but I respect only people. If they are worthy of it! Our mother was. And much as I like it, worth immeasurably more than the desk."

Mered backed off. "You're right. Mother was troublesome, but worthy of respect. I commend you for handling her funeral." He looked somber and suddenly his voice became sweet as honey. "On second thought, don't go yet, brother. I would have your advice. How long should I wait to see the king? If I tell him the satrap is dead and he's found alive, it would mean trouble for me."

"Suddenly you seek my counsel?" asked Melchior. "Do you want to be satrap so badly?"

Mered chuckled. "The city would be lucky to have me! Well, what are your thoughts?"

"If you visit the king you must give him accurate information, and lacking that, there's not much good in going. You would be wise to wait 'til you know more. You might send your servants to search for him. Perhaps in the cave country north of the river."

"An excellent idea! Good night to you, brother."

The next day Mered sent his servants to scout for the satrap while Melchior resumed his studies. Working with Gaspar, Melchior soon determined that only eight of their fellow astrologers had survived the Great Death. They called them together, and since many were young and inexperienced, it was no surprise when both Melchior and Gaspar emerged as leading candidates to head the school. But consumed as he was with his Messiah studies, Melchior threw his support to Gaspar. So it was that seven months after Dodi's death, Gaspar was elected the head of the school of astrology in Seleucia.

The startling announcement Seleucus had made regarding the sun was soon forgotten. Life in Seleucia slowly returned to normal. Weeks turned into months. Melchior's studies of the prophecies continued, and he became more convinced than ever that the stars would somehow play a role. But he saw nothing out of the ordinary in the heavens, and as Gaspar found new purpose in running the school, Melchior wondered if the prophecies that had given such meaning to his life would ever be fulfilled.

CHAPTER 16
Voyage of 'The Baysan'

§

ALIMA WAS EXCITED BUT ANXIOUS as she stood with her family near The Baysan's gangway. When she saw Musa motioning for them to board, she turned to her mother and brothers, eyes brimming with tears. "I will miss you all; and I'll do my best to find father."

Jun hugged her close and touched her cheek to Alima's. "I know you will, my daughter, but I beg of you, be wary of the Romans. A promising future awaits you and your young man. Don't put it at risk for your father's sake."

Alima nodded and hugged her mother tightly. Then she kissed Waled and Akram before taking Sameer's arm to board. As soon as they were on deck, Musa gave the order to raise the sails. The wind was blowing in their favor, just as he had predicted. With Sameer and Balthazar by her side, she waved toward shore until the ship turned west and her family was lost from view.

When they were well underway Captain Musa showed Alima to the little room her brothers had built. It wasn't big but had a small bed and would afford her privacy and protection from the elements. As the days past, she found herself returning there often to rest and to weave.

As the days passed, Alima fell into a new routine and rarely felt bored. She liked watching Sameer and Balthazar help the seamen, and occasionally fished with them off the stern when they were free to do so. More than anything, she enjoyed looking toward shore, trying to figure out where they were and searching for other ships in the distance. Rather than monotony, she found each day brought new sights and anticipation of the days ahead.

A week after leaving Qana they sailed into Eudaemon in late morning. Musa promptly sent his crew ashore for fresh food and water. "You'll enjoy leave for the rest of the day if you bring it back quickly! We sail at first light."

The crew had their work done within a few hours and Alima watched as they left the ship laughing, her brother Sameer among them. Just then Balthazar walked up behind her.

"Aren't you going with Sameer?" she asked. "I'm sure he would enjoy your company."

Balthazar shook his head. "I think he won't want company for what he has in mind," Then he slapped himself on the side of the head. "I'm sorry. You didn't need to know that."

Alima smirked. "With three brothers, do you think I don't know how men like to spend their time?"

Balthazar looked at her quizzically. "Some men, Alima, not all. And is that how you think of me? Like one of your brothers?"

Alima was surprised by his question and wasn't sure how to answer. What was he to her after all? A good friend for sure. No-one but a true friend would spend so many drachma to protect her from an unwanted marriage. That was all she could think to say right now. "No, not as a brother. I think of you as my true friend."

Balthazar looked as if he wanted to say more, but he only nodded. He seemed satisfied with her answer, and she was glad. He'd been so kind to her these last few weeks. She had always looked upon him as the son of the neighbor trader, but now she knew him as much more. She knew his temperament, his goodness, his wisdom, and his strength. "I'll never be able to thank you for what you've done for me and my family. Paying the bride price as you did to free me from Umar. Allowing the pretense of our betrothal, saying you'll help search for father, even buying me new clothes for the journey. No words can thank you enough."

Balthazar smiled and took her hand, "There's no need to thank me. I hope that if my sister had been in your situation, someone would have done the same. Not that I think of you as my sister either! I mean, well . . ." and stuttering he concluded, "I hope you know what I mean. I think of you as my true friend, too." Then he went down into the hold of the ship to check on Melwah, and his amphorae.

Sameer returned to the ship late at night and fell down on the deck in a heap outside Alima's cabin door. She almost stumbled over him when she came out the next morning, and started laughing when she saw him. "What's the matter, little brother? Too much drink last night?"

Sameer groaned and rolled over. Alima moved on, knowing it wouldn't be long before Musa had him on his feet to help the crew. They set sail at sunrise, and as expected Musa roused Sameer as he made his rounds of the ship.

So far, the voyage had been uneventful. The Gulf of Berbera had delivered sure currents and westerly winds drove them on with only a few gusts and light showers. Soon they would be sailing through the Bab-el-Mandeb Strait to the Red Sea where Musa said the weather could be unpredictable. The winds would likely shift, and there would be more reefs to contend with. The ship would do a lot more tacking until they reached the Egyptian port of Berenike on the western shore of the sea.

A few days out of Eudaemon they sailed through the strait, and Musa posted archers along the port and starboard decks. He said they were to keep watch for Nabatean pirates who had been attacking ships in the Red Sea for decades. "Sound the alarm bell if you see their flag," ordered Musa. "I'll tell you when to let fly the first volley." But the first day past the strait stayed quiet with no unusual sightings, and the winds soon died down. They sailed on very slowly and after four days, Musa pulled the archers. "Don't worry, men," he said. "I think we're too far south for the Nabateans to bother us. I'll post you again when we're closer to Berenike."

Since Berenike was still weeks away, they all had to conserve food and water. This had never been a problem for Alima, who ate sparingly, but for the men who labored hard all day it was much harder. She knew the water would be rationed so those who worked hardest received the most. Alima was glad to see Musa fairly apportioning water and the occasional draft of beer to his men. I can see why they like him, she thought.

So far, she'd witnessed very little grumbling, and she was sure she would have noticed it as watching the men had become her main pre-occupation. She'd been around hard-working, barely clad men her whole life, so she wondered why she suddenly found herself aroused watching the shirtless men maneuver about the sails, pulling on the heavy rigging and jumping to obey the Captain's orders.

The men included Balthazar, of course, who helped wherever he could. And now she found herself attracted to him in a whole new way. She had never felt this way about Sahl. She remembered how the village women in Khalan talked about their husbands; what they liked about their men and that their wifely duties were pleasurable. But she had found little pleasure in watching Sahl move or walk or even in their couplings. She wasn't sure why.

She had always thought love and attraction to her husband would come naturally in time. But in the three years of her marriage it never had. Was it a flaw in her or his age or his generally cold attitude? She had sometimes seen older men around town, both in Qana and Khalan, and they had been pleasing enough to watch. But she had never felt the sensations of interest that drew her eyes to Balthazar.

She enjoyed watching every movement of his body. The way he flexed his arms when holding the rigging, and the way his thighs glistened with sweat in the afternoon sun. Maybe he'd always had a muscular build, and she had just never noticed it. But now watching him every day, she realized how well-proportioned he was. She admired the shape of his head and strong chin, and the easy manner that set him apart from the others. She tried to keep herself from thinking of him. Of how his dark brown eyes looked in his tanned face, and how his laugh lit him up from the inside like a candle glowing in the dark.

She felt embarrassed by her thoughts, as if anyone could look at her and know what she was thinking. To avoid giving herself away, she spent more time in her room when the heat of the day was hottest. But though Balthazar was out of sight, it was impossible to keep him out of mind. How would she ever talk to him again if she thought of him as she did? I'll find a way, she told herself. I'll stay closer to Sameer. That should help.

But she soon realized that Sameer had ideas of his own for how to spend his time, and little of it included her. After dinner, he played dice with the crew under the ship's torches or fished until his line went slack, so there was little time left for her.

What else can I do? She wondered. She had quickly completed the small weaving projects she'd brought along. She had a few beads and some leather cords to make necklaces, but that close work was only possible in daylight, and it was difficult to spear the beads while the ship bobbed and rocked in the sea.

Day after day she had little choice but to watch Balthazar work half-naked with the crew, and day by day she found herself increasingly thinking of him. I must do something different, she thought. She tried to avoid eye contact and spent many daylight hours mending the clothes of Musa and his crew. But the nights often felt like they would never end. Occasionally, when she felt sure all but the night watch were asleep, she would leave her cabin to walk the deck, holding tightly to the rail, listening for the splash of fish and watching for the torches of far off boats. It was on one such night, when she stood at the rail looking out to sea that she was startled to hear a strange sound.

What is that, she wondered? A big fish? The moon and the stars were clouded from sight and a low fog shrouded the water. She could hardly see two paces beyond the rail. But she was wide awake so she stood silently listening. Listening for any sound that presented itself. And suddenly she knew what it was. A small ship was approaching. She recognized the sound because it was a type of fishing vessel her father had built, and she had often sailed with him on the bay to test them. Something is wrong, she thought. A small ship would not approach a large one like theirs without fair warning and never at night. She ran quickly to Musa's bell amidships and rang it soundly. "Alarm! Alarm! Wake up! Pirates!" she screamed at the top of her lungs.

The ship came to life before she had rung the bell three times, and she looked up to see Balthazar at her side. "Run to your room and bar it. No matter what, don't look out or show yourself 'til Sameer or I come to you. Do you understand?"

"Yes." She ran quickly, for already she could see men climbing over the rails. Musa shouted for his men to engage, and her thoughts returned to Khalan. Like that awful day, men with swords, knives, slashing, shouting, screaming in rage as they attacked. Her body shook as she barred the door, but when her body collapsed onto the deck she found herself praying. "Oh please, Great One. Please don't let this be like Khalan. Not like Khalan."

She repeated her words over and over as the fighting raged outside her little room. I hid like this then, she thought. Should I be hiding again? She heard cries of anguish, surprise, and big splashes. What's happening out there? Were Balthazar and Sameer all right? Every fiber of her being wanted to go out, to see if she could help. But she remembered Balthazar's words and her promise. So she did as she had done before, steeling herself against the noise and pain, and waited for the fight to end.

Then came a sudden quiet. Was it over? Were her loved ones still alive? In nervous dread, she waited with her ear to the door. There was nothing for some time, then a low murmur. Please let them be alive! Please. Suddenly, she heard a voice.

"Alima! It's me, Balthazar. The battle is won."

She unbarred the door tentatively. There he stood, bloodied by a few cuts and bruises but otherwise unharmed.

"Oh praise the earth and stars!" she said hugging him tightly. "You are alive! And my brother?"

"I'm here!" Sameer stood behind Balthazar, grinning widely to show off the loss of two teeth."

"The women will never look at you the same again," she said before she could stop herself.

"But what does it matter, with these muscles to admire?" Sameer shot back.

Alima smiled and walked out onto the deck. "Where are all the pirates?"

"We surely didn't let them go" said Sameer. "They came for a fight and we gave them one. Tonight all the fish will enjoy a Nabatean meal!"

"You threw them all overboard?

"Every damn, dead one!" answered Sameer.

Captain Musa walked up from behind him. "It'll be a cold day in Hades before I show mercy to one of those bastards! And by the way Alima, I must thank you for the warning bell! I won't ask why you were up at such an hour, but I thank you for saving our skins!"

"And you thought she would be bad luck!" said Balthazar.

"It's true. But I'm glad to be wrong." Musa looked at her over Sameer's shoulder. "You are welcome to sail with me any time."

The next few days passed quietly as the winds blew steadily in their favor, and Alima's thoughts wandered. For a change, the nights brought dreams not only of Balthazar but of Berenike. Jumbled visions of strange men and women played on the edges of her mind, but when she woke she remembered only the faces of Balthazar and her father.

Would they find him in Berenike? The dreams unsettled her for she could not tell if they were good omens or bad. She yearned for the comfort of a warm embrace but found none. Her brother was busy helping the crew and Balthazar seemed too absorbed in the stars to pay her any mind. She felt abandoned by them both.

One night Musa called the three of them together on the forward deck. "We should sight Berenike by morning, and I want you to know a few things before we go ashore. We'll stay about a week, while our sails are fixed and we unload cargo. I hope we won't have to wait long to get it done.

"Why should we have to wait at all?' Asked Sameer.

"Because many ships come with the summer winds, Berenike will be crowded. And the influx of ships keep the Roman coffers full. Every ship must pay a tetarte, for the privilege of docking in their port."

"How much is the tax?" asked Balthazar.

"Twenty five percent of the cargo value. It's high, but at least the Romans put some it into the port. I must admit that the docks are well maintained."

"Still, twenty five percent is a lot of money," said Balthazar.

"It is. There are a few more things you should know. Be careful where you fill your canteens. Berenike's ground water is brackish so try not to drink it. There's usually good water in the qualts, but be careful or you'll find yourself with a stomach sickness that can keep you on your back for months."

"Don't worry! I can find my way to good water like a camel!" said Balthazar easily.

"That may be, but you're not the one I'm concerned about," said Musa looking toward Alima.

"Thank you for worrying about me, but I can find good water as well as any of you!" Alima sounded exasperated.

Musa threw his hands up in mock defense. "Please, please! I'm sure your betrothed will watch over you well enough."

"Of course, I will. Unless Sameer is with her, we'll travel together always."

Alima bit her lip. She had hoped for some time to herself, but now unless she could get Sameer to escort her, she would be hand in hand with Balthazar until they sailed! How could she do so without revealing her feelings?

"There are just a few more things." Musa continued. "Keep your eyes open near the docks and you may be rewarded with a sighting of elephants."

"Elephants!" The threesome exclaimed together.

"You mean, those huge animals with the big floppy ears?" asked Alima.

"Those are the ones. The Romans first brought them from Africa over a hundred years ago to train them for battle. Then about fifty years ago, they opened breeding camps here. Now they train them near Rome, but the breeding camps remain. Don't be surprised if you see some elephants near the docks, since they transport them on special ships, called elephantegoi. I see some almost every time we're in port." Balthazar, Sameer and Alima looked hopeful they might be so lucky.

"Now I have one last thing to say and it is the most important." Musa paused, looking at each of them directly. "We're no longer in Arabia. Berenike is a Roman territory and their laws prevail. Be careful who you talk to, what you say and how you say it, especially if you ask about Mehir. I'll inquire discreetly from my friends, but it we must take care. We cannot have our ship delayed for any reason!"

"Thank you, Musa," responded Sameer. "We promise to be careful."

Early the next morning, Alima stood near the bow looking west as Berenike appeared on the horizon. All morning she watched as the city grew larger until, by mid-afternoon, the houses of the city were in clear view. To starboard a peninsula of land jutted into the sea several miles north of the city. There were some large houses built out toward the cape with a few small fishing vessels anchored about. She wondered if there was a reason, then she remembered Musa talking about the silt that built up because of currents south of the cape. That must be why he was piloting the ship well south of it toward the docks on the port side.

As they sailed closer, Alima's eyes were drawn west to a large white building on the highest point of land. It shone with the light of the sun, and she couldn't keep her eyes off it. She called out to Musa who was nearby. "Captain, what's that white building? Up on the hills to the west. It looks like the sun is shining right through it!"

"It's the Temple of Serapis. Quite a sight, isn't it?" He strode past her, shouting orders to his crew as the ship slowed its approach. It was larger than both Qana's and Eudaemon's ports, and built to accommodate ships of many sizes. Soon, she noticed some Roman soldiers directing Musa to a berth. Musa kept the bow of the ship into the wind as they slowed to a crawl, and soon the crew was throwing lines out fore and aft to secure it. He had obviously done this many times, and his timing was flawless. The ship came to a gradual gliding stop, and before long, Musa was giving his crew a well-deserved leave. Like the men, Alima couldn't wait to get off the ship. As soon as she saw Sameer, she walked up to him eagerly. "I can't wait to see the city! Can we leave for the market right now?"

"I don't see why not. I'm hungry as a beast!"

"Then let's go," said Balthazar as he approached. A full meal is just what I've been dreaming of."

Alima blushed. Food wasn't what she'd been dreaming of, but she was hungry just the same. She followed the men down the plank, and stepped ashore. She felt as if she was still rocking, and took Sameer's arm to steady herself, determined to enjoy her first walk on land in many weeks.

As Musa had predicted, Berenike was crowded, but Alima was not cowed by it. On the contrary, she was intrigued by the many different faces and types of dress. She immediately recognized the red tunics of the Roman legionnaires who ran the docks, for she had seen a few in Qana. But as they neared the market, she saw other men dressed in free flowing togas and leather sandals. "What country are they from?" she asked Sameer.

"They are Romans too, but not of the army."

Alima noticed other men of darker complexion who were barefoot and bare chested. They wore white linen skirts from their waists to their calves, but what drew her attention most was their painted faces. They had smudged black kohl around their eyes like women, and she bent close to Sameer and asked, "Are those Egyptian men?"

Sameer nodded as he gazed steadily ahead. Seeing men adorned like women was a new and unfamiliar custom. She had never seen women or men paint their faces in this manner, and she often found herself staring as she tried to figure out what she was seeing. She recognized the henna dye they used to color their lips and nails, but she had no idea what they used to cover their lids with shades of green and blue.

Some of the women wore single strapped linen dresses that were almost sheer. Many wore adornments in their hair and on their bodies, and Alima couldn't help admiring their various anklets, bracelets, necklaces and rings made of beads and metals. Some women were strikingly beautiful, with high cheek bones and slim figures, and she could tell Sameer was entranced. She laughed as his eyes followed their every movement, especially the sway of their walk.

Soon the mouth-watering aromas of the open air eating places drew their attention from the crowd. There were many choices available: beef, chicken, salted pork, dried catfish, even snails if they wanted to spend a day's wage for a meal.

"Let's stop here," said Sameer. "That chicken smells very good."

They sat down to watch the meal cooked in front of them and ate it quickly once it was served.

When they had finished Balthazar looked at Sameer. "Would you let me take Alima to the Temple of Serapis tomorrow? I've decided not to sell my spice here so I'm free to show her around the city." Then looking at Alima he added, "If she wants me to take her, that is."

"I'd love to see the Temple! But you must come with us, Sameer!"

"I'd like nothing better, but I might ask around about father. I'll let you know in the morning."

"All right," said Alima sounding let down.

"I'll do my best to make it an interesting day," said Balthazar. "Or perhaps you'd prefer a different escort? Maybe one of those Egyptians with the smudged eyes?"

Sameer laughed aloud, spitting out the last of his beer, as he looked at Alima. She was laughing, too. "No thank you," she said quickly." A plain eyed man from our country will be just fine."

Through torch lit streets they traced their way back to The Baysan, where the men bunked down on deck, and Alima on her straw covered bed. Her body quickly readjusted to the rocking, and before she knew it she was waking to the shouts of the crew. She hopped up and went out hoping to find fresh water. She wasn't disappointed. Musa had brought several full amphorae aboard and poured water into two large tin pitchers to be shared by all. She waited her turn, and was grateful to get a cupful to drink and another to wash up with.

She went back to her room, washed, combed and re-plaited her hair and put on a clean dress. Realizing how plain she looked in comparison with the Egyptian women, she decided to wear a few pieces of beaded jewelry. She wound some around her neck, placed some on her wrists and twisted some into her hair. Then judging her appearance worthy of a visit to the temple she stepped out into the daylight. She found Balthazar standing next to Melwah, and Sameer on the dock.

"Good morning," she said, bowing slightly to each of them. "I'm ready for our trip to the temple. Are you coming brother?"

"I am. Musa said he'll ask about father, so I'll wait to see what he learns. I'm afraid I must be the third wheel with the betrothed couple after all!"

Taking his arm and pulling him aside, Alima whispered. "Why do you taunt me in front of Balthazar?"

"I'm just teasing," said Sameer. "But Balthazar is one of the finest men I've ever met and you would do well to find someone as good."

Alima looked suddenly glum. "Teasing or not, I'm still in mourning and you needn't remind me the betrothal is a fake."

Losing his temper at her apparent touchiness, Sameer raised his voice in rebuke. "You're still in mourning? Really? No one would know it to look at you! Aren't you forbidden to wear adornments?"

Alima flushed. "I . . . I guess I forgot amidst all the excitement. I will remove them."

"Wait! You don't need to," said Sameer. "Wear what you please. Why you would mourn a man like Sahl I don't know. If I were a woman,

I would shorten my mourning, and enjoy the freedom afforded me without parents to remind me of rules and traditions!"

Alima looked surprised. "I will gladly honor our customs, brother. I had thought to fit in with the Egyptian women when I put these on. To look nice for you and Balthazar. But you're right; I shouldn't be wearing them yet." Head down and looking determined, she re-boarded the ship, removing her beads as she did so.

CHAPTER 17

The Temple of Serapis

§

"WOMEN! I'LL NEVER UNDERSTAND THEM!" exclaimed Sameer when Alima was out of earshot. "Did you hear me, man?" He elbowed Balthazar who was looking at the sky.

"What? … did you say something?"

"Yes. I was saying I can't understand women! I gave Alima an excuse to wear her beads and she decides to take them off anyway."

"Ah! I think Alima likes our customs. She would never take a short cut round them, and I think she was embarrassed at her lapse in judgment."

"You may be right, but Musa and the crew think she's betrothed to you. I'm sure they expect her to be wearing adornments."

"Then perhaps it has more to do with what she expects of herself."

"What do you mean? Every woman's first concern should be with what others expect, especially their men."

"I'm not sure about that. I knew Sahl, and I think it was hard for Alima to know what he expected. But she found ways to be proud of herself, to expect things of herself. Haven't you noticed other women who are the same?"

"How do you mean?" asked Sameer.

"Well, think of your mother. She takes pride in her cooking and in the work of her hands, in work unrelated to her men. My mother and sister were that way too. Why should Alima be different?"

"It's true my mother delights in her cooking, and in the compliments she gets. But she's cooking for us men! Sewing for us!"

"Yes, but what if she cooks for a female friend, or for your sister? Don't you think she would take the same pride and care?"

"I suppose," said Sameer.

"Well, that's what I mean. How she spends her time and uses her talents shows what kind of person she is."

"You seem to know a lot about women," said Sameer.

Balthazar laughed. "I certainly do not! But I like to watch people. And I've noticed Alima goes out of her way to do things in certain ways. The way she gathered spices in Khalan, the way she tended the garden, the way she dresses, even the way she walks. She was particular about each thing in a different way. Seeing her mourning through to its conclusion may be part of that. It's just her way."

Alima returned moments later, her adornments removed.

"Alima, would you like to ride Melwah?" asked Balthazar. "It will be good for him after so many weeks on the ship."

"Thank you but I'd rather walk today."

"Very well." said Balthazar who proceeded to mount and urge Melwah forward. By noon they were at the western outskirts of the city, and climbing toward the Temple. It was built on the highest point of land in Berenike, and as they walked, a sweeping view of the city appeared before them. To the east, they could see the city center, the harbor and beyond that the cape that curled into the sea like a half moon. To the west and north, the terrain sprawled in a seemingly endless series of hills and desert interspersed with well-worn trails and the occasional Roman praesidium. To the south, the land flattened into a desert-like plain that hugged the sandy coast.

When they reached the hilltop, once again they marveled at the imposing white structure. After securing Melwah's reins to a nearby tree the friends began to circle the temple grounds. They saw many artisans etching hieroglyphs and cartouches in portions of the building's façade and were surprised to see many Roman inscriptions near depictions of the Egyptian deities.

"Why are there Roman writings on an Egyptian temple?" asked Alima.

"Because the Romans like to leave their mark wherever they go," said Balthazar quietly. Alima and Sameer nodded as they walked past some Roman soldiers and ascended the steps to the main hall.

With few worshipers about, they walked unhindered past statues of various gods and goddesses and an altar of libations. There were a few more small rooms where flickering torches warded off the shadows, but they held little appeal and the threesome decided to leave in search of a place to eat.

Not far from Melwah they found a quiet spot, away from the artisans and Roman guards. They shared water from their canteens and some salt-dried fish and fruit; and after finishing, Balthazar lay down on his back to peer at the sky. He stayed that way for quite some time, while Sameer and Alima continued to enjoy their food.

"I wonder why the Egyptians have so many gods and goddesses," said Alima to Sameer. "I like the idea of a female goddess, but I think our Prophet Zarathustra's idea of one god is much better. Even if he is male, it makes more sense to me."

Sameer frowned and shook his head. "Why do you question such things? What difference does it make, one god or many? Besides, women aren't meant to judge the rightness of gods and goddesses, are they, Balthazar?"

Balthazar sat up at the sound of his name. That unusual star he'd been watching would have to wait. "It's true that our country won't allow women to play a role in worship, but I hear there are places where women are priestesses and even run temples. Our creator, Ahura Mazda, made both men and women with minds to reason and question. Don't you ever wonder how beliefs arise ... why people worship as they do? Why shouldn't Alima wonder as much as any man?"

Sameer raised his hands in unison. "Because the gods are unknowable, and beyond my understanding. I leave those questions to the wise men of the world. They know of these things. We should stick to what we know and care about. I know ship building! And if I were a woman,

I would stick to what a woman should care about, my family and my man!" He looked very self-satisfied.

"Well, maybe you don't care about such things, but I do," said Balthazar. "That's why I want to study the stars. Many think the gods have written the answers to our questions, even our lives, in the stars if we but know how to read them."

"Is that why you spend so much time watching them?" Sameer chided.

"Partly. Today I'm looking because I've seen something amazing. An unusually bright star!"

"There's nothing unusual about that!" said Sameer. "There are many bright stars in the sky."

"Yes, but this star seems to be moving."

"Maybe Serapis is trying to send us a message! Maybe he doesn't want us to question the nature of the gods." Sameer joked.

"Perhaps. But if that's true, he's a naive and shallow god, for men will never stop questioning."

"Why do you say that?" asked Alima.

"Because I think it's our nature to be curious, to wonder why. We want to make sense of the world. The Egyptians have obviously decided that just one god wasn't the answer because they have so many."

"Can you explain what you mean?" asked Alima.

"I mean look around you. There is so much to fear: sickness, storms, the quaking earth, the violence of men and the terror of our imaginings. Like the sea monsters the crew told us about but never saw. We seek protection from the unknown and from evil, and find it hard to imagine one god can control it all, save us from it all. So men like the Egyptians create many gods to do what they think one god cannot."

Sameer shook his head. "It seems like a waste of time to think about such things, but it's your time to waste." He rose and walked away, signaling the discussion was over.

Balthazar took Alima's hand as she rose and she held onto to it gratefully while she addressed him. "You're an interesting man, Balthazar of Khalan. I know you're fascinated by the stars but I see now it goes beyond that. Your questions run deep like mine."

Balthazar bowed his head in acknowledgement of her comment but said nothing as he let go of her hand. "Would you like to ride Melwah back to the ship?" he asked.

"I would. The walk here was longer than I expected." Balthazar helped her into the saddle and they returned in silence, though Balthazar tripped several times as his eyes strayed often to the eastern sky.

The rest of their time in Berenike was uneventful. Musa and his crew loaded new cargo and fresh provisions while Sameer and Alima watched the elephants in a pen near the northernmost dock. And they all laughed at Balthazar who spent most of his time playing with Melwah and staring at the sky.

The night before they set sail, Sameer and Alima asked Musa if he'd had any luck asking about their father. "Not much. I'm sorry to say. I heard only vague guesses about where the Romans might be building ships. Some told me the coast near Caesarea, others said Crete. Still others said Rome itself. If they've taken your father there, I fear you'll not see him again." Musa scratched his beard as he went on. "But I had one bit of luck, when I spoke to an old beggar on the dock. He said that a few years back a Roman ship docked here with an old Arabian slave on board. He remembered the man because the Romans guarded him so carefully. He figured the man must be special. But he couldn't tell me anything more. I'm sorry."

"Thank you for asking," said Sameer. "That may have been our father, but it doesn't tell us much. Maybe we'll have better luck at the next port."

"Maybe," said Captain Musa. "But don't count on it."

CHAPTER 18

Caesarea Maritima

§

THE BAYSAN SET SAIL AT dawn. With good winds and no storms to impede them, it cut swiftly through the waves toward Arsinoe. Archers were posted day and night to watch for pirates but saw none. They sighted a fleet of Roman ships over the course of two days, but Musa gave them a wide berth and they sailed on without incident. As was her custom, Alima enjoyed looking toward shore, hoping to spot a shipbuilding site, though she doubted her father could be found that easily.

Mainly she kept to herself wondering why the sky held Balthazar's attention and she could not. Since their trip to the Temple, he'd been so absorbed in the stars that he hardly ever spoke to her. Had she offended him? She had held his hand for one long moment near the Temple. Surely he must know that she cared? Or would she only ever be a true friend? The question hung in her mind like a ripe fruit just beyond her reach.

South winds sped them through the northern waters of the sea. They were making good time toward Arsinoe. Why then were the captain and crew so tense? Her answer came soon in a series of coral reefs port and starboard that seemed to stretch for leagues. Several times she held her breath as the winds pushed them toward the reefs. But Musa knew his ship and piloted the ship steady and clear to Arsinoe.

After docking, Musa immediately arranged for them to join a large caravan heading to Pelusium. Alima had never seen so many camels in one place. Over fifty thousand of them, including Melwah, lined up waiting to take on riders and supplies. It took many days to unload

Balthazar's amphorae and to select the largest, fittest camels to carry them. When their fees were paid and the caravan was ready to depart, they said goodbye to the crew of *The Baysan* and headed toward The Great Sea where a new ship and crew awaited them.

Alima traveled with a large group of women and children, and rarely saw the men who walked at the head of the caravan. She began to miss her sailing days and the week in Berenike. Balthazar seemed to understand her in ways no man ever had and she yearned to spend more time with him.

The days dragged on without him, and the frequent haboobs made them feel even longer. She had lived with these storms all her life but confronting them in the open desert and as part of a large group was a new experience. When they saw one coming, the whole caravan quickly corralled its camels to the nearest high point of land or within an oasis if one was near. After commanding all their camels to koosh, they would cluster around the children, sit down and press themselves against the sheltered side of each animal. They used water from their canteens to wet their noses and carefully covered their faces with scarves. Most of the sand would be thrown over them and all would be well. But every storm threatened danger, and she would never forget when a child became separated from their group and was lost. Alima wept with the mother when the child's body could not be found in the great mounds of sand left behind.

Finally, after weeks plodding through the desert, Alima spotted Pelusium in the distance at the far north-eastern edge of the Nile. When the caravan finally halted, she was reunited with the men.

"I missed you, brother," said Alima as she hugged Sameer.

"As well you should!"

Musa laughed and shook his head. "I envy your youthful pride."

Balthazar said nothing, his attention once more absorbed in the sky. The three of them followed Musa toward the dock where they found *The Serafina* ready and waiting. They boarded quickly and within a few days, after all their cargo had been transferred, set sail for Caesarea Maritima.

Alima was mesmerized by the clear azure water of the Great Sea. Again they sailed within sight of the coast and she found fellowship with Sameer looking for fish off the starboard side. How she wished that Balthazar would join them, even if for just a few moments.

As they neared their destination, Alima wondered if he'd fulfill his promise to search for her father once his spices were sold. She would have liked to ask him but found her energy diminished by a harrowing fatigue. The wind, the waves and the caravan trek had taken a toll. Oh, for the journey to be over! She felt selfish to think it, but wished the quest for her father wouldn't take them much farther. And if they couldn't find him? It was a thought too terrible to take in.

Despite the mild weather, the sea was choppy as the ship neared Caesarea, and *The Serafina* rocked in the wake of a steady southwest wind. The sandy Judean coastline stretched north and south as far as the eye could see. There were no natural coves or visible harbors, but Caesarea had become a huge maritime port nonetheless. Musa said that Herod the Great had built the harbor fifteen years before with the help of Roman engineers, and so he'd named the port, Sebastos, the Greek equivalent of Augustus, after his Roman benefactor.

The port was impressive; and per his habit for detail Musa told them how man-made islands of concrete, dirt, and stone were deposited on the open seabed and enlarged by sinking pre-set caissons of concrete to construct the huge horseshoe shaped breakwater. She noticed that the southern breakwater made a graceful L-shaped arc away from land, first west from shore then north. The northern breakwater extended straight west in a perpendicular angle to the shore and was about half as long as the other.

Near the mouth of the harbor on the south breakwater, stood a tall lighthouse with a series of smaller towers built at intervals along the wall. Opposite the lighthouse, on the north breakwater, was a series of towering statues. Viewed together, the harbor entrance was quite a sight, and *The Serafina* was headed straight for it.

As they sailed closer, many buildings came into view. Alima could see what looked like an amphitheater to their starboard side. It was built on a wide peninsula of land south of the breakwater. And just ahead and north of the breakwater, stood a palace with a pool overlooking the sea. It was surrounded on all sides by covered walkways. Alima wondered who lived there, but since Musa was now busy piloting his ship, her question would have to wait.

Her eyes scanned the harbor trying to take it all in. So many large ships in one place! Qana, Berenike and Pelusium all paled in comparison. Could her father be somewhere close? Surely such a large harbor must have a shipyard nearby.

The Serafina dropped anchor just north of the breakwater entrance. They would need to moor overnight, until they paid the Roman tax and were granted permission to dock. Alima watched as Musa, his first mate and Balthazar rowed a small boat to shore to look for the port administrator and pay the required taxes.

"It's hard to believe we're finally here, isn't it?" Said Sameer as he joined her.

"Yes," said Alima her face to the shore.

"We must talk, sister. I've been thinking about the future, about what we should do if we don't find father."

"I've been thinking about that, too," said Alima.

"Good. Then maybe you'll agree we need a plan ... for our return home. We don't have enough money to continue searching forever or to travel much farther."

"I know."

"Father's been gone well over three years. We saw no trace of him on our voyage, and there's a good chance he may not be here either."

"We knew finding him would be difficult."

"Yes, but I thought we'd find out something as we sailed. Other than that vague comment from the beggar in Berenike we learned nothing at all!"

Alima looked him in the face. "I know our money won't last forever, but we've come so far. If we don't find father here, then we'll think what to do next. Father may be right here, in this city! It's too soon to talk about going home. Much too soon!"

"But what if he's not? We can't ask Balthazar to set his plans aside forever. He's done so much already. And it looks as if you are little closer to him now, than you were in Qana. You must know he hasn't asked about making the betrothal real."

"Ah! Is that what this is about? You want to get me off your hands?"

"That's not fair! You know I want what's best for you! It's just . . . I thought there might be a seed of something lasting, so I'm surprised you haven't grown closer."

Alima looked into the wind. "I'm sorry, Sameer. I know you care about me and I'm thankful. But Balthazar confuses me. Sometimes I feel there is a seed, as you say, of something lasting. But at other times, there's nothing."

Alima bit her lip and her face tightened. She wasn't comfortable talking with her brother about Balthazar. Women only spoke of men with other women. How well she remembered speaking to her sister in the years before her marriage. They'd shared their fears and hopes, talked about the boys in Qana, who they fancied and didn't. Would she ever find someone as close to confide in? Her thoughts skipped to Balthazar. Like Baysan, he listened to her and seemed to value her ideas. He didn't judge or make assumptions about what she should or shouldn't do. It amazed her, and made her feel good.

"Alima! Where is your head?" Sameer broke her reverie. "I asked you something."

"I'm sorry. I was just thinking how much I miss Baysan."

"What has that to do with anything? I miss her too. But we're talking about Balthazar. I need to know. How do you feel about the man? He wouldn't have paid the bride price he did if he didn't care about you. Would you like me to speak to him? Perhaps, I can persuade him. Maybe it's not too late!"

"No! Please no. There was a time before Berenike, when I felt his eyes on me, and I thought of him as well. But something changed after our trip to the temple. He hardly ever talked with me after that."

"But you were the one who wanted to keep things formal." Sameer responded quickly.

"I know. I wanted to abide by our customs. But after the temple, things changed. Maybe I was deceiving myself. Maybe he never felt anything more than the loyalty of a good friend. Now, I feel awkward when I'm near him, like I'm a stone around his neck."

"I'm sure that's not how he feels. I could have sworn he looked at you as a man does when he's looking for a woman of his own. But you're right. He seems different, preoccupied. He's got his face to the sky every chance he gets."

"Exactly! Do you remember in Berenike, how he talked about a bright star that looked like it was moving? And ever since he's been like a man obsessed!"

"He is that. He never helped the crew much after that either," said Sameer.

"But what does it matter? If he wanted our betrothal to be real don't you think he would have said something by now? So you are right. We should make our own plan, and Balthazar should feel free to make his. But there will be no talk of leaving until we explore Judea. Not until we know if father is here."

Sameer nodded. "All right. But I mean to have a talk with Balthazar. If only to determine how long he'll help with the search."

Balthazar returned to the ship that afternoon. While Musa made plans to dock, Balthazar drew Sameer and Alima aside. "Do you remember Musa's warnings before we docked in Berenike?"

"Yes," they said in unison.

"Well, he said we must be even more careful here. King Herod rules Judea by Roman authority and owes his allegiance to Caesar. Many respect him for his great buildings, but he's hated by the Jews. And now many say he's gone mad. That's his palace on the heights, with the pool overlooking the sea."

"Oh!" said Alima. "I wondered who lived there."

"You may think it beautiful, but Musa says that palace weeps blood. Herod has killed his wife, his brother, and two of his sons. Musa told me a joke he heard from the sailors: that even Caesar thinks it's safer to be one of Herod's pigs than one of his sons!"

"But our search for father shouldn't take us anywhere near the king," said Alima.

"Let's hope not," said Balthazar.

"So how do you think we should search for him?" Sameer asked.

"First, I've got to sell my spice. Then I'm free to help you. Musa said there used to be a shipyard up north of town." He pointed in that direction. "It might be a good place to start."

Early the next morning, Musa brought the ship through the breakwater and headed straight to the section of the quay devoted to unloading cargo. With the assistance of hired help, Balthazar's amphorae were unloaded and transferred to one of the port's many warehouses. Traders stood in groups along the dock hoping to buy and sell spices, oils and other commodities, and Balthazar spoke with most of them before deciding to sell to a Roman named Marius. Due to the high quality of his cinnabar, they readily agreed on a price which afforded a good profit. It would go a long way to support him in the months and years to come. After signing the bill of sale, he congratulated himself on a successful deal and cleared his mind to help his friends.

That evening, Musa approached Balthazar at the bow of the ship. "Well young man. What do you say? I can tell you've become a skilled bargainer! Such a good price I hear you struck! Perhaps we should go into business together. I plan to leave for Jerusalem soon. My wife always wants a piece of silver from the Jewish artisans there. Would you like to come along? Perhaps you can find some items to resell when we return to Qana!"

Balthazar was taken by surprise. "It's an interesting idea, but I haven't given any thought to leaving yet. When do you leave for Jerusalem?"

"In three days. I usually spend some months in Judea before heading home when the winds are more favorable. I always go to Jerusalem and to Alexandria too, if there's time. That's a city you would like. There's a special place there where men observe the stars. What do you say? I'd be happy for your company, and promise you a good share of any profits."

"I don't know." Balthazar responded cautiously "A little extra gold would be welcome, but if I go to Jerusalem, I won't be coming back this way. I am heading east to Parthia. There's a school of astrology there too, in a city called Seleucia."

"Better than Alexandria?" asked Musa looking skeptical.

"I don't know. But I hear they counsel kings and priests alike. And I want to study where the Babylonians did."

"I understand. But how does your woman like the idea of traveling so much farther? It will take you many more months to reach Parthia and she already looks very tired."

Balthazar realized he hadn't included Alima in his comments. "She knows of my interest in the stars. But we haven't decided on a departure date. As you can imagine, we have plans to make and things to do. We need to get our land legs back, Captain!" Balthazar smirked, hoping Musa would ponder all the possibilities for a young couple, newly engaged and beginning on a life journey.

"Oh, my man! To be young again and in your sandals! A lovely bride and the glories of the marriage bed. Yes, I'm sure you have better things to do than follow me to Jerusalem. But if you change your mind, you can always get word to me here at my ship."

"Thank you for the offer. Above all, I thank you for a successful journey and your guidance with the Romans." He kissed Musa on both cheeks.

"It was my pleasure young man! I wish I had a son like you. Such a good head for business and not afraid of hard work. That's a rare combination. Do you know where you'll stay? I can make some suggestions." Balthazar listened carefully as Musa told him where they might find lodging.

As the sun sank beneath the sea, he stood alone on the torch-lit deck, looked to the eastern sky and found that now familiar star. In his mind he saw the sky as it was that morning in Berenike. It looked at first like the other eclipses he had seen, but he soon realized it was much more. There was a beautiful glow coming from the edges of the moon and he could not look away. He continued to gaze and when it was over, two stars emerged from behind the moon instead of one. He was transfixed and soon noticed one star was much brighter than the other, and most amazing of all, it seemed to be moving! It wasn't a shooting star. No, this was something else. It moved slowly, and he might not have noticed it at all if he hadn't been watching so closely. There was something special about it. He felt it in his bones, and that was why he couldn't keep his eyes from the sky. Even during the day when it was all but impossible to see. If only Mehir could be found soon so he could make his way to Seleucia.

Early the next morning, after bidding Musa and the crew goodbye, he packed their belongings on Melwah, and set off with Sameer and Alima to find lodging. By late morning, they had found an inexpensive room in the poor part of the city. It wasn't as clean or private as an inn, but it was in the part of town Musa had recommended.

The house was a small mud and brick hut with a central wall that divided the family area on one side from the extra room on the other. Each side had a separate entrance and a small high window framed in wood for fresh air. Sameer and Balthazar would share one end of the rented room, and Alima the other. And fortunately, there was a curtain which divided the space, so Alima would have a bit of privacy to dress. The owners, Noah and Judith, had three young children and seemed welcoming enough.

While Alima and Sameer moved their belongings inside, Balthazar got Melwah feed and water. It was the first time he'd been alone with the animal since the caravan to Pelusium, and Balthazar stroked his side and inspected his hump and hooves as Melwah slurped from the small trough outside the hut. When he was done, Balthazar handed him a few nuts and seeds as a treat. Tomorrow he would buy some wheat and oats to make up for the deprivation of recent weeks.

"What do you say, Melwah? We've come a long way, haven't we? Did you like being a part of that caravan? You carried your load so proudly and look no worse for it. But our wanderings aren't nearly done, so don't get too comfortable." Balthazar led him to a nearby tree and commanded him to koosh. "Good boy. Stay and rest. I shall be doing the same very soon."

CHAPTER 19

The Search Goes On

THE HUT WAS SMALL BUT cozy thought Alima as she sank onto the narrow straw bed, and gratefully surrendered to the sweet oblivion of sleep. Early the next morn, light streamed through the window stirring her to wake. She sat up cross legged, examining her surroundings and wondering what the household customs might be.

She had briefly met Noah, the man of the house, when they paid their board. Balthazar said he was named after an ancient man, long revered by the Jews. The story went that Noah had saved all mankind and animals from extinction by building a boat before a flood covered the earth. She tried to imagine such a horrible event, and understood why the man would be extolled. But mainly she was glad to be here, for it struck her as a good omen to be lodging in a house linked by name to a boat builder.

When the men woke, Alima was already heating a pot of water for tea over the small fire pit outside the house. When the tea was ready, she served it to the men then joined them on a log near the fire pit.

"Are we agreed then?" Balthazar asked Sameer. "We'll each take a portion of the coast road to look for boat yards? And before we leave, we'll ask Noah if he knows of one."

"I can't think of a better way," said Sameer. "I'll be happy to head south, which will cover the longest distance."

"Then I'll go north. Alima, unless you're too tired, could you browse the markets for food? Maybe explore the city and the area west of town. If you can memorize what you see, perhaps we can draw a map later."

Alima smiled. "I'll be happy to! Will you be home by sunset?"

"I can't speak for your brother, but I hope to be," said Balthazar.

"As will I," said Sameer. "Is there more tea?"

Alima poured each man another cup and Sameer shared some dried berries and a portion of bread taken from the ship. It wasn't very tasty but would keep their stomachs from growling 'til they could get more. After the men left, Alima prepared herself for the day, washing from a water bowl that had been left for them. When she was done, she put on a clean dress, fixed her hair and head scarf and went to thank Judith. She found her kneeling over her baby boy and cleaning his bottom just inside the open door. Though Arabic was her first language, she had learned Aramaic as a child and was trying to remember it. She watched silently as Judith washed her son and put his little tunic on over his bare bottom. He's so beautiful, thought Alima. And active too, for he squirmed out of his mother's arms as soon as she was done dressing him.

Judith laid him on a reed mat nearby and bowed low to Alima when she rose. "Good morning and welcome! We're happy to have you share our house."

"We're happy to be here," said Alima smiling and bowing in return. "Thank you for the water. I always like to start the day with a wash!" She held out the bowl to Judith.

"Please keep it for your stay. The well is just down the road." Judith indicated the direction with her hand.

"Thank you. Your baby is so beautiful! How old is he?"

"Ten months."

"He really moves around doesn't he?"

"All the time! Just like his father . . . can't stay still. See?" Judith pointed to the little one who had rolled over several times and was already several feet from the mat she had set him on. "I'm going to work in my garden today. Would you like to help?"

"I would, but the men want me to go to the market. Can you direct me?"

"It's that way." Judith pointed southeast. "Just follow the crowds toward the eastern gate."

Alima bowed. "Thank you! Maybe I can help you in the garden another time."

"You would be most welcome," said Judith.

Alima was proud that her first attempts at Aramaic had gone well. After setting the water bowl in the hut, she took the path Judith pointed out, and soon found herself on a wide stone-paved boulevard, lined by many large buildings. The houses weren't baked clay and straw brick like Judith's, but stone block houses of varying colors and sizes. She passed a public bath, then an amphitheater built in the round Grecian style. Just beyond it was a construction site where many men labored, and she slowed her pace a bit to see what they were doing. Some of them were pouring a soft mixture of pebbles, mortar and ash into pre-made wooden frames, while others dismantled frames to expose the hardened material and smooth out the facade. On the finished side of the building she saw men applying stucco and colored tiles, and still others attaching thin slabs of marble to the walls. It must be the home of a very wealthy person, she thought, walking on. Though she hated the Romans for taking her father away, she could see they were ingenious when it came to building.

The streets became more crowded as the sun rose higher and she was able to understand little bits of conversations from listening to the passers-by. Some of them spoke of a caravan route that ran through Caesarea, from Tyre in the north to Egypt. No wonder she could hear so many different languages. There were many soldiers in the streets, too. Sameer had told her not to draw attention to herself, so she lowered her eyes and pulled her headscarf down whenever she came near them. The locals kept their distance too, but didn't seemed fazed by their watchful eyes. How well they hide their resentment, she thought.

Eventually, she saw the market and stopped to purchase a reed pen, ink and a small roll of papyrus to make Balthazar's map. She stored her purchases in a cloth bag, and wound her way past the food stalls stacked full of every kind of staple. Barley and wheat, figs, dates, grapes and pomegranates, and several types of beans, lentils and peas. She saw fresh picked olives and oils for sale, as well as many spices. Though most people made their own bread, there were some flat breads for sale, along with a thicker bread called challah, fennel and fig cakes, and some sweet breads.

After determining the stalls with the best prices, she bought some flour, as well as some almonds and pistachios, which she knew her brother loved. Continuing on, she found an artisan who made beautiful jewelry and decided to buy a bracelet for Judith. She selected a wide wooden bracelet intricately carved on the outside with a smooth inner surface. She haggled on the price, walking away at one point until the seller pursued her and they agreed upon an acceptable sum. She had had no close friends in Khalan, so the hope of making a new friend filled her with anticipation. Maybe I can help with her little boy, she thought. What a joy it would be to hold him!

As she examined the wares in the nearby stalls she thought back to the home she'd shared with Sahl. Would she ever have a house of her own again? One that she could make comfortable for a man she loved?

It was already late morning and her stomach growled, so she bought some bread and a glass of goat's milk along with some olives, and sat down next to some local women to eat. She relished the taste of the fresh bread and when she had finished it, bought a fig cake to eat with the last of her milk.

She observed everything and listened as best she could to the women around her. It was impossible to understand every word, but she noticed how their tone changed when soldiers rode by. The undercurrent of fear and anger was palpable. The city's atmosphere was not as calm as it had first appeared.

Feeling rested, she set out to explore. She spent the day roaming the eastern sections and finding the main roads out of town. Later in the afternoon, when she had memorized enough for a map, she headed back to Judith's house after buying a duck at the market. Her day had been successful. She was anxious to know if the men had been too.

Like Alima, the men had spent the morning walking. They had traveled only a short distance together before Sameer grew talkative. "Can you believe it? We're finally looking for my father! I want to thank you for staying to help."

"I promised I would, and only dishonorable men forget their promises. I hope we can find him soon," he replied in a serious tone.

"I do, too. The sooner we can get some answers the better. And that reminds me, now that we're alone, I must pose you a question. I watched on The Baysan how you often looked at my sister. I can't help thinking that you like her. Would you have an interest in making the betrothal genuine? You're a good man, Balthazar, we would welcome you into our family."

Balthazar kept walking, but slowed his pace. "I'm not sure how to answer you. Yes, I think Alima's beautiful, clever, and hard working. She would make anyone a fine wife. But I told her when we fled Khalan that I had no plans to marry. And I told you the same before we spoke with your Uncle Nibal. That hasn't changed. I'll stay until we've searched for your father, then I plan to move on."

"But what if we don't find him here? How long are you prepared to help us?"

Balthazar grimaced and continued walking for some time before he spoke again. "I know how much it means to you, and I know there'll be sadness if you can't find him, but we could look in all the ports along the Sea and never find him. I would never say this to Alima, but it's possible we may not."

"I know. I've been telling her we can only search for a little while in Judea before we'll need to go home. But it would be helpful to know how long you can help. She'll be disappointed enough if we don't find father. I don't want her disappointed in . . ."

Balthazar suddenly looked angry. "In me! Is that what you were going to say? You don't want her to be disappointed in me?"

Sameer put his hands in the air. "I'm sorry, I didn't mean that..." But he said nothing more.

The two men walked in silence until Balthazar renewed the talk. "Sameer, I think your father is valuable to the Romans. They'll take care to keep him working. But he's an old man. Sickness or death can come at any time. I don't want to disappoint either of you, but I'm not prepared to search endlessly. If we don't find him near Caesarea, I will be leaving."

"I understand. You've done more than most men. You need not do more."

Balthazar could tell from Sameer's somber tone that he wished otherwise. "I'm sorry." Balthazar said glumly. "Perhaps we'll have good fortune for a change."

"Yes, let's hope for that," said Sameer.

They soon came to a point where the road forked. "I'll see you tonight," said Balthazar. "Good luck!" He continued north along the coast road for some time but could see no shipyard where Musa had predicted one. Maybe it had moved? The port was distant but still within sight when a thought occurred to him. Perhaps Marius, the trader, would know if there were local shipyards. He headed back toward the port considering how best to inquire. He found Marius, along with several other traders, standing outside the amphitheater. Marius recognized Balthazar right away, and walked over to greet him.

"Good day to you, Marius," said Balthazar politely, as he continued walking to draw Marius away from the others. "I came to ask if you might have an interest in future trades if I make this a regular stop in my travels?"

"Yes, indeed. Your spice is much better than what I often see. That's why I paid you what I did. I'm not like some who try to buy the best for the least. Such a short-sighted way of doing business! I might make a quick profit but then you would take your business elsewhere for the next trade. I like to trade with men I can depend on to give me consistently good quality. So you think to be selling more of it, do you?"

"Most probably. But I may ship it to Rome, myself. How would you feel about taking delivery from me there instead?"

"I suppose. My son handles the business there. You would make delivery to him. If you can deliver the same quality, I could give you a letter with my mark stipulating the agreed price. Of course, if my son were to find the quality wanting he would lower it. But tell me, how would you do this? Musa doesn't sail to Rome."

"He doesn't. I'm considering buying or building a ship here, and hiring another captain to pilot it. Do you happen to know if there are any ships for sale in port? Or perhaps I'd be better off having one built?"

Marius's eyes opened wide. "My, my! Your gold must be weighing you down if you're thinking of buying or building a boat! There's only one yard near here and it builds ships for the emperor alone. But there may be some bargains in port if you don't mind buying an older ship."

"I see." Balthazar replied, feigning disappointment. "So the only new ships being built are all Roman ships? I'm surprised by that. I hadn't noticed any shipyards in the harbor, though I figured there must be some nearby. Or perhaps they are all being built near Rome?"

"Many are built near Rome, but not all. There are shipyards in various places throughout the empire, wherever it suits the Emperor. And here, well there are no yards near the breakwater, but if you walk twenty leagues north along the coast, there's a large one where Gaius is building a small fleet, merchant men and attack vessels alike, at least so I hear."

"Is that so?" said Balthazar, hoping to keep the conversation going.

"Yes. The Emperor prefers to build here because the labor is cheap. The shipyard is out of sight of the locals, so not to invite sabotage, which is not unknown among the Jews." Marius said these last words condescendingly and Balthazar understood the remark as the slur it was intended to be.

"I understand your meaning." He answered playing along. "A man can never be too cautious."

"Exactly!" replied Marius. "And Gaius is that above all. But ambitious, too; and knows how to stack the odds in his favor."

"Stack the odds?" Balthazar queried. "In what way?"

"Well it's common knowledge among us traders. We hear most of what happens, so it's no secret, I suppose." Balthazar could see that

Marius was happy to repeat the latest dockside gossip, and widened his eyes urging Marius on. "When the emperor placed Gaius in charge a few years ago, one of his chief tasks was to build a new fleet. Gaius is the kind of man who likes people to owe him. In fact, he often goes out of his way to do favors, so he can lengthen the list. Anyway, he helped a friend secure a post as head of the southern fleet, the one that patrols the waters out of Berenike."

"I know the one." Balthazar interjected.

"Yes, well in return for his friend's appointment, Gaius asked the man to look for experienced ship builders, anyone who might assist at the yard here. And the fates cooperated, for such a man fell into his hands some years back when a family member committed a crime that implicated him. It was a stroke of luck that allowed him to impress the man, who now labors at the shipyard north of here."

"A stroke of luck, indeed," said Balthazar casually, hiding any hint of interest in his information. "I take it Gaius is taking full advantage of it?"

"You ought to believe it! He has ambitions to be the next procurator of Judea and completing all the ships on time may help him get the post." Marius looked over toward his friends at the amphitheater and noticed them walking away. "I'm sorry, but I must be going. I have another boat to meet." He pointed to a large merchant ship that was just docking at the quay.

"Yes, of course." Balthazar walked away feeling pleased but angry. Why hadn't he thought to ask Marius sooner? He couldn't wait to tell Sameer and Alima, and turned toward Noah's house to await their return.

When he got back, he saw Judith working a little patch of land behind the house. He walked into the garden, bent down and began pulling weeds as Judith was doing. If the garden wasn't tended, the weeds would soon overwhelm the plants which looked very dry indeed. Judith looked at him in surprise, but silently accepted his offer of help with a smile.

Her two daughters, who looked to about four and six in years, were helping as best they could at the other end of the garden. Half working, half playing, they nudged each other impishly every few minutes, and appeared to be making a game of it, to see who could pull the most weeds the fastest. Soon they stood up, ran to Judith and pulled her over to their patch.

"Now let's see," said Judith. "Your weed pile is big Miriam, but yours is even bigger Rebecca! Well done!" Judith raised Rebecca's arm above her head. "The winner!" Judith announced.

Miriam started to pout. "We'll have none of that my girl. Come. You both did well." Judith took them by the hand into the house. Soon they returned with smiles on their faces, each eating a handful of figs. Judith knows how to reward her children, he mused. He remembered his own father and mother playing similar games. Chores were never a drudgery after that.

He continued working in the garden until it was cleared, then went in search of water. As he searched the shelves for a cup, Alima entered and Balthazar turned, happy to see her.

"Let me help you," he said, relieving her of the heavy sack that hung on her back. "Have you bought out all the stalls in the market?" he teased.

"Of course not! Though if I'd had a male companion or a mule along, I might have!"

"Woman, are you comparing me to a mule? Have I ever given you reason to find me stubborn or obstinate? I thought you might regard me just a little higher in the animal kingdom!"

Alima laughed, but changed her tone quickly as she looked at him levelly. "Why do you call me 'woman'? My name is Alima!"

The reprimand stung, for he had only meant to tease her. She'd obviously taken it differently. But no sooner did he ponder the etiquette of the exchange then he saw her smiling again.

"And as far as how I regard you," she continued, "I hadn't really thought about you that much! I mean, at least not in animal terms. Let me think. What animal are you most like?" she queried aloud as she set the duck on the small wooden table and began to pluck at its feathers.

"You can run quickly and quietly, so a rabbit could make sense. And then there's your eyesight. It's very good. You can see the stars so far away, and you're always on the look-out for a good trade, so you could be a hawk. Or perhaps you could be an owl, for like them you silently survey your surroundings wherever you are, and your decisions are usually wise ones. But oh, the mule! A mule is so loyal. It's true they can be difficult at times, but they are ever ready to carry the heaviest burdens. And that is you, is it not? You've been helping me carry my burdens ever since we left Khalan. So if you do bear a mulish resemblance, is that so very bad?" she asked with a disarming smile.

Balthazar smiled back, unbalanced by her analysis, but drawn in as he admired how she'd twisted his understanding of a lowly animal into the highest compliment. *How does she do it?* Embarrassed by her words, he bent to avert her eyes and bumped his forehead into hers. Looking up to apologize, he found them anyway. *Those beautiful brown eyes.* They seemed to thank him, question him, desire him, all in an instant. They held for a moment, then each of them drew away.

"Sorry. I 'm getting in your way," he said quickly. "I'd best go wait for Sameer." He left the house hastily for the safety of the garden. *She has a way about her,* he thought. *Only this morning he told Sameer he had no interest in marrying, and yet at times like this he felt his very being calling out for her.*

A while later, Alima emerged from the house holding a well-plucked duck by its neck. Balthazar lay prone on the ground, eyes again to the sky. "I'll take this to Judith. I hope she hasn't started cooking yet." She didn't wait for his reply, but strode purposefully past him shaking her head.

Despite his apparent distraction. Balthazar had heard her. "What is she thinking?" he wondered. Did she respect his interest in the stars or think him foolish? Her shaking head suggested the latter. He looked again to see the now familiar eastern star that kept moving steadily toward them. Should he show it to her again? He'd mentioned it once at the temple in Berenike. He had felt close to her then. There were times when he felt so close to her, and others when she felt as far away as the stars.

CHAPTER 20

A New Friend

§

ALIMA KNOCKED LIGHTLY AND JUDITH beckoned her in. "Please enter."

She held the duck in one hand and some spices, apricots and figs in the other. "I brought these for you. Perhaps we could cook them for dinner?"

"Thank you! I'm afraid I don't have much in my cupboard." Judith looked at the food as if it was a treasure. "It's been some time since we could afford meat. Mostly we eat what we grow in the garden, but it's not always enough for my children." Alima noticed tears glistening in Judith's eyes.

"We're happy to help. You rented us a safe place to lay our heads, and at a fair price, so we are thankful."

"You're the first people to rent from us in over a year. Many northerners used to stop on their way to Jerusalem. But since the uprisings and crucifixions, that has changed."

"It must be difficult," said Alima.

"Yes," said Judith, her forehead wrinkling. "My Noah is a carpenter. He used to work for a wealthy Roman in town, but many of our people were let go after the last uprising. Noah was one of them. Now he looks for work each morning, but doesn't always find it. We are grateful for your rent." She sat down on the floor and began to caress the brow of her sleeping baby.

Alima knelt down next to her. "Life can be hard. I lost my husband and all my belongings in a tribal raid on our village. I escaped with

Balthazar, and went back to my family only to learn my sister was dead and my father missing. It was a terrible time. But I found reason to hope."

"Yes, hope usually gets us by, doesn't it? But then again. . ." Judith shook her head. "Have you ever seen a crucifixion?"

"No," said Alima with a shudder.

"You're one of the fortunate ones. I have seen many over the years and on those days, I wondered if hope was a fool's refuge."

"It can seem that way sometimes. But then I see little things that make hope seem no delusion. I watched you cleaning your son this morning, tickling him and laughing, forgetting the cares of the world. Hope rises in such moments, when love abounds."

Alima hugged Judith, then sat back on her haunches wondering how those words had come to her in Aramaic, the language she hardly remembered. I must follow my own advice, she thought. I mustn't give in to despair, even if we don't find father, even if Balthazar leaves.

"Thank you," said Judith as she rose from the floor. "Thank you for reminding me of what's important! Maybe hope is the best gift of men. It reminds me of an old story my mother told me about the mother of our prophet, Samuel. Would you like to hear it?"

"Very much," said Alima.

Judith nodded. "There was a woman named Hannah. She was married for many years to her husband, Elkanah, but bore no children. Elkanah also had a second wife who bore him several children, and the second wife would humiliate and provoke Hannah because she was barren. As you can imagine, Hannah felt tormented. She prayed constantly to God but no children came. One day, Hannah went to the temple, and was approached by a priest who mistook her prayerful murmurings for drunkenness. Hannah defended herself. 'I'm an unhappy woman, she said. I have neither wine nor liquor and was only pouring out my heart to the Lord.' The priest was moved by Hannah's story and told her, 'Go in peace, and may the God of Israel grant you what you asked.' Hannah left the temple renewed in hope. Soon after, she conceived and bore a son, Samuel, who she consecrated to the Lord's service. I always thought that the priest gave Hannah such a great gift when he renewed her hope. Then I realized that it was God speaking through him. It was our God, Yahweh, who rewarded Hannah's faith and let her know she was loved. Our God is a great and merciful God, Alima."

Alima's eyes brimmed with tears as Judith finished her tale. "You have no idea how much that story means to me. I don't know your God, but maybe I should. Thank you for sharing your story," she said quietly. "Speaking of gifts, I have one for you. I hope you like it."

Alima took the bracelet from a pouch attached to her waist and handed it to Judith who gently brushed her fingers over the carved vine and smiled. "Thank you. It's beautiful! I have seen some like it in the market but never thought I'd own one. Did you know that this carving has a great meaning for us Jews?"

"No. I bought it because I think it's lovely."

"It is, but it's also meaningful. This carving symbolizes the tree of life."

"I've never heard of that. Is there a story connected with it, too?" Alima asked.

"Yes, but it's a long one."

"Then maybe you can tell me another day when we have more time?"

"Maybe." Judith squeezed Alima's hand. "I should start cooking! Noah will be home soon, and he will be delighted to see duck for supper. The herbs and dried fruits you bought will make it a sweet delight."

"Can you excuse me, Judith? I must see if my brother has returned."

"Go ahead. I'll put the duck on the spit. And thank you."

Alima walked outside to see Sameer sitting on a log next to Balthazar. Would their news be bitter or sweet?

CHAPTER 21

A Roman Shipyard

"I TELL YOU SAMEER, IT must be him!" said Balthazar. "The story is just too similar to be anyone else."

Alima heard the word 'father' and couldn't help interrupting. "You have news of my father? Why didn't you tell me? Why would you keep this from me?"

"I wasn't trying to keep anything from you," said Balthazar. "I was waiting for Sameer so I could tell you together."

"But you didn't wait for *me*! I was only steps away!" she sounded insulted but took a deep breath. "Tell me what you've found."

Balthazar related the events of his day. He spoke of his short fruitless walk, his decision to speak with Marius, and what he learned of an old Arabian man enslaved in return for a promotion to a friend of the port administrator. "There's a good chance the man is your father!" finished Balthazar. "And that's he's working in a shipyard not far from Mount Carmel."

"This is the news we've been waiting for!" exclaimed Sameer. "How far is Mount Carmel?"

"About twenty leagues from here. Judith said if we leave at dawn we should be there when the sun is high."

"That's good. We might be back in a day," said Sameer.

"If the weather is good," returned Balthazar. "What do you think? Should we go tomorrow?"

"The sooner the better," said Sameer. "What should we say when we get there? If the shipyard is like Caesarea's port, it'll be well guarded. They're too concerned about sabotage."

"You're right," said Balthazar. "I think we must tell them you're looking for work."

"Only me?"

"I'm not a skilled shipbuilder like you. And besides, if they hire you right away, who will come back to tell Alima?"

"I didn't think of that. You think they might hire me on the spot?"

"They might. We must be prepared in case they do."

Alima sat quietly as the men planned their departure. "I wish I could go," she said when all was decided. "I can handle the walk."

"I know," said Sameer. "But having you along while I search for work would seem strange. They might suspect something, and we don't want to give them any reason to question us."

"Sameer's right, Alima. You should stay here."

"I understand. But it will be hard to watch you leave."

"We'll take care, and I'll try to remember every detail so I can relate it when I return. Will that suit you?" asked Balthazar.

"It will have to. If you see father, do you think we can tell Musa before he returns to Qana?"

"We can try," replied Balthazar. "Musa's going to Jerusalem soon. But he said I can always get a message to him through his crew on *The Serafina*."

Alima smiled. "That would be wonderful!"

"Then it's settled," said Sameer. "I have a good feeling about this. I hope I'm not wrong."

The next morning, the men left as the sun rose. Following Judith and Noah's directions, they soon found the bumpy coast road that skirted the sea through sandy fields of high tufted grass and rock. The gulls swooped low above their heads as they left the city behind, and before long they came upon a long raised aqueduct that paralleled the road. It ran straight for many miles then veered off to the northeast.

"This must be the aqueduct Noah talked about last night," said Sameer. "He said the Romans built it under Herod's direction to carry water from those heights down to the city."

"I can see a mountain in the distance," said Balthazar. "It must be Mount Carmel. We must skirt its western edge to reach the shipyard."

"It looks like we still have a long way to go," said Sameer. "Are you sure this road goes past the mount? It looks like the mountain ends at the sea."

"Noah swore the road narrowly hugs the shore around the point. Do you see that steep ridge far to the northeast?"

"I see it."

"There's a valley called Jezreel northeast of that ridge. It's the only natural pass through the mountains, but taking that route would take much longer.

"Noah and Judith should know," said Sameer. "But I wish we could walk on the other side of the aqueduct, so it would block the wind." The warm sea breeze they had first welcomed had morphed into a westerly wind that pelted their faces with sand whipped from the beach below. Their faces took on a red marbled hue as the sand accumulated in their beards and brows.

Despite the heat, they tightened their headscarves and trudged on with heads bent low. The exertion of the hike made talking difficult, so they spoke very little and drank sparingly, knowing their water must last the entire trek.

Eventually the winds quieted and they were able to loosen their scarves, walk upright, and enjoy gentler breezes as they looked about. The beach stretched north and south to their left. Gazing inland through the aqueduct's arches they observed groves of olive and fruit trees, and high fields of grain.

By mid-morning, they stopped for a short respite on a rise that afforded a view of the coast. Caesarea lay far behind them. Just ahead, rose the massive cliffs of Mount Carmel. They drank enough water to quench their thirst and began again, occasionally breaking into a short run when the road was level. After walking another league they rounded a bend that blocked Caesarea from view. They had reached the narrowest part of the road, squeezed between the mount's limestone walls and the crashing waves of the sea.

Before long the road widened as the land curved inland. They trudged on for half a league along the shores of a large bay until they saw a deep water cove. "Look there. Do you see that?" Balthazar asked, his eyes fixed on the opposite shore of the cove. "It looks like a big warehouse. Can it be the shipyard?"

"It's got to be," said Sameer. "There are ramps extending from the building into the water. And the ships at anchor look new. They're building the ships inside." They continued that way, fording the stream and watching carefully for sentries. "That building is big!" exclaimed Sameer as they moved closer. "It looks at least twenty meters high and maybe sixty meters wide."

When they were within a hundred yards of the building, the shrill sound of horns brought them to a quick halt as a small contingent of soldiers approached on horseback. "Down on your knees!" ordered the commander in Aramaic as he drew near. "What's your business here?"

As they dropped to their knees, Sameer stammered, "I . . . I come in search of work. Do you need shipbuilders?"

"Maybe. Is that your trade?" the guard queried.

"Yes! I've worked for many years in my home city."

"And where is that?"

"Okelis, on the coast of Arabia." Sameer answered.

"I've heard of Okelis," said the guard. "And what of your friend here?"

Balthazar looked up at the guard. "I'm from Khalan in the Hadramaut Kingdom. I'm a trader, not a shipbuilder. I buy and sell spices and have done some business with Marius in Caesarea. I came with my friend as a courtesy. I seek no work for myself."

"Hmm. What are your names?"

"I am Balthazar and my friend is Sameer."

The Romans searched them for weapons and found only Balthazar's sling and two small, dull knives. But they took them anyway, and escorted the men down to the shipyard. "Sit here until we call for you," said the guard. They sat together on a narrow wooden bench outside the first arched entry of the warehouse. The front of the building was comprised of a series of wide arches, and both men itched to see what was happening in the huge edifice behind them. They weren't restrained but the expressions of their guards, left little doubt that they shouldn't move.

They had a good view of the sea and the bay that served as the yard's port. Balthazar counted fifteen ships at anchor, and watched keenly as one ship was gradually moved from its dry dock into the water on a moving ramp. He squinted his eyes perusing each ship's deck for Sameer's father. He didn't know what Mehir looked like, but he figured he could pick out an old man among so many young ones. Sameer did the same but they both knew that Mehir was most likely inside the building.

Several hours went by and still they sat, baking in the afternoon sun. Every now and then they sipped a little water from their pouches but did not speak. They remained vigilant, however, only occasionally closing their eyes against the sun's glare, until a soldier led them into the building that echoed with pounding hammers, and the groans of men moving heavy timber.

Large brick-face pillars divided the building from front to back into eight parallel bays. The last bay on the south side was used as a storage area, with tools, canvas, and other materials stored in neat rows. The seven other bays each sheltered a ship under construction. No wonder they can build ships so quickly, thought Balthazar. As they reached the rear, their guard stopped to address an officer who sat at a table examining scrolls. The men conferred briefly in Latin, then the officer rose from his seat. He was a tower of a man with broad shoulders and a muscular build. Balthazar could see no fat on his body, and guessed from his complexion that he might be of mixed Roman and Egyptian ancestry.

The officer looked them over from head to toe. "So I hear one of you is looking for work. Which of you is Sameer?"

"That's me." said Sameer. "I've built all kinds of boats and ships since I was a boy. I am a skilled builder."

"Are you a Jew?"

"No, sir. We're followers of the prophet Zarathustra."

The officer nodded then looked to Balthazar. Walking closer, he stood with a sardonic grin, his face only inches from Balthazar's and pumped both fists open and closed in unison, "And you? Along for the walk, you say? A long way to come for that I think."

Balthazar understood the physical menace for what it was, but refused to be intimidated. "I'm engaged to his sister, and she bade me come with him for safety sake. We're not from this region, so we don't know the country nor its dangers. I would be looking for a new bride if I hadn't agreed."

"Hah! Women are the same the world over, are they not? Always worrying, always demanding. My wife offers sacrifices to the gods when I leave Rome but I always wonder if she prays that I return or that I don't!" The man laughed aloud at his own joke. "But such is the life of a man long married. How I envy you a youthful woman. For your sake, I hope she's easy to please and worth your time."

"She is," said Balthazar, unintentionally emphasizing his last word and realizing as he said it, how true it was.

"It sounds like the woman has bound you. Such is the pity. And because I'm feeling good today, you will see her again. You'll be free to go after I make a decision on your friend."

He turned to Sameer. "The timing of your appearance is fortunate. One of our older builders died in an accident yesterday and you could take his place, but I want to judge your skills first. Come." The Roman led Sameer to the next bay where a team was finishing a deck. "Get up there and do as they say. My foreman will watch and let me know if you're fit."

Balthazar remained where he was while Sameer worked. Finally, the foreman jumped down with Sameer and gave a thumbs up to the officer.

"Hah!" smiled the officer to Sameer. "You get to live!"

Sameer and Balthazar looked at each other quizzically. "My jest," said the Roman. "You are hired under these terms: You must start now and work for six months. You will live in the barracks east of here and get three meals a day. You work from dawn to dusk . Wages are paid in denari at the end of three months. There are no leaves, but you will have your nights to yourself. We do have small . . . entertainments in camp." He paused to look at Sameer. "Are you agreed?"

Balthazar could see surprise written on Sameer's face and understood his dilemma. Could the old builder who died in the accident have been his father? If so, he might be taking this job for naught. And how could he work for so many months and leave Alima alone? Would Balthazar be willing to stay with her? There was no chance to talk but what choice did he have?

"Yes, I agree," said Sameer with only slight hesitation.

"Good!" said the officer to Sameer. "I will take you to your crew."

"And you ..." said the officer as he looked at Balthazar. "This guard will escort you to the road. See that you leave directly. I pluck the eyes of spies, and have no patience for liars."

The guard was already prodding him out the door, so Balthazar waved a quick farewell to Sameer, and followed the guard to the road. And mindful of the officer's threat, he did not linger.

The shadows of dusk closed in quickly. Balthazar picked up his pace hoping the exertion would warm him against the evening chill. He trained his eyes on the ground to avoid tripping in the uneven light, and felt at a loss to explain to Alima how the day had ended. Tense with anxiety, he imagined how the conversation might go:

Alima: Did you find my father?
Balthazar: No.
Alima: What do you mean?
Balthazar: We watched for him for hours as we waited to speak with the Roman officer in charge but never saw him.
Alima: Where's Sameer?
Balthazar: He took a job at the shipyard, just as we planned.
Alima: Without knowing father's there?
Balthazar: Yes. You knew it was a possibility.
Alima: Yes, but I thought maybe you'd have an idea if my father was there.

Balthazar: We did too, but it didn't happen. In fact, the officer told us one of his old builders died in an accident yesterday. It could have been your father but how could we be sure?

Alima: You mean Sameer took the job and my father could already be dead?

Balthazar: Yes, but your brother had no choice. The officer told him he had to start right away if he wanted the job.

Alima: I understand. When will we see him again?

Balthazar: Not for six months.

Alima: Six months?

Balthazar: That was the term of hire and they give no leaves.

Alima: No leaves? I've never heard of such a thing!

Balthazar: Great Caesar wants his ships built quickly so the Romans don't give leaves!

Alima: But what if something happens to him? How will we know?

Balthazar: We won't. But he's a grown man; he can take care of himself.

Alima: You say that, but I've seen how the people around here look at these Romans. I've heard from Judith how cruel they can be.

Balthazar: It's true. They can be cruel. But we were there for many hours and saw no cruelty. I think they will treat their builders well.

Alima: I don't like it. I think you should have stayed with him. Gotten a job yourself...

Balthazar: But we talked about this, remember? I don't have skills like Sameer, and he had to demonstrate how he could work. Besides you can't stay here alone, in a strange land! Sameer would want me to watch over you.

Alima: I can take care of myself!

Would it really go that way? He hoped not. Yet when he arrived at the hut in the small hours of the morning he had a strong sense of foreboding. He was tired, hungry, and cold with a head that pounded like a hundred galloping horses. He wanted to sleep and explain it all in the morning. Maybe when he was rested he could make her understand. But as soon as he entered, Alima rushed to him. He explained how the day had gone. She listened quietly, gave him a piercing look and walked to her bed without a word. Finally closing his eyes, Balthazar considered that it had gone exactly as he'd feared.

In the morning, he woke to the sound of crowing cocks and a sky that threatened rain. He walked outside to find Alima tending the fire. She handed him a cup of tea.

"Thank you," he said cheerfully, hoping for a similar reply, but she said nothing.

"Will you not speak to me?" he asked. He wanted to make her understand, to smooth things over if he could. "We did our best. The Romans gave us no chance to confer or discuss the situation. We weren't ready for the way things worked out." He waited quietly. Still nothing.

His tea tasted sour. "What would you have me do then, woman? We all agreed Sameer would work there, and that's what he's doing. Is there nothing I can do to please you?" Balthazar was reminded of the Roman officer's words the day before.

After several moments of silence, Alima spoke up. "I remember once before asking you not to call me 'woman'! My name is Alima. And what would *please* me? I would have you go back and work with my brother. He's the one who may need help, not me. If you can't do that, then you might as well take yourself off to that star school you always speak of, for you're no use to me here!"

Balthazar was taken aback. "Do you mean that? You don't want me to stay?"

"Yes, I mean it!" Alima replied angrily. "I'm capable of working here. I can weave, I can sew. I can harvest honey and sell it. And I'm sure Judith will let me stay on. I'll be safe here alone."

"But I can't go back to the shipyard. The Roman in charge would surely suspect me of spying, and it would put Sameer in danger."

Alima started crying and walked off toward the well. Balthazar tossed what remained of his tea on the fire, and felt he might as well be dousing what was left of their friendship. "Then I'll be on my way," he said in a low voice, and walked into the hut to pack.

Book Three

CHAPTER 22

A Star in the East

§

JUST OVER SEVEN MONTHS HAD passed since the Great Death. Melchior and Mered coexisted in the estate but hardly spoke. Aside from his stars, Melchior found pleasure only in Bina's food and the company of his nieces and nephews. One day, his eldest nephew ran into the house shouting aloud. "Have you heard? They've found him! They've found him!"

"Found who?" asked Melchior who was sitting in his usual garden spot.

"The satrap! He was living in a cave north of Ctesiphon."

"That is news! Who found him? How does he fare?"

"Some shepherds found him. They say he was mad and babbling. That he hardly knew who he was."

"So the rumors were correct. Does the king know?"

"He must. The satrap died soon after they found him and messengers were sent to the king. Excuse me, but I must tell father."

"Yes, yes! Go on."

The next day as Melchior sat studying scrolls in the garden, Mered came to him. "I hear my son told you of the satrap's death?"

"Yes, he did." said Melchior.

"As you might expect, I plan to visit the king, to seek appointment as the new satrap. But I'd like your advice. I must offer him a gift worthy of my request. It must be something unusual! Do you have a suggestion?" Mered sounded almost a supplicant, and after so many weeks of silence Melchior was surprised by his friendly tone.

"I do indeed! If you want the king to take notice, it must be a gift no one else can give. It cannot be gold, or gems, or even another concubine, though he might enjoy those well enough."

"All right, you have my attention. What gift could be better than those?"

"Knowledge," said Melchior. "Information of the sort no one else can give."

"What knowledge could be so valuable that the king would make me satrap for sharing it?"

Melchior smiled. "The knowledge of the great king who will come."

"You speak in riddles brother, for they all think they're great, do they not?"

"That is true enough, but this one will be a king like no other. He'll be born in Judea, and rule a kingdom beloved by God. The portent would be strong for any nation who aligns itself with him against the Romans."

"Acch! You're talking that Messiah nonsense again! You have spoken of this king for years, and where is he? What makes you think this knowledge won't be received by the king with a sword to my neck? And if by chance he doesn't kill me, that he won't laugh me out of the palace?"

"He won't . . . because I have good reason to believe the Messiah's coming is near! The prophecies say his coming will be announced by a star, and I've seen it! In fact it was on the anniversary of our mother's death, and Gaspar agrees with me that it's a *very special star*. That's the knowledge no one else can give!" Melchior could see a new interest in Mered's expression so he continued. "For years our kings have tried to extend their influence into Palestine and Judea. Don't you remember father telling us about the time our army, under Prince Pacorus, captured Jerusalem and put Antigonus on the throne?"

"Yes, but that was over thirty years ago! And it didn't work out well, did it? Herod fled to Rome and brought an army of Romans back to defeat us! I dare not remind our king of that!"

"That's not what I'm suggesting. But this star likely portends changes in Judea that the king will want to know about. Herod is old. Probably in the last years of his reign. The time could be right for a new and power-ful Jewish king, and I'm sure our king would rather be his ally, than his enemy. Think about it, Mered! The value of such an alliance, one that will be possible with the advance knowledge of the messiah that no one else knows!"

"I don't know," said Mered looking doubtful. "I know the king likes intrigue and the chance to ally himself with a new king against the Romans would exert an overwhelming charm. Let's say I'm willing to believe you. How can I convince the king?"

"Remind him that his counselor, the great Seleucus, believed in the prophecies. Tell him that Gaspar and I have seen the signs of the Messiah's coming, an unusual star, and that if he'll sponsor us, we'll go to Judea to find him. In the meantime, you can play the humble servant by recommending people worthy to be satrap. Phraates will remember you, because you offered him information no one could give, and didn't try to buy your appointment as most others will."

Mered still looked dubious. "I don't know. Maybe some gold or a beautiful concubine would be wiser after all?"

"It's your decision. But I know King Phraates seeks advantage over the surrounding kingdoms through prophecy and omen, and this infor-mation may give him that. Since Seleucus's death, there are no more experienced astrologers in all of Parthia than Gaspar and I. The King knows it. I venture he'll believe us!"

Mered stroked his beard. "I'll consider what you've said."

A short time later, Melchior watched as Mered galloped off in the direction of Ctesiphon, across the river from Seleucia. For generations, Parthian kings had wintered there and Melchior recalled the palace in his mind's eye. The unusual architecture of the long entry hall, the great throne room and the carvings in the vaulted arch over the King's throne. Each were designed to awe and distract visitors and petitioners. But those who kept their wits despite the surroundings and spoke wisely were much more likely to have their pleas met. Which type of suitor will Mered be? He wondered.

Melchior didn't see his brother again that day. But when the sun was high the next day, Mered ran into the house yelling at the top of his lungs. "I've done it! I've done it! You're looking at the new satrap!" Dahab fawned over him and his sons and daughters praised him with song and dance. It was a festive scene which Melchior listened to from a distance. He waited for Mered to come to him, and it didn't take long, for as soon as the family's adoration subsided, Mered came carrying two glasses of wine. "Come brother, we must drink together! The satrapy has returned to our house. The job our father did so well is *mine*!"

Melchior accepted the cup and raised it high. "Here's to you then, brother. Well done. Very well done. May I ask how it went?" Melchior raised his eyebrows in expectation.

"I was received much as you predicted. The King was weaker than I've ever seen him. And distracted . . . by what I've no idea. But as soon as I mentioned the prophecy, his attention was secured. He asked for proof of the prophecy, as I knew he would. But when I told him you and Gaspar and Seleucus all believed it, and I mentioned the new star, he was convinced."

"Then what?" asked Melchior. "Did he offer you the satrapy then? Or did you ask for it?"

"Neither. I left the king to ponder the knowledge, as you suggested, and presented him a scroll with a list of names for satrap, with my own at the bottom. He reviewed it briefly but I could tell his mind was wandering, so I left and bid him good health as I departed."

"Then I confess, I am confused," said Melchior with a questioning look. "How do you know you're the new satrap?"

"Ah! This is the best part of my story. I left this morning feeling good for I had gotten his attention and not his scorn. Which as you know, I was worried about. Until now I've always thought those prophecies the delusions of our mother and her ancestors. But I realized that it didn't matter if the King shared those delusions, as long as it got me the satrapy!"

"That sounds like you. Always the pragmatist. But I still don't see how that makes you the satrap."

"Because, brother, as I rode home wondering how long it would take him to act, a messenger overtook me on horseback. I was approaching the bridge on the Ctesiphon side of the river when he hailed me from behind and gave me this scroll with the royal mark. He bid me accept the King's appointment, which of course, I did. It's effective immediately!"

"Then I say again, well done! When do you move into the palace?"

"As soon as Dahab and our servants can arrange it."

"Bina stays with me," said Melchior looking serious.

"Yes, of course. She's your slave, not mine. Though I may borrow her to cook from time to time."

"We can arrange that. Congratulations, brother. I will miss you all."

"Now, now. It's only the children you will miss."

Melchior cocked his head. "It's true I will miss them the most. But satrap or not, you're still my brother. I'd like to serve as your counselor and astrologer if you'll let me." Then in a serious tone he added, "It's within your power to be the best satrap since father. Remember his work. Remember to make the people your priority."

"Pleasing the King is my priority," countered Mered shaking his head. "If I can help the citizens without angering the king, I will do so." He finished off his wine and strutted from the room.

Melchior sat back on his bench, his mind a storm of questions. Did I make a mistake helping Mered? If I hadn't, he would surely think me against him. But am I now a friend? Can I ever be his true counselor? Melchior's doubts grew and he decided he would talk it over with Gaspar the first chance he got.

Three days later, Mered and his family were packed and heading to the satrap's palace. Melchior wasn't surprised by the quickness of it. The satrapy had been Mered's ambition for a long time and Melchior was now questioning whether he should have assisted. The next day, he pulled Gaspar aside at the school. "We must talk."

"I know about Mered," said Gaspar. "News like that travels faster than a sand storm."

"I have some concerns," said Melchior.

"*Now* you have concerns? I told you Mered wouldn't be my choice for satrap."

"I remember, but I thought having him in debt to me might be a good thing. Now I'm not so sure ..."

"Has he done something dreadful already?"

"No. It's just the way he acted after his appointment. He told me the King's desires are his priority. I fear the citizens will hardly be considered. And I don't think he'll feel much loyalty to me now that he has the power he wanted."

"Why are you surprised? I've heard from others that he's been doing whatever he could to keep the King happy for years."

"That may be. But mercurial and selfish as he may be, I thought having him as satrap was better than a stranger."

"Maybe yes, maybe no. I've known many strangers who were good men. But it's too late now. Perhaps we can encourage him to make improvements, if not for the people at least as a tribute to himself. The plague has left our city in a bad way, and even if he does very little it will be a help. "

"Sadly, that is true. By the way, did you know that as part of Mered's plan I offered to journey to Judea on the king's behalf?"

"You what?"

"You heard me! I'm positive this star is announcing the Messiah! The unusual manner of its appearance and the strange way that it's moving has convinced me. We must follow it to Judea. We need to find the messiah."

"It's an amazing star, but to make such a long journey! Now that I'm head of the school, I'm not sure King Phraates will let me go away for so long."

"I've asked Mered to press our cause. Phraates will have to answer us eventually."

But days passed, then weeks, and the astrologers heard nothing from the King or Mered. Melchior enjoyed having the estate to himself and spent his evenings watching that brilliant, moving star. How well he remembered its sudden appearance in the constellation of Aries the Ram. He knew that another astrologer, Claudius Ptolemy, thought the Aries constellation held great portent for the people of Judea. So of course, he often looked there for signs of anything new.

On the day he sighted the star, he had walked up to the date palm orchard in the early morning darkness and stood near his mother's grave. He made a small sacrificial offering to Yahweh on the permanent altar he'd built, then sat down to meditate and watch the stars before sunrise.

What he saw that morning was something he'd never seen in all his years of star gazing. The planet, Jupiter, emerged in the east as a morning star. He noticed that the moon, the sun and even Saturn were all present within Aries. This was important since he knew that when Jupiter and Saturn were attendants to the rising sun, there was portent of kingship. Then as he watched, the moon eclipsed Jupiter, and when Jupiter emerged from behind the Moon another brilliant star emerged as well. It was as if Jupiter had multiplied itself! How could that be? One star is eclipsed by the moon and two emerge from behind it? It mesmerized him in wonder! Then he noticed a small but discernible movement of the new star as it moved away from Jupiter. It shone as bright as a comet and he sat watching it for hours until it faded with the rising sun, then returned to his house, changed clothes and went to find Gaspar.

The words had tumbled from his mouth. "Gaspar, have you looked to Aries today? It is a marvelous sight! Unbelievable in portent! A new star! I think the sign of the Messiah has finally arrived!"

Gaspar laughed aloud. "Yes, I've seen it! How could I not? I saw it immediately after the eclipse. You really think it's associated with the prophecies?"

"Yes! Don't you remember: 'A star shall rise out of Jacob'? It's impossible to be sure, but as I watch its steady movement, it's as if the star is asking me to follow it!"

"Melchior, my friend, come back to earth! Your mind must be wandering." Said Gaspar.

"I was remembering my first sighting of the star."

"It was a day we shall never forget, and now another wonder has transformed you! You've left caution at the wayside and it's wonderful! You really want to make such a long journey?"

"Yes! Before my mother's death I would never have thought to do it. But I tell you, there's something peculiar about this star! It's not natural. And last night I had a strange dream."

Gaspar's mouth opened wide as if he would speak, but no sound came.

"What wrong?" asked Melchior. "You look thunderstruck."

"I feel as if I am, for I too had a dream last night! Like none I've ever had. Tell me yours," said Gaspar.

"I dreamt that a young man dressed all in white spoke to me. He stood before me saying, 'Delay not. Follow the star to Judea.' It was as you say; like no dream I've ever had. No one else was in it, and I woke with the oddest feeling that he actually came to me, as if I was awake. I didn't have to struggle to recall. The message was clear as day."

"Our minds can play games with us in dreams."

"Yes. But truly, this felt more like a message than a dream, like the man had come to visit me. I know I was sleeping, so I can't explain it or why it has stirred me so. I feel an urgent need to follow his instructions! Now tell me yours?"

"Exactly the same. Word for word. I've been questioning my sanity all day. And I, too, felt I might have been awake."

Several days went by. Melchior asked Mered once again to speak with the King about Judea. Each day as they waited for the king's decision, Melchior and Gaspar watched 'their star', and Melchior was becoming convinced that some greater power was at work. He had never seen a star born and knew no one at the school who had, so he considered it odd that it should happen while he watched. Finally, one day he felt he must act.

"Gaspar, it's time for a decision. I know it'll be a risk for you to go without the King's permission, but I need only yours. Will you give it to me? I need to inter my mother's bones and am convinced delay is not an option!"

"I promised I would go with you and when I make promises, I fulfill them. I'll inform the King of my need to go, and remind him of the importance of our journey. He already knows and likes the man who will take my place."

"Are you strong enough for the journey?"

"These last months have been trying, but I would never let you go on such a momentous journey without me. My one request is that we bring along plenty of water, for my thirst is often very great. It's one of the things that changed after my illness. That and my continual urge to pee!"

Melchior laughed. "I can arrange the water, and you can pee from your camel anytime, if you don't mind hearing Bina call you an animal."

"If she rides ahead of us, she'll never know! So let us begin our preparations. I'll send a messenger to the king. Short of imprisonment or death there is nothing he can do to stop me!"

"Thank you!" said Melchior, clasping Gaspar's shoulders. "We'll take Bina with us, and I'll ask Amro's son Asher to join us. Amro says he's a good hunter and should be a great help."

Melchior returned immediately to tell Bina and Amro. Bina was not happy at the prospect of traveling so far, but Amro welcomed the responsibility of caring for the estate, and left immediately to find Asher. Within days he learned that not only was Asher willing, but he brimmed with enthusiasm for the journey. It was exactly the reaction Melchior had hoped for, because Asher's youth and positive manner would surely combat the tedium of the trek.

Now only the final preparations remained. Melchior bought camels and saddles, plus several donkeys as pack animals, and because the trek would be a long one, searched for food that would keep. Most of it was salt dried fish and meats, nuts and dried fruits, along with some grain and dried beans. He hoped Asher's well-honed hunting skills would occasionally allow them fresh fowl and meat.

New water bladders were essential to keep his promise to Gaspar, so he bought the best he could find. Finally he purchased tents and blankets, for if he had to endure months sleeping on the ground, he wanted to be warm and dry. He bought a large tent for himself and Gaspar, and a smaller one for Asher and Bina. Asher was accustomed to sleeping under the stars, but Bina wasn't, and Melchior was concerned about her. Though she might deny it, he knew her hips ached, for she rocked as she walked and sometimes winced when she rose after sitting. The long rides might be painful, and he wanted to allow her some comfort at day's end. Before long, he had everything they needed, including the much sought permission from King Phraates.

One day after Melchior informed his brother of their coming departure, Mered surprised him with a visit. "Good day to you, brother," said Mered. "I came to bid you farewell, and I have good news to convey!"

"What could be better than hearing the King gave Gaspar leave for the journey?"

"A purse of course!" replied Mered. "Your journey will be an official one."

"Well then, I must thank you indeed. Gaspar and I had figured to spend our own drachma on gifts."

"No need for thanks; I shall find a way for you to repay me later!" said Mered as he handed over a large purse of gold nuggets and two canisters of spice. "Nice eh?" asked Mered. "The spice is from my own storehouse, from the same stores preferred by King Phraates!"

"It will make a fine gift," said Melchior.

"There's one more," said Mered as he handed his brother a bolt of cloth. "Look at this wonderful purple cloth! It's prized by every king because of the expensive dye used to make it."

"This is a surprising bounty," said Melchior.

"If your trip secures a new alliance for Parthia, all gifts will be worthwhile!" replied Mered. "I want your mission to be successful and pray you'll take time to explore the land of our ancestors. You must stay long enough to do justice to the bones of our mother."

Melchior didn't believe a word of this. Mered had never shown pride in their ancestry, and now he wanted Melchior to believe it mattered? More likely he wants to keep me away from Seleucia, thought Melchior. He laughed at his brother's deviousness. "Surely King Phraates will be anxious to hear my report, so I won't have much time to explore. But I thank you for helping secure his support."

"There's one more thing. At the urging of his Roman queen, Phraates bid me give you this letter, which makes you an official delegation. He requires you to call on King Herod to present his gift as a sign of good will. Phraates knows that Herod has no great liking for him, but desires to keep up at least the appearance of respect between our kingdoms."

"I suppose I shouldn't be surprised considering the influence of Queen Thermusa. I hadn't counted on traveling as an official delegation but it may make our journey easier."

"How fortunate that you agree! Here is Phraates' gift for Herod." He handed Melchior a small leather pouch filled with gems.

"Very well. I'll keep this with me at all times, and you may tell the king we shall call on Herod as soon as we arrive in Judea."

"I will. May your journey be successful," said Mered, as he took his leave.

Melchior mulled over the King's demand. Calling on Herod had not been part of his plan, for he could only imagine how the news of a rival Jewish king might be received. If Herod was as violent and conspiracy driven as people said, they would need to be very careful indeed. On the other hand, official documents might lend some safety and importance to their journey. He wrote a short letter to Gaspar explaining Mered's news, confirming their departure, and asked Bina to deliver it.

Afterward, Melchior walked to his mother's grave. It was time to move her remains to the ossuary. It was a task he preferred to do alone, and in a solemn way. So he put his mother's old prayer shawl over his shoulders, and knelt down facing west, the direction that would lead him to Jerusalem and the new temple. He raised his head to the sky and prayed: "Oh Lord! Soon, I will leave this place with my mother's bones, bound for your holy city. Please guide our steps, and keep us on the path you would have us walk. Protect me and my friend Gaspar, and our servants, Bina and Asher. My mother was a good woman, Lord, righteous and obedient of your commands. Show me a good place for her bones."

"And Lord, if you have sent your Messiah into our world, help me to find him. As I begin my journey, I place my trust in you. I have seen a special star in the firmament, and will follow it in the hope it is your guiding light. Amen."

Melchior rose from his knees, picked up the shovel he'd brought, and spent the next few hours digging. The intervening year had done its job of returning Dodi's body to the earth, and he easily retrieved her bones from the remnants of cloth she'd been buried in. The limestone ossuary he'd commissioned from a local artist was delicately carved with her name in Hebrew. He took the gabled top off the ossuary, and reverently placed his mother's bones within it. Then he closed the ossuary and carried it home to await their journey.

CHAPTER 23

Journey to Judea

§

THE FOURSOME LEFT SELEUCIA EARLY on the first day of the week. Three men and one old woman astride camels, with seven more pack animals, including three donkeys packed tight and high. What they called 'their star' had continued its now familiar movement west-northwest, and the constancy of its direction led them to choose the Royal Road as the perfect route. Built five hundred years earlier by the Persian ruler, Darius the Great, it ran almost 550 leagues from Persepolis, east of Seleucia, west to Sardis near the Aegean Sea. Some called it the Silk Road because east of Persepolis, it connected to routes leading to India and China, but Gaspar preferred 'The Royal Road' because they traveled in search of a messianic king.

They accessed the road in Ctesiphon and would follow it west to Asia Minor, then southwest to Damascus, into Palestine and southeast to Jerusalem. It might not be the most direct route, but it would likely be the quickest, and the value of its many caravansaries could not be underestimated. After examining his maps, Gaspar estimated their trek to Damascus would take three months, then maybe another month to Jerusalem. The prophecies predicted the new king would be born in Judea, but exactly where was uncertain. They would need to consult with priestly scholars, preferably the High Priest in Jerusalem, to refine the scope of their search.

Gaspar had traveled this road as a youth when he left Media, but he could tell that it was all new territory to Asher, who seemed captivated by each bend in the road. Determined to get to know the young man,

Gaspar rode next to him on the second day of their journey. "Asher, my boy. How do you like the traveling life so far?"

Asher grimaced. "My rear doesn't like it much, but I'm eager to see new lands."

Gaspar snorted. "Ah, yes! The riding . . .in a few days your body will mold itself to the saddle and you'll feel better."

"I hope so," said Asher. "No one in our family ever had the money for a camel or horse, and my father hardly ever uses an ass, so riding is new to me. Is all the Royal Road this bumpy?"

"No. Some of it's paved with cobbles but most of it is hardened dirt and sand like this. Five hundred years of caravans and armies have pounded it down. Is this your first long journey?"

"Yes, sir. I've only ever herded sheep before this."

"I see," said Gaspar. "So did your father give you any advice?"

"Only to heed to you and Master Melchior. But I've heard stories from the old shepherds. They said to beware of animals and bandits. That's why I'm keeping a keen eye on the road".

"No wonder you watch it so intently," said Gaspar. "This road is well traveled so I doubt we'll have trouble with animals, but they were right to warn of bandits. They often lie in wait for travelers."

"My bow will be ready," said Asher. "And I'm a pretty good shot."

"That's what I hear," said Gaspar. "Maybe you should ride lead. If you see anything unusual, let out a hoot, so we can all be ready if trouble comes."

"I will, sir. Any bandits who attack us will be sorry men indeed. I may never make this trek again and I aim to finish it alive!"

Gaspar laughed at the young man's determination. "We do, too!"

"It was a good idea to hire him," said Gaspar later when he drew his camel alongside Melchior. "He's a smart one."

Melchior nodded. "He's an untested rider but he's learning quickly. I'm not so sure about Bina." The two of them looked back to where she rode, clinging haphazardly to her camel.

"She should be in front where we can see her," said Gaspar.

"You're right. I see now why she was dreading this trek, but there's no turning back now."

Later that evening, Gaspar approached Bina by the fire. "That was a good meal you made tonight."

Bina raised her eyes to him. "You're welcome, Master Gaspar. Unfortunately, there are no second portions. Master Melchior told me to make our food last as long as I can."

"That's as it should be. Still, I marvel at how you make food taste so good. Even here on the road."

"I learned that as a girl," said Bina. "We were poor, so my mother taught me to make the best of every bit."

"A lesson you learned well," said Gaspar. "May I ask how you are surviving the journey? Your face speaks of pain. Is it constant?"

"It comes and goes. I try to start anew each day for it does no good to dwell on yesterday's pain. And sometimes I pretend I'm not me."

"That's a trick I'd like to learn." said Gaspar.

"It's simple: I keep my eyes on the little things around me, the animals that scurry as we ride, the snakes and lizards, the birds. I imagine myself one of them. Free to wander where I like. To fly high into the sky or to burrow under the rocks into a cool, quiet place. It soothes me and makes me feel as I did when I was young, before I was sold. Sometimes I do it for hours and before I know it, the day's ride is over and it's time to cook."

"I see," said Gaspar. "I will have to try it the next time I'm in a place I don't want to be."

"Oh!" said Bina. "I didn't mean . . ."

"I think you did, but it's all right. It may not have been your choice to come, but I'm glad you're here. There is no cook in Seleucia, slave or free, who is so admired for her cooking as you. In truth, I'm surprised the King hasn't stolen you from Melchior by now."

"Oh no!" cried Bina. "I would never want to leave Master Melchior!"

"And you won't," said Gaspar. "I just want you to know how valued you are. Melchior thinks of you like family."

"I know," said Bina quietly, looking away. "I would never serve another; still . . . my days are not my own."

Bina began to collect their bowls, as Gaspar considered her words. She had acknowledged his compliment but in a most unexpected way. Was she unhappy? Melchior had never said so and he had seen nothing to think it true. The next morning, he watched her prepare porridge for breakfast. She put the same effort into her work as ever, with the same excellent results. Nevertheless, he decided to speak with Melchior when an opportunity presented itself. Right now he had to find a way to survive the trek himself. The last few days had brought strange sensations in his feet and hands; tingling and sharp pains, like someone was striking him with a hot arrow. It must be from riding all day, and like Bina, he would make the best of it.

They quickly developed a routine. Each day they rode 'til mid-day when they'd stop to eat and rest out of the sun. Asher would scout for shade, a copse of trees, or an outcropping of rock, and if none could be found, they'd sit on the shady side of their camels.

Each night they found a place to camp before nightfall and pitched tents together. If they were especially tired, they would take an extra day recouping their strength in a spot that afforded water and shade. Asher used those opportunities to hunt small game and birds, which were a welcome addition to their meals.

One day south of Arbela, in northern Parthia, they had just come over a rise when Asher rode back yelling and pointing. "Look, look!" he repeated several times. "There's a large way station ahead!"

"Do you think he wants to stop?" Gaspar asked Melchior lightheartedly while Asher was still many paces away.

"Like my sister-in-law at a market. Shall we have a little fun with him?"

Gaspar nodded. "Poor boy! So much of his life spent with sheep!"

They stifled their laughter with difficulty as Asher rode up. "Such a large caravansary!" said Gaspar. "What do you think, Melchior? Shall we stop for a few days?"

"I don't know," answered Melchior. "It will be expensive, and we've been making good time. Maybe we should keep moving."

Gaspar said nothing, pretending to ponder his course of action. He could tell Asher was hanging on their every word, and the longer he waited the more anxious the youth appeared, shifting in his saddle and fidgeting with his reins. Gaspar decided to end their little game with a smile. "Yes, it will cost many drachma, and I suppose we'll lose some time, but it'll be worth it. We've earned a little rest."

Bina clapped and Asher whooped. Gaspar took the lead as they rode toward the caravansary which was set a hundred paces back from the road. Built of roughly hewn stone, it looked like a large square fort with a front gate big enough for their high-packed camels to pass under with ease. The courtyard beyond was a hubbub of activity. Scores of people and animals milled around the enormous water cistern and trough that dominated its center, while others strolled through stalls on the perimeter. Some stalls offered shelter, others served as a market and one as entrance to a public bath.

Since the caravansary functioned as an inn, the astrologers decided to share the cost of all it offered. After providing for their animals they secured shelter in semi-private alcoves that jutted to the right and left off a long interior passageway. The place was dark, and would have felt like a cavern if not for some oil lamps and openings in the vaulted ceiling that allowed the sun to stream in.

After their morning meal the next day, they all headed toward the bath which Gaspar realized was sourced from a local qualt. There was one pool for the men and another for women, which Bina entered with delight. Gaspar observed Asher watching several young women enter the female bath with their mothers, and elbowed Melchior. "It seems the young man wants a woman," said Gaspar quietly to his friend.

"I noticed, but is that our responsibility?"

"No, but I remember how my father gave me a nudge in that direction, and it helped me get over my reluctance with women."

"You, reluctant? I hardly think it possible!" exclaimed Melchior.

"We were both young once, or have you forgotten?" They spent most of the morning in the bath, alternately soaking in the pool, sitting on the steps, and stretching out on benches surrounding it. The warm water relaxed his muscles and Gaspar's feet stopped tingling. After toweling off, Gaspar joined Asher who sat alone on a sunlit bench.

"I have a question for you, Master Gaspar," said Asher.

"What would that be?"

"I've heard that in some caravansaries there are places where men and women consort. Is there a place like that here?"

"I believe there's a place like that behind these baths. Why do you ask?"

"I was just wondering. I saw some girls before, and well, do you think any of them work that way?"

"Not those girls. They were with their mothers for good reason; to keep them from meeting young men like you. They would never be permitted alone with a man until after their betrothal."

Asher looked downtrodden.

"Look son, I meant nothing against you. Good mothers watch their daughters closely, and every young man can be a threat. I'm sure your parents protected your sister in that way; didn't they?"

"Yes. Before she married, my father would have skinned any boy who tried to be alone with my sister."

"Precisely! I've never taken a wife, but I know a good woman can make a man's life very pleasant. Not only through domestic attentions, good food, a clean house, but as a helpmate. A good woman engages not only your body but your mind. Have you ever engaged girls in conversation?"

"I've spoken with some girls at weddings, friends of my sister mostly. But only to say a few words."

"Have you ever lain with one?"

Asher looked surprised. "No, sir. Never. My parents were never able to arrange a betrothal. Maybe one day."

"It will come, my boy. But believe me, you will want to befriend a girl first. The laying, well, every animal can do that. But the mind...

AH! That is something else again. Yes, the body is what excites, what attracts. But the mind, the companionship . . . those will give lasting pleasure."

Asher nodded. "My father has told me much the same when he catches me watching girls. Still I feel that it may never happen. My father tried to arrange a betrothal, but a boy from a wealthier family won the bride."

Gaspar could see the boy looked despondent. "Asher, there are girls in this place. You can talk to them or do other things as you like, but either way you pay for their time. Would you like to meet such a girl?"

Asher looked at Gaspar with uncertainty. "You mean you would arrange it for me?"

"It's not the best way to meet a girl, but I will if you wish it."

"Yes! I do wish!"

"Come with me then," said Gaspar.

Asher followed Gaspar into the adjoining dressing room where two servant women helped them don clean clothes. Asher was clearly uncomfortable. "Relax, son," said Gaspar. "These women are only here to help us dress." After the servants left, Gaspar continued. "Now let's see about seeking some female companionship." Gaspar led Asher to a nearby alcove where he spoke quietly to a man in attendance.

"What is your going rate?" Gaspar asked the owner of the small brothel.

"I can make a special offering, sir." The man replied eyeing them both. "We usually charge five drachma per visit, but for you and your son here, I will reduce it to four. My girls are very accommodating, I promise you!"

"We'll pay two for my son only, and we shall want a girl who is quiet and respectful." Gaspar was emphatic as he clasped Asher's shoulder. "Someone close to his age and who will talk to him as much as he wants."

"I know just the one." the man responded, agreeing to the price. Gaspar paid and the man led them to a nearby room, nicely appointed with hand woven rugs, mellow lantern lights, a bed and a chair.

"I'll wait with him until the girl arrives." Gaspar told the man.

"As you wish," came the reply.

Gaspar looked at Asher. "I have made the arrangements, but must give you some advice borne of my years. You should treat the girl as you would want a woman in your family treated. With tenderness. Talk to her. Ask what she likes. Be good to her and do only as nature prompts you. If talk is all you want, that's good, too. Don't feel ashamed to take your time. Do you understand me?"

"Yes, sir," said Asher. They waited only a few moments before a beautiful girl stood before them. She looked about seventeen in years with a slender build, long dark hair, and brown eyes touched with flecks of gold. She wore a loose gauzy tunic from her neck to her thighs that left little to the imagination. "Go ahead, then," said Gaspar. "I'll be nearby should you have a problem." Gaspar watched them enter the room and close the curtain that served as a door, before moving on.

CHAPTER 24

Asher Meets a Girl

§

THE GIRL TOOK ASHER'S HAND and led him to the bed. He sat on the edge of it, watching her every move, not quite believing this girl was here for him. He wanted to speak, but his mouth was too dry. She bid him stand and moved in front of him as if to remove his clothes.

No," said Asher, suddenly finding his voice. He wanted the girl. So very much; but not like this. "Please, let us sit. Not on the bed. I want to talk."

The girl frowned. "You not want me? I young but can please. I know how."

"I'm sure you do," said Asher smiling. "But, this... I'm not" He began to fumble for words. How to explain himself?

The girl watched his face, then nodded and took his hand. "Come." She pointed to the floor. "If you want sit, we sit. If you want talk, we talk. You put head this pillow, or my lap. As you like."

Following her lead, Asher sat on the floor, and thinking it might be pleasant, stretched out with his head on her lap. He looked up toward the arched ceiling. This is better, he thought. He didn't want some girl he had never met directing him on what to do, especially about his body. He wanted to control himself. Now maybe he could.

She began to weave her fingers through his hair, and he felt entranced as her fingers ran softly from his forehead to his neck. 'That feels good," he said to her quietly. He felt strangely comforted and soothed. "Where are you from?" he asked. "I can tell from the way you talk, you're not from here."

"I from Greek," she said, as she started massaging his neck and shoulders.

"How long have you been in this place?"

"Ten months," she answered. "Last year, my parents die, so I live with my uncle. But he no want me. Sold me to man who runs this place. I shamed woman now."

On hearing this, Asher sat up and looked into her eyes. She looked away, so he put his hand to her chin and gently turned her toward him. "You have no reason to be shamed. Your uncle did wrong to sell you."

"I think maybe he do because I not serve him well. Not cook well. Not clean well."

"No. I think your uncle sold you because he likes silver more than people. You are his family. No matter how you cook, or serve, as family he should care for you. A good man would not do such a thing to his kin."

Her eyes glistened with tears, so he took her hand and squeezed it. She sniffled and he offered her his sleeve. She laughed and refused. He continued to hold her hand, thinking about her situation. She was at the mercy of men who paid for her. Men like himself. But at least she was sheltered, fed and clothed. Was it better than living on the road, like many orphans, who begged to survive? He wasn't sure.

"Is it very bad here?" he asked.

She hesitated. "I see you at bath with two men. Why you with them? Are you their servant? Or in debt?"

"No, I'm not their servant and I'm not in debt!" said Asher emphatically. "I'm a shepherd and those men are astrologers. My father works for the short one. "

"Astrologers? What that mean?"

"It means they are learned men who study the stars." Asher pointed toward the sky.

"I understand. But why they need you?"

"They hired me to go with them to Jerusalem. I scout and hunt for them. They are paying me well." Asher told her proudly.

"You lucky have such job."

"Yes, I am. I always like working, even in the fields. I take good care of my sheep." As he finished speaking, his gaze went from the girl's face to her body and lingered there.

Feeling his eyes on her, the girl smiled. She pulled him closer and this time he did not resist. Before he knew it, his arms were around her, he was kissing her and pulling her toward the bed. It felt so good to touch her. He quickly shed his tunic and lifted hers off too. Such smooth skin and hair that smelled like flowers. This was how it should be. A natural wanting, not just an arrangement. They continued kissing, pressing together. She was breathing faster and moaning a little. But her moans sounded pleasurable, so he continued running his hands along the curves of her body, gently caressing her back, her breasts, her buttocks. Almost without realizing, his body joined with hers and he experienced a spasm of pleasure unlike anything he'd known.

He searched her face. Did she feel the same? Her eyes were closed but she looked content so he closed his too, and sleep found him quickly. When he woke he was pleased to feel her still in his arms.

It felt strange to be lying with a girl he'd never met before, but oh so good. His years numbered seventeen and he'd wondered when this might happen, even talked about it with his brothers, but no opportunity had ever presented itself. He had liked a few girls from his village, but they were betrothed to men of worthier means. And his long absences away in the hills didn't help. He had often dreamed what it might be like. But this was no dream. This was real and she was beautiful.

For some time, he lay looking at her, wondering what her name was, combing his fingers through her hair as she had done. When he ran his fingers lightly over her chest, she opened her eyes returning his gaze. She smiled but he became embarrassed when he realized she was studying him. What does she think of me? Does she like me too? "Thank you," he said to her quietly. "It was..."

"Yes, I know," she responded. "Your first time."

That wasn't what he was going to say. How had she known? He wanted to tell her how wonderful it was. How beautiful she was. Then almost as if sensing his thoughts, she added, "It was good, and . . . you good man. I like."

He reddened. He wanted to say he liked her too, but didn't want to stammer. "Thank you," he said finally, regaining his composure. "What's your name?"

"Corinna," she replied, as she kissed him again.

"What does it mean?" Asher managed to ask as he nuzzled her neck.

"Beautiful. My mother told me Corinna means 'most beautiful.'"

"She gave you the right name," said Asher, returning her kisses with ardor as he became aroused again. Soon, Corinna surprised him by climbing on him, and they settled into a steady rhythm that became more pleasurable and powerful with each passing moment. This time Asher found he could control himself better, and waited until he was sure Corinna was ready before finishing. Afterward, he held her close, enjoying every moment.

"When you leave here?" asked Corinna.

"In three days," said Asher. "Maybe we can meet in the square if you have free time."

"They watch me closely. Will you stop this place on way home from Jerusalem?'

"I'm not sure. Maybe." Asher replied.

"Oh. Maybe," said Corinna. Then she quickly turned away, picked up her tunic and left the room. Had he said something wrong? Done something wrong?

Feeling bereft from her sudden departure, Asher rose, dressed quickly and went in search of Gaspar. He was no longer in the brothel, and Asher found him with Melchior and Bina shopping among the market stalls. It was already late afternoon and he realized he must have been with Corinna for several hours. How was it possible that the time had gone so quickly?

As soon as Gaspar saw him, he slapped Asher on the back. "Glad to see you came up for air, my boy! I don't have enough money to pay for another session like that this trip, so I hope you enjoyed yourself?"

Greatly surprised by the question, Asher still managed to respond, "Yes sir, very much. She is a beautiful girl. And I . . ." He lapsed into embarrassed silence.

"Glad to hear it." Gaspar replied knowingly.

Asher watched as Gaspar, Melchior and Bina surveyed the items for sale. It was a small market, but well stocked. Melchior gave Bina some money for whatever she might want. She decided on a new headscarf to replace the old, wind-worn one she'd been wearing. "Thank you! I like it very much," said Bina as she put it on.

"It looks good on you," said Melchior. "I see your robe is threadbare in spots. Perhaps when we get to Judea we can get you a new one."

"Maybe," she said shyly.

Asher heard her reply and was reminded of Corinna. That word can mean so much, he thought. He and Gaspar continued to browse the market as Bina and Melchior walked off. "Do you need anything, Asher?" asked Gaspar. But Asher's attention was riveted on a girl who was walking in the courtyard behind the market. She was dressed very modestly, with a full veil that covered half of her face. Nevertheless, Gaspar could tell she was the one Asher had met in the brothel. "Asher!" Gaspar called the young man's name loudly to get his attention. "Here. Take this and go buy the girl something nice."

Asher accepted the coins Gaspar offered bowing low. "Thank you!" He said and walked directly to Corinna as Gaspar watched.

"How are you?" he asked, not sure what else to say.

She shook her head. "You see me only little time ago. How you think?"

Asher turned red realized she was making fun of him. "But you left so quickly, I hope I didn't offend you. I wanted to talk more. To get an answer to my question."

"Question?" asked Corinna.

"About your life here."

She looked away. Was she afraid of something, someone? "It's all right. You don't have to talk. I just want you to know, I like you very much and I hope no one hurts you."

Corinna smiled and drew him aside from the crowd. "Thank you for your care," she said almost in a whisper. "So far, I have the luck. No-one hurts me, but I worry. I see most old men, not young ... not nice like you. Sometimes they too old for enjoy girl, understand? I think that why they want me. To help be bull again . . . but when it no help, they angry and I afraid."

Asher took her hand. It upset him to think she must be with so many strangers every day. As he looked into her eyes, she suddenly started to pour forth a torrent of words that he tried hard to understand. "I ... I no want be here. I want life like my mother. Want husband, family, but will no happen for me . . . because I am pornai, Ash. . Ash . . ."

"Asher." He completed his name for her.

"Asher." She repeated. "Greek law say pornai can no marry. I see many families come baths. But no family for me. Family world no my world." She crossed her arms across her chest as if to signify how separate, how alone she felt.

Asher understood. He'd sometimes felt alone sitting on a secluded hillside with his sheep his only company. As if the world was passing him by. What great things went on in Seleucia and Cistephon while he wandered the hills? But he still had a family and his freedom. This journey was his chance to see the world and he was loving it. What could he do to help Corinna feel as he did?

"Maybe you can be part of that world again," he said. "Maybe there is a way."

Corinna's eyes widened. "A way?" she asked.

He replied with a question of his own. "Maybe. Do you know how much your master paid for you? If we can repay him, well. . ." he left the rest for her to understand.

"You tease!" said Corinna. "Why you want do for me? We meet today only."

"Yes, but I think you're a good person. And I'm not afraid to ask my friend. Nothing may come of it, but I can ask. Right now, I'd like to buy you something in the market. It will be my gift to you no matter what."

Corinna looked amazed. "You very kind. I no get gift for many years, so I like," she said smiling broadly.

"Good," said Asher as he took her hand. They walked past several stalls and Corinna looked at the offerings as if for the first time. She finally settled on a long wheat colored robe. It was plain except for a few colored beads sewn into the edge of the neckline, but Asher could tell that it would complement her skin and hair well.

"It will look beautiful on you!" he said, encouragingly.

"I like very much," she said.

"You would look good even in a camel blanket," he said with a smile, hoping she would understand his compliment.

"Thank you, Ash . . .Asher. But camel blanket too hot for me."

Asher laughed as he paid for the dress, and handed it to Corinna. "Can you wait here, please? I want to speak my friend," he said, pointing to Gaspar who was completing a purchase of his own.

"Must hurry," she said, looking anxious. "I have little time for walk."

"I'll try to be quick." He strode over to Gaspar with purpose in his step. "Gaspar! We must speak. It's important."

"What is it, my boy? You can't want to be with that girl again so soon! Even a young man like you needs to rest his loins!" said Gaspar laughing.

"It's not that. Something more important. That girl ... Corinna. She's nice, Gaspar. Really nice, and I want to help her. She told me her uncle sold her to the brothel owner when her parents died a year ago. I'd like to help buy her freedom. I know it may cost many drachma, but I could use the money you promised me for our journey. If you'd pay me in advance, that is."

Gaspar looked at Asher, then to Corinna who stood at the edge of the market, admiring her new robe. "Asher, do you know what you're asking? You hardly know this girl! And the silver we will pay you is meant to secure your future. It will be enough to buy some land and maybe a herd of your own. Do you really want to give that up for this girl you only met?"

"Yes!" said Asher.

"But do you realize that once she's free, she'll have no obligation to stay with you? You may like her, even think you love her, but she may spurn you and go off with another. Think this through, son. It's not something to decide so quickly."

"I understand," countered Asher. "But I keep wondering, what if she were my sister? If my parents died and my sister was sold into bondage, and had to lay with men every day to make her master wealthy, I would do whatever I could to help her. This seems right. Even if she doesn't choose to stay with me, I'll have other ways to earn money. Please, Gaspar. Please help me."

"You're really sure about this?"

"I am," said Asher.

"Then, I must speak with Melchior. He's paying part of your wage, so he must be part of the decision. If we succeed, we must be prepared to take her with us. That means buying another camel and more food. It cannot be decided lightly and I won't promise you anything."

Asher bowed. "I understand. We'll wait for your answer."

Asher ran to Corinna and told her what Gaspar had said.

Corinna looked into his eyes. "You kind man." She stood on her toes, put her hands on his shoulders and kissed his cheek. He wanted to kiss her lips but kissed her forehead instead. Then he watched as she walked back to the brothel, rubbing the soft cloth of her new dress against her cheek and disappeared from sight.

CHAPTER 25
A Minor Complication

§

GASPAR FOUND MELCHIOR FINISHING UP his feed purchase with Bina. "Can we speak? It's important."

"You look concerned," said Melchior as they walked away from the noisy market.

"I am. You remember I told you Asher met a girl at the brothel earlier?"

"Yes, and?"

"It went well enough, maybe too well. There is a complication."

"Already? By my stars, the boy was only with her for a few hours. How can there be a complication?"

"Asher has a very good heart. He may or may not be in love, but at the least he was touched by the girl. She's young and beautiful, and was sold into the trade by her uncle when her parents died. Asher wants to give up the pay we promised him to buy her freedom, and asked us to arrange it."

"I see," said Melchior stroking his beard. "Does he realize the girl may be using him? That he may never see her again afterward, and he'll be giving up a tidy sum."

"Yes, I told him as much, but to no avail. It seems clear it's his idea not hers. He's a caring young man. Reminds me of myself in younger years. I fell easily too, but I never met a girl who made me want to sacrifice like this."

"Am I right in thinking you're on his side?"

"I suppose." Gaspar answered dryly. "I don't know what kind of girl she is, but I'm impressed by his willingness to be so giving. In all my years, I've never seen the like of it. But if we succeed, we'll need to take her with us. It will mean another person to feed, to care for. What do you think? Can we afford it?"

"We can, but it pains me to think the boy may be sacrificing his future for a girl he hardly knows. I suppose it will do no harm to approach her owner. If he's not willing to part with her, that will be an end to it. But we must determine how much we're willing to pay so the negotiation doesn't get out of hand. How beautiful is she?"

"Very."

"That will make it harder."

"No doubt."

"We can at least try. Will the boy hold it against us if we fail?"

"I think not!" replied Gaspar forcefully. "He'll be disappointed, but I think he'll understand. On the other hand, we'll assure his loyalty for trying. We really need his help for the rest of our journey. We're not as young as we used to be."

"Truer words were never spoken. Well then. You have my agreement. Why don't you approach her owner? Make it look like I'm the interested party and you're the go-between. Don't tell him we want to purchase her freedom; just say I require her for myself. We'll wait for him to set a price. And let's not say anything to Asher until we reach a conclusion."

"Very well."

Gaspar found Corinna's owner at the door to the brothel. "Hello, my man. The business we conducted earlier was most satisfactory. After my son spoke of Corinna's charms, my traveling companion happened to see her in the market, and now desires her for himself."

"Ah, yes! She is quite a pearl. I'll be happy to let her entertain him. She has several hours open, so she can attend to him immediately."

"No, you misunderstand me," said Gaspar. "He desires her for himself, always."

"He wants to buy her from me?" Corinna's owner responded, clearly surprised. "But he hardly knows her! And didn't your boy tell you that she's inexperienced? Such a wealthy man as your friend will surely want someone more skilled than that one! She still cries for her family, and I can't promise that she would know how to keep him satisfied."

"My son told me as much, but you needn't concern yourself with that. My friend wants her for his harem. If the girl is lonely, she may find the company of other women comforting." Gaspar let the man ponder his words before pressing his offer. "So what do you think? Are you willing to part with the little nymph? Your headache could very well be your gain, if we can reach agreement."

Corinna's owner made a face but took only a short time to deliberate. "I will consider your request, but I tell you, the price will be high. The girl is beautiful, and I must cover the cost of her purchase and keep these last months."

"Decide on a price and tell us on the morrow," replied Gaspar.

"I will."

Gaspar returned to Melchior with the news. "Good," said Melchior. "I've already asked about another camel. There are several for sale of good quality, but it won't come cheap." They fell into quiet conversation, preparing for the possibility of another rider.

That night, the foursome ate their meal together in the courtyard. Surrounded by other travelers, they reclined on blankets around a large fire pit in a corner of the yard. The air was still and the sky cloudless. The fragrance of roasting meat and vegetables tantalized them, as they searched the night sky for their favorite star.

"What do you make of that star, Asher?" asked Gaspar. "That bright one in the eastern sky? I'm sure you've noticed us watching it."

"I see you watching it," said Asher. "But I don't understand why. Does it have a special meaning?"

"You could say that," said Gaspar. "It's a very unusual star and it's guiding us on our journey to Judea."

"How can that be?" asked Asher.

"We first saw it many months ago in an unusual eclipse of the planet Jupiter. Then we noticed it's been moving steadily ever since. We've never seen a star quite like it, and we think it holds kingly portent."

As they sat looking up at the star, they were approached by a young man, a fellow traveler who had noticed their skyward glances.

"Pardon me, sirs. I couldn't help hearing your conversation. I'm a star gazer too, and noticed that same star emerge many months ago just as you described. I haven't been able to shake the feeling that it means something momentous. What do you make of it?"

Melchior was the first to reply. "That's a very good question. Is it not Gaspar?"

"Most certainly!" replied Gaspar. He'd never imagined the star would have much import to anyone else and was surprised to be questioned about it.

"Then tell me, please! I first saw it early in the morning in the eastern sky immediately after what I judged to be an eclipse of a planet. I'm no astrologer and I have no instruments to study it, but I could swear it has been moving westward!"

"You're right. The star is moving. How extraordinary that you noticed it, and yet you're not an astrologer?"

"I'm not, but I hope to be. My name is Balthazar. And who do I have the pleasure of meeting?"

Both men rose and bowed. "My name is Melchior."

"And I am Gaspar. What is this you say about wanting be an astrologer?"

"I'm on my way to Seleucia on the Tigris. I've heard of a school there, started by the Babylonians, where men have studied the stars for centuries. Do you know of it?"

"Know of it?" Both men exclaimed.

"It's our life!" said Gaspar excitedly. "We both study and teach there. And when our old friend, Seleucus, died in the great death over a year ago I became its leader."

Balthazar clapped his hands to his head. "Is that so? It's my great pleasure to meet you both. May I ask, are you heading to Seleucia? If so, I would be honored to ride with you."

"No! We're going to Jerusalem to ..."

"To inter my mother's bones," interrupted Melchior. "She died over a year ago. We've been traveling three weeks and this is our first caravansary stop. It's been a welcome change from the open road. But come, let us walk away from this throng so we may speak more easily."

The three men walked to a quieter corner of the courtyard, leaving Bina and Asher to eat by the fire. As soon as they found a comfortable spot to sit, Balthazar looked to Gaspar. "So you are the head of the most famous astrology school in Parthia!"

Gaspar laughed. "Yes, I am. But the King and his nobles can be difficult, and now that I'm gone I find I miss it very little. To me it's more rewarding to study the stars under the night sky with friends than it ever was with the king hanging on my every pronouncement."

"I agree," said Melchior. "Here we can study the stars and divine their meaning without fear of noble displeasure."

"Is it as bad as that?" asked Balthazar. "I always imagined you would speak as the stars prompt you and be done with it."

"It's never that easy," said Melchior.

"He's right," said Gaspar. "We glean information from our studies to inform King Phraates, and he rarely confronts us except if he's prompted by his Roman queen, which happens quite often of late. At those times we must present our findings with great care."

"I see. You must couch your predictions in ways that don't offend?"

"That's right," confirmed Gaspar. "We try to give our King insight into the inclinations and desires of other kingdoms. Are the stars aligning for our success or theirs? Is this a propitious time to engage in combat or would next year be better? That's the kind of advice he seeks. And of course, if he has questions about his wives and family. Should he take a new wife? Which of his sons might usurp his throne? Parthia has had a sad history of upstart sons and brothers challenging the King, so of course he seeks confirmation that all is well . . . or not."

Balthazar nodded. "I heard the very same about King Herod when I was in Judea."

"What did you hear?" asked Gaspar. "Is there an astrologer counseling him?"

"I wouldn't know. But I heard that he has killed many of his relatives for fear they will usurp his crown." "We've heard that he trusts no one. What a bitter way to live." said Melchior.

"You travel from Judea, you say? You don't speak like a Judean." said Gaspar.

"You have an ear for language. I'm from Arabia in the Hadramaut Kingdom, north of Qana."

"Then you're a long way from home!" said Gaspar. "Has your longing to study astrology drawn you all this way?"

"Not entirely. After my family died in a raid on our village, I came to Judea to sell my spice and to help a friend. I made a good profit on my cinnabar but my friend . . . didn't want my help anymore, so I left for Seleucia. Meeting you is the first good fortune I've had since Judea.

"We extend our sympathy on the death of your family," said Melchior. "Death is never easy, but sudden violent death is worst of all. Gaspar and I lost family and friends in the Great Death, and sometimes those memories still haunt me. I found my faith has helped me greatly."

"Is that so? Then your God must be a special one! I wondered about what happened to my family, too. Why my friend and I were spared. I still don't understand it."

Melchior and Gaspar were both visibly drawn into Balthazar's story. "Can you tell us, Balthazar, how you survived? And who survived with you?" Gaspar couldn't help his curiosity.

Balthazar recounted the story. "Alima and I both asked ourselves why we were the only ones saved."

"Those questions may never be answered," said Melchior. "I believe that my God often uses men as instruments of his will. Perhaps it is so with you. If there was purpose in your survival, it will be revealed to you in time."

Balthazar shook his head. "That's an interesting idea, but I'm not sure I believe it. I try to do what's right when I confront hardship, yet I'm found wanting and plagued by doubt. Now I want only to learn what the stars can teach."

"Found wanting when you tried your best? Do I detect the hand of a woman in your doubt?" asked Gaspar. "We can surely teach you about the stars, but about women? That may be more difficult."

Balthazar raised his brows and smiled ruefully. "Yes, a woman figures in my doubt. But you bring me low, indeed! I thought you astrologers would approach life with certainty. Am I wrong?"

"Yes, you are wrong," said Gaspar. "Nothing in life is certain, and the older we get the more we know it's true. Still, some things happen that seem beyond mere chance. Those are the things we seek to understand through our stars. Like meeting you here. I don't think it was mere coincidence, do you?"

"It's strange enough, I'll give you that," said Balthazar. "Did you say you left Seleucia three weeks ago?"

"Yes. But we travel with our guide, Asher, Melchior's slave woman and many mules and camels. You'll surely travel faster alone than we did," said Gaspar.

"I know. But now that I think on it, why should I go on alone? You're likely the most learned astrologers in Parthia and I know the roads to Judea. I'd be happy to help out if you'd let me join you and teach me as we go. What do you say?"

Gaspar looked at Melchior. Balthazar was obviously eager to learn about the stars, and they were both well equipped to teach him. But now for the second time in a day they were challenged to enlarge their little caravan.

Balthazar noticed their indecision. "Believe me sirs, I am an easy traveler. I have my own camel and can pay my way for food and water. And if you like, we can negotiate a fee for my studies as well. Though perhaps you will find my assistance in hunting and setting up camp to be as valuable."

"You're pretty sure of yourself, aren't you?" Gaspar laughed aloud. "I like that in a man! What do you say, Melchior? I think it may be no accident that we met Balthazar as we spoke of our star. Perhaps he's meant to follow it as well?"

"Perhaps. Yes, Balthazar. You're welcome to join us," said Melchior. "But you must pay your way. Make sure that you have purchased what you need before we leave."

"And when might that be?" asked Balthazar.

"The day after tomorrow. There will likely be six of us including you."

"Six? I thought you said there were four of you?"

"It's a long story. We may have a young woman joining us, a girl who worked at the brothel here."

"Ah! I understand," said Balthazar.

"I doubt it," said Melchior raising his brows. "We'll explain it, if it comes to pass, but it's not what you may think."

"Then I'll try to withhold my judgment. I find that to be a good policy in many cases."

"A very wise statement from such a young man. If you're as quick to learn about the stars as you are a student of human nature then you will surely rise to great heights," said Gaspar.

"Thank you!" Balthazar accepted the compliment graciously.

"Good. Now let us rejoin the group," said Gaspar. "The night is still young and my nose has been calling me back to the food for some time!" The three men walked back to the fire pit where they ate and conversed about the stars well into the night.

CHAPTER 26

Freedom for a Slave

§

LATE THE NEXT MORNING, CORINNA'S owner found Gaspar and Melchior in their quarters still shaking off sleep. They rose from the cushions where they reclined. "Good morning. This is, Melchior, the friend on whose behalf I approached you. Please sit."

Melchior looked him over from head to toe for he always liked to appraise those he did business with. Though go-betweens were not uncommon, doing business in person was preferable in his mind.

"Good day to you, sirs," Corinna's owner replied. "I've considered your request and am prepared to part with the girl for a pittance. Only a thousand drachma."

"I see, well that seems high to me." Melchior replied. "I've bought girls just as beautiful for half the price in Seleucia. Perhaps I should wait 'til I return there to find another for my harem."

Corinna's owner pouted and rocked head side his to side. "So soon you trifle about the sum! I might be willing to sell her for less, if payment can be made in gold."

"How much less?"

"Two hundred fifty less."

"Seven hundred fifty drachma still seems high." Melchior raised his eyebrows and considered whether he should parry to lower the price again. Rather than verbal sparring, he decided to delay his answer a bit. His father had taught him and Mered that timing and a little acting could make all the difference in a negotiation. He slowly stroked his

beard in apparent consternation over the new number, then rose and
walked about the small alcove in a very measured rhythm as he mut-
tered. He never looked toward Corinna's owner as he paced, and maintained a look of marked disinterest. He thought in his mind to say no
to the deal for he wanted his face to show itself true. He was about to
tell the man so, when Corinna's owner jumped up saying, "Don't be too
hasty. Don't say no before you hear my final offer!"

Melchior maintained an uncaring facade. "And that would be?"

"Six hundred and no less!" Corinna's owner replied hastily.

"A much better price, for a girl who's no longer a virgin. I am agreed."

Pulling a small scale from his saddle bag along with a bag of gold
pieces, Melchior weighed the equivalent of six hundred drachma, poured
the gold into a small leather pouch and held it tightly. Corinna's master
reached out his hand, but Melchior held it fast, "Not yet, sir. You shall
have payment as soon as you deliver Corinna. And of course, make your
mark that I am her new owner. As it happens I have a piece of papyrus,
so there is no need for delay."

The man scowled, but eyed the bag of gold. "Very well. I shall go for
her now. Perhaps you would like to come fetch her? She has little in the
way of personal goods, but she may be more cooperative if you explain
her purchase. She's an emotional girl, and I don't want her making a
scene in front of my customers."

"I will go," replied Gaspar. "As soon as you sign. Will you dictate,
Melchior?

Gaspar unrolled the papyrus and wrote the words Melchior wanted,
then watched as Melchior and the brothel owner made their marks.
Melchior took the papyrus, handed Gaspar the gold and watched as the
two men walked away. This is good! He thought. We will leave tomorrow and the girl will have little time to change her mind. If she decides
to leave us, at least it will be when she's closer to her home country.

Within minutes Gaspar returned with Corinna carrying a few small
bags. She looked anxious as her eyes scanned the room.

"I can see you're looking for Asher," said Melchior kindly. "Do not worry. He will be here soon. And on his behalf, I welcome you. My name is Melchior," he said bowing. "This is my friend, Gaspar. Asher works for us."

"I happy meet you," said Corinna bowing low.

"What did the brothel owner tell you?" asked Melchior. "Did he say I bought you for my harem?"

"Yes. But that not what Asher tell me at market, so I not sure what believe. When my uncle sold me, he say he send me to school in new country. It was lie. I hope Asher no lie."

"Asher did not lie. But I understand your worry. Your uncle should have protected you, cared for you. Instead he sold you. It was an awful betrayal. I do not have a harem and never will. Gaspar only said that because some slave owners don't like selling if they think their slave will be freed. Asher paid for your freedom. It was his idea. There is no harem."

Corinna's eyes opened wide. "No harem?"

"No harem," repeated Melchior again. "Asher bought your freedom."

"Asher...so kind! This is good! But, how I live, eat? I have no money. My only family is uncle who sold me. I never want see him again! "

"You won't have to," said Melchior. "But it's not for me to decide what you do. Now that you are free, you must make your own choices. . . I hope you will choose wisely, but only you can decide what you want."

"I understand. Try be wise. Must thank Asher first. He do this for me?"

"Yes," said Melchior. "Asher has given all his wages from our journey to free you. But, one thing I must insist upon. You must leave with us tomorrow. You can travel with us as long as you like until you decide where you want to live."

"Thank you, sir. I be happy leave this place! Maybe I help cook, serve on your journey. Where you go?"

"To Jerusalem in Judea," said Melchior.

"I never leave Greece 'til I come here," said Corinna. "I had friends who go Jerusalem. They pray at temple."

"We plan to see that temple," said Melchior as Bina walked into the room. "Corinna, this is my servant, Bina. She has served me well since I was a child."

Bina smiled and bowed to Corinna. "I welcome you, Corinna. You will find no better master."

"Bina, I think you misunderstand," said Melchior. "Corinna is not my slave, nor my concubine." Bina looked toward Gaspar. "Nor is she Gaspar's. She is a free woman and will be traveling with us to Judea. But she will share in the chores as we travel."

Bina looked taken aback. "A free woman? . . . But I thought."

Melchior nodded. "I can imagine what you thought. Corinna was working in the brothel but not anymore. Asher bought her freedom with his wages."

Bina frowned then turned toward Corinna. "I..." she stuttered. "I welcome you," said Bina, still looking confused and a little downcast.

"Well then," said Melchior. "Corinna, you will be under Bina's care for the remainder of our trip." Melchior put his arm on Bina's back to show his approval. "Bina can teach you many things and will direct you on how to help us."

"Thank you! You kind people. I never can thank." Corinna knelt down on both knees and with her hands brought together as in prayer, bent down to the ground in front of them, first to Gaspar, then to Melchior and lastly to Bina. When she looked up, she asked, "When Asher come? I want thank him, too."

"Very soon! In the meantime, why don't you and Bina get acquainted?" Melchior put his hand on Corinna's shoulder and bid her rise.

Bina took a few deep breaths before stepping forward. "It will be nice to have you as company, Corinna. I help find firewood, stoke the fire, and cook the meals. Can you help with those things, child?"

"My mother teach me cook, sew, weave, but I do what you need."

"You have a willing nature. I'm sure we can put your talents to good use. Come take a walk with me, so we can talk a bit."

When the women returned a short time later, Asher was polishing Melchior's belt. He smiled when he saw Corinna and rose to greet her hesitantly. Melchior noticed his uncertainty. "Go ahead, Asher. Don't let the girl stand there unwelcomed!" That was all the encouragement Asher needed, for he ran quickly to Corinna, bowing and grasping for her hand.

Corinna looked up at him with tears in her eyes. "Thank you! I know you only two days and you . . . you change my life! I bless the stars that brought you."

"I can show which one!" Asher said quietly. "Melchior and Gaspar found a special star that may lead us to the new king in Judea. If you stay with us, maybe you will see him, too."

Corinna looked surprised. "You see special star?"

"Yes, we've been following it! I can show you when the sun goes down. As for the new king, I only know that he's supposed to be special, too. Melchior calls him 'The Messiah' and says he is destined to be a great king like King David and Solomon. Have you ever heard of them?"

"Yes. My Jewish friends in Greece speak of them. They say King David win many battles and Solomon very wise."

"Yes. That's partly why I came on this journey. I've never seen a king. Not even King Phraates in Parthia, so even if the king is a Jew, he will surely be someone to remember!"

"I want see him, too," said Corinna.

"I was hoping you would . . . but Melchior and Gaspar said it was your decision. Now that you're free, you can come and go as you please, but I'd like you to stay with us . . . with me."

"I have no place to go, so I happy to stay. . . One thing I promise. . . I be honest. You my friend, and friends no lie. If I not want stay, I tell you."

Asher nodded his head. "I understand."

"What would you like me to prepare for our meal tonight?" Bina asked aloud, directing her question to Melchior.

"There's no need to cook tonight, Bina. We'll eat in the square as we did last night. And by the way, another person will be joining us for our journey. His name is Balthazar."

The band of six left the caravansary in the early dawn hours. Melchior, Gaspar, and Balthazar rode high on their camels as the star seemed to precede them high in its westward course. It had deviated very little from its original path, and continued to shine ever more brightly as the days passed.

One night as the three men sat by the fire, Gaspar scrutinized the cloudless sky. "My friend, I must confess this journey is a surprising experience. Each day we watch our star move slowly across the sky, and each night it shines so brightly it gives competition to the North Star. I'm at a loss to describe it, and I know now how you felt ... that we were meant to follow it."

Melchior smiled. "So you don't think me mad to lead us on this quest? I still have my own doubts."

"Do not doubt, my friend. Remember the dream? It was no coincidence that we both had the same dream, on the same night! And remember how your mother said that together we would find a way? That the Lord would show us the way?" Gaspar stood up and started shaking his feet.

"What's wrong?" asked Melchior.

"It's my feet. They tingle and feel numb, as if they aren't part of my body. They've been bothering me since we left Seleucia and it's been getting worse each day."

"Why didn't you tell me?"

"Because there's nothing to be done for it. I can still ride and walk well enough."

"Very well. But you must tell me if gets worse. We can shorten our rides if you think it will help."

"Thank you, but it's not necessary. Besides, the sooner we get to Judea, the better." Drowsy and yawning, Gaspar limped off to his tent as Melchior watched the sky. Bina had bid everyone goodnight hours ago, but Asher and Corinna remained, sitting quietly within the glow of the fire. Corinna sat within the spread of Asher's legs, her back resting against his chest, his arms entwined loosely about her, both gazing at the fire. It was clear to all that they were entranced with each other.

"What's the matter, Balthazar? You look exceeding sad tonight." said Melchior as he observed the young man.

"Do I? I was looking at Asher and Corinna and couldn't help thinking of my friend, Alima."

"Your friend?" asked Melchior. "From the look on your face I would say she is something more than a friend."

"She might have been once."

"Sounds like you miss the woman."

"I do miss her. Do you plan to ride through Caesarea on your way to Jerusalem?"

"I'm not sure. We must examine Gaspar's map to determine the most direct route. Does your friend live there?"

"She was staying with a Jewish family there when I left. If we travel that way, I would like to check on her, to be sure she's all right. . ." Balthazar looked to the sky. "The sky is so clear tonight. Can you tell me what that cloudy patch is there? I've seen it many times on clear nights and always wondered what it is."

"Ah yes! That glowing band is called the Milky Circle. A Greek named Aristotle, was one of the first to describe it in his great writing 'Meteorologica'. At times it appears low in the sky and at other times it's quite high. . . .Hey you two!" Melchior called to Asher and Corinna, hoping to draw them into the conversation. "I know you only have eyes for each other, but look at the sky tonight. Is it not a beautiful sight?" Corinna and Asher looked up as Melchior suggested.

"Do you see the Milky Circle?"

"Yes," said Asher. "And I've seen it before. When I'm out on the hills with my sheep, the sky often looks like this. It makes me feel . . . not so alone."

"I like, too," said Corinna. "My country has story of Milky Circle. We say it road to Mount Olympus. . . Path to the gods."

"Melchior told me about that." Said Asher. "He has taught me about many stars, and told me the bright star we're following may lead us to the Messiah, like the Milky Way leads to your Mount Olympus."

Melchior was proud of Asher's progress in learning the stars and he was glad the youth perceived his knowledge to be as important as his physical prowess. He'd seen many boys who relied solely on their strength and fighting skills to impress women. In his experience, it was often the men who developed their intellect along with their bodies, who were most successful in wooing women.

"It's time for sleep. The morning will come quickly and we've many leagues to go." He watched Corinna enter Bina's tent, as Asher went off to a third tent with Balthazar. So far, the two men were getting along well and he was glad. Despite the relative calm of their journey, Melchior felt an inner urge to press on with their trek. He wasn't sure why, but like Gaspar, he was beginning to think that the sooner they got to Judea the better.

CHAPTER 27

Change in Caesarea

§

THE SUN SHONE BRIGHTLY AS Alima and Judith labored in the garden. The days were growing shorter and it was time to harvest the plants they had nurtured over the summer. "Come, girls," said Alima. "Carry this basket into the house. Your mother and I need your help today."

"Thank you," said Judith as she rubbed her bulging belly. "I feel older and older each time my womb carries anew."

"Have you a name in mind for this one?" asked Alima.

"Noah and I have talked, but have no decision yet. Our son is named for Noah's dead father, Isaac, who is descended from the House of David. I think if this should be another boy, we'll name him after Noah's grand-father, Matthan."

"Why not your own father?" asked Alima.

"Because we usually name our children in tribute to a family member who has died. My father is still alive, at least, I think he is. He lives a good distance away and I haven't seen him in a long time."

Alima looked over to where little Isaac was playing in the dirt. "Your son will need a thorough wash when we are done. Will you let me bathe him for you?" asked Alima.

"With pleasure!" said Judith smiling. As the women continued pluck-ing beans from the yellowing plants they heard a horse approaching at a clip. "We hardly ever get riders in this part of town," said Judith, look-ing wary. "He seems to be slowing. I hope ..." But the words died on her tongue as the horseman rounded her hut and stopped a few paces away."

He looked down at them from his horse. "Is this the house of Noah, husband of Judith?"

"I am Judith. Has something happened to him?" she asked with furrowed brow.

"Come round the house away from your children," said the rider. "My news is not good."

Alima ran to Judith, whose hands were shaking. "I can take the children inside."

"No. I want them with me. They are my strength! Come to momma, girls." Miriam and Rebecca ran to their mother. Judith picked Isaac up, and held him tightly then looked stoically to the rider. "Tell us your news."

"I am sorry, but your husband Noah, is dead. Crushed by a stone as he was working on a house near the amphitheater. The foreman bid me tell you, so you may retrieve his body. "

Judith's legs sank beneath her and the children began to cry.

"Poppa's dead? He's dead, momma?" cried Rebecca in between sobs. "Why is he dead, momma?" She joined her sister Miriam in a chorus of sobs that brought out the neighbors from nearby huts. The more the girls cried the more upset little Isaac became.

Alima put her hand on Judith's shoulder. "I can watch the children while you go. Do you have a way to bring his body for burial? It may not be easy."

Judith turned her tear stained face to the messenger. "Is his body badly mangled?"

"Yes. It is not the usual practice but since you are with child, I can arrange to take it to your gravesite. You must still meet with the foreman, however."

"If you can take him to the potter's field, I would be most grateful. I have no money for a proper grave," said Judith as tears flowed freely down her face.

"I will do it," said the man. "Can you follow me now?"

"I will. Go with Alima, girls. And take your brother. I must go with this man."

Alima took Isaac from Judith's arms. "Come, girls. Your mother has something important to do, and she must do it alone."

Three days later, after Noah's body had been buried in the potter's field, Judith and Alima sat together after supper. It was already dark outside and the children had been put to bed.

"What will you do now?" asked Alima tentatively.

"If Noah had a brother, I would be expected to wed him, but he has none."

"Do you have family nearby?"

"No," said Judith. "My family lives a good distance away in a town called Nazareth. I have no way to earn a living here in Caesarea, and I can't travel by myself with the children. If my time should come early, it would be bad."

"Have you delivered early in the past?"

"Yes. Both Isaac and Miriam came early."

"Then the sooner we get you to Nazareth the better," said Alima.

"But the roads can be dangerous. It would be foolish to make the journey alone with the children."

"I will go with you."

"That would be a blessing, but what if your brother returns? Aren't you afraid you will miss him?"

"He has four months left to work at the shipyard, and you will be better off with family around to help you, especially after your babe arrives."

"You are a good friend, but getting to Nazareth won't be easy. It's on the other side of the Carmel range."

"Oh! . . . Well, I have a little extra silver. Perhaps we can hire a neighbor to take us?"

"I'll ask around. Noah's friend, Nathan, might be willing to help."

"How far is it to Nazareth?" asked Alima.

"A two day journey, but the children can't walk that far and I get more tired with each passing day. We should try to hire a wagon to take us."

"I agree."

"It's too bad your Balthazar isn't here. He seemed so kind. He might have helped us, don't you think?"

"Yes. He would have," said Alima looking suddenly very gloomy.

"Didn't you have an agreement of marriage? I thought he was your betrothed," said Judith.

Alima shook her head. "The story is a muddle. After my husband died, Balthazar paid my bride price so I wouldn't have to marry my wicked cousin."

"Was he so bad? This cousin of yours?"

"Yes. And Balthazar, gave his own land and much spice to free me of him."

"He must have had feelings for you. To do something like that."

"I thought so. But I was never sure. And then we argued because he left Sameer to work alone at that shipyard. In a fit of anger I told him to leave."

"Did you mean what you said?" asked Judith.

"I thought I did. But later . . . I realized how rash I had been. I let my fear and anger speak when I should have had faith in him. I should have trusted him."

"Do you love him?" asked Judith.

"I do," said Alima. "But now it's too late. He's gone to Parthia and I shall never see him again."

Alima and Judith asked around for days trying to find a man willing to take them to Nazareth. First Judith asked Noah's friend, Nathan. "I'm sorry, Judith. I would take you if I could, but the foreman won't give me leave from work. I'll ask my cousin." But the cousin had to take his family to a far city for the census. "I'm sorry, Judith. I would help you if I could." It went likewise with several others, until one day Judith looked at Alima and cried. "I'm worried, Alima! I haven't found any man who can take us to Nazareth, and my belly grows bigger by the day. What shall we do?"

"Our plight is no reason for indecision," said Alima. "I have enough silver to buy a small cart and a donkey. We'll make the journey ourselves."

"But the road can be perilous. How can we protect ourselves?"

"My brothers taught me how to use a sling, and I'm a good shot. I can take the head off a rabbit at a hundred paces, and a man is much bigger than that."

"All right," said Judith still looking uncertain. "I suppose we have little choice but to go alone."

Alima had no trouble finding a cart and a healthy donkey for a reasonable price in the market. "Can we be ready by daybreak?" Asked Alima after she rode home in the cart.

"I'm sure we can," said Judith. "Come, girls. Get your robes and scarves together. Your sandals, too. We're leaving for Nazareth in the morning."

Judith gathered their clothes while Alima packed food, filled canteens from the well and began to pack the cart. Early the next morning they were ready. "Hop up, girls," said Judith. "Miriam, I'm handing Isaac to you. Promise to hold him tightly; I don't want him to tumble out."

"I will, momma," said the child.

It was early fall and the days were getting cooler, so Alima placed a warm blanket around the children after they were settled in the cart. "We can move the blanket aside when the sun comes up. Are you ready for our adventure?" she asked.

"Yes!" said the girls together.

"Will we ever come back momma?" asked Rebecca.

"I don't know," said Judith. "We might if your grandpa can help us next year. I'd like to move your father to a proper grave. But we shall see what the future holds." The children sat at the front of the cart with their belongings behind them.

"Would you like to walk or drive?" asked Alima.

Judith looked thoughtful. "If you are agreed, I'll walk first. My energy saps as the day goes on."

"Then I shall drive," said Alima as she jumped onto the cart's bench. "Hold tight to your brother. Miriam."

"I have him," said Miriam.

"We're ready!" chimed in Rebecca.

"Then let us begin!" Alima cracked the whip on the donkey's hind quarters and the wagon surged forward. Judith took a long look back toward the house before turning around and echoing Alima's words. "We're off to Nazareth. Let's pray the Lord will keep us safe on our journey."

Alima had made a new sling from plaited flax in the last week. Now she placed it in her lap, a stone ready in its cradle. Many more stones lay within arm's reach in the cart. Like Judith, she had hoped for a man to attend them, but lack of one was no reason to be unprepared. She could protect them as well as any man if the need arose, and kept a keen eye to the road as she drove. It brought back memories of her journey from Khalan with Balthazar. It had been an awful time. A time of death, of devastation. But today she remembered it with a yearning. How she wished Balthazar was still here.

Although Judith's pregnancy was advancing, it seemed to be no hindrance to her endurance, for she kept up well with the cart. And because she knew the roads, she advised Alima when to speed up, when to slow down, and when they should watch for bandits. They followed the Via Maris toward the Carmel Mountains. Through the early morning hours, Judith walked briskly, teasing the children from time to time, keeping them happy and smiling. But Alima could see her tiring as time passed, and slowed the cart by late morning so Judith might tred more slowly.

The road was level and paved with cobbled stones at the start, but as they got farther from Caesarea, it became rough and uneven. "They must have had a lot of rain here," said Alima struggling to keep the cart steady. "This section is badly rutted."

"It's washed away in places," said Judith. "I'll walk behind you. Try to keep the cart toward the middle where it's more level. It will be disaster if we lose a wheel."

Alima tried her best to keep the wagon moving steadily but it was slow going as it rocked side to side. "Hold on children!" said Alima. "This is going to be bumpy!" They were at the highest point of a hill and the road was so rutted that Alima feared the cart would tip. There was perspiration on her brow as she slowed the donkey to a walk, but she drove past the most dangerous area, and picked up speed again as the road improved toward the bottom of the hill. "That was a tough one," said Alima breathing a little easier. "If we hit a spot like that again, the children should get out." But it was never necessary and they rolled on for another hour until the sun was high overhead.

"What do you say we stop to rest?" asked Alima. "The children must be hungry and we all need a rest."

"I was thinking the same thing," said Judith.

Alima pulled the wagon off to the side of the road where there was some shade and a few rocks and bushes. "Come children. Time to get out," she said. The girls hopped out as Judith grabbed Isaac and urged the children to relieve themselves behind a large bush.

Alima did likewise, then scurried to lay a blanket by the side of the road and unpacked a little food. She set out a canteen of water along with some bread, figs and a little cheese. The children were hungry and grabbed for the food like hungry wolves. "Girls, please! You're not animals!" said Judith. "Go slow and leave some for the rest of us."

"Sorry," said Miriam.

"Sorry, momma," said Rebecca.

"That's better," said Judith. "When we get to your grandfather's house, you must be more careful. You must always say please and thank you. I want you to make me proud. Can you do that for me?

"Yes, momma," said the girls in unison.

"What is grandpa like, momma? I don't remember him," said Miriam.

"I'm not surprised. You were only a baby when we saw him last. He's a fine man; very big, and very kind. I think you'll like him." said Judith smiling.

The group ate in peaceful companionship. As soon as the girls were done eating they began to run and play as Judith nursed Isaac and told Alima about Nazareth and some of her girlhood friends.

"Nazareth sounds like a nice town," said Alima.

"It always seemed like a big family. We rejoiced in the good times and wept through the hard times together."

"Were there many of those?" asked Alima.

"Enough," said Judith. "The worst was when King Herod's men came to collect taxes. There was one year after a bad drought when several families couldn't pay, and the soldiers took their children in payment. A boy here and a girl there. All the Jews in Nazareth wept for them. I lost one of my best friends, Sarah. She had just turned sixteen, and they took her on her birthday. I'll never forget the look in her mother's eyes."

"An awful thing to be sure," said Alima. "I have wept for lack of a child, but to lose a child like that . . ."

"I swore that I would die rather than lose a child that way," said Judith. "But I understood once I had children of my own. You can't give up. You must live for the others who depend on you. That was one thing about my Noah. He had his faults, but he always kept a roof over our heads and the taxes paid."

"He loved you," said Alima. "Anyone with eyes could see that."

The women talked as the girls played, until Judith was done nursing. "Can you take him from me?" asked Judith. "I must relieve myself before we move on." Alima took Isaac from his mother's arms and called to the girls. "Come Miriam! Rebecca. Into the cart with you. We'll be moving on."

Suddenly, Judith screamed. The girls stopped running and looked toward their mother in fear.

"What's wrong, momma?" yelled Miriam. They began to run toward her.

"No! Don't come near! Alima, keep the children away," said Judith in a strangled voice. "There are snakes. I've been bitten."

"Get back in the cart, girls. Do you hear?" Alima handed Isaac into Miriam's hands. "Hold your brother. I'm going to help your mother." Alima grabbed her sling and walked carefully toward Judith where she lay slumped on the ground.

"Judith, I'm coming for you. How many snakes? Can you see them?"

"Three of them. Near my feet."

"I've got my sling. I can see them, but I'm getting you away from there first." Alima could see three vipers slithering across the ground just a pace or two from Judith's feet. "I'm going to hold you under your arms and pull." Alima watched the snakes as she grabbed for Judith and began to pull with all her strength. "I've got you. I'll move you as far as I can."

"Where are the snakes? Are they still near me?"

"No, they're sliding back under a rock. I don't think they'll bite again."

"I ... I feel strange. I think my foot is swelling."

"I'll keep pulling. You're going to need all your strength to get into the wagon." Alima pulled Judith to the side of the wagon, turned her on her back and pulled up her robe. She could see two bites on Judith's leg, which was swelling badly and turning an ugly shade of purple.

"Girls, we've got to make room for your mother. Rebecca, move some of the supplies back. Miriam you hold Isaac. I'm going to get your momma into the cart." Though Judith was clearly dazed, Alima helped her to stand and managed to push her up and into the front of the wagon where she lay behind the wagon seat. "Judith, I'm going to try to suck out the venom. It may be your only chance."

"No, it's too late. . . . I need you to watch over my babes."

"But Judith. It might help."

"No. Listen . . . there's no time. Promise to watch over my babes. Let me hold their hands, while . . ."

"But Judith, tell me . . ." Before she could ask her question Judith's body went limp.

"Momma! Momma! What's wrong with momma?" asked Miriam. The children began to cry.

"Your momma's sick, girls. Very sick from the snake bites."

"Will she die like poppa? Oh please say she won't die, too!" cried Miriam.

"I hope she won't, but I don't know. Maybe we can get your momma help in the next village. Will you help me like big girls? Can you hold your brother while I drive? We must go quickly."

"Yes! Let's go quickly. Let's get help for momma!"

Alima drove on for several hours, higher and higher into the mountains as she looked for another town. Judith had told her that Nazareth was on the other side of the Carmel range, beyond the Plains of Esdraelon, and she remembered her mentioning another town when they got through the pass. She was in the pass now, but how far was the town? The children were quiet, looking sleepy, so she kept going, and every now and then stopped to look at Judith. Her friend's body was barely warm and her breath was so shallow that Alima feared it wouldn't be long before the vipers' venom took its toll.

What would she do if Judith died? The children would be orphans and in her charge, unless she could find kin in Nazareth. The afternoon sun was sinking and she could see storm clouds in the distance. That's all we need, thought Alima. A big rain to finish off the day! Why was life so hard? Judith had spoken with such hope, of her children, of her God. And Alima had wanted to share in that hope. But where was Judith's God now? Tears ran down her cheeks as she pulled the donkey to a halt. The children had fallen asleep on their mother's body. She put her hand on Judith's head and felt the awful truth. Her friend was getting cold.

She looked up to the sky and called out from her heart. "She called you Yahweh, Lord! Where are you? She said you loved them. If this is true, I ask you, please, help me care for her children! I don't know what to do! If you exist, if you hear me, show me what to do. Help me!" Alima shook her head. She must be mad to be talking to a dead woman's god. So many questions. Should she turn back or press on to Nazareth? In Caesarea, she might wait for her brother, but in Nazareth she might find the children's grandfather. But what is his name? Where does he live? She had been Judith's friend for months but how little she knew of her. There was the story about the friend named Sarah taken by the Romans. That at least she remembered. And that Noah's father and grandfather came from . . . what did she say? The house of David, whatever that means.

She rode on for a short time as the sun sank lower. Just when she was thinking to pull off the road, she spotted some houses on a hill to her left. She snapped the whip sharply against the donkey's rump. "Get on with you!"

Trees were already throwing long shadows in her path, and the children were beginning to stir. On and up the lonely darkening road she drove, until she reached the approach to an ancient village. She passed several long abandoned huts whose stones had tumbled and broken into bits. But there was life here, too. She smelled smoke and meat roasting. The hill was enveloped in darkness when she pulled the cart up in front of the first place she saw light.

"Children, wake up," she said gently. "Miriam, Rebecca. Come on. Let me take Isaac."

"Are we there, Alima? Are we in Nazareth?"

"Not yet, but we're getting close. We must spend the night here. Come with me, please." She scooped Isaac up as the girls climbed out. Strangely they said nothing about their mother. Perhaps they think she's still sleeping, thought Alima. She led the way to the house, knocked soundly, and was greatly relieved when an old woman came to the doorway.

"Please, I must ask for your hospitality. We're on our way to Nazareth and need shelter for the night. Have you a place? A room I can rent, or a stable where we can lay our heads?"

"Where is your man?" asked the woman. "Surely, you didn't come alone with the children?"

"There is no man. We tried to get someone to take us, but no one could. Many have left Caesarea because of the census, and then my friend's husband died. We had no choice but to travel alone."

"Oh you poor woman! Come in, come in. That's right, children. Come warm yourselves by the fire and share my meal."

"Thank you. You are very kind."

"It's what I'm here for my girl."

"My name is Alima, and the children are Miriam, Rebecca and Isaac."

"My greetings to you all. I am Elizabeth. You mentioned a friend, is she with you?"

"Yes, but would you to step outside, so we may speak alone?"

The woman frowned. "Will the children be all right by themselves?"

"I think so. Girls, watch your brother. I'm going with this nice lady to get our pack."

Alima bowed to the woman as she stepped outside. "You are so kind to take us in. But I must tell you, I am not the children's mother. Their mother is my friend, Judith, who lies in the wagon." Tears slid down Alima's face. "She was bitten by vipers . . . and died a short time ago. She was with child."

The woman cupped Alima's face in her hands. "Oh my girl! What a hard day. I grieve with you and the children. Do they know?"

"Not yet. The boy is too young but the girls. . . I'm not sure they understand. They fell asleep. Maybe they think their mother sleeps, too."

"You said your name is Alima?"

"Yes."

"That's not a Jewish name."

"Judith was a Jew but I'm from Arabia; I was brought up to follow Zarathustra."

"Ah, yes. I've heard of that prophet. Your people and mine, we both believe in doing good. Let me help you take your friend from the wagon. Then we'll find a way to tell the children."

"You will help me do that?"

"I will."

Elizabeth followed Alima to the cart, and as Alima climbed into it, Elizabeth reached for Judith's legs. "Do not blame yourself, my girl. The viper took her because it was her time. There is nothing you could have done."

"But she was my friend! And now I fear for the children. What will become of them if I can't find their family?"

"You seem a good woman. Can you not care for them yourself?"

"Me? . . . Yes, I can. It may not be easy, but I can."

"Motherhood is never easy, my girl. It often invites great sacrifice, even when the children are your own."

"I know. I saw Judith sacrifice for her children, but I envied her for it. I thought I would gladly stand in her shoes to be a mother. It was what I wished and longed for. If I cannot find their kin in Nazareth, I may get my wish, but not in the way I thought."

"Life has a way of testing us, surprising us. But you have inner strength, Alima. Do not doubt. You will mother the children well if that be the way of it."

"I never used to doubt, but lately . . ."

"Believe in yourself as the Lord believes in you! Make your plan and carry it out. You will go on to Nazareth and search for their kin. And if you don't find them, you will be their mother. Your friend could not have chosen better. Now, let us move Judith to my stable where she will lay until her burial."

Elizabeth held Judith's legs above the edge of the wagon as Alima struggled to lift her body up. "I'm not sure I can do this," said Alima. "She's heavier than I thought."

"Just ease her out to me a little at a time. I will hold her while you jump off."

"But she's so heavy. I don't think . . ."

"Believe me child, I'm stronger than I look."

Alima frowned but did as she was told. Little by little she pushed Judith's body into Elizabeth's arms, and surprisingly, the old lady had no trouble holding her. In fact, she seemed to cradle Judith in the few moments it took Alima to jump from the wagon and regain her hold under Judith's arms. Together, they carried Judith's body to the stable, where they laid her on a large pile of hay.

"Let's go feed the children, now," said Elizabeth.

"And tell them about their momma," added Alima.

"Yes. And when the time is right I'll come back to prepare her body for burial. I have the oils and spices to do it properly. Is that agreeable?"

"That would be most kind."

It rained in torrents during the night, but quit by early morning. It was then, with the children by their side, that the women buried Judith's body in a cave behind the stable. When it was over, Elizabeth sat with the children on the wet grass. "The Lord will remember your mother, children. She was full of love for you and abounded in hope and kindness. You have lost your mother but the Lord will be with you always. Believe me when I say, the Lord will watch over you all your days. Come now. Let us warm ourselves by the fire."

"A warm fire sounds good," said Alima as she shook off the dampness from her cloak. "Children, Miss Elizabeth has prepared some barley with onions and some fresh bread for us to eat before we leave for Nazareth. Come on then. There's a bowl for each of you, and cups of nice fresh goat's milk." Alima held Isaac close as she coaxed him gently to eat and drink. It was a new experience for the child who'd been nursing at his mother's breast until yesterday. When all of them were satisfied, she bundled the children into the wagon.

"Thank you, Elizabeth. I will never forget your kindness."

"It was the Lord's will that I be here," said Elizabeth.

"And it was my great good fortune," said Alima as she climbed onto the wagon's seat. "Until I saw the glow of your hut, I thought we'd have to sleep in the rain, and I feared greatly for the little ones."

"I know you had fear and doubt. But the Lord helped you to care for them."

Alima looked up in surprise. "But how can you know that?"

"Because you prayed for his help didn't you? Farewell, my girl," said Elizabeth as she waved.

"How could she know that?" wondered Alima as she watched the old woman walk back to her hut and disappear into a heavy fog. "Farewell,

Elizabeth!" yelled Alima through the mist. "I'll try to stop on my way back from Nazareth." She smacked the whip against the donkey's rear, turned the wagon around and headed back down the hill. When she reached the Via Maris, she turned east toward Nazareth. Within moments the sun broke through the clouds, burning off the fog.

"Wave to Miss Elizabeth, children!" said Alima. "She's probably watching us from her doorstep."

The girls stretched out their hands. "Where's her house, Alima?" asked Miriam. "I don't see it."

"Me, either," said Rebecca

"It's there, on the hill! Look closely." She stopped the wagon to show them, but it was as they said. The fog had risen, the cave was clearly visible, but there was no hut, no stable, no other houses, only the tumble down ruins of the ancient village.

CHAPTER 28
Setbacks

$

ONE MONTH LATER, THE LITTLE band of travelers was nearing Damascus, and everyone was well except for Gaspar. Each night Balthazar watched him walk around their campsite, shaking his feet and rubbing them with oil. He wasn't surprised when Gaspar suggested stopping for a few nights at an inn. They spent several days in the city, enjoying the amenities of civilization, hot meals, public baths and giving their animals a well-deserved rest. But the day soon came to resume their journey. As Gaspar, Balthazar and Asher packed the animals, a horse drawn cart rumbled down the road at a hasty pace. One of their donkeys, frightened by the sudden close encounter kicked up its hind legs, forcing Gaspar to jump back onto the rusty iron spoke of a broken wheel.

"Ay!" Gaspar yelled aloud. "You stupid animal! Look what you've made me do!"

Balthazar ran to his aid. "That looks nasty. We must pull the spoke from your foot and clean it quickly."

"I know. I know. Go ahead. Get it over with!" said Gaspar grimacing in pain.

"Do you want us to send for a physician? The innkeeper may know where to find one." said Balthazar.

"No! Just send Asher for the others. The women can bathe my foot and bind it up."

"But a physician…."said Balthazar.

"Just do as I say!" said Gaspar heatedly.

As Asher ran off to find the others, Balthazar did his best to comfort Gaspar by wiping his rapidly perspiring brow. But the man's pain and worry was written in the lines on his face. A man who couldn't walk was often as good as dead. Even mounting an animal was infinitely more difficult if you couldn't put weight on a foot.

"I guess I won't be much help packing today," said Gaspar when Melchior came running.

"What's new in that?" said Melchior, trying to make light of it. "Let's get that rusty spoke removed!"

"It hurts like a son of a bitch!" said Gaspar.

"Do you want some wine first? I'm afraid it's all I have for the pain," said Balthazar.

"Does it have any mandrake in it?"

"Sorry, no. Do you still want it?"

"You had best believe it."

Balthazar withdrew a pouch from his saddle bag and filled his tin cup to the brim. Gaspar drank it down in one gulp.

"Another?"

"Yes." Again Gaspar drank it quickly.

Moments later, Asher returned with the women. Corinna carried a pitcher of water and a wide bowl, while Bina held a towel and some cloth.

"Are you ready?" Balthazar asked.

"As I'll ever be." Gaspar looked away and grunted loudly as Balthazar attempted to extract the rusty spoke.

"It must be caught on some bone," said Balthazar. "Do you want me to continue?" Though he was very pale, Gaspar nodded. Pulling with all his strength, Balthazar finally succeeded as Gaspar fainted into the arms of Melchior who sat behind him. Corinna poured water over the bloody wound, while Bina held the bowl beneath his foot. When Gaspar came around a few moments later, Bina was already wrapping his foot in clean white cloth.

"You must bind it just right," said Melchior. "Enough to stop the bleeding but not so much as to turn his foot blue."

"She's knows that well enough," said Gaspar testily. "How many times has she done the same for you and Mered's family?"

"Yes, but not for any wounds as grievous!"

"I'll be fine." But when Bina was done binding his foot, Gaspar closed his eyes in exhaustion.

The rest of the day passed uneventfully as the troop headed southwest from Damascus on the road to Ulatha. Though Gaspar was still in pain, Melchior and Balthazar tried to cheer him. "We're getting closer!" said Melchior.

"We'll be in Judea before you can finish the next bladder of wine!" said Balthazar.

Gaspar cussed in response. "You piss ants! I need mandrake, not wine!"

Balthazar was starting to recognize the sign posts he had passed on his way toward Parthia, and knew the road would take them through some scenic country. They were about four leagues beyond Damascus when they noticed a snow capped mountain in the distance. Since Gaspar looked exhausted, they decided to camp in an area where several other groups were also stopped.

"How's your foot?" asked Melchior as he and Balthazar helped Gaspar from his camel.

"It throbs, but my usual numbness is setting in, and this time I welcome it!"

"I can understand that. Would you like me to examine it? The bandage is starting to seep," said Melchior.

"No need for that. It'll hurt more if you unwrap it. Let's just wrap a little more cloth around it."

"So be it," said Melchior.

Balthazar frowned, thinking Gaspar would be better off to look at the wound, but kept his own counsel. As Melchior finished binding more cloth on the foot, Balthazar offered Gaspar more wine. "I have plenty to share."

"I knew there was a reason I liked you!" said Gaspar.

Bina and Corinna fixed an evening meal over a fire they shared with other travelers, and served Gaspar where he sat outside his tent. That night, Gaspar cried out in pain so often, that Balthazar was glad to be up and about at dawn.

The next day they made good progress and soon the great Mount Hermon, which they had seen in the distance the day before, loomed large to the northwest.

"Quite a sight isn't it?" said Melchior.

"Indeed," said Balthazar. "I admired it as I travelled east. I wonder if we might talk about our route. Will we travel through Caesarea?"

"I checked Gaspar's maps and it appears there is no direct road south from here to Jerusalem. So when we reach Ulatha we'll head west to the Via Maris, then south into Caesarea. I know Herod has a palace there, and with any luck we can see him there instead of Jerusalem."

Balthazar looked stunned. "You're calling on King Herod? I thought you were following the star to find the Messiah?"

"That is our purpose, and I would avoid Herod if we could. But before we left Parthia, King Phraates bid us call on him. So we must meet with the man whether I like it or not."

Balthazar appeared serious. "Must I come? I have no desire to meet the man."

"You needn't come. Gaspar and I can see him without you."

"Good! Then I shall visit my friend Alima while you're at the palace. I've worried about her ever since I left."

"Very well." Melchior looked up to the darkening sky. "I've noticed our star seems to be turning southward. It's leading us toward Jerusalem, just as we thought it might."

As Melchior watched his star, Balthazar drew his camel alongside Gaspar. "I think we should stop and have a look at your foot. Your bandage is soaked through with blood again."

Gaspar looked down in surprise at his dangling foot.

"Didn't you realize you were bleeding so?" asked Balthazar.

"No," said Gaspar, looking puzzled. "Else I would have stopped earlier. Well, let's attend to it."

Gaspar and Balthazar commanded their camels to koosh. "We must clean Gaspar's wound!" Said Balthazar. "Bina, can you fetch some water? Do you have more clean cloth, Melchior?"

"Yes! I got some extra from the innkeeper in Damascus."

"Good! Asher, help us get Gaspar off his camel." They found a low flat rock by the side of the road and helped Gaspar walk to it. When he was seated, Bina unrolled the blood soaked cloth from his foot. It was obvious that the wound was starting to fester.

"I'll need to clean it well," said Balthazar. "If we leave it like this, it will only get worse. Brace yourself. This is likely to hurt."

"What else is new? Please remind me to kill that donkey later, will you?"

Balthazar drew out his knife and wiped it with a small piece of Melchior's cloth. Then he poured a little wine over the knife and began to scrape around the edges of the wound. Gaspar gasped and sweat beaded on his forehead as Balthazar went deeper and wider, scraping out the pus that had developed so quickly. "Do you feel faint?" Balthazar asked quietly, not wanting to embarrass the man.

"No. But are you finished?"

"Almost." When Balthazar had cleaned the wound as well as he could, he directed Bina to pour water on it and bind it as she had done before.

"Thank you," grunted Gaspar, who looked ashen. "This was a very bad bit of luck. Remind me to castrate that donkey later, will you?"

Balthazar laughed. "I can do that, but you must tell me. Is that before or after you kill him?"

According to plan, Balthazar and his friends traveled west from Ulatha to Tyre where they rested for a day and found a physician to look at Gaspar's still festering foot. The physician pulverized some poppy pods and sprinkled a little of the powder around the edges of the wound. Then he gave Gaspar some wine mixed with mandrake. When Gaspar became sleepy, the physician cleansed the wound as quickly as he could before rewrapping it. "Tell him to keep it clean. And here's a little extra poppy powder. The coloring around his wound is not good, so the pain and pus may likely continue."

Balthazar knew what the physician did not say. That a wound like Gaspar's which didn't heal, and continued to fester, might mean the loss of the foot or worse.

As soon as they could get Gaspar on his camel, the little caravan headed south on the Via Maris. They watched their star as closely as ever, and realized that it was now south and east of them. Balthazar could see that Melchior and Gaspar were eager to correct their course. "How will you determine our final destination?" he asked one day as they neared Caesarea. "We're getting closer to Judea, but the star is so bright that at night it seems to glow for miles in all directions. How can we narrow it down to a single town? It doesn't seem possible."

"You raise a good question." said Melchior. "For which I have no answer. But the Lord has brought us this far, and as my mother predicted, we trust he will show us the way."

"You are remarkable men indeed. For months you've journeyed and you still have no idea where you will end up. You have done it all based on trust in an unseen god? I have trouble understanding this."

"Balthazar, my friend! Have you learned so little since we met? What do you think has been happening all these months?" asked Gaspar as he spurred his camel close to Balthazar's with his crop. "Was it not extraordinary how we saw the star in the first place? And that it moves? And that we met you at a way station in the middle of the desert both looking at the same unusual star?"

"Yes, but . . ."

"No buts, my friend! Those are not the only unusual events we have witnessed. Perhaps we never told you that Melchior and I both had the same dream the night after we saw the star. In our dream, a glowing man in white directed us to follow it. We both felt it was more than a dream. As if the man were talking to us, yet we knew we were asleep. Such a thing is not mere coincidence. I am the son of a Magi priest. My father interpreted dreams and never did I hear of two men having the same dream on the same night with the same message!"

"It is beyond our understanding," added Melchior. "Has there never been a time in your life when you sensed an unseen hand playing a role? Directing your path?"

"Only once, when my village was destroyed. Alima and I both wondered why we alone survived."

"Gaspar and I wondered the same thing after the Great Death. Then he convinced me there must be a reason. That we had things to do yet."

"Like this quest?" asked Balthazar.

"Yes," aid Gaspar. "Not until the man in white appeared in our dreams did we understand. For some reason we were meant to follow this star. Maybe you survived the attack on your village for the same reason."

"It's a curious thought. But I can tell you that I haven't had any strange dreams."

"No glowing man in white?" asked Gaspar laughing?

"Not so far," said Balthazar.

"Be sure to tell us if you do. This has been a journey filled with unusual events. I wouldn't be surprised if there are more to come," said Gaspar.

They rode into Caesarea by the end of day. Balthazar recognized the road and realized he wasn't far from Noah and Judith's hut. Would Alima welcome him back? Perhaps he could persuade her to come with him to Jerusalem. He became more and more anxious until finally he spurred his camel forward and yelled out. "My friends! I must ride on to see Alima."

"Ah, yes. The friend!" said Gaspar. "Are you sure that's all she is to you?" Gaspar grinned widely.

Balthazar frowned. "And whose business is it but mine if she is?"

"Sorry, sorry! I meant no offense," said Gaspar.

"Don't let the old man rile you," said Melchior. "It's his way of teasing, irritating though it is. I think we should go on to the city. What think you, Gaspar?"

"Yes. My foot is numb and oozing again. I would sorely like it tended to."

"Would you like me to do that now?" asked Balthazar. "A little delay won't mean much."

"No, you go on," said Melchior. "Bina can help with it. Go find your friend and come to us when you're done. We'll pitch our tents on the edge of the palace grounds."

Balthazar waved as he rode off. Though he'd only stayed at Noah's house a few days, he remembered the way as if it was yesterday. When he saw the place, he commanded Melwah to sit, jumped from the saddle and ran to the garden side of the house shouting. "Alima! Alima!"

The hut seemed strangely quiet. He heard no crying baby or giggling girls. Could Alima be inside weaving or sewing? He called again, "Alima!" as he pushed open the door of the rented room, but only empty space greeted him. The place looked deserted. He walked out. There were no warm embers in the fire pit. He ran to the family side of the house. "Noah! Judith!" he called out, but again got no reply.

Surely some of the neighbors must know where they are. He ran to the first hut he saw and yelled out in his best Aramaic. "Is anyone home? Anyone?" He ran from house to house, and finally found someone home, some distance from Noah's. The woman he encountered looked frightened and brandished a club.

"I mean you no harm," said Balthazar as he put his hands up and bowed. The neighbor still looked uncertain but lowered the club. "I must know." Balthazar continued. "Has something happened to Noah and his wife? And what of the Arabian woman, Alima? Do you know where she is?"

He had to repeat himself again more slowly before the woman nodded and replied. "Noah's dead. Crushed in an accident at work. Judith buried him in the potter's field."

"This is terrible news," said Balthazar putting his hand to his head. "Where have the women and children gone?"

The old lady frowned. "Most of the neighbors have gone away because of the census. The Romans want to count us for taxes, so we must travel to the towns of our fathers."

"Is that why Judith left with the children?"

"I cannot say. She is with child again. I heard she went to live with her family."

"So she won't be coming back?"

"I think not."

"When will the new baby come?"

"I think not for some months."

"Do you know the town where her family lives?"

The woman shook her head. "No. I did not know her well."

Balthazar looked grim. "And the Arabian woman? Do you know if she went with Judith?"

"I'm sorry. I didn't see them leave. That house has been empty for many weeks."

"Thank you," said Balthazar as he tried to take in the bad news.

He found the others where Melchior said they would be, camped on the outskirts of the palace grounds. Looking toward the port he noticed *The Serafina* still docked where she had been two months earlier. That's strange, thought Balthazar. Musa should have sailed by now. Was it possible Alima had gone back to the ship? His hopes rose on the thought.

Balthazar saw Asher approach and called to him. "Greetings Asher! I don't see Melchior and Gaspar; have they gone to call on the king?"

"Yes. But they won't find him. I heard from some sailors that the king left a few weeks ago for Jerusalem. I venture they'll be back when they learn the same."

"Can I ask you to feed and water my camel? I didn't find Alima where I thought she'd be, and I want to seek her near the docks. I won't be long."

"As you will."

Balthazar walked quickly to *The Serafina* and yelled up to one of the sailors from the dock. "Hey there! Is Captain Musa about? I would speak with him."

"Sorry, Balthazar! He's not back from Jerusalem, and we're all a sight worried. It's not like 'im to be so many weeks late."

"How long has he been gone?"

"He left three days after we docked and said he'd only be gone two weeks. He's more than two months late and we've missed the date for our sail to Alexandria. This has never happened afore."

"It doesn't sound like Musa. Have you sent anyone to find him?" asked Balthazar.

"Not yet, but the first mate will be leavin afore sunset."

"That's good. Can you call the mate for me? I must speak with him."

"I'll get 'im for you. Come aboard if ya like."

"Thank you." Balthazar boarded the ship and walked around its deck while he waited. There was no sign of Alima, and he knew she would have shown her face if she'd heard him. The first mate came from below carrying a pack, looking for all the world as if he'd lost his best friend. "What can I do fer ya, Balthazar? I'm in a bit of a hurry. Must leave for Jerusalem ya know."

"I heard about Musa. I'm heading to Jerusalem myself but not for a day or two. I've come to ask about Alima. Have you seen her? I thought she'd be at the house we were renting but the place is deserted."

"No, I haven't seen 'er since she left with you after we docked. I thought you were betrothed. How did you come to be separated?"

"It's a long story. But I'd like to leave a message for her. If she comes by, please ask the crew to tell her I'm going to Jerusalem and will be back. Can you do that? It's important."

"I'll leave word. The men will tell her if they see her, you can be sure of that. Good journey to you, Balthazar."

"And to you. I hope you find Musa."

"Me, too. I don't know what we'll do if I don't."

Balthazar returned to the astrologers' encampment to find Melchior and Gaspar sitting around a small fire. The look on Gaspar's face told Balthazar it was time to attend to his foot, but Gaspar put his hand up as Balthazar approached. "Yes, my foot hurts, and yes it should be cleaned. But first, you must tell us what sours your countenance so. Did you not find your friend? Or would she not speak to you? You must confide in this old astrologer if I'm to counsel you properly."

Balthazar frowned. "You are right on the first count, Gaspar. I did not find her. The owner of the house where she was boarding died some weeks ago, and the wife, Judith, left town with her children. The neighbor I spoke with has no idea where Alima went."

"Did she go with this Judith woman?"

"The neighbor couldn't say. She said the Romans have ordered a census for tax purposes that requires all Jews to return to the town of their fathers. The neighbor had no idea where that might be for Judith." "Too bad," said Gaspar. "I know how much you wanted to see your friend. But is that the only thing that worries you?"

Balthazar went on to explain Musa's disappearance.

"Two friends lost! I'm sorry to hear it. But perhaps the man is conducting business in Jerusalem and nothing is amiss."

"I suppose it's possible, but unlikely. The man's as dependable as the sun and the moon, and as timely. I fear some ill has come to him," said Balthazar with a heavy sigh.

"Each of us has an appointed time, and it could be his. But there's no use worrying, Balthazar. What will be, will be."

"My head knows that but my heart is another thing entirely. Now tell me, did you see King Herod? Or must you look for him in Jerusalem?"

"Alas!" said Gaspar. "King Herod has preceded us to Jerusalem. But our audience with him is not nearly as important as the other things we must do there."

"Such as?" asked Balthazar.

"We must speak to high priest at the Temple and find out what the prophecies foretell regarding the Messiah's birth place."

"And, we must find a holy place to lay my mother's bones," added Melchior. "She wanted to rest among her people and I hope to find a place near Jerusalem."

"When shall we move on?" asked Balthazar.

"At first light.

Two days later, the little caravan approached the Damascus Gate on the northwest side of Jerusalem. Balthazar noticed that not only was Jerusalem a walled city, but it was built atop the slope of a hill with a valley to the east. "Are we heading right to the Temple?" asked Balthazar when they were still a ways from the gate.

"First thing in the morning. Tonight, we must find a place to stay," said Melchior.

"But there are people everywhere! Why don't we camp outside the city so we don't have to waste time searching for rooms?"

"That's a thought. What do you think, Gaspar? Shall we pitch our tents out here somewhere?"

"I'd prefer a place near a stream. I'm always parched and we'll need water for the animals."

Balthazar hailed a man he saw resting by the side of the road. "Hey there! Do you know where we can find water for our animals?"

"If you follow the wall east of the city then south, you'll come to the Gihon Spring. It's in the valley not far from the eastern wall. Keep walking east."

Thanking the man for his help, they steered their animals off the road and to the east as they followed the city's northern wall. Off to their left was a hill where several crosses stood, evidence of recent Roman justice.

"I've heard of the crucifixions," said Balthazar. "But these are the first I've seen. It's gruesome even from this distance."

"Yes," said Gaspar. "That's why the Roman's leave the bodies on display, as warnings."

"Do the authorities crucify people in your country?" asked Balthazar.

"Not in Parthia. But they did in Media, where I was born. It was one memory I was glad to leave behind."

The group moved on until they got to the eastern wall, then headed south. The sky was already darkening when they found the spring and a place to camp near an olive grove. As Asher, Bina and Corinna began to pitch the tents, Balthazar and Melchior helped Gaspar from his camel. Despite their care, his wounded foot was steadily worsening, and he couldn't walk unaided. They found a spot for him under an olive tree, then helped the others with the tents and searched for kindling.

"I fear for Gaspar," said Balthazar quietly when they were beyond the man's hearing.

"As do, I," said Melchior. "We clean the foot regularly, yet it worsens. This morning I noticed an ominous purple color in his lower leg. I fear there is poison in him and I'm not sure what more we can do."

"When you get your audience with Herod, you should ask if the royal physician will see him."

"I will. Come. Bina will be waiting on these sticks for her fire. By the way, I want you to come with us when we see Herod."

"I thought you said you wouldn't need me."

"I did, but I will need your help with Gaspar. Please say you will come."

"As you wish."

CHAPTER 29
Jerusalem

§

EARLY THE NEXT MORNING, MELCHIOR, Gaspar, and Balthazar rode into Jerusalem. There was no mistaking the Temple Mount which gleamed on the heights just beyond the eastern wall. "I'll ask to speak with the chief priest when we get to the temple," said Melchior as they prodded their camels up the narrow climbing street to the Mount. "We must find out what is prophesied about the Messiah's birth place, and the Chief Priest will know better than anyone." When the road became too steep for the camels to negotiate they dismounted and found a stable.

"Excuse me, sir," said Melchior to the owner. "We've come to visit the temple. Can you tell us how we may enter?"

The man looked the threesome over from head to foot. "You are foreigners, yes?"

"Yes. We come from Parthia and Arabia," said Melchior.

The man squinted his eyes at them. "You are not Jews?"

"No, we are not," replied Melchior.

"Then you must enter through the Court of the Gentiles. But first you must immerse yourselves at the Mikveh. There is one down the street. But not you," said the man pointing to Gaspar.

"Why not me?" asked Gaspar in surprise.

"Because of your foot. I can see that it bleeds. You are unclean and may not go into the baths or near the temple. It is forbidden."

Gaspar's expression turned sour. "If I can't come with you, what would you have me do, Melchior? I will not wait in this stable with these flee ridden donkeys!"

"I will not ask you to. Especially not after your last donkey encounter," said Melchior with a frown. "Balthazar, will you escort Gaspar back to camp? I'll go on my own to the temple."

Balthazar nodded.

As the two men headed back, Melchior put his hand on the stable owner's shoulder. "Thank you for your advice. My friend's foot is not healing, and I'm glad he can rest today. Can you tell me how to find the Court of the Gentiles?"

"Through the Hulda gates on the south side of the mount. The double gate will lead you into the tunnels then up to the plaza and the Gentile Court."

"Thank you. Please feed and water my camel while I'm gone." He found the mikveh pool easily enough, and though the water felt good, he did not linger. As soon as he judged himself clean, he dried, dressed and headed to the Hulda gates. As he approached the south wall of the Mount, he saw a large wide staircase and two sets of double arched gates in the wall just beyond the stairs. He followed the jostling crowd through one of the gates into a long candle-lit tunnel. It was painted with geometric patterns, and he wondered what other artistic embellishments might await him.

The tunnel became steeper as he moved along until he was climbing a set of stone steps up and up and up. It would have been an impossible climb for Gaspar, and he was glad his friend had returned to camp. Soon he emerged into the Court of the Gentiles. It was a large open plaza completely enclosed by pillared courts. In the middle of the plaza was the temple building, set apart by a balustrade, and more stairs and walls. Rising above the walls, he could see the Holy of Holies, the highest building in the temple complex. The Ark of the Covenant had been there once, but that was before the Babylonian exile. The tablets were gone now, but the smoke of sacrifice still rose in the air; the people could still reach out to their God.

He turned, wanting to explore the grounds before he offered his own sacrifice. On the southern side of the Gentile Court was an imposing red-roofed structure. It was higher than the other three sides and supported by huge columns. He walked to its eastern edge and found a small space where he could look out over the marble wall to the Kidron valley below. What a beautiful setting! He gazed about for a long time wanting to absorb the majesty of the place.

But the squeal of animals and the bartering of the multitude pulled his attention back to the plaza which was rimmed by the tables of money changers and animal vendors. How can they operate a market in such a holy place? He wondered. The people needed to buy animals for their sacrifices, but why here? He wandered over to a moneychanger's stall and watched as men exchanged various coins for shekels and half-shekels. Apparently nothing but the shekels were accepted as payment within the temple grounds.

He could hear people bargaining for the choicest year-old lambs and the whitest turtle doves. Once the deals were struck the men led their animals and families up a staircase to an upper courtyard. He could hear singing coming from somewhere beyond its doorway near the Holy of Holies.

He got in line to change some of his money. "How much for four half-shekels?" he asked when his turn came. "Eight drachma," came the reply. He made the exchange and turned the shekels over in his hands. Within his grasp he held the means for making a pleasing sacrifice but no amount of study at his mother's knee nor knowledge of the prophecies would make up for the fact that he'd never been circumcised. How strange, he thought. In Parthia, he'd always sought to hide his Judaism but now more than anything he wanted to acknowledge it.

He walked over to a seller of lambs. "Sir, I am a gentile, but would like to offer a sacrifice. Is it permitted by the law?"

"It is. But you must bring your animal to one of the priests, and he will offer the sacrifice for you. What can I sell you?" asked the man. "I have nice choice lambs. The priests will offer up special prayers when you give a lamb like this. And I will make you a very good price."

"Will you now?" said Melchior who felt oddly defiant. He wrangled a bit before agreeing on a price. "Where should I take the lamb?" asked Melchior as he finished paying with his shekels.

"You see that sign?" The man pointed to a post near the balustrade surrounding the grand staircase.

"I see it," said Melchior. "But I'm not sure what it says."

"It says 'Under pain of death only Jews may enter here.' said the man. "You may not go beyond that balustrade. But if you pull the bell chain over there, a priest will take your animal for sacrifice."

Melchior did as the man instructed and waited patiently with his bleating lamb near a doorway in a corner of the court. It wasn't long before a young, ornately robed priest came to the doorway.

"Rabbi, I give this lamb for sacrifice in memory of my mother, Dodi, a Jewish woman of Parthia."

"I shall offer prayers in her name," said the young priest as he reached out to take the roped lamb from his grip.

"Before I release him, Rabbi, I must ask to speak with the Chief Priest. It's a matter of great importance."

"The Chief Priest! Humph! That is impossible. He's busy in the Temple, and he doesn't speak with Gentiles. Just give me the lamb and be gone!" said the young priest with growing irritation.

"You don't understand, Rabbi. I must speak with him; I have an important question to ask. Perhaps you can tell me. . ."

"I have no time to answer questions! I'm here to take the animals and that only will I do. Now give me your lamb!"

"I cannot, Rabbi! Listen, please. Perhaps I should introduce myself, I am ..."

"I don't care who you are, you foolish goy! I've work to do. So give me the lamb and leave, before I call a guard."

With his free hand, Melchior pulled a piece of papyrus from his robe and held it in front of the priest's face. "Do you see the royal seal on this letter? It's the seal of King Phraates of Parthia. He has sent me to call on King Herod, but before I do, I must speak with your High Priest. Call him now or when I see the king, I shall tell him about a certain uncooperative young priest by the goyim door."

The young priest's demeanor changed almost instantly. "Oh! Surely, you misunderstood me, sir. I'll get another priest to take your lamb, and will escort you myself to meet the high priest in a more suitable place." The priest called to someone beyond Melchior's sight. "Zechariah, can you take over for me? I must attend to a special visitor!"

Melchior watched as a kindly old priest came to the door and took hold of the lamb. "I'm happy to offer your sacrifice to the Lord, my son. Did you say you do this in memory of your mother?"

"Yes," said Melchior surprised that the old man had heard him. "Her name was Dodi, and she was a good Jewish woman, a descendant of the exiles to Babylon. She always wanted to come here . . ." his voice trailed off as his eyes began to water.

"Be at peace," said the old priest. "And be assured, the Lord will heed your sacrifice and remember your mother. Have you found a place to lay her bones?"

"Zechariah! We have no time for this!" cut in the young priest. "This man is an important guest and must see our High Priest. Just take his lamb and move along, will you?"

The old priest began to shuffle off when Melchior shouted out. "Wait, Rabbi! How did you know about my mother's bones?"

The old priest turned to face Melchior. "I just had a feeling when I saw your eyes. You cannot place her bones within Jerusalem, but you may find a goodly place in Bethlehem." Zechariah turned and walked off with the lamb before Melchior could utter another word.

The young priest closed the door behind him and waved Melchior down the staircase. "Follow me, away from this rabble."

Melchior followed the priest to a shaded area in the long red-roofed portico he had noticed earlier. "Please join me," said the priest as he sat back on a wide stone bench. "My name is Caiaphas. Who did you say you are?"

"I am Melchior of Seleucia, counselor to the satrap and King Phraates of Parthia."

"I see," said Caiaphas. "Why do you wish to speak with Chief Priest Joazar? I am one of his assistants, and will help you however I may."

"My fellow astrologers and I have traveled far in search of the Messiah. We have seen his star and followed it, but we must know what the prophets foretold about his birth."

The young priest looked surprised. "If you are Parthian, how do you know about our Messiah?"

"As I said, Rabbi, my mother was a Jew, descended from the exiles to Babylon. She raised me on the Mosaic Law and told me of the prophecies."

"Tell me about this star you have seen," said Caiaphas.

"I would be happy to, but I must insist we include the Chief Priest in our discussion," said Melchior.

"Very well," said Caiaphas with a stony expression. "Wait here. It may take some time." Caiaphas walked off as Melchior closed his eyes.

Some hours later, Melchior felt a firm hand on his shoulder and woke with a start. A group of about ten men, all priests as far as he could tell, stood before him with serious faces. The young priest Caiaphas was the first to speak. "Melchior of Seleucia, I would present to you our Chief Priest, Joazar, son of Boethus."

Melchior stood and bowed low from the waist. "Greetings, Rabbi Joazar. Thank you for coming to speak with me. I have here the seal of my King, Phraates IV of Parthia." Melchior held up his letter of commission. "King Phraates bid me and my fellow astrologers call on King Herod. But before we do, we seek your wisdom of the prophecies concerning the Messiah who is to come."

"I see only you," said Joazar. "Where are these others you speak of?"

"Gaspar and Balthazar are back at our camp. My friend, Gaspar, injured his foot and could not enter the temple because it still bleeds. He is impure."

"I see. It's good that you follow our laws!" said Joazar bobbing his head. "Caiaphas tells me you have seen a prophetic star. Tell me of this."

"About nine months ago as we observed an eclipse in the constellation of Aries the Ram, a constellation that holds portent for the people of Judea. It was still dark as the planet, Jupiter, emerged in the east as the morning star. The moon, the sun and even Saturn were all present within Aries. This drew our interest because when Jupiter and Saturn are attendants to the rising sun, there is portent of kingship. As we watched, the moon eclipsed Jupiter, and when Jupiter emerged another brilliant star emerged as well. It was unheard of and yet there it was!"

"Very interesting," said Joazar. "But what made you think it was the star announcing our long awaited Messiah?"

"For two reasons. Not only did the star appear in an unusual way, but we soon realized it was moving to the west, toward Judea. It didn't move swiftly, but slowly and steadily, as if it was asking to be followed. And then there were the dreams."

"What dreams?" asked Joazar.

"My friend, Gaspar, who heads the astrology school is the son of a Magi priest. His people are well known for interpreting dreams, and on the night following the star's appearance, both Gaspar and I had the *very same dream*. In it, a glowing man in white spoke to us. He said: *Do not be afraid. I am a messenger of the Lord on high. Today you have seen His star in the Heavens. Follow it. For the scepter shall not depart from Judah, nor the ruler's staff from between his feet, until tribute comes to him.* So we made plans for our journey and when King Phraates made us his official delegation to Herod, we left in haste."

"Our people have awaited the Messiah for centuries. If what you say is true, a new era of power and glory will come to Judea. What questions do you have for me?" asked Joazar.

"The star has brought us here but we don't know what the prophets foretold about the Messiah's place of birth. What can you tell me?" asked Melchior.

Joazar nodded. "Seven hundred years ago our prophet Micah said: "But you, Bethlehem, least among the clans of Judah, From you shall come forth for me one who is to be ruler in Israel; whose origin is from old, from ancient times. Therefore the Lord will give them up until the time when she who is to give birth has borne, and he shall take his place as shepherd by strength of the Lord . . . his greatness shall reach to the ends of the earth."

"Where is this town, Bethlehem?" asked Melchior realizing that the old priest, Zechariah, had also mentioned it.

"It's in the hills about two leagues south of here," said Joazar.

"Thank you. I will go with my companions immediately after our audience with King Herod."

"Perhaps I can help with your audience," said Joazar. "Caiaphas, go now to the king's palace. Tell him I have an important visitor and that we must see him. Bid him receive Melchior and his friends with me, on the morrow, if it please him to do so." Caiaphas ran off. "I'll send my messenger to you as soon as I know when the king will see us. Where can we find you?"

"We're camped outside the eastern gate near an olive grove in the Kidron Valley. We have three tents and many camels."

"I know the place. I'll send my messenger as soon as I have news." Joazar whirled around and walked off, his priestly retinue trailing at his heels.

Melchior left the temple grounds and returned as quickly as he could to his camp. After relaying the news of his visit, he called Asher to him. "Asher, I have an important task for you. You must leave immediately for a little town called Bethlehem. It's in the hills about two leagues south of here. I want you to scout around quietly. You must look for a baby boy, born within the last few months."

Asher looked at Melchior. "I can do that, sir. But then what? Should I come back here? And what if there's more than one child? There could be several born within the last months. What then?"

"Good questions all. This baby will be special. The star that has brought us here is special so I want you to look for . . . unusual things. I can't tell you what they may be, but you'll know. When you find the baby, pay him homage, for he will be a great king someday. And afterward, wait for us on the road outside Bethlehem. I expect we will be there within a day or two, as soon as possible after we see Herod."

"I can do that," said Asher, still looking uncertain. "Do you have any idea where the babe may be found? Or the names of his parents?"

"None. You must search out every possible place, houses, inns, wherever a family might live. If you can find the village midwives, they might be able to direct you to anyone them have helped."

"Very well," said Asher. "I'll need some food and water."

"Yes, of course. Bina! Prepare a pack for Asher. Enough for a few days, and quickly please! He's going on a short journey and we'll be joining him soon."

As soon as Asher left, Melchior called everyone together. "I have grave concerns, my friends. Due to the ass of a priest I met at the Temple, I was forced to announce our commission from Phraates. It was the only way I could think to see the chief priest and learn more about the prophecies."

"Why should that give you concern?" asked Balthazar. "You would have announced your commission to Herod eventually."

"Yes, but I didn't want him to know of our search for the Messiah. He already suspects rebellion lurks in every corner. What his jealous mind will stir up at the news of another king I dare not imagine. He's an evil man, and we must be ready to leave for Bethlehem immediately after we see him."

"But that's likely to be at night, and the roads are unknown to us! Are you willing to risk the possibility of robbery or worse?" asked Balthazar

"I fear we have no choice. Now that the Chief Priest is arranging our audience, Herod will know of our search for the Messiah. It wouldn't surprise me if that arrogant priest Caiaphas shouts it from the rooftops just to make himself look important."

"Would it not occur to this priest that Herod's jealousy will be stoked when he considers what the Messiah's kingship may mean to his dynasty?"

"I don't think so. Caiaphas struck me as a selfish man. He sees and hears only what behooves his interests."

"Even if it means endangering the new king ordained by God and prophecy?" asked Gaspar.

"Even then."

"Then I understand your concern," said Balthazar. "What must we do?"

"We must break camp as soon as we hear from Joazar's messenger, and establish a meeting place outside the western wall. Bina and Corinna can watch over our belongings while we meet with Herod. Then we'll join them and make haste to Bethlehem."

"Will the women be safe alone? Perhaps I should stay with them?" asked Balthazar.

Melchior frowned. "I want you with us. I told the priest to expect three of us, so three of us there will be."

"As you wish," said Balthazar with a sigh.

When the sun was midway across the sky the next day, a messenger approached on horseback calling out Melchior's name. "Melchior! Melchior of Seleucia!"

"Over here!" he yelled in return. "I am Melchior of Seleucia."

The man drew near and spoke from his saddle. "Rabbi Joazar, sends his greetings. He said King Herod will see you and your fellows at sunset today. Joazar will meet you at the Phasael Tower before sunset to escort you."

"How will we know which is the Phasael Tower? I saw several when I was at the temple yesterday," said Melchior.

"It's the largest of the three towers north of the palace. You'll find it easily." The messenger rode off as quickly as he'd come.

"Well, my friends!" said Melchior looking to Gaspar and Balthazar. "We've an appointment with King Herod, so let us make haste. But first we should bathe, and make ourselves presentable. We cannot see the king stinking like the mangy dogs we look."

"Speak for yourself!" said Gaspar. "My foot is the only part of me that stinks. The rest of me still looks like a Grecian god. Don't I look the stuff of dreams, Balthazar?"

"Not of mine!" said Balthazar laughing.

"I should hope not! More likely it's your lady friend, Alima? Or has our mysterious man in white finally come to you?"

"Still no man in white for me," said Balthazar. "As for Alima, my dreams of her remain fleeting. She comes and goes in them ere I can say a word. How would you interpret such dreams, Gaspar?"

"Our dreams are strange and amazing things, my friend! They can be the bridge to the nether world, or to the gods, or to our deepest desires. My interpretation? The fact that you dream of her at all is telling. She comes and goes? That means she is just beyond your reach. You seek her because you want her. And you would speak with her or you wouldn't notice that you can't say a word. You want my counsel?"

"Surprisingly, I do."

Gaspar nodded. "So be it. Think well on what you will say to her 'ere the time comes when you have the chance."

Balthazar nodded in a thoughtful way, then rose and walked off to wash himself in the stream.

"He has much to consider," said Gaspar.

"Yes, he does," agreed Melchior. "Come. Let me help you to the stream."

CHAPTER 30

A Shepherd Leads the Way

§

ASHER GUIDED HIS CAMEL WITH speed toward Bethlehem. There was no direct route, so he travelled west then south at the first fork, and by late afternoon was on the outskirts of the village. He slowed his camel to observe the place. Bethlehem was built on a hill with rocky outcroppings that suggested there might be many caves in the area. This is good, thought Asher, for he hoped to find a cave to sleep in come sundown. He could also see many sheep roaming the fields to the east. I'll go that way when I'm done searching the town he thought. Maybe I can find some fellow shepherds willing to share their fire with me.

As soon as he entered the town he dismounted, reasoning it would be easier to look through open doorways as he searched for the baby. He walked slowly, up and down each winding little road, watching, listening. The village was crowded like Jerusalem, and he began to realize how difficult a task he'd taken on. How was he ever going to find one particular baby when there were so many people about? He looked for the signs of babies. Swaddling clothes hung to dry outside a hut. Mothers singing in low tones. Babies crying. Each time he heard what sounded like a baby he would dawdle near a doorway waiting to hear if the baby's name was mentioned. Was it a boy or a girl's name? He tried not to draw attention to himself, but it was difficult. More than once the man of the house caught him watching and yelled at him to move on. What a discouraging task! The sought-for baby could be inside someplace sound asleep and he would never know it!

Melchior had told him to watch for the unusual, so all the while he stayed alert. What should he be watching for? Melchior had said he would know when he saw it, but he wasn't so sure. Several hours passed and he'd seen nothing out of the ordinary and no baby boys of the age he sought. Frustrated and tired, he decided to look for a place to spend the night as the sun set behind the western hills. He would begin again come morning by searching out the local midwives.

At the far reaches of the village, the sun was setting, yet the sky still seemed bright. How can it be, he wondered? A few moments later after the sun had set, it still wasn't dark. Looking up, he realized a star was casting its light directly over the village. Was it Gaspar and Melchior's star? It might be, but it seemed much closer and brighter than it had been during their journey, almost as if he could reach out and touch it.

He headed toward the fields of sheep he'd seen earlier where he knew he'd feel at home. Past tufts of high grass and low trees he plodded with his camel until he saw a group of five shepherds gathered round a fire. He waved and shouted, "Greetings!" in his best Aramaic. Balthazar had taught him a little of the local language, and he wanted to remember all he had learned. He stopped several paces away, put his hands up and bowed. "I'm a shepherd, too. I have food to share. May I join you?"

One of the shepherds motioned him over, and rose to greet him. "Come, lad. The night is cool and the fire is warm. Did you say you have food to share?"

"Yes," said Asher as he tied his camel's reigns to a nearby bush. "I have some food in my pack. Let me get it."

"This is good," said the old shepherd. "The rabbits were too quick for us today and our stomachs are growling."

"I'm happy to share what I have," said Asher as he squatted down to lay out the food Bina had packed for him.

"Such a cool night," said the old shepherd as he raised his hands toward the fire.

"It is cool. But not as cold as my hills in fall."

"And where might your hills be, lad?"

"In Parthia, south of Seleucia."

"Parthia? That's a far distance. What brings you to our country?"

"I came with some friends in search of a special baby and it took us five months to get here."

"A special baby? Is that so?" the old shepherd stroked his beard. "What's your name boy?"

"Asher."

"Welcome, Asher. I am Josiah. Your food looks good, but are you sure you want to share it all? This is a hungry lot you see before you!"

"I can see that," said Asher as the others eyed his food. "I'm glad for your company and to share your fire. So, please tell them to help themselves." He started to munch on a piece of salt-dried fish and poured himself some water from his canteen. Josiah motioned for the others to partake and the men who had watched him curiously began to help themselves.

"Now about this special baby. Is it a boy child you seek?" asked Josiah.

"Yes," said Asher swallowing some fish.

"How do you know he is special?" asked Josiah. "And what makes you think he'll be born in Bethlehem?"

"I know very little of him. But my friends are astrologers, and they have studied the prophecies. They found a star in the heavens they say foretells the baby's birth. They call him ..."

"The Messiah! Yes, we know."

Asher stopped eating and looked at Josiah. "You know the baby we're looking for? You know the Messiah?"

"Yes. We know him. We saw him on the night of his birth. It was a wondrous night, not many days past. Would you like to see him too?"

"Oh Yes!" said Asher excitedly. "But wait . . . how do you know it's really him? I was walking through town earlier and there are many babies in Bethlehem. How do you know this baby is the Messiah?"

"Because of what we *saw*. It was two weeks ago tonight that we sat round this fire. The night was very still. We heard no birdsong, no wolves, and no wind at first. Then the wind began to blow, just a little rustle at first then greater and greater. It whipped up the fire in our pit. The flames twisted and whirled high into the sky as if it was dancing. As it settled down, we heard much birdsong, which never happens after dark. It was as loud as dawn! Then we heard voices singing. Beautiful voices! First one, then two, then a multitude. I'll never forget it. The most beautiful harmonies! Moving, lilting, rising, falling on the wind."

"Out here in the dark of night? Who was singing?" asked Asher sounding mystified.

"That was the strangest part. The singing came from the sky itself! We looked all around and saw only a star. So bright and so close! Then we saw him - the angel of the Lord. He was dressed all in white and appeared before us just beyond the fire, glowing like a star himself. We were sore afraid and fell with our heads to the ground."

"What happened then?" asked Asher in amazement.

"We would have stayed like that all night, but the angel told us not to be afraid, so we looked up. His hands were stretched out to us, friendly like, and he had a huge smile on his face. He said: *'Behold, I proclaim to you good news of great joy that will be for all the people. For today in the city of David a savior has been born for you who is Messiah and Lord. And this will be a sign for you: you will find an infant wrapped in swaddling clothes and lying in a manger.'*"

"We wondered at his words. We've heard the prophecies of a Messiah since we were children, but never thought we'd live to see it. The angel disappeared before our eyes, but then we heard voices! Many voices coming from the sky praising God. They said. *"Glory to God in the highest and on earth peace to those on whom his favor rests."* It was unbelievable, and we knew we had to find the baby right away."

"How did you find him?"

"We followed the singing. The voices led us to a cave where we heard a baby crying. Come, we will take you to him."

CHAPTER 31

A Date with King Herod

§

IN JERUSALEM, MELCHIOR, GASPAR AND Balthazar waited on their camels outside the Phasael Tower. They had no trouble finding the place built as it was upon the western wall in the highest part of the city. After washing and primping for their audience they had taken down their tents, packed and ridden to the western side of the city. The women would wait for them there, on the other side of the wall from where they waited now, across the square from Herod's palace.

"Gaspar, would you like to do the talking or shall I?" asked Melchior.

"I was ready for that task, but am much in pain. Would you mind doing the honors?"

"Not at all," said Melchior. "But we should discuss it, to be sure we are in agreement. I think we should try to keep the visit short. Just long enough to be cordial. We can present the gifts as we leave. And remember; we're not Herod's astrologers, nor his counselors. We have no obligation to toady or help him with his political problems. If he asks us for such we shall sweetly demur."

"I agree completely. I trust you'll say as little as possible about our search for the Messiah?" asked Gaspar.

Melchior smiled. "You may depend on it. I hoped he would not learn of it, but that is impossible now."

As they finished speaking, three men approached them from the Mariamne Tower across the court. "That's Chief Priest Joazar in the middle," whispered Melchior to his companions. "The young priest to his right is Caiaphas. I don't know the other."

"Good evening, Melchior," said Joazar.

"Good Evening, Rabbi. Caiaphas. It is my pleasure to present my fellow astrologers, Gaspar and Balthazar."

"Good evening," said Joazar. "You may dismount here. My servant, Ben, will take your camels to the king's stable."

"Very well," said Melchior. He and Balthazar proceeded to dismount, then assisted Gaspar. "Will we have far to walk?" asked Melchior.

"We enter the palace at that door, but the king will receive us in the Caesareum at the other end of the palace. It's a fair walk."

"Then might we call for a chair? Gaspar has trouble walking."

"Assuredly. I will call for one as soon as we enter."

"Very good." Melchior looked to Gaspar. "Come, my friend. Let us help you." With Gaspar between himself and Balthazar, the three men made their way slowly across the stone courtyard to the palace entrance, where the great doors opened immediately. Joazar spoke with the head servant as soon as they entered. "Fetch a chair and two carriers for our guest."

Melchior surveyed his surroundings as they waited for Gaspar's chair. The walls were built of white marble, all cut exactly alike and so finely secured that the seams between the slabs were hard to see. Beautiful paintings adorned the upper walls and ceiling which was vaulted so high he had to strain his neck to see it all.

Within moments two slaves came running with a gilded chair lift which they set on the floor for Gaspar. As soon as Melchior helped him mount it, Joazar clapped his hands. "The king awaits us in Caesar's wing. We must not keep him waiting." Then he led the way through the palace.

The place was aglow with candlelight and torches, and Melchior marveled at the sheer number of rooms and the quality of workmanship that had gone into the building and its furnishings. They passed atriums and gardens, bed chambers and eating areas, porticos and pools, small groves of trees bounded by canals, ornamented walkways and dove-courts filled with tame pigeons. The entire palace was filled with furnishings embellished with glittering stones of every color and size, brazen statuary and ornate columns and pillars. As far as he could tell, the two wings of the palace appeared to be mirror images of each other, separated by a large courtyard and circular pools. He continued to gaze around until Joazar raised his right hand, and the chair carriers set Gaspar down in what appeared to be a huge dining hall. He helped Gaspar from the lift, and the audience began.

"Hail to you, my king!" said Joazar bowing low before Herod's throne.

"Hail to you, great king!" mimicked Caiaphas.

"Ah! Chief Priest Joazar, and the groveling one, so good of you to come. I see you have brought honored guests from afar. Please, present yourselves." Herod waved them forward. "There is no need for shyness."

Again supporting Gaspar, the three astrologers walked forward together, linked in a human chain of friendship. When they were within ten paces of Herod, they bowed as one. As agreed, Melchior took the lead. "King Herod, we come in peace, a delegation of King Phraates IV of Parthia. Truly, now that we have seen Jerusalem, and your wonderful achievements in Caesarea, we understand how well deserved is your title 'Herod the Great'. I am Melchior of Seleucia. And these are my friends and fellow astrologers: Gaspar of Media and Balthazar of The Hadramaut Kingdom in Arabia. Together we serve as astrologers and counselors to King Phraates. Thank you for receiving us." The threesome bowed again.

Herod came down from his throne with some difficulty and walked over to them, now joined by Joazar and Caiaphas. "Come sit, gentlemen. You have come a long way, so rest and be comfortable." He wore a pained expression but led the way to a cluster of couches. After reclining carefully, the king spread his fingers out in a fanlike gesture. "Join me! Wine for us all, Caiaphas! Quickly! Something must help this pain in my lower regions and today it will be wine."

Melchior laughed to himself watching the priest forced to play the part of a servant. He could tell Caiaphas wasn't happy, but he felt no pity for him. The priest poured wine from a silver vessel into glasses on the huge dining table and brought them one by one to each man, serving the king last with a low bow.

"Now tell me about Phraates," said Herod. "How is your sovereign?"

"He is well, your majesty," said Melchior.

"Is he enjoying the slave girl Augustus sent him? She is very beautiful."

"Thermusa is his queen now, and she has made herself indispensable to the king. And her son, Phraataces, has grown into a strong young man."

"Strong enough to be your next king?"

"That is doubtful, your majesty. He has several older brothers in line to inherit before him."

"So you say. But one never knows what can happen to brotherly relations, isn't that right, Joazar?"

"That is true, your majesty. Accidents, pestilence, war; unexpected death may intervene at any time."

Herod smiled. "And motherly intervention, yes?

Joazar put his hands up in a sign of indecision. "I suppose it is possible that a mother's love could . . . change the line of succession."

Herod cupped his chin with his hand. "I met Thermusa years ago. Yes, that one bears watching. But tell me, why has Phraates sent you to me? Before the Pax Romana he was one of my enemies."

"I know that, your majesty," said Melchior. "But King Phraates has become an admirer in the years since. He has great respect for those who secure prosperity for their people. And Phraates knows how hard it can be when the forces of rebellion swirl and provoke from within."

"Is that so? Perhaps, like me, Phraates has encountered his own share of rebellion? It is the only way he would understand the difficulties I face. Even within my own family! But I don't let minor difficulties with relations blur my vision. You may tell your king that I hold him in regard as well."

"I shall be happy to, your majesty. And may I tell him the reason for your esteem?"

"You may, indeed. He has done an admirable job of controlling the trade routes from China. His coffers must be over-flowing with the wealth of it. Of course, he is descended from a line of clever men. His father, Orodes, defeated my friends, the Romans, some years back. Not an easy thing to do."

"Quite right, your majesty. When you were a mere child, Orodes defeated Crassus at Carrhae. But your friends were smart enough not to try it again."

"The Romans are clever men, too, and I've learned over the years that a man would be foolish not to value their alliance. But let us speak of another matter. What's this I hear from Joazar, that you seek knowledge of the Messiah prophecies? That you search for the place of his birth? Tell me more."

Melchior nodded. "We have seen an unusual star, your majesty. One that may portend the long awaited Messiah."

Herod's face hardened, as he turned to face Joazar. "You are the High Priest. Can this be true? Do the prophecies say that a star will announce the Messiah's coming?"

Joazar appeared confused as if not sure how to reply. "Some say so, your majesty. Others think the star refers to the messiah himself. It is hard to be sure."

"I see," said Herod, squinting his eyes. He looked back to Melchior. "And why is King Phraates interested in honoring the Jewish Messiah? I would not have thought it to be of interest to him. After all, I hear he is not especially welcoming of Jews in his kingdom. He wouldn't be trying to subvert my rule, by allying himself with a pretender to my throne?"

Melchior could see the tone of the audience becoming hostile. He must not allow it. "Not at all your majesty! I told you, King Phraates honors you greatly. If what you say were true, would we announce ourselves? Would we bear you gifts? No! I tell you we saw a star which as astrologers we believe holds portent for the kingdom of Judea. Of course, there is another possibility. I heard in Caesarea that one of your concubines is ready to give birth. Is this true?"

Herod's face softened. "It is. My physician attends her now in Caesarea. But what has that to do with anything?"

Melchior adjusted his body on the couch so that the king might feel his full attention. "Because, your majesty, we deal in forecasts which are always subject to revision depending on the movements of the celestial bodies. It's entirely possible the star does not portend the messiah, but the birth of your son, the future king of Judea."

Herod smiled. "What an interesting thought! I must consult with my own astrologers on this. Still, if your first prediction is correct . . ." Herod ran his tongue along the edge of his wine glass. "The birth of the Messiah would be a momentous occasion for all of Judea? Isn't that right, Joazar?"

Joazar nodded. "Yes, your majesty. It would usher in a time of great power and glory for all Judea, in which you would surely share."

"Share, Joazar? I thought you knew me better. I am not much accustomed to *sharing*. But, if there is a new Jewish king born in Judea, I too would like to honor him, as I honor any sovereign. What do the prophecies say, Joazar, about the Messiah's birth?"

"Seven hundred years ago the prophet Micah said: *But you, Bethlehem, least among the clans of Judah, From you shall come forth for me one who is to be ruler in Israel; whose origin is from old, from ancient times.*

Herod raised his brows. "Bethlehem eh? It's a little backwater of a town, but the great King David came from there after all, did he not?" asked Herod rhetorically.

"He did, your majesty," said Caiaphas.

"I did not mean for you to answer that, you idiot," said Herod pointing a crooked finger into the young priest's face. "Be quiet or you shall join my son, Antipater, in the tower." Caiaphas looked down in embarrassment and retreated to a corner of the room where he sat silent and sulking. How wonderful, thought Melchior. To see that arrogant priest receive a heaping dose of humiliation seemed right, even if it did come at the hands of Herod.

"Come, let us enjoy some repast," said the king. "I have prepared a small feast in your honor. But you must promise to return to me after you find this Messiah. Tell me where he is, so I too may go and bear him homage. Will you do that?"

"Most certainly, your majesty!" said Melchior bowing. But he looked away as he walked to the table. *Does he think me mad? Telling him where he can find the messiah would be like escorting a wolf into the pen of a captive lamb.*

He followed the king and the others to a low dining table where they reclined on couches while the servants poured wine and brought plates full of choice meats, cheese, fruits and grains. *I must distract him,* thought Melchior. Gently, he moved the conversation in new directions, inviting Gaspar and Balthazar to join in. They spoke with Joazar and the king on topics of general interest but eschewed further talk of politics or the Messiah. The Judean countryside, the conditions of the roads, their caravansary experience, and the beauty of the temple were all discussed in varying detail. Caiaphas sat next to Joazar but remained silent throughout, and when the meal was over, was the first to excuse himself.

"I must leave, your majesty," said the young priest. "I must be in the temple early tomorrow."

"Well, don't let us keep you," said Herod.

"I must leave as well," said Joazar. "We thank you for your hospitality, my king! Be assured we will inform you as soon as we have any news from Bethlehem."

"Will you be going there yourself?" asked Herod.

"No. I have responsibilities here, but I will send one of my men."

"Good! Then I can expect to hear from both of you!" said Herod pointing to Melchior and Joazar.

"For good or bad, you shall hear from me," said Joazar. "I want to make sure the child is not some imposter put forward by a family looking for riches and influence. We have not waited all these centuries to fulfill the prophecies only to have some pretender usurp the power of the true Messiah."

"I couldn't have said it better myself," said Herod smiling. "Melchior, will you and your friends be departing as well?"

"Yes, your majesty. But first we would express our thanks with some gifts." He pulled out a piece of beautiful purple cloth, which had been rolled up and tucked within a fold of his robe. "For you, your majesty, from King Phraates. And this." He handed over a small purse of polished jade gem stones. "You have many gems in your palace, but this jade may hold special properties."

The king emptied the stones into his hand and rolled them around. "They are lovely. What properties do you speak of?"

"They are known for their healing power, your majesty. You must place your favorite stone between two purple candles and let the candles burn for a spell. Afterward, when you carry the stone as an amulet, it may auger healing."

"Thank you! I need healing," said Herod. "I have been much afflicted of late."

"May I make a special request, your majesty?" asked Melchior. "Gaspar injured his foot some days ago and like you has been in great pain. Do you have a physician in the palace who might attend him?"

"Your Majesty, it is not necessary," said Gaspar looking surprised and angered by the request.

"I'm sorry, but your request is impossible. My physician is in Caesarea tending to my concubine. I hope he returns soon, for I require him myself! I am in grave pain, which seems to worsen by the day."

"I'm sorry to hear that, your majesty," said Gaspar with a sigh. "Let us hope the child she bears you is healthy and hardy."

"Yes. That is my hope. I shall await your return from Bethlehem. And if my physician is back by then, and in my pleasure, I shall have him look at your foot."

The group walked out in the same stately procession as they had come, with Gaspar held high in the chair and Caiaphas preceding them all out the door.

They left the city by the western gate, rejoining Bina and Corinna where they had left them. "Did you encounter any trouble?" asked Melchior.

"No, Master," said Bina. "Everything was quiet. Some soldiers rode by but no-one else."

"Good. Then to Bethlehem we go! See there! Our star shines bright as ever."

"It looks close, doesn't it? Like it's dropped lower in the heavens," said Balthazar.

"Like a baby drops in the womb before he comes," said Bina.

"Only a woman could think of that!" said Gaspar. "But it's a curious comparison, considering the reason we follow the star. Melchior, what did you think of Joazar's comments about the Messiah? I could understand him wanting to send a man to Bethlehem. But it seemed strange that he's already questioning if the child may be an imposter."

"I agree," said Melchior. "If the child is questioned by the leadership of his own people, the prospects for his reign will not be good. As for Herod, I have no doubt that he'll try to dispose of any competition. We must make haste to find the babe before they do!"

Some two hours later the little caravan was on the outskirts of Bethlehem looking for Asher. The star's light made it easy to scan the roadside and before they had passed the pillared guidepost of the town, Asher came riding toward them waving and hooting.

"I've found him! I've found him!"

"Excellent!" said Melchior. "You've done well my boy. Is it far?"

"No. His family is living in a cave at the edge of the village."

"A cave? The future king of Judea?" asked Melchior. "That doesn't sound like the kind of place where I thought we'd find him."

"They said it was the only place they could find. The village is crowded because of the census."

"Well, what are we waiting for? Lead the way!" said Gaspar.

Asher circled his camel around and led them into the fields where his shepherd friends tended their sheep. He waved to Josiah and a few others as they continued on.

"You've made friends already?" asked Balthazar. "That didn't take you long."

"They were the ones who brought me to him," said Asher. "I'd still be searching if not for them." They rode along the edge of a stream until they came to a cave on the edge of the village. Asher put his right hand up to slow the procession. "The babe may be sleeping. Let's dismount here lest we wake him."

Asher had called the place a cave, but to Melchior it looked more a stable. In front of its wide low entrance lay two donkeys, several milking cows, a few goats and an old dog, but he heard no mewing or barking and surprisingly sniffed no stink. In fact, the place gave off a fragrant aroma like the jasmine tea Bina often made.

As the group commanded their camels to koosh, a man emerged from the cave. "What have we here, Asher? Are these the astrologer friends you spoke of?"

"Yes, Joseph!" said Asher with a wide smile. "The short one is Melchior, the tall one is Gaspar, and the dark, good looking one is Balthazar." The three men bowed in sequence.

"What an interesting description," said Melchior.

"But so true!" added Gaspar. "And you would be?"

"Joseph. The father of the babe you seek. My wife, Mary, is nursing him inside."

"It is with great joy that we greet you, Joseph! We have travelled very far in search of your son," said Melchior.

"So Asher has told me, but in truth, I don't understand how it can be. Perhaps you can explain it when Mary is ready to receive you?"

Melchior smiled. "With pleasure. But it is late, perhaps we should wait 'til morning?

"No, the night is young, and you forget that we're new parents. The night often becomes day, if the babe so wills it. I'll call you as soon as Mary takes him from her breast."

Melchior bowed. "Very well. Would it be acceptable for us to pitch our tents out here? We promise not to disturb you."

"By all means. You will surely not be noisier than the animals! Besides, we'll be happy of the company. It's been a while since Mary has had a woman her age to talk to."

Melchior helped Gaspar get settled under a nearby palm tree as Balthazar, Asher and the women began to set up camp. "Let me help you," said Joseph, bending to help Melchior pull one of the tent skins taut. "This is always easier with extra hands."

"It surely is," said Melchior with a smile. Before long, all three tents were standing and a fire was burning in a pit.

"Mary's ready to receive you, now," announced Joseph soon after.

"We'll be right there." Melchior went to his saddlebag and withdrew a canister of frankincense and a bag of gold.

"Let me carry something," said Gaspar. "I may be lame but my hands still work."

"I have something to give as well," said Balthazar, holding up a silver canister. "It's very high quality myrrh."

"Fitting gifts all," said Melchior. He approached quietly, trying to judge the capacity of the shelter. The entrance was about nine paces wide, but it looked much longer inside, so he proceeded slowly and solemnly as he thought befitting. When he could see everyone had entered, he greeted the baby's mother, Mary, who looked to be about Corinna's age. "Good lady, thank you for welcoming us at such a late hour."

Before she could say a word, he knelt on bended knee before her and her son, as the rest followed suit behind him. "I am Melchior of Seleucia. In the name of the most-high God, who led us with a star, we bear homage to your son, the Messiah!"

"Thank you. But I must ask you, how did you come to know we were here? And why do you think my son is the Messiah?"

"My mother, Dodi, was descended from the exiles to Babylon. She taught me about the law, the prophets and the prophecies. When Gaspar and I saw an unusual star, we thought it might be the sign that augured his coming. And then, of course we had the dreams."

"What dreams?" asked Joseph who sat at Mary's side.

"The night after we saw the star, Gaspar and I had dreams. They were so unusual that we were prompted to speak of them. In our dreams, a glowing man in white said he was a messenger of the Lord, and that we should follow the star we'd seen in the heavens. You can imagine our astonishment when we realized we'd both had the same dream!"

"Was that the reason for your journey?" asked Mary.

"Yes. That and the fact that when she died, my mother asked me to inter her bones in the land of her ancestors. I have her ossuary with me still."

"I'm sure you will find a good place for her before you return."

"I must. But tonight, I give glory to the Lord who led us to your son. May his kingdom reign in glory and peace forever as the prophets foretold. In his honor, I bear a gift of the finest frankincense." He set the canister down in front of the manger where the baby lay sleeping, then sat on the straw-covered floor nearby.

Gaspar limped forward with difficulty. "Greetings, Mary and Joseph. I too thank you for receiving us. I am Gaspar, son of a Magi priest, and counselor to the king of Parthia. With Melchior, I studied the prophecies and followed the star. With a happy heart, I do him homage and offer you this gold. I hope it will be useful as he grows." He placed the bag next to the frankincense and sat down next to Melchior.

Finally, Balthazar approached. "My greetings to you both. I am Balthazar of Arabia. I am no special person, but I honor your son, because I too was drawn here by the star and a prophecy Melchior told me: *For a child is born to us, a son is given to us; upon his shoulder dominion rests. They name him Wonder-Counselor, God-Hero, Father-forever, Prince of Peace.* I have heard of many kings but none that truly seek peace. Power and riches? Yes. But peace forever? Such a king will be a true blessing to his people. So I honor him in the hope that his kingship will be a light to all nations. Please accept this canister of myrrh as a sign of my good will."

A bright smile lit Mary's face as she reached to pick up the sleeping baby. "On behalf of my son, Jesus, and my husband, I thank you for your gifts and fine words. We are poor people, and I don't know how this kingship you speak of will come to be. But I trust in the Lord, for He has done great things for me. I too have seen a messenger of the Lord. A glowing man in white. And Joseph, well, he can tell you about his dream later. The Lord is watching is over us, of that I have no doubt. I see there are some women among you. May I greet them as well?"

"Bina, Corinna, please come," said Melchior. "Mary and Joseph want to meet you." The women walked forward and bowed before Mary, announcing their names in turn.

"I am happy to meet you," said Mary. "Would you like to see my son?"

"Oh yes!" said Corinna bending down to touch the baby's fingers. "He beautiful baby. Can I hold?"

"Of course. If you sit down, I'll hand him to you."

Corinna held him carefully, cooing and laughing as Bina sat next to her, quietly waiting her turn. After a little time, Mary asked Bina, "Would you like to hold him too?"

"If I may."

"But surely," said Mary, who moved the baby from one woman to the other.

"Good little boy child!" said Bina, who was all smiles. "See how he watches me, Melchior? Just like you did as a baby."

"Were you Melchior's nurse when he was born?" asked Mary.

"Yes. I was a young girl when Melchior's father bought me in Samaria. Melchior's family has been very good to me. But this! Getting to hold the little king, this I will never forget."

"I'm glad," said Mary. "Joseph, do we have any food or drink to share with our guests?"

"Unfortunately we have only a small rabbit. It's not much but we can certainly share it."

"Thank you, but we're not hungry, are we?" Gaspar looked to Melchior and Balthazar.

"Not me," said Melchior.

"Nor me," said Balthazar. "Though I dare not speak for the others."

"Corinna and I ate as we waited for you in Jerusalem," said Bina. "Besides it will be morning soon."

"I saw some plump pheasant in the field as I watched for you today," said Asher. "Come daylight, I can try to catch a few to roast with the rabbit."

"A good thought. Let's wait for morning to eat," said Gaspar. "But I am parched! Do you have any water, Joseph?"

"Our pail is almost empty, Joseph," said Mary. "Can you fetch some?"

"I'll go," said Balthazar. "If you can point me to the well."

Joseph nodded. "Follow the path to the right, into the village and past the inn. The well is only a little further on in the square. Here's our pail.

"Good," said Balthazar as he took the pail from Joseph. "I'll be back soon."

CHAPTER 32

Balthazar Goes to the Well

BALTHAZAR MADE HIS WAY ALONG the path past the inn. The night was calm, the air was warm, and despite their hurried departure from Jerusalem, he felt unexpectedly at ease. He hadn't found Alima, and he worried about Musa, but those concerns seemed small compared with the events of this night. Two Kings! He'd been with *two* kings, as different from each other as birth from death. He hadn't wanted to meet Herod, yet it had happened, and the man had lived up to his reputation. Herod had demeaned and threatened the obsequious Caiaphas with a pleasure bordering on delight, and despite his stated intention to honor the Messiah had agreed with Joazar's suspicions that the child could be a pretender. Balthazar was glad when the audience ended.

The infant was an entirely different kind of king, if in fact a king he was. Balthazar had come with no expectations of the Messiah, and if his companions had any, they had surely been tossed to the wind. What kind of king is born in a cave? And to such poor parents? If the child was destined for kingship it was surely as unusual as the star that had guided them here. Yet, he found himself wanting to believe. In the prophecies, the dreams and the child.

When he got to the well he set Joseph's leather pail down on the rock ledge. The place was silent except for the water wheel that creaked as he lowered the rope and its skin bucket into the depths. He waited to hear it splash, pulled it up and poured the water into Joseph's pail. Realizing it was only half full, he lowered the rope once again.

"Come back, Rebecca! Please come back! I didn't mean it!"

The child's voice jarred him. He turned his head to see who might be calling when he felt a sudden jolt from behind. "Whoa, little one!" He said, letting go of the rope. "Who are you running from so late at night?"

My sister!" said the little girl sniffling. "She was mean to me. She pushed me out of the bed we were sharing!"

Balthazar pulled a cloth from his tunic, and squatted down to wipe her dirt and tear smudged face. "I'm sure she didn't mean to hurt your feelings."

"Yes she did! She always teases me."

"What does she say to tease you?"

"She says my ears are big! It's mean, and I don't like it!"

Balthazar patted her on her shoulder. "It is mean, but she's wrong. I think you have beautiful ears."

"You do?"

"Yes, I do. And I think your name is lovely too. Is it Rebecca?"

"Yes."

"Rebecca is a beautiful name. What's your sister's name?"

"Miriam."

Balthazar looked at the child more closely. "Miriam? Do you have a little brother named, Isaac?"

"Yes."

"And your mother is Judith?"

The little girl sucked her breath in. "Yes but . . . she's dead! Just like my poppa."

Balthazar frowned, and wrapped his arms around her as sobs wracked her little body. "It's all right, Rebecca. I cried when my momma died, too."

Rebecca sniffled and looked up at him with big brown eyes. "Your momma died, too?"

"Yes. My momma, and poppa, and sister. All on the same terrible day."

"Were you lonely?" asked Rebecca.

"I felt very lonely, and angry! Do you feel angry sometimes?"

"I guess. I fight a lot with Miriam."

"Where is Miriam? Can you take me to her?"

"I don't want to!" said Rebecca stamping her feet. "She was mean and I'm hiding."

"Not at night, little one. It's not safe to hide at night. You might get lost or attacked by wolves. But come daylight, you can play and hide all you want from Miriam."

"I can?"

"Yes, but first you must take me to your family. Do you remember the way?"

"I think. We're living with a lady Alima met at this well."

"Alima? Alima's here?"

"Yes. She's taking care of us since momma died."

Alima, here? He could hardly believe it! "Take me to her, Rebecca. Please."

Rebecca took Balthazar's hand and led him to a little house down the road from the well. He could see Alima standing in an open doorway with Miriam by her side. Her hair was loose about her face. How beautiful she is! . . .

"Rebecca! Come back here, right now!" said Alima. Rebecca dropped his hand and ran forward. He watched from the shadows as Alima stooped to look at the child.

"Why are you weeping, Rebecca? Are you hurt?" asked Alima.

"No. I wept because the man asked me about momma."

"What man?" asked Alima.

Balthazar stepped out of the shadows. "This man. She ran into me at the well."

"Balthazar?"

"In the flesh." He walked close to her.

"But how?"

"By some miracle I think . . . I will tell you all of it in a moment. First, we should attend to the girls." He smiled down at Rebecca. "It's seems that your little charge was hiding from her sister. A little quarrel borne of sisterly affection?"

Alima raised her eyebrows and glared at Miriam who was hiding her face in the folds of Alima's robe. "Mmm. Not at all surprising." Alima lifted Miriam's face up to the starlight. "What do you have to say to your sister, Miriam?"

"I'm sorry, Rebecca. I didn't mean to push you out of bed."

"Or?" said Alima.

"Or to say your ears are big," said Miriam.

"And what will you promise her, Miriam?" asked Alima.

"I promise not to do it again."

"Will you give Miriam a hug, Rebecca?" asked Alima. "I think she really is sorry."

"I guess." Rebecca offered a begrudging hug before quickly pulling her arms back.

"Now go back to sleep girls," said Alima guiding them into the house. "We're guests in this house, and I don't want your squabble to wake our hostess." Alima listened for further signs of argument before turning to Balthazar.

"I . . . I can't believe you're here! I'd thought never to see you again!"

Balthazar shuffled his sandals in the dirt. "Do you remember the star I watched so much after Berenike?"

"How could I forget?"

"Well, I heard two men speaking of it when I stopped at a way station on my way to Parthia. We started to talk, and it turned out they were astrologers! From the same school where I want to study. They were coming here to Judea."

"So they invited you to join them?"

Balthazar shrugged. "In truth, I invited myself along. I was anxious to learn from them, and . . ." He took her hand. "I wanted to see you again."

"Did you stop in Caesarea? I never saw you."

"I stopped, but the house was deserted. I asked around and heard from a neighbor about Noah's death. But she could tell me nothing of you or Judith."

Alima took a deep breath. "After Noah's death, Judith was destitute. She had no money, and she was with child again. She decided to go to Nazareth to live with her father. I couldn't let her go alone."

"It was just the two of you with the children?"

"We couldn't find anyone to take us. So I bought a wagon and a donkey with some of the silver Sameer left me. I couldn't let her go alone with the children!"

"That sounds like you."

Alima blushed and pulled him by the hand. "Come sit with me." She led him to a bench on the side of the house. He sat on one end of the bench and she on the other.

"Can we sit closer?" he asked. She smiled and moved so that her back was against his chest. "That's better." He put his arms round her and laid his chin atop her head.

Alima tuned her face to the sky. "I don't know what to make of this starlight," she said. "I have thought of you often when I look to the heavens, but never have I seen nights so luminous as in this town!"

There's a good reason!" He raised his right arm and pointed to a star directly overhead. "That's my star! It's the reason the night sky glows, it's the reason I found the Messiah, and it's the reason I found you. It's one amazing star!"

Alima turned to face him. "I don't know this Messiah you speak of, but if his star is what brought you back, then I will praise him! I have missed you. And I'm sorry, truly, for sending you away."

"I've missed you, too. Very much. I . . . I hope now that we've found each other again, we can find a way to stay together."

Alima turned to face him. "I hope so, too."

"Good." He let his breath out as if he had been holding it for a long time. "So tell me, how is it you came to Bethlehem? You said you were heading to Nazareth."

"We were. Judith and I left with the children, but she was bitten by vipers when we stopped to eat. She died before we were half way to Nazareth."

He wiped the tears from her cheeks. "I'm sorry. I know she was your friend. Were you alone with the children?"

"Yes I was alone, and I was frightened. Not for myself, but for them. I didn't know the road and I could see a storm coming. But then something miraculous happened. I can't explain because I'm still trying to understand it. But we found shelter with an old lady, the children were safe and I was able to bury Judith."

"And you got to Nazareth safely?" He ran his fingers through her hair.

She nodded. "Mmm. We got there the next day only to discover that Judith's father had died some months back."

"What did you do then?"

"I wasn't sure what I should do, until I remembered the words of the old lady."

"The one who sheltered you?"

"Yes. She renewed my courage. She said I should believe in myself the way the Lord believed in me. It helped me. When I learned Judith had no kin left in Nazareth, I considered returning to Caesarea, but I decided to come here when I heard Noah might have kin here. So I loaded the children in the wagon and started south. It was an arduous journey but we made it. Unfortunately, I've not found any relations here either."

Alima suddenly jumped to her feet. "Oh my! The sun is coming up! I must get back before the household wakes."

Balthazar grabbed for her. "Wait! Don't leave yet."

"Come with me," said Alima.

He smiled. "I'd like to, but I must get back, too. My friends sent me in search of water a long time ago. They probably think me well lost by now. I will come back for you."

"I should hope so," said Alima. "I would like to see this Messiah of yours."

CHAPTER 33

Asher Makes a Decision

§

ASHER SLUNG HIS BAG OVER his shoulder, picked up his bow and quiver and slapped his hand against his belt. His sling and stones felt secure. There was only one thing more he wanted with him. "Will you come with me, Corinna? Help me catch some game?"

Corinna looked at Mary. "He wants me help him. You want me here, or go Asher?"

"Go on," said Mary smiling. "There'll be more chances to change the baby later."

Corinna got up. "I come, Asher! Moment please." She wrapped a shawl around her shoulders and followed him out of the cave. When they were well away from the others, she tapped him on the shoulder.

"Why you need me hunt? Is not woman's work."

"I know. And I don't need you exactly. I want you." Asher smiled. "We've had no time alone in a very long time, and I mean to change that."

Corinna tipped her head and raised her brows. "You want lay with me? You promised hunt. We need food."

"And we shall have some. The pheasants should be in this field down yonder. We will bag some birds, and after we will celebrate."

"Celebrate? What means 'celebrate'?"

"You will see. It's a surprise." Asher smiled broadly as he kissed her hand. "Quiet now!" He pointed to a spot twenty paces ahead where a brood of pheasants probed the ground with their bills. Then in a whisper: "Look at those fat ones. I'll aim for those first."

Corinna hid herself behind a bush. With an instinctive grace Asher set his body, drew an arrow from his quiver, nocked it, set his fingers and drew back. Then he watched and waited. He wanted to impress Corinna, so not any shot would do. When he released, the arrow flew straight, through one pheasant into the next. He took some twine from his bag and handed it to Corinna. "Tie them together with this, and hold them close. We don't want to lose them to a wandering cat."

Asher walked ahead, looking for his next catch. Corinna followed. They did not speak. Up and over several hills covered with meandering sheep and goats. He spotted Josiah and waved, but walked on. They continued to the hills on the other side of Bethlehem but saw nothing and circled back. "See how we've been rewarded for our diligence?" said Asher. A brood of pheasants scratched the ground just paces from where he'd bagged the first ones. "There's something here they like."

He grabbed the sling from his belt, slipped the loop over his finger and loaded a stone into the cradle. Then he raised his arm up and whirled the sling about his head. Around and around, faster and faster. When he released, the stone flew out hard, felling the plumpest bird in the brood. He let fly another stone before the birds reached the sky and whooped as yet another fell to the ground. "I'm ready to celebrate! Are you?"

As Corinna tied the four birds together, Asher pulled a small blanket from the bag on his shoulder and spread it on the ground. Then he sat and beckoned Corinna to join him. "I like when the day begins with a successful hunt."

"You good hunter, Asher. I never see birds taken so quick."

"My father taught me how to hunt when I was young, and I've been practicing all my life. When you're out in the fields, if you don't catch, you don't eat."

Corinna smiled and patted his belly. "Why you not fat if so good hunter?"

He raised his index finger in front of her face. "Are you making fun of me? I'm a good hunter, but I share my kills with the other shepherds. Seven of us herd in the hills south of Seleucia and we all help each other."

"How?"

"We share our food, our fires, even our shelter. Some years back, we built a small hut together, and we sleep there when it's cold. It's good that we don't have to be alone all the time. We talk and sing, play tunes. My friend has a small reed pipe and he makes beautiful music with it."

"I like music," said Corinna.

"Me too. I tell you Corinna, the night I got here, when Josiah brought me to see the baby, I heard something amazing. Josiah told me the story of the night when Jesus was born. He said he saw an angel and heard heavenly voices announcing the baby's birth. And when he brought me to the cave, I swear I heard it too. It floated on the wind. It didn't seem real somehow, but I know I didn't imagine it. There is something extraordinary about this baby, Corinna. I can feel it in my bones."

"You think he king?"

"Yes, but not the usual kind of king. I can't explain it. It's like when I look at your face, I know you are special. I feel in my deepest being that we are meant to be together. That my life has changed because of you. I feel the same way when I look at that baby. He is special. And I think that maybe he will change my life like you have."

Corinna blushed. "I change your life?"

Asher drew her close and kissed her lips gently. "How do you doubt it? I love you, Corinna. I have loved you since I first saw you." He drew her close and kissed her again.

Corinna ruffled her hands through his hair. "I love you, too. You want make love?"

"I want," said Asher drawing back to look at her face. "But more than that I want you to be mine. I want us betrothed. Will you be my wife, Corinna?"

Corinna's eyes grew wide. "You want me as wife? Oh, yes! I want. I want love you, I want your babies. We make good life!"

Asher kissed her again, sliding his hands along the curves of her body. How good, how right it felt, but he forced himself to stop.

Corinna looked up at him. "What wrong? Why you stop?"

"Because I want to go back and tell the others. I want to celebrate!" He took a deep breath and rose to his feet pulling her up to him. "Come. Let us announce the good news!"

Asher ripped the blanket off the ground as Corinna picked up the birds. With her hand in his, they ran toward the cave. He began to hum. Corinna hummed after him. Back and forth, one after the other they repeated the same tune faster and faster until out of breath Corinna stopped. "You make love with music!" She said smiling up at him.

"We will discover many ways, my love, before our days are done."

CHAPTER 34

The Man in White

BALTHAZAR RETURNED A FEW HOURS later to find Alima waiting with the children by the bench. "Good morning, girls! All friends again?"

The sisters shrugged.

"As I thought! But you must promise to behave today. No arguing. We're visiting a family with a new baby, and you must be quiet round him, understand?"

"I told them that already, didn't I girls?"

"Yes, Alima," they replied together.

"These people are very friendly. And speaking of friendly people, Alima, you never told me how you came to be staying where you are. Rebecca said you met the woman at the well?"

"It was the first place we came to. We needed water and I reasoned it would be a good place to ask about Noah's family. Sarah was one of the first women I met, and after a while she asked if we had a place to stay. When I told her we didn't, she invited us in. Sarah's very kind."

"She must be to invite a strange woman with three small children to share her house."

"She's widowed and says she likes the sound of children in her house again. We're getting along very well, and I've already told her about you."

"Have you? And what was it you told her?"

"That you were no stranger, and that I love you. It was the proper thing, since I'm living under her roof."

Balthazar nodded and smiled. "Can I carry Isaac?"

"That would be wonderful!" said Alima. "He's much heavier than he used to be."

"By Pollux that be the truth!" said Balthazar as he took the child from her arms. They walked in amiable silence toward the hillside cave where the others awaited. In the broad light of day, Alima looked even more beautiful than she had the night before. There was a bounce to her step and a liveliness that he did not remember in months past. It may be only temporary he thought, but motherhood becomes her.

"Balthazar, my boy! Is this the lovely Alima?" yelled Gaspar, as they approached the camp.

"She is!" said Balthazar with a hint of pride in his voice. "Alima, I would like you to meet my companions. This towering, curious chap is Gaspar. Melchior sits to his left. The young man there is Asher, and the girl next to him is Corinna. The lady stirring the pot is Melchior's servant, Bina. The best cook the world has ever known!"

"I wish it was true!" said Bina waving her wooden spoon in the air." Welcome to you, Miss Alima! Little ones!"

"Thank you," said Alima. "I would like you to meet the children. This is Miriam, Rebecca, and little Isaac. Can you bow to our new friends, girls?"

Miriam and Rebecca bowed together, as Alima took Isaac from Balthazar.

"Welcome children! Welcome," said Melchior. "Are you hungry? We've some nice fat pheasants and a rabbit roasting over the fire. Would you like some?"

"Yes, please!" said Miriam.

"Oh, yes!" added Rebecca with wide eyes.

"Bina, can you fill some bowls for them?" asked Melchior.

"Most surely, Master," said Bina. "Come sit girls, and I'll serve you some food."

Alima carried Isaac round the other side of the fire and found a place next to Corinna. Just as she was getting settled, Joseph emerged from the cave with Mary and the baby.

"Is this the baby I've heard so much about?" asked Alima.

"Yes, this is our son, Jesus. I am Joseph and this is my wife, Mary. Welcome, Alima. Balthazar told us about you. What a blessing to be able to celebrate our son's birth with so many good people. And so much good food! Thank you for the birds, Asher. Four pheasants in one morning is quite a boon!"

"Today was a good day for hunting, but for another reason as well," said Asher rising. "While I have your ears, I would make a happy announcement. This morning I asked Corinna to be my wife. And she said yes!"

"Oh my!" said Gaspar. "Didn't I tell you, Melchior?"

Asher pulled Corinna by the hand to stand with him and continued in a strong voice. "Corinna, in the company of our friends, I betroth myself to you and swear to take you to wife." He took a small piece of polished stone from within his tunic and held it out to her. "I found this stone a long time ago in the hills of Parthia. It isn't rare, but for years have I polished and cared for it. See how it shines? I offer it to you now, as a symbol of my love."

Corinna took the stone from his hand, kissed it and held it high above her. "Before eyes of friends I say be good wife always."

Gaspar clapped his hands. "This calls for celebration, my friends! Carve the pheasants! Plate the figs! What else have we to offer, Melchior?"

"I can cook some lentils with onions!" said Bina.

"And I retrieved our water pitcher from the well!" said Joseph, poking Balthazar in the ribs as he rose to pour some water.

"Sorry about that, Joseph," said Balthazar drawing him aside. "When I discovered Alima was in Bethlehem I fair forgot what I was doing."

"Very understandable. I used to forget what I was doing, too, when I first set eyes on Mary."

"Have you any advice on how to speak to women? As an old married man?" asked Balthazar in a whisper.

"I'm not that old am I?" asked Joseph.

"I didn't mean it that way! It's just that, sometimes I say the wrong things. Now that I've found Alima, I don't want to lose her."

"Then tell her so. Share your feelings," whispered Joseph.

"You think it's that simple?"

"I'm a simple man, Balthazar, so yes."

Balthazar helped himself to some food and found a spot to eat close to Alima. He noticed that everyone was eating, except for Gaspar. "Can I get you a plate, Gaspar?"

"No thank you. I will get my own."

"Bina, please help Gaspar fill his plate," said Melchior.

"No, Bina! I told Balthazar I will help myself and I will."

Melchior shook his head. "No need to get testy, old friend."

Everyone watched as Gaspar struggled to his feet and limped slowly to where the food was set out on the ground. "See, no need to worry about me," said Gaspar as he bent over to fill his plate. But the words were hardly out of his mouth, when he lost his balance and fell with a thud into the food.

"What a donkey's ass I am!" shouted Gaspar as the men came running.

"Can I help you?" asked Joseph.

"We'll do it." said Melchior. "Balthazar, Asher, help me move him."

"I'm sorry. I should have listened to you!" said Gaspar. "I didn't mean to ruin the feast."

"You haven't," said Joseph. "No small accident can take away the day's gladness." Joseph raised his water cup into the air. "To you, Asher and Corinna! Much happiness on your betrothal! And to you, Balthazar and Alima, who found each other again here in Bethlehem!"

"Thank you, Joseph! But we should take a look at Gaspar's foot," said Balthazar. "I don't think we've cleaned it since before our audience with Herod."

"You had an audience with King Herod?" asked Joseph in astonishment.

"Yes, by commission of our king," said Melchior. "I assure you, we would not have sought him of our own accord. Perhaps the time has come for us to tell you of it."

"We should," said Gaspar. "But damn it, can you lift me out of the food first? I like pheasant but not when I'm sitting on it!"

With Asher's help, Melchior and Balthazar pulled Gaspar up and settled him some paces away. Bina brought some water and fresh cloths, and after cleaning the remnants of food from his clothing, helped Balthazar remove Gaspar's foot bandage. Not only was the wound festering, but it reeked, and the group was forced to cover their noses as Balthazar cleaned it. Gaspar was in so much pain afterward, that he retired to his tent.

"His foot looks bad," said Joseph in quiet tones as he rejoined the group around the fire.

"Very bad," agreed Balthazar. "The leg gets blacker every time I look at it, but I don't know what more can be done. I fear for him."

"As do I," said Melchior. "I pray for his healing."

"You speak of prayer like a devout Jew," said Joseph.

"I pray and sacrifice like a Jew but I was never circumcised. I'm a gentile in the eyes of your priests. You see, my father wasn't Jewish and after the massacre of five thousand Jews in Parthia, he insisted my mother teach us in secret. He was afraid for us. But our ancestry, the law, and the prophets were important to her, and to me. It's why I traveled so far to find your son. And it's why I'm worried about King Herod."

"I don't understand," said Joseph.

"I'll try to explain. We followed the star believing it would lead us to Judea but we didn't know what the prophecies said about the Messiah's birthplace. So I went to the Temple to find out and to offer a sacrifice in my mother's name. When I brought my animal forward I asked to speak with the Chief Priest."

"That was brave of you! Trying to speak with the chief priest is like trying to speak to the king himself!" said Joseph.

"As I discovered! The arrogant priest I spoke with, denied me at first then met my request with a threat. I reasoned he would only heed me if I showed him my commission from our king. It worked, but it had unfortunate consequences. Consequences that may have put your son in danger."

"How is that?" Asked Joseph.

"Because the Chief Priest accompanied me to my audience and told the king of our search for the Messiah."

"So King Herod knew you were coming to Bethlehem?" asked Joseph.

Melchior put his hand on Joseph's shoulder. "Yes, I'm sorry to say. We knew his reputation for jealousy and murder is well deserved, especially when he perceives a threat to his rule."

"But my son is a newborn! And a poor one at that," said Joseph. "What threat can he present to the king?"

"None that's immediate. But I doubt that matters to Herod. The threat need not be real or immediate for him to act upon it."

"Melchior is right," said Balthazar. "Herod asked us to come back to tell him where we found the child. He said he wants to come honor him, too, but we don't trust him. And it's not only Herod you must be wary of. The Chief Priest is concerned that your son could be an imposter."

"An imposter! Why would anyone pretend to be the Messiah?"

"That is not so hard to explain," said Melchior. "Plots and intrigue are common in sovereign courts and the parent who controls the child king is often as powerful as the king himself."

"But we are poor, simple people. We know nothing of kingly courts. Nor do we want to."

"It may seem unbelievable, but you must beware," said Melchior. "For the safety of your family, we urge you. Do not stay in Bethlehem for long."

"But Mary is not yet purified! We wanted to do that in Jerusalem before returning to Nazareth."

"When?" asked Balthazar.

"According to our law it should be done forty days after the birth of a male child."

Balthazar and Melchior exchanged glances.

"You don't think we should go, do you?" asked Joseph as he looked at Mary.

"No," said Melchior. "Must Mary be purified in Jerusalem?"

"No. She can do it in the mikveh here, or in any natural stream or body of water. Perhaps we will change our plans."

As the men finished speaking, they heard Gaspar groaning in pain from his tent. Joseph shook his head in sympathy. "My grandfather, Matthan, died from a wound like that. We're all carpenters in my family, and my grandfather cut himself one day while cutting some timber. It was a painful way to die."

"Many pardons for interrupting," said Alima. "But did you say your grandfather was named Matthan?"

"Yes. My family is descended from the House of David. That's why we came here to Bethlehem, to register for the census. Why do you ask?"

"Because my friend, Judith, told me her husband was descended from the House of David. And that his grandfather was named Matthan."

"Was her husband's name Noah?" asked Joseph.

"Yes," said Alima.

"Did they live in Caesarea?"

"Yes. That's where I met them."

"Noah was my cousin!" exclaimed Joseph. "Do you hear this, Mary? Alima knew your friend Judith and my cousin, Noah."

Mary looked at Alima. "Are those Judith's and Noah's children?"

"Yes," said Alima. "Balthazar, my brother and I rented a room from them in Caesarea. When my brother and Balthazar left, I lived with Judith and helped with the children. Noah died in an accident soon after. Judith died on our way to Nazareth, and when we got there, I learned that Judith's father was also dead."

"Such a sad tale. Judith was a good woman and an old friend," said Mary.

"She told me that Noah's grandfather was named Matthan. I remembered the name because it was the name they had chosen if the new baby was a boy."

"You mean Judith was with child when she died?" asked Mary.

"Yes. It was a dreadful day. For me and the children."

"Why did you come here?" asked Joseph.

"Because Judith's friends told me Noah might have family here. I brought the children here in hopes of finding their kin."

"And now you've found Joseph," said Mary.

"Yes."

"Come, Mary, we must talk of this," said Joseph.

"All right. I can see my son is searching for his next meal. We'll rejoin you later." said Mary. She rose with Jesus and followed Joseph into the cave.

"What a remarkable place," said Alima looking to Balthazar. "I come here and find not only you, but family for the children."

Balthazar nodded. "Yes. But your countenance tells me something is amiss."

Alima looked into his eyes. "You know me well, but my worry has nothing to do with you. Finding you Balthazar, has brought me great joy. Please believe that!"

"I want to. Why then the wrinkles on your brow? I thought you wanted to find their kin."

"I judged it right to do so."

"Then why do you look so sad?"

"Because I've come to love them."

"I know how much being a mother means to you, and you may not have to give them up. Joseph and Mary are poor, newly married and far from home. They may decide that caring for three more children is not within their means."

"It's a slender reed of hope but I will hold it."

Soon after Joseph exited the cave and approached them. "May I speak with you, Alima?"

She nodded.

Joseph sat down by Balthazar and Alima. "Mary and I are uncertain what to do about the children. They are beautiful, and I do feel responsible for them, but they would be a handful."

"So, you will let me keep them?" asked Alima excitedly. "I will be the best . . ."

Joseph put his hand up. "Please wait! I haven't finished. You seem a good woman, and I mean you no offense, truly! But what do we know of you? Are you Jewish?"

"No. I was raised according to the teachings of the prophet Zarathustra."

"I suspected as much," said Joseph shaking his head. "It is unfortunate."

"Balthazar and I may not be Jews, but we are good people, Joseph!"

"I do not doubt that. Many gentiles are good people. But you're not married and you're not a Jew. The children are. Noah and Judith would want them raised in the law, and with understanding of the covenant. Can you teach them those things?"

"No, but I love them, Joseph! Judith knew me, and trusted me with them. Doesn't that matter?"

"Judith had a good heart, and yes, it matters that she trusted you. But I think the children would be better off with parents who can teach them God's laws and who understand their ancestry. Mary and I may not be able to raise them, but we have friends in Nazareth, who can. They are childless and would make loving parents. When we return to Nazareth, we shall give the children to them."

Alima put her hands together as if in prayer. "Is there nothing I can say to change your mind?"

Joseph swayed his head from side to side. "We will seek the Lord's guidance and give you a final answer in the morning."

"Very well," said Alima.

Balthazar could tell she was troubled. "Perhaps it's best not to say anything yet to the children. Would you like to return to Sarah's house now?"

Alima nodded. As he took her by the hand, he realized that the day he envisioned so happily had turned very gloomy indeed.

Balthazar woke with a start in the middle of the night. He felt as if he had not slept at all, and he knew why. The man in white, the glowing man so often mentioned by Melchior and Gaspar had spoken to him in a dream. He threw off his blanket and ran to their tent.

"Gaspar! Melchior! It's happened! He finally spoke to me!"

"What has you so crazed?" asked Gaspar with a weak voice.

"The man in white, the angel! He spoke to me in my dream! He said 'Rise and go forth' so I came to tell you."

Gaspar struggled to sit up. "Will you help me up, Balthazar? I have no strength."

Balthazar pulled him to a reclining position and propped a saddle-bag behind him. "Is that better?"

"A little. Now tell us. You heard from the man in white? The one we saw in our dreams?"

Balthazar sat next to Gaspar. "Yes, and it's just as you said. He spoke to me, not as in a dream, but as in life. I remember his words so clearly!"

"Do you hear, Melchior? Sit up damn you! The man in white has spoken to Balthazar!"

"Yes, yes! I hear." Melchior sat up yawning. "So tell us. What did he say?"

"He said: *Do not fear. I am a messenger of the Lord God. Do not return to Jerusalem. For Herod is going to search for the child to destroy him. Rise and go forth to your home by another way.*"

Melchior raised his hands up. "See there, Gaspar! My warning to Joseph rings true. He said 'Rise and go forth'? Did you wake immediately?"

"I did for I felt the urgency of his warning. We must leave here now," said Balthazar. "And there's something else. Your star, the one we followed. It's vanished! Go see for yourself."

Melchior stuck his head out of the tent, then rose and walked outside. He was gone only a few moments before returning. "You're right. The star is gone and the night is dark as any other. We must tell the others."

"I'll tell Joseph and Mary, and go for Alima. Will you rouse the others? Gaspar is in no condition." Balthazar ran to the cave and yelled into it. "Joseph! Mary! I must speak with you!"

"You may enter," said Mary. "We're already awake."

Balthazar walked in and was surprised to see Mary and Joseph dressed as for their own journey.

"What wakens you in the dark of night? Is it Gaspar? Is he worse?" asked Mary.

"He seems weaker, but that's not the reason for my intrusion. I had a dream that concerns your son."

Joseph walked up to Balthazar. "From the angel in white?"

"How did you know?"

"Because he spoke to me as well. What was his message?"

"He said we must not return to Jerusalem, that Herod is seeking to destroy your son. He bid me rise and said we should go home by another way. I woke immediately for even in my sleep I felt the need for haste."

"My message was similar," said Joseph. "He said: Rise, take the child and his mother, flee to Egypt, and stay there until I tell you. Herod is going to search for the child to destroy him." I felt the same urgency, and we prepare now to leave. Have you told your companions?"

"Yes. I'm going now for Alima and the children. Will you take them with you?"

Joseph shook his head. "No. We would have if we were returning to Nazareth, but this changes everything. I don't want to put them in danger."

"May I offer a suggestion?" asked Balthazar.

"Please do," said Joseph.

"I'm going to pledge myself to Alima. We love each other, and I think she will not refuse me. The bride price is already arranged. After we marry, I will take her with me to Parthia so I can study with Melchior. You know his Jewish ancestry, Joseph. Would you let us take the children, if Melchior will teach them? We would be good parents."

Joseph scratched his head but did not hesitate long. "I will consent if I hear Melchior's promise."

"Very good," said Balthazar. "I'm going to fetch Alima. We'll ask Melchior when we return."

Not long after, he stood in the open doorway of Sarah's house calling out. "Alima! Alima, are you there?" He had to call several times before she came to the door. He could see Sarah in the house not far behind.

"Balthazar, it's still the dark of night. Is something wrong?"

"Yes! Get your things! And the children's. We must leave Bethlehem. Quickly!"

Alima looked at him in alarm. "What's happened?"

"You trust me don't you?"

"You know I do. But what has that to do with leaving?"

"I've had a dream. It's difficult to explain but I know we must act upon it."

"What kind of dream?"

"I had a dream like Gaspar and Melchior. A man in white, what the Jews call angels, spoke to me. He said Herod is trying to kill Jesus. He said we must leave, and not return to Jerusalem. Joseph had a similar dream. We must go."

"Very well." She turned to Sarah who stood behind her. "It's time for us to leave you. Can you help me get the children ready?"

"Now? In the middle of the night? What madness is this?"

"It must be done. We would wait 'til morning if we could. Please help us."

"I don't understand, but so be it." Sarah went inside to rouse the children.

"Will you hitch the donkey, Balthazar? The wagon's behind the house and the donkey is in the field."

Within minutes, Balthazar had the wagon waiting, and when Alima emerged with the children, he helped them into it. "Do you have all their clothes and some food?"

"They never had much," said Alima. "Sarah has given us some food. It will have to do until we can get more. And by the way, you know how I like a plan; may I ask where we are going?"

Balthazar laughed. "You may ask but I do not have an answer. Did you say your goodbyes to Sarah?"

"No, but I'll be quick." Alima handed Isaac to Balthazar and ran to Sarah who stood in the doorway. "How can I thank you for your hospitality and friendship? I will never forget you, truly."

"I hope not!" said Sarah. "The children were a joy, and you are a good woman. I hope you will be all right with this Balthazar of yours! What kind of a man takes his woman away in the dark of night?"

"Do not worry, Sarah. He will take good care of us." Alima smiled.

"I hope so." Shaking her head, Sarah put her hands on Alima's shoulders. "Peace be with you, my girl. I pray the Lord will watch over you and those little ones. Take care." Sarah hugged her and stepped back into the house as the wagon jerked forward.

The drive up to the cave was a bumpy one and Balthazar struggled to keep the wagon upright. But he moved steadily until he stopped within view of the cave. His companions had broken camp. The tents were down and except for Gaspar, who dozed against a tree trunk, the others scurried to pack the animals.

"Stay in the wagon, girls, until I call for you," said Balthazar. "I must speak with Melchior, Alima. Then we should bid farewell to Joseph's family." As Alima and the children waited, Balthazar strode to where Melchior held tight to his mother's ossuary. "May we speak? I have a favor to ask which involves you and the children."

Melchior yawned. "I overheard Joseph say he and Mary were taking them to Nazareth. Is that still his plan?"

"No. He doesn't want to put them in danger, but the final decision may depend on you."

"On me? In what way?"

"I told Joseph I'm going to pledge myself to Alima. He said he will let us keep the children, if you are willing to teach them the Law of Moses."

Melchior drew back. "You want me to teach them? I love children but have never endeavored to teach them. It's a job for a woman."

"That may be, but you remember the Mosaic stories and the words of the prophets. Please, Melchior! It may be the only way that we can keep them . . . the only way Alima will get to be a mother."

Melchior smiled. "Then I will do it. And I can use my mother's scrolls to help me."

"Thank you. I must ask one more thing. Will you promise this to Joseph and Mary?"

"Yes."

Balthazar walked over to the wagon. "Alima, bring the children to the cave. It's time to say our goodbyes."

Alima looked stricken. "How can I give them up? They are just starting to trust me, to feel safe with me."

Balthazar looked into her eyes. "You said you trusted me. Come."

Alima closed her eyes, took a deep breath then spoke up strongly. "Come girls. We must visit baby Jesus and his parents." Carrying Isaac, she followed Balthazar and the girls into the cave. Melchior was already there cooing to the baby near Joseph.

"Joseph, has Melchior given you his promise?" asked Balthazar.

"Yes, he promised he will teach the children about our laws and the covenant. Mary and I are grateful. We know you and Alima will be good parents to them."

Alima looked at Joseph in shock. "You will let us keep the children?"

"We will. And we offer our congratulations to you and Balthazar."

Balthazar smiled and walked to her side. "I am pledging myself to you, Alima. I love you! Here and now, before these good people, I ask you to be my bride."

"Your bride? The betrothal is real? Finally real?" Tears streamed down her face.

"Yes. Finally, blessedly, wonderfully real! Will you still have me?"

"Yes! Oh yes!" Alima set Isaac down and hugged Balthazar with a strength he had not seen in her. When she released him, he kissed her on the forehead then smiled at the others over her shoulder. "It's been a strange night, but a good one."

"Yes it has," said Alima, squeezing his hand.

Joseph called the children to him. "Miriam, Rebecca! Come quickly! And bring Isaac. Say goodbye to your little cousin, Jesus. We must part, but perhaps you will see your cousin again someday."

"Maybe we can teach him to play hide and seek with us," said Rebecca.

"I'm sure he will like that," said Mary. "Where are the rest of your companions, Balthazar? It's time we say farewell."

"I'll get them." Balthazar strode from the cave calling the others. "Come everyone! Come say your goodbyes."

Balthazar grabbed Asher as he approached with the women. "Will you help me escort Gaspar? He is very weak." The two of them walked to where Gaspar sat, dozing. Balthazar had to shake him several times before he woke. His face was white and his lips bloodless. "It's time to leave, Gaspar. Mary and Joseph want to say their goodbyes. Will you come?"

"If you . . . help me." His words came haltingly and were difficult to hear.

Balthazar grabbed him under his right arm and Asher under his left. Together they pulled the big man to his feet, and walked him into the cave. He was breathing with difficulty.

"Where would you like to sit?" asked Balthazar.

"Near . . . the babe," said Gaspar. "We came so far. I want these . . . last moments close to him." Gaspar looked at Mary.

"Gentle Gaspar. Your company has brought us much pleasure. Though you suffered, you never. . . "

Melchior laughed aloud.

Mary smiled. "Well, almost never let it overcome your spirit. Would you like to hold my son before you leave? I don't recall you ever got the chance."

"I would," said Gaspar with a dull smile.

Mary brought the baby to him and when she realized how weak he was, helped him hold the child in his arms.

He began to whisper. "Greetings, little king. Prophets called you the ancient one. But that seems wrong. You are the new life . . . come to bring joy. I regret nothing of our journey. Not thirst, not heat, not even . . ." He coughed. "Our wretched donkey!" Gaspar closed his eyes and bent his head to kiss the baby's brow. "Thank you, Mary and Joseph, for this honor."

"The honor was ours," said Mary as she took her baby back.

"Speaking of donkeys. How is yours, Joseph?" asked Balthazar. "Is he up to the journey that awaits you?"

"His best days are behind him, but he is all we have."

"Then please accept the gift of my camel. Melwah is a gentle animal, agreeable and fleet of foot. He will carry your family in safety wherever you go."

Joseph shook his head. "I cannot! He is too valuable and you will need him yourself."

"We have a wagon and a donkey, and many other animals to choose from. Please take him. You will need a dependable mount now more than ever."

"Thank you, Balthazar. I fear you are right in that. I promise to treat him well."

"Before we part, may I make a request?" asked Melchior. "When my mother died, she asked me to take her bones to Jerusalem. She wanted me to bury her near her ancestors. But I had no time to find a grave, and now again we leave in haste. With your permission, I would bury her in this cave. I think she would like the idea of resting where the little king was born."

"It seems a goodly spot and I doubt the animals will object," said Joseph.

"I noticed a depression in the floor at the back," said Mary "It might be the right size for an ossuary. Do you have it with you?"

Melchior held up the box. "Can you show me the spot?"

Mary led him to the back wall and pointed to a small hollow in the floor.

"This will work." Melchior knelt down and carefully lowered the ossuary into the crevice. "I must find some dirt to cover it with."

"Over here," said Joseph. "There's a small mound of gravel and stone that's fallen from above. Will this do?"

"It will do very well." Melchior scooped a huge handful of stone and gravel and dumped it into the hole to cover the ossuary. Then he stamped it down 'til it was level with the cave floor. "I would offer a prayer to the Lord. It won't take long." Bending his head he spoke aloud for all to hear. "Oh Lord God! I call upon you to bless my mother's resting place. She was a woman of faith and wisdom. Because of her I found the Messiah. Bless me with your wisdom too, so I may instruct the children entrusted to me, according to your will." He looked upon the gathering. "It is time to part my friends, or the angels warning may be for naught,"

"Melchior is right," said Joseph. "We must make haste. Will you bring your camel to the cave entrance, Balthazar?"

As the group rose to leave, there came a sudden, loud cry from Gaspar. "What blessing is this? Look at my foot! My foot is healed!"

Balthazar and Melchior stooped down to look at the foot, as the others crowded round. The stink which had been ever present was gone. Balthazar unwound the bandage, carefully un-twirling the bloody cloth little by little. When the last of it was discarded, the whole assembly cried out in awe. No longer did they see a blackened stump, with a gaping oozing wound. The foot was smooth, pink and unblemished.

"It's unbelievable!" cried Melchior.

"A true miracle!" said Bina.

"How can it be?" asked Joseph.

Mary looked from her baby to Gaspar. "How do you feel, Gaspar?"

Gaspar stood up, placing the full weight of his tall frame upon both feet. "I have no pain! No numbness! Truly our journey has been filled with wonders." Tears streamed down his face as he stooped to kiss again the babe who slept in Mary's arms. "Goodbye little king. And thank you. Thank you for giving me a new life."

"It is the first of many wonders," said Asher from behind. "For he is no ordinary babe and he will be no ordinary king!"

Journey to Judea

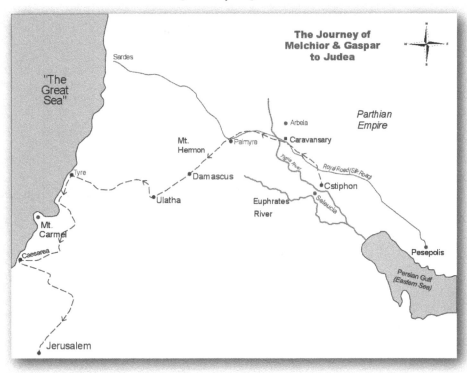

The Voyage of 'The Baysan'
&
The Caravan Trek Home

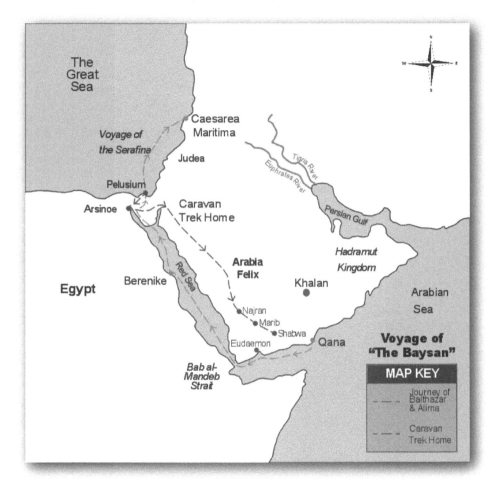

Book Four

CHAPTER 35
Heading Home

§

"WHERE ARE YOU, OLD FRIEND?" asked Gaspar. "Your wear the face of one far away."

"Do I? I was watching Balthazar bid his camel goodbye, and it came to me that life holds many farewells. They are never easy and the final farewell is always the hardest."

"As sure as the sun rises that farewell was coming my way. But I held the child, and lo! I am a man reborn! I wish it was in my stars to stay by his side 'til he is grown! What a king he will make with power like that!"

Melchior nodded. "You may be right, but that is a discussion for another time. Today, we must decide our course of travel. Balthazar, you said the angel told you to go home by another route. Is that correct?"

"That's what he said."

"Well, Herod knows we came from the east. It will be easy enough for him to post watches along the roads heading that way. That leaves us with two choices, south to Egypt or west to the sea. What think you?"

"There might be another way," said Balthazar. "Would you consider going west to the coast road, then north to Caesarea? Musa's ship is still there. If he's returned, I could persuade him to take us to Alexandria or to Arabia. We could find our way to Parthia from there."

Melchior shook his head. "It's too risky, my friend. Caesarea would put us right under Herod's nose. His palace is within sight of the port!"

"Yes, but he would never expect us to depart that way with the Romans patrolling the port as they do."

"He wouldn't expect it because it's madness! Besides you don't know if Musa is alive or dead. No, I think we must head south to Egypt. And the sooner the better."

"Then I think we must part ways," said Balthazar. "Alima's brother and maybe even her father are north of Caesarea. I owe it to her to return and wait for them."

Alima spoke up from behind him in the wagon. "No, Balthazar! You do not owe me that. After you left for Parthia I realized what you said about Sameer was true. He's a grown man, capable of finding his way home, with or without us, or my father."

"But what if Sameer returns to Judith's house and finds you gone as I did? He may never return to Qana. He may search for you in Judea until he dies."

"Then so be it," said Alima. "Much has changed since Sameer left to find my father. We're to be married and have children to care for. I have no wish to put them in danger. Besides, I'm sure he'll think you're watching over me, which is truer now than ever."

"So you're willing to leave without waiting for Sameer and your father?"

"I am. We must look to the future, Balthazar. You and the children are my future. I will not put you in peril."

Balthazar turned to Melchior. "Egypt it is then, but the coast road may still be our best route. Musa told me it runs north - south all the way to Egypt and it's the favored route of caravans. If we happen upon Herod's men it will be easier to mingle and disguise ourselves among other travelers than on a lonely inland route."

"He's right," said Gaspar holding the map out for Melchior to examine.

Melchior scanned the papyrus and nodded. "Very well. Gaspar, why don't you and Asher lead the way? I'll ride at the rear. Balthazar, you take the middle with the women and children."

They took the ridge road south from Bethlehem through the highlands of Judah. The road was rugged but Melchior pressed his friends to keep moving. It was not easy, especially when the children began to complain, but he had no intention of being caught by Herod's men. The morning hours took them past Bethsura to Hebron, where they took a road to the west. They lost a wagon wheel in the village of Marisa, but no one was hurt, and they moved on quickly after fixing it with the help of the village smithy. Through the long dusty afternoon they pushed on, trying to put as many leagues between themselves and Bethlehem as they could.

Like the others, Melchior remained watchful for soldiers and any sign of Herod's scouts. He hoped Joseph and Mary had gotten away safely, and wondered if they had taken the same road. A few times, when the path afforded a long view of the road behind, he looked back for them, but to no avail. The sun's last twilight rays were barely visible above the Great Sea as they rode into the ancient city of Ashkelon. The day that had begun amid a rush of warnings and wonders was ending in the quiet embrace of the sea and sand.

They camped in an isolated spot and departed at dawn the next morning. For two days more they journeyed south on the Via Maris, through Anthedon and Gaza, Jenysos and Raphia, until they crossed the border into Egypt. Only then did they slow down knowing they were beyond Herod's reach.

"What do you think, my friends?" asked Melchior as they sat around the fire that night. "Where should we head next?"

"There are several possibilities," said Balthazar. "We can continue along the coast road to Pelusium. There are always a multitude of caravans to join there. Or we can join a caravan in Petra, but getting there will mean turning south through the desert, a much more difficult trek. Or we can head south to Arsinoe and find a ship sailing for Qana. *The Baysan* may still be docked there, though who would pilot it I cannot imagine."

"I like the idea of a sail, so Arsinoe would be my choice," said Gaspar.

"It sounds inviting, but why should we go to Qana?" asked Melchior.

"You mean, besides Alima's mother's cooking, and the hospitality of their house?" asked Balthazar

"That sounds like enough reason," said Gaspar. "Do we need another?"

"Only our wedding feast!" said Balthazar. "What say you? Will you celebrate my union to Alima in Qana?"

"It would be our pleasure," said Melchior with a smile. "I only hope we can find a ship in Arsinoe willing to take us there."

It took them a week to reach Pelusium and four more days to Arsinoe. Having a wagon and three children meant slow going, but Melchior enjoyed watching them play and tell stories. It reminded him of days gone by with his brother. How good those days of innocence had been, before Mered's ambition and thirst for power had become the overwhelming need.

Thoughts of Mered necessarily moved to thoughts of the Messiah. His brother had never believed the prophecies, thinking them the delusions of a downtrodden people. How would Mered respond when he heard the Messiah was born in a cave to poor parents with a manger as his cradle? And what did it auger for his kingship that his family had been forced to flee Judea? Then Asher's words echoed back to him. 'He is no ordinary babe and will be no ordinary king.' Asher might be right. How else did one explain the star, the dreams and Gaspar's miraculous healing?

But his mind vacillated between doubt and belief. He had always thought the Messiah would be the king who threw off the yoke of Roman oppression and ushered in a reign of peace and glory. Was such a kingship possible, considering the baby's humble beginnings? Moses and David had both come from simple people. Would this Jesus follow a similar path? Melchior wanted to believe it, but he was confused, and struggled to think how he might explain what he had found to Mered and King Phraates. And above all he felt a strange stirring inside himself. He had openly declared himself a Jew to Joseph, and pledged to teach the children all he knew of the laws and covenant. How can I go back to what I was before?

As soon as their little troop arrived in Arsinoe, Balthazar made his way with Melchior to the port. As he had imagined, *The Baysan*, rocked in her berth where he'd last seen her so many months ago. He hailed one of the crew and with Melchior made his way up the gangway when an old sailor called his name.

"Balthazar! How are you son? Never expected to see you back so soon!"

"Our plans have changed since we saw you. Alima and I must find passage back to Qana."

"Only the two of you?"

"No, I've some friends with me. There are ten of us. Four men, three women and three children. This is my friend, Melchior."

"Good day to you, sir. You're all looking for passage? That'll be near impossible my boy! No ship I know has room for that many passengers. It's all about cargo."

"Even if we're willing to pay well above the going rate?" asked Balthazar.

"Even then. You would do well to join a caravan. I hear there's one leaving soon for Shabwa."

"There are no other possibilities for sailing?" asked Balthazar.

"There might be, if your group was only men, but the women are always bad karma. We were all shaking our heads when Musa boarded your woman, Alima, but she found favor with the gods, so we feel a might different now."

"As you should, for she save saved the ship that night."

"I remember it well. Fortunately the bad karma she held was for the pirates and not our crew."

"Then, I suppose we must find our way to that caravan. Where can we find the master?"

"Due east of here, in a large tent with a red flag waving atop. Before you leave, Balthazar, have you any news of our captain? We expected Musa over a month ago, but have heard nothing."

Balthazar explained the little he knew of Musa. "I'm sorry I can't give you better news."

The man shrugged his shoulders. "It's more than we knew before. Safe journey to you.

"Thank you. I hope Musa returns to you soon."

The men set off in the direction the sailor had pointed to and thanks to the high-flying red flag, found the caravan master's tent with little trouble. Tariq was a large man and irritable. He wore the clothes favored by Himyarites which immediately set Balthazar on edge. Though many Himyarites lived in southern Arabia, Balthazar had not come face to face with one since the deaths of his family. He took a burning dislike to the man, which was reinforced by the way Tariq complained about everything: the weather, his animals, his demanding wives and the rising cost of spices.

Balthazar picked up on his comment. "You find time to trade in spices?

"When I find an opportunity for profit." Came the unexpectedly short reply. Tariq went on to brag at some length about how efficiently he ran the caravan. Balthazar and Melchior listened with growing impatience before managing to negotiate a rate to join the caravan.

"Let me explain our formation," said Tariq before Balthazar could explain that he already knew. "Rope your animals together, tail to head, no more than eighteen in a file. Your camels should lead, with donkeys to the rear. The children can ride, but the rest of you must take turns walking and riding."

"We have an old woman among us who may not be able to walk far," said Melchior.

"She need not, as long as she rides one of your camels, not mine. Remember any camel who cannot continue will be left behind, so be sure to distribute their packs and watch for blisters and pack sores. We'll assess a fee at each city for your portion of food, water and fodder. We aim for seven leagues a day but much depends on weather and water. We begin at daybreak day after tomorrow. Any questions?"

"Only one," said Melchior. "Who is your next man? We should know, just in case."

"Just in case?" Tariq sniggered. "Abdul is my manager. He can settle disputes, collect duties and fees, but he is not me, and never shall be. Anything more?"

"No. I've done this before," said Balthazar.

Tariq raised his eyebrows. "Good. Then we shouldn't have any misunderstandings."

"I don't like that man," said Balthazar when they were well away from Tariq's tent.

"I could tell. He whined like my sister-in-law, Dahab, but I thought perhaps there was something else behind your rancor."

"I know you're an astrologer but are you a diviner as well? How could you tell?

"I have learned to read men's faces, my boy. It's part of my trade. We predict what we see in the stars, but we must always watch how our patrons react to our words. Do they like what we're telling them or not? Especially as regards the king. Do we see joy and eagerness in his face or fear, hatred and anger? If we see an emotion that may create a problem we can couch our predictions . . . how shall I say? In better terms. Understand?"

"I think so."

Melchior nodded. "So what about the caravan master made you angry, for I'm almost certain it was anger that I saw."

"He's a Himyarite. A Himyarite tribe destroyed my village and killed my family. I know because I saw some of their dead bodies. Tariq wore the same style of clothes and had a talisman hanging from his neck just like the ones I saw on the Himyarites in Khalan."

"Could he be from the same tribe that attacked your village?" asked Melchior.

"He could. Do you understand now why I don't like him?"

"I do."

The men made their way back to camp and told their companions when the caravan would leave.

Since we are trekking again so soon," said Gaspar, "what do you say we take a respite in the time we have left? My body is crying out for water?"

"I thought your thirsting days were done," said Melchior.

"They are. What I propose is a day at the baths, if we can find one. I haven't bathed since we submerged in that icy, cold stream near Jerusalem."

"Nor have I," said Melchior.

"None of us has," said Balthazar. "There hasn't been time."

"Then come along men!" said Gaspar. "We're going to the baths."

The Journey Home

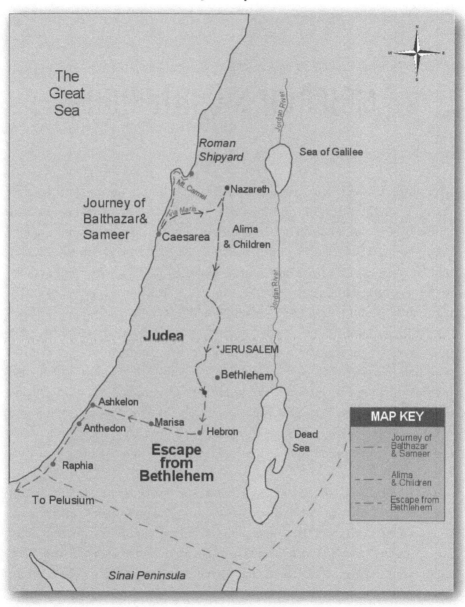

CHAPTER 36

Melchior's Confusion

§

MELCHIOR WALKED BACK FROM THE baths in a better mood than he had gone. Though he had not imbibed like his drunken companions, he had enjoyed every other offering of the bath, including some female companionship. It had been a long time since he had done so, and its effect had been unexpected. Rather than regretting it as he often had, today he felt energized and renewed. Yes, the visit to the baths had come at the right time, and he hoped the feeling would last.

Still, looking at his rowdy friends, he wondered if it might have been wiser to attend them in the pool, rather than the young woman who had ministered to him so pleasingly. Would the women folk accuse him of shirking his duty? He could already picture their shaking heads and raised fingers. But blast it all! Couldn't Gaspar have exerted some influence on the younger men in his absence? But that was a ridiculous thought! He had no doubt Gaspar had led them down the boozy path to befuddlement.

Melchior tried not to look reproving as arm over arm, Balthazar and Asher sang their way into camp. Alima and Corinna came out of their tent looking even more troubled than he had expected. With stony faces they watched as Balthazar and Asher slapped each other on the back before sauntering off to their shared tent. To his surprise the women didn't follow their men, but walked instead toward him. Was it something other than anger he saw in their faces? His full gut felt empty as they stopped just paces away.

"I am sorry, Melchior, but we must deliver sad news," said Alima with tears in her eyes. "It's Bina."

"What happened?" he asked, already knowing from the look on her face.

Alima recounted the afternoon's tale. How they had gone to the bay with the children. How Bina had been washing Isaac at the water's edge when they were attacked by a crocodile. How Bina had grabbed the boy and run so fast and far. "She saved Isaac! She saved him, Melchior! He would be dead now if not for her."

He nodded. "Bina always loved children. But I don't understand. You say the croc didn't get to them? Then what happened to her?"

"I told her to run as I tried to distract the monster. She was quick at first, but I could see it was hard on her as she ran on. Isaac is heavy, and the sand was deep. She slowed her pace but did not stop, even when she could have. I think the fright and exertion were too much. We found her slumped here in camp only a short time later."

"Take me to her."

Melchior knelt down next to Bina's body, shaking his head. How could it be? Only hours ago she had been cooking, laughing and lively as ever. His lips trembled. *Where was I when she needed me?* While he had been bathing, lounging, fornicating, this slave woman who had cared for him since childhood had been caring for another child, and dying. Suddenly, he felt Gaspar's wobbly hand on his shoulder. "I'm soooo . . . sorry, old friend. Thisss . . . this is . . . a greeeevous loss."

Melchior looked up at him. "You should sleep it off, Gaspar."

"Don't tell me what I shhh, shh. . . ould do, Melll ... chior! Bina was . . . my friend, too!" Gaspar sniffled, and Melchior could see his eyes were wet.

"Well then, tell me for I don't understand."

"Tell you ...what?" Gaspar mumbled through thick lips.

"Why is the Lord punishing me? Have I not done all that was asked? I saw the star and followed it! My mother died and I reburied her in

Judea! After years of studying the prophecies and the stars I found the Messiah! And this is how I am rewarded?" His voice shook with anger.

Gaspar sat, opened his water bladder and poured it over his head. He was silent for some time before speaking again. He sounded almost sober when he did. "Why do you blame this on your Lord, my friend? Bina was old. It was her time, as it will be mine and yours someday. But a reward? What did you expect?" Gaspar shook his head as he closed his eyes.

Melchior let the last remark pass. "I know she was old. But she was a special part of my life, Gaspar."

"She was your slave."

Melchior glared at him. "You know she was much more to me!"

"Then why didn't you free her the way Asher did Corinna? I never told you, but after Corinna joined us, Bina talked to me."

"She did?"

"Yes. She said she would never leave you . . . but her slavery still chafed. She wanted to make her own decisions like any free person. She wanted her time to be her own. She didn't understand why you gave your gold to free Corinna but did not do the same for her who served you for so long."

"I keep asking myself that. In truth, I never thought of it 'til these last days. And there were times, I thought I saw the question in her eyes. As if she was asking: 'Why not me?' I planned to surprise her when we returned to Seleucia. But I should have told her! I should have..." Melchior began to sob.

"I see," said Gaspar. "You feel guilty for not telling her, and you're blaming it on your God."

Melchior rose and for the first time in his life looked upon Gaspar in anger. "You foolish drunkard! How dare you say such a thing? You who accept no God! Worship no God! And yet you judge me about mine? I thought you were my friend, Gaspar." He walked away.

The rest of the night passed quietly. Melchior spoke to no-one and no-one spoke to him. Whether it was his grief, his glower, or his restless eyes, he cared not. The silence was a relief. He could think in the silence. He had to bury Bina in the morning and must decide how to go about it. Most in his class of society wouldn't care a whit to bury a slave. They would throw her in a pit and be done with it. But Bina had been family to him. True, she had been born a Samaritan, but that had meant nothing to him. She had always respected him. So despite his growing doubt and uncertainty, he would bury her as a Jew.

After supper, he began to prepare her body. He filled a bowl with water and found a clean cloth to perform the ritual cleansing. As he wiped her body down, his mind wandered back to the day he and Bina had prepared his mother's body. How he had depended on her then. When the cleansing was done, he blessed her body with drops of oil and sprinkled some frankincense and myrrh that Balthazar had given him. Then he unwound a small piece of cloth to shroud her upper body. It was the unused cloth he had been saving for Gaspar's foot, but it was all he had. He wrapped it around her head and neck and used one of her old robes to wrap the rest of her. Then he lit a torch to keep animals away, and threw a blanket around himself as he waited for the dawn.

When the sun rose, he felt calmer. He had no desire for food, but drank some water, before calling to his companions. "My friends, if you would honor Bina, please come to her burial." The men came out of their tents one by one.

"Have you dug her grave yet?" asked Asher yawning.

"Not yet," said Melchior.

"Then I will help you," said Asher.

"So will I," said Balthazar.

"And I," said Gaspar.

The three men followed Melchior to the ground he had selected and began to dig. Though the soil was sandy, it took some time to dig a hole, deep enough. When they were done, they were all sweating and thirsty.

"I need some water," said Gaspar rising from his knees.

"Thank you for your help," said Melchior.

"I did it for Bina, not you," said Gaspar as he strode off.

Asher and Balthazar exchanged glances but stayed to help Melchior finish the burial. Soon after the soil had been levelled over her body, Gaspar returned with the women and children. Except for the children who chattered among themselves, they stood somber and silent.

"Will you say some words?" asked Asher.

"I will try." Melchior raised his head to the sky. He wanted the right words to honor Bina but nothing came to him. For a long time he was mute. It frustrated him. Tested him. It would not do! Finally, in anger he burst out: "Why Lord? You know all things, so why did you take her before she had a chance to taste freedom? She was a good woman. She wasn't a Jew but are Jews the only ones who matter to you? If there is a life after death, then I beg you to receive her. And tell her that I loved her, because I never got the chance."

CHAPTER 37
Corinna's Past

§

ASHER LEFT CAMP AFTER BINA's burial. They had used up their salted meat soon after leaving Bethlehem and the rapid pace of their journey left no time for hunting. They were subsisting on nuts, fruit and grains, and he wanted more.

Fish and fowl were his quarry so he carried a sling, a bow and a net, hoping opportunity would present itself in the marshes to the east. He poked his way through the reeds, surveying the land for prey, and watching for reptiles. So far, except for the leeches that clung to his legs, he was enjoying the solitary hunt and wetland vistas. After sloshing through several empty pools, he spotted a large raft of ducks on a pond ahead. He drew an arrow from his quiver, nocked it, fixed his stance and let it fly. One duck fell. But any chance for another was lost as the startled flock rose skyward. He retrieved his kill and waited for the flock to return, but when his wait went unrewarded, decided to fish instead.

With his duck over his shoulder, he moved upstream hoping to find a place where the water was deeper, and fish might hide among the rocks. It took him some time, but he eventually found a place. Unfortunately, the stream had a shelf edge and no rocks where he could step out into the current. So he stripped a long branch from a nearby bush, tied his net to it with some braided reeds and extended it as far as he could into the current. He held it out there, occasionally changing arms, waiting, and watching for the glint of fins below the surface. Finally, he felt the weight of a catch and pulled the net from the water. Three fish wiggled their greeting. It was time to head back.

By the time he returned, the women were back from the bath and greeted him with smiles.

"These will make a hearty meal," said Alima.

"That is my hope," said Asher. "Will you teach Corinna how to clean them?"

"I can do that," said Alima. "But she may already know how. She said Bina taught her many things over the last months. Will you help Balthazar with Isaac while we work? I think he could use a little help." The loudly wailing child was perched precariously on Balthazar's shoulder as he tried to play with the girls.

"Let me have Isaac," said Asher holding out his hands.

"With pleasure," said Balthazar. "The boy doesn't seem to like me right now."

Asher took Isaac, sat him on his knees and began to sing. The child's eyes fastened on him, and soon the crying became a low whimper. Asher continued to sing and soon Isaac began to smile, then to giggle as Asher tickled him on his tummy.

Balthazar drew closer. "How did you do that? I tried to make him smile but nothing seemed to work."

"I like to sing," said Asher. "I sing to my sheep when they're restless. And I've watched my older sister sing to her babies, so. . ."

"You are a wonder!" said Balthazar, clapping Asher on the shoulder.

"Are we ready for the caravan tomorrow?" asked Asher as he continued to hum to Isaac.

"I think so," said Balthazar lowering his voice and gesturing toward Gaspar and Melchior. "They've been packing all day. Not together though. They're like oil and water today."

"Do you think they'll make it up?'

"I hope so, or this caravan may prove very unpleasant."

Just then Gaspar walked over to join them. "I see it's been another successful day for you Asher. We will never starve if you are close at hand."

"I hope not!" said Asher smiling. He looked over to where Corinna and Alima were cutting up his kills. "Did the women enjoy the bath?"

Balthazar nodded. "Alima said it was good, except for an incident as they were leaving."

"What happened?"

"Alima said several men were entering as they left, and one of them approached Corinna."

"Approached in what way?"

"How do you think? He said he remembered her from the caravan-sary. He complimented her on her 'special gifts' and asked if he might enjoy them again."

Asher stopped humming. "What did she do?"

"She told him he was mistaken; that she was not the girl he thought. But Alima doesn't think the man believed her. It could be a problem in the future,"

Asher's face grew serious. "Why could it be a problem? We're leaving tomorrow."

"Because he is the caravan master. His name is Tariq."

Asher shook his head. "She's a free woman! This Tariq had better not touch her, or I swear I will smite him."

Gaspar cut in. "Asher, think back. Corinna's owner sold her to Melchior. He thought she was going to be a concubine in Melchior's harem, so the papers we got show Melchior as her owner. They do not say she is a free woman. Melchior must grant you papers to show that when our trek is done, and the money you owe him is earned."

"Yes. But what difference does it make? She is free! We are betrothed and this man has no right to taunt her with her past!"

"You're right," said Balthazar. "But he's the caravan master. Tariq can make trouble for all of us if he chooses."

"Then what's to be done?"

"You may not like this idea," said Gaspar. "But it may be the best way to protect Corinna. Let her stay in the tent with Melchior and me. Once this Tariq realizes she belongs to Melchior, he should leave her alone."

"If you think it will keep her safe, I will allow it. I will do anything for her, I swear it!"

Later that night, as the women were putting the children to sleep Asher decided to ask Melchior for his help. He explained how Tariq had spoken to Corinna and how he was concerned for her safety during the journey ahead.

"I don't understand," said Melchior. "What has this to do with me? She is your betrothed and your responsibility to protect."

Asher nodded. "She is, but Gaspar reminded me that her papers still show her as your property."

"Did he now?" Melchior shot an irritated glance at Gaspar.

"Yes, I did," interrupted Gaspar quickly. "Tariq is a mongrel dog, Melchior. He will sniff around the women if we let him, but he won't knowingly violate your harem once he knows of it."

"The plan has merit, but it's your plan, Gaspar! I have no wish to be part of it. Enjoy your harem, Gaspar."

CHAPTER 38
The Caravan Begins

§

ALIMA STRAPPED ISAAC TO HER chest and burrowed her nose in his hair. Miriam and Rebecca shared the camel in front of hers. They wouldn't like riding together, but Alima cared not. They were too young to walk and she wanted them where she could see them. They were her children now and she meant to do right by them.

The men ran up and down the line, securing tethers and checking packs. Hundreds of camels roared, growled, and snorted their impatience to move. Miriam and Rebecca covered their ears, but the cacophony didn't ease until the command to start repeated down the lines. Their path would take them southeast into the desert, first to Al-Ula, then south to Najran, Ma rib`, Shabwa and Qana. The trek was over five hundred leagues, and would take over two months, but she would be with Balthazar and the children. What more could she want?

Corinna rode behind her with Gaspar walking at her side. The men had decided she would travel as his concubine and sleep in his tent to help assure her safety. Balthazar had asked Alima if she, too, would feel safer with Gaspar. "Tariq cannot be trusted, Alima. But he dare not violate another man's harem."

Alima had shaken her head. "I've had enough of pretending for my lifetime. Besides, if I must be in a harem, it will be in yours. " Her remark had brought a smile to his face and a gratifying reply.

"Then you shall travel as my wife and sleep in my tent. If that Himyarite bastard dares to bother you, he will see my vengeance."

The first weeks of travel went smoothly. The camels trod from sunrise to sunset, with breaks each afternoon when the sun was hottest. So far, the weather obliged. Cool breezes brushed their faces, and no storms hindered their progress. But it was late spring; the monsoon rains were already late.

The children were adjusting to the new rhythm of caravan life. Miriam and Rebecca had complained about riding together, until Balthazar told them they must prove their ability to share a saddle before they could ride alone. Now they sat quiet as butterflies on a desert flower. Even Isaac seemed happier. The child who had refused almost every kind of sustenance after Judith's death was now taking sheep and goat's milk from a cup along with bread, fruit and grains. He was gaining weight and trusting her like a mother. More and more she felt that she was. Considering the time needed to care for the children, she was relieved not to cook. The cost of the caravan included charges for food, so they ate what the cooks made, whether they liked it or not.

Alima could tell that Melchior in particular disliked the food. What a changed man he seemed since Bina's death! He had appeared happy enough when she met him in Bethlehem; considerate and courteous though quiet. And his willingness to instruct the children about Judaism had certainly earned her gratitude. He had already begun to instruct them during some of their evening stops. Yet she sensed a sadness in him. Balthazar had described him as a man of purpose. The Melchior she saw these days looked listless and lonely. When they traveled he was disturbingly silent, and on the infrequent days when they rested, he showed no inclination to talk with his old friend Gaspar, to watch the improvised entertainments or join in games. Amid the commotion of caravan life Melchior's reserve took on a chilling tone.

Three weeks from Arsinoe they arrived in the oasis town of Al-Ula. How beautiful, thought Alima. The town sat in a narrow valley, rimmed on the west by high red sandstone cliffs. Date palms stretched far into the distance and spring-fed pools reflected sky and rock in a patchwork of mottled blue and red.

From her camel she beckoned Balthazar to come closer. "This looks a pleasant place. Do you think we'll stay a while?"

"I think so. The next stage of our trek will be the longest, so we must rest while we can." When the camels halted, Alima unstrapped Isaac and handed him to Balthazar. She dismounted and found a kiss waiting for her as Balthazar handed Isaac back.

"Will you find some time for me in the days ahead?" he asked, nuzzling her neck.

"Don't tell me you are jealous of the children."

"How can I help it? I see how you kiss them and stroke their brows. It is enough to drive me mad. But I have considered it, and have made a decision. You may continue to shower them with your affection on one condition."

Alima cocked her head. "And that would be?"

"That you promise me the same one day soon."

Alima smiled broadly. "I do promise, when we are wed."

"So my madness must continue?" Balthazar dropped his head in what Alima knew was a sign of feigned frustration. "A man must always know where he stands with his woman."

She laughed. "And now you do. But I promise to make the wait worth your while."

Balthazar kissed her again on her brow. "I shall see that you do!"

She helped the girls from their camel as Balthazar went to help the men. The children had to be thirsty after the afternoon's hot ride so she poured them all some water. One after the other, they gulped it down.

"Can I help?' asked Corinna bending down to play with Isaac.

"We've run out of water," said Alima shaking the last drop into Miriam's wooden cup. "Will you ask Gaspar to walk us to the well?"

"No need," said Corinna. "Many women at well. We take children. Be safe."

Alima shook her head. "The men will not like it, Corinna."

"Gaspar busy with camel. We go." Corinna pulled a leather water bucket from her pack, picked Isaac up from the ground and walked off in the direction of the well.

Alima looked on in dismay. "Come girls, we must catch up to her." After collecting their canteens, she took the girls by the hand and ran after Corinna. They got to the well just in time to see the caravan master walk up behind the younger woman.

"Thirsty are you, sweet one? I am too. But I thirst for more than water." He ran a finger along the nape of Corinna's neck. "Yes, one day soon I will show you how much I can drink."

Corinna jumped, and turned so quickly that she spilled the water bucket. Isaac began to cry. Some of the local women moved to the other side of the well.

Tariq looked surprised to see a child in Corinna's arms. "You have a son, my sweet? Could he be the fruit of my loins? I think his age makes it possible."

"He is my son," said Alima forcefully as she took Isaac from Corinna and looked straight at Tariq. "Corinna is no pornai. She belongs to Gaspar of Seleucia. "

"Is that so? And who is this Gaspar? I don't believe I've met the man."

"He's an advisor to King Phraates of Parthia. Corinna is a concubine in his harem, not a water trough. You'd best prepare your neck for a sword 'ere you speak to her like that again."

Tariq came closer, so that his face was but a hands length from Alima's. "A spirited one. I like that. And who might you be, little mother? I find one water trough may be as good as another when one is parched." He did not wait for an answer but puckered his lips and snickered. As he turned to leave he pointed to Miriam and Rebecca who stood just behind Alima. "Such lovely girls you have there! Perhaps they are thirsty, too?" His loud laugh echoed back as he strutted away.

Alima shook with fury. "That man is evil." She looked to Corinna. "I told you not to come alone. If Gaspar had been with us that would not have happened."

Corinna put her hands together and bowed. "I sorry. Make mistake. Will no do again." Tears ran down her cheeks.

"Who was that man?" asked Miriam. "You don't like him do you?"

"No, child. I don't. But he is the caravan master, so unfortunately we will see him again. You and Rebecca must promise not to go near him. Can you do that for me?"

"Yes, Alima," said Miriam.

"And you, Rebecca?"

"Yes, Alima. I promise," said Rebecca.

"Good." Alima took a breath and patted Corinna on the shoulder. "Don't worry. We will be all right. But we must stay near the men. All of us." When the bucket and canteens were filled, the women returned to camp, settled the children down for a rest and called the men together.

The men were enraged when they heard what had happened at the well. Asher looked especially angry and pulled his knife from its sheath. "Asher, Wait!" said Gaspar. "The man is a mongrel, but so far he has done no real harm. His words alone are no cause to kill."

"Gaspar's right," said Balthazar. "He's a Himyarite bastard but he's done nothing to warrant a knife."

"Not yet," said Asher. "Must we wait until he does? The man is a menace, and not just to Corinna."

Balthazar looked at the others. "Asher's right. All the women, even the girls are in danger. We dare not leave any of them alone."

Gaspar looked at Corinna. "You should have waited for me, Corinna. I took you into my tent to protect you but I cannot if you walk off alone."

Corinna lowered her eyes. "I very sorry. Will not do again. That man is bad. Very bad." Asher walked up behind her and put his hand on her shoulder. Corinna put her hand on his.

"Corinna understands," said Alima in the girl's defense. "She is right. Tariq is evil. If you could have seen how he looked at Miriam and Rebecca as he walked away. "

"You and the children will not leave my side!" Said Balthazar as he pulled out a knife from his tunic. "Alima, I want you to carry this knife, in case we get separated. Do you hear?"

Alima took the knife from his hand. "I hear you, Balthazar. I will gladly slice him to pieces if he ever touches my girls."

CHAPTER 39

Danger in the Desert

BALTHAZAR'S ANGER WAS PROFOUND. NOT since Khalan had he felt such rage. In the days that followed, he watched over Alima and his girls, as he now called them, with the eyes of a hawk. Everywhere they went, he went. If he was busy with the men, Alima knew to stay by his side. He told the girls they could not stray. No running and hiding, no seeking and startling 'til the caravan was done.

He was relieved to see Asher and Gaspar so attentive to Corinna. Though it was uncommon for men to accompany their women as they were, it was necessary, so they weren't bothered by the social customs. When the women carried water, so did Gaspar and Balthazar, when they washed clothes, so did the men, and when the women bathed so did they.

They stayed in Al-Ula three days, and Tariq did not bother the women again. Balthazar was glad but could not drop his guard nor feel secure in his family's safety. That would not come until the caravan was far behind them.

The next weeks were exhausting as they pushed across the desert at a harrowing pace. Further and further south they went. Each day felt like the last, with nothing but sand, sky, and an occasional rain storm to mark the passing of days. The weeks dragged on. Finally one afternoon, Balthazar spied some rocky peaks in the distance. He called up to Alima on her camel. "We're coming to a town! I think Najran is beyond that ridge. I overheard some men talking at supper. They say it is a good place."

"Did they say any more? I would know the particulars, my love."

"Ah yes! I forgot you are a woman who likes the fine points. Let me see. They said it's nestled in a sprawling oasis, has many palm groves, plentiful orchards and many fresh water springs. Does that satisfy you, Princess Alima?"

She smiled at him. "Yes it does, Prince Balthazar. I hope we will stay some days. The children and I are ready for a rest."

"As we all are."

Two leagues on, they passed the ridge, and there was Najran, just as he'd pictured. Hundreds of flat-roofed clay houses populated the city, some of them with eye-catching white edges. Here and there he saw men sitting on their roofs with their women, and he imagined himself there with Alima, enjoying the breezes rolling off the rocks.

When camels stopped, he went through the familiar routine of unleashing the animals, taking them to water and pitching tents. Now however, he did so with Alima and the children in tow. And when he was done, he brought them to an oasis pool to bathe. Many of his fellow travelers were doing the same. The women and children were at one end of the pond, the men at the other. As far as he could see he was the only man bathing with his family, but he dared not forget Tariq's threat.

The other bathers reminded him of festival revelers as they lounged under the palms, laughter erupting like bubbles from an over-fermented cask. Even Melchior, who had been so sour of late looked content as he soaked in the freshwater pool. With his eyes still on his family Balthazar swam toward him.

"How are you, my friend? You have been so solitary these past weeks. . . I wonder . . . is something weighing on you?"

"Perhaps a little. It has been a trying time, has it not?"

"Mmm. The long days have been hard. But the Bedouins have lived the nomad life for centuries; I'm sure we can endure it another month."

"True enough. You think like a scholar, my boy. You will make a splendid astrologer one day."

"I'm eager for it."

"Are you? I remember feeling that way once, but my eagerness is gone. I fear what we may find back in Seleucia."

"But surely your position is secure? Didn't you say your brother is the satrap?"

"I did. What I did not tell you . . . is that we do not often see eye to eye. I'm sure he considers our brotherhood a trick of nature, for we are nothing alike. The tenuous bond we share is nurtured more by mutual suspicion, than love. We speak when we must and do things for each other only to secure private goals. We are not Cain and Abel, but we're not far from it."

"Who are Cain and Able?" asked Balthazar.

"The first sons of the first parents on earth. Their brotherhood ended in death."

"Your thoughts are dark ones, Melchior. Come swim with me to Alima. And think on this: If your brother is not family to you, choose a new one. The children have no grandfather . . . Does the title suit you?"

Melchior looked confused. "You want me to act as Grandfather? To your children?"

"Yes. You are teaching them like one. Do you think it a foolish notion?"

Melchior shook his head. "Not at all. I am complimented that you should ask. I only hope I can do justice to my role as their teacher ..."

"It is a responsibility I have no doubt you will live up to," said Balthazar. "Now will you join us?"

"I will. And thank you for your trust, Balthazar. It is a beautiful day, is it not?"

The remaining days in Najran were equally beautiful. Monsoon rains drummed on their tents at night, but by morning the skies were clear. Melchior began to spend more time with Balthazar and his family, and Balthazar was glad. They strolled through the city each morning and rested by the oasis pool in the afternoon. At night while the children slept, Balthazar and Alima held each other. He had often wondered how she would feel in his arms. Now he knew and thanked Melchior's Hebrew God for returning her to him.

Many days of travel followed, but the going was easier, for they were on the edge of the Rub'al Khali near the fertile land the Romans called Arabia Felix. High rock peaks, fertile slopes and plentiful rainfall lay ahead. Yes, Balthazar knew these lands and their history. The Queen of Sheba had ruled here; had brought gold and incense to Solomon from here, and traders like his father had bought and sold spice along these trails for centuries. The familiarity brought him comfort as each day brought them closer to Qana.

Three weeks later the caravan wound its way toward the city of Marib. The waters of the Wadi Adhanah were full from the spring rains. "Do you see the Great Dam, Alima? The Sabaeans built it over seven hundred years ago, and it's still spilling water out to the surrounding fields!"

Alima looked at the dam in the distance. "It is amazing!"

"Isn't it? The locals can control how much water goes to the fields by opening and closing the dam's sluice gates. It's a feat of engineering even the Romans would admire."

They camped on the eastern outskirts of Marib and stayed two short days before moving on. The caravan master had not come near the women since the men had instituted their watch pattern but Balthazar maintained his vigilance. The camel train continued east then south into the Do'an valley toward Shabwa. We're almost to Qana, Balthazar thought as he looked to Alima. We're almost man and wife.

"Have you ever been here, Alima?" He asked as the camels halted on the plain west of the city wall.

"No. Until I met you I had only ever been to Qana and Khalan."

He smiled. "You are a world traveler now."

"I am, but it will be good to see Qana and my family again."

"Have you thought about what you will say to them?"

"You mean about Sameer and father? I hope we can tell them together. We had good reasons for not returning to Caesarea. When they see the children they should understand."

"I hope you are right. . ." he paused. "You remember the Temple of Serapis?"

"In Berenike . . . of course I do."

"There's another temple here in Marib. Would you like to see it?"

Alima shook her head. "I don't think so, but thank you for offering to take me."

"You enjoyed Serapis; I thought you might like this one, too."

"Six months ago I might have. But since Judea, Judith's Hebrew god is the only one I want to learn about. Anyway, the girls need to run and play. And Isaac looks sick; I want him to rest near the tent."

"Then that's what we shall do."

That night, they enjoyed an unusually good meal of roasted duck and barley. Melchior, who had been sitting with them each night for supper, even complimented the cook to his friends. "That was a wonderful meal. Not as good as Bina's, but almost. Duck was always one of her specialties."

"She had a way with food," agreed Balthazar.

Melchior belched loudly and the children laughed. "I think I have eaten enough for one night. Would you girls like to play before you sleep?"

The girls looked to Alima. "May we, Alima? Please?" They jumped up and down waiting for an answer."

"Yes. Go ahead. But stay with Melchior. Do you hear?"

Balthazar, Alima and Isaac remained as Melchior escorted the girls outside the large eating tent.

"How is our boy Isaac? He doesn't look sick anymore," said Balthazar.

"You're right. A little shade and water made a big difference."

"It sounds like he had the sun sickness. We must take care to keep his head covered."

"I try but he keeps pulling off his scarf. We must find a way to keep it on him."

"We'll think of something." They walked around talking to other young parents, trading stories about child rearing and listening to how they protected their children from the sun. Sometime later they returned to their campsite to see Melchior walking out of his tent alone.

"Where are the girls, Melchior?" asked Alima.

"I don't know. I left them here just moments ago."

"Why did you leave them alone?" Alima asked sounding upset.

Melchior scratched his head, but began to look worried. "I promise you I was only gone a few moments while I went to retrieve a piece of papyrus. I was going to show them how to write on it. They can't be far." He began to roam the grounds calling their names. "Miriam! Rebecca! Where are you?"

Alima and Balthazar called out also, but got no answer. "This isn't good, Alima," said Balthazar. "Where are the others? We may need their help!"

"They went to the Shabwa Temple," said Melchior.

"Then we must search ourselves. Alima, take Isaac back to look in the supper tent. Can you search around the pool, Melchior? I'm going toward Tariq's tent."

"Do you really think he would take them?" asked Alima.

"I do, and he will pay for it if he has."

Balthazar ran as quickly as he could to Tariq's tent. Even in the darkening sky he could find it because of the red flag that waved above it. He didn't bother to announce himself but pushed the flap aside to enter. No-one was in it. Not Tariq, not the girls, and neither of his two servants. Coming out he searched the area around the tent, calling the girls' names as he went. "Miriam! Rebecca!" He called again and again.

After some minutes he heard Melchior calling to him. "Balthazar, I found them! They're safe."

He walked in the direction of Melchior's voice and found him standing with his arms around the girls.

"Where did you find them?" asked Balthazar.

"They were near the pool."

Balthazar squatted down to look at them. "Girls what did I tell you about going off by yourselves? Especially at night?"

"But we didn't go by ourselves, Balthazar. We were with a boy."

"What boy?"

"I don't know his name, but I think he's a servant of the caravan master."

"Why did you go with him? You know we don't want you anywhere near Tariq."

"We know, but Tariq wasn't with him. It was only the boy. He said we had to go with him right away or we would miss the mermaid."

"The mermaid?"

"Yes. We were waiting by Melchior's tent, and the boy asked if we wanted to see a mermaid in the pool. He said he would show us where she was. But when we got there the mermaid was gone. The boy left. Then we heard Melchior calling us."

Balthazar and Melchior exchanged glances. "Someone wanted us away from our tents," said Balthazar. "We must hurry back. How fast can you run, girls?"

The men raced the girls back to their campsite and found Asher, Gaspar and Corinna talking by the fire pit.

"Have you seen Alima and Isaac?" asked Balthazar.

"No. We wondered where everyone was. Has something happened?"

"I can't explain now, but something is not right." He ran at once to his tent, poked his head in before turning around a yelling to his friends. "Someone struggled in our tent! Our clothes are scattered and one of the blankets is ripped. Gaspar, can you stay with Corinna and the girls while the rest of us look for Alima and Isaac? I fear someone has taken them."

"Yes, of course. We'll go to my tent and won't leave until we hear your voice. Come ladies."

Balthazar raced Asher and Melchior back to Tariq's tent.

"You think Tariq has taken Alima?" asked Asher.

"Yes. I think he told his servant boy to call the girls away knowing we would separate to search for them," said Balthazar.

"And you think he took Alima when she returned to your tent?" asked Melchior.

"I do. There was no one in Tariq's tent before, but he may be there now. We must look again."

When the men got near Tariq's tent, Balthazar put up his hand. "Shh. Let us listen first." He waited only long enough to hear Alima's sobs before rushing inside. What he saw reminded him of Khalan. Alima sat sobbing in the middle of the tent, her robe pulled up around her waist. Tariq's body lay next to her, a knife embedded deep in his chest.

"Alima! How? How did he get you?"

"He surprised me in our tent. I wanted to leave Isaac there but he wouldn't let me. He said he would kill Isaac if I didn't come with him. But Isaac soon started crying, and Tariq became enraged, so he tossed him into some shrubs near the pool. Like he was a piece of dried wood. You must find him. Don't worry for me. Go find my boy!"

Balthazar nodded. "Melchior, will you stay with her while we look for Isaac?"

"Yes. Hurry! I'll stay with her."

Asher and Balthazar ran from the tent. "We should get a torch. It's too dark to search without one," said Asher. "I'll fetch one from the supper tent while you start looking near the pool."

Balthazar hurried on as Asher ran to get a torch. "Thank you for the full moon tonight, Lord," he said aloud. It was the first time he had consciously prayed to Melchior's Jewish God but somehow it felt right. He needed help to find Isaac, and if Melchior's God had helped Alima on her way to Nazareth, maybe God would help him, too. The moon's reflection off the water brightened the area enough that he could easily search the edge of the pool. Isaac was no-where near the water's edge, but where was he? Asher returned just as Balthazar was starting to move his search further back from the water.

"Hold it high, Asher. You look left and I'll look right. Alima said Tariq threw him into the bushes, so let's pay close attention to those areas first."

"Let's look over here," said Asher pointing to an area of deep brush. "They might have walked past this area going from your tent to his."

"All right," said Balthazar. "Let's look."

Asher held the torch high above the bushes as they worked their way around the brush. The area was long and wide, and they tried to look far into it but with all the new growth it was hard to see past five paces. "Do you see that?" said Asher. "There's a spot about seven paces in where the branches are bent. I think something is weighing them down."

Balthazar used his arms to part the brush as Asher held the torch above their heads. "Watch that torch," said Balthazar. "Some of this brush is dry as tinder."

"I know," said Asher. "Do you see anything yet?"

"I think . . ." Balthazar walked a few more paces and bent down. "It's him! It's him, Asher. He's hurt but alive." Balthazar pulled him out amid a burst of curses and grunts, for the child was entangled in a thorn bush. When they were beyond the worst of it, Balthazar brought Isaac to the pool and lay him by the water's edge. Then he scooped some water into his hands and poured it on the child's face. Isaac's body shivered. Balthazar poured more water on him, and used his hands to wipe the blood from his face.

"Is he bleeding much?" asked Asher.

"No. He has some scratches from the thorns, but I don't see any deep wounds." Just then Isaac opened his eyes and Balthazar used his hands to smooth the boy's hair. "It's all right, Isaac. You're safe. I'm taking you to Alima."

CHAPTER 40
Ghosts of Khalan

§

MELCHIOR FELT RESTLESS AS HE waited with Alima. There was no deny-ing she was shaken, and he felt responsible. If only he hadn't left the chil-dren alone! But how could he help her now? He couldn't, *wouldn't* just sit and wait! Slowly, he washed the blood from her hands with water from his canteen. Then knowing the knife belonged to Balthazar, removed it from Tariq's body and put it within the folds of his tunic. "Come out-side," he said to Alima. "Why should you look upon this wretched man's body when you can breathe the fragrant air of the desert night?"

"Is it fragrant, Melchior?"

"It is. Come breathe of it. When Isaac is back and things are righted, the air will help you put this memory behind you." He escorted Alima from the tent, removed his cloak and laid it on the ground. "Sit with me. We'll wait for Isaac together."

"I fear for him, Melchior. He's so little and Tariq threw him away like he meant nothing! What if he's dead?"

"Then you will mourn him as any mother who loses a son, but I do not think it will happen."

"Why not?"

"Balthazar told me about Judith. How you traveled so far with the children after her death. I have questioned the Lord greatly of late, and cannot presume to know his ways, but why would he help you care for the children then only to take Isaac from you now? No, I think Isaac's days on this earth are far from numbered."

A few moments later, two boys approached as if to enter Tariq's tent. Melchior leapt up in front of them. "Where are you going, boys?"

"We are Tariq's servants. I want to look in my master's tent," said the older boy. "He took something from me and I want it back."

"If this is true, you shall have it. But I have questions for you first. Sit down." The boys sat where Melchior pointed. He was about to begin his questioning when Balthazar arrived with Asher. "Alima! Melchior! See who we found!"

Alima jumped up. "Oh Balthazar! You found him! Is he all right?"

"He is. Sit down so I may hand him to you." She sat back on Melchior's cloak and Balthazar gave Isaac into her arms.

"Oh, my boy! Are you all right? I was so frightened for you." Her eyes ran down the length and breadth of him, looking for cuts, breaks, bruises.

"He has a big bump on the back of his head and many scratches from the thorns, but I think he will be fine," said Balthazar.

"Praise God!" said Alima. She looked into Isaac's eyes. "I love you, little boy. You know that, don't you?" Isaac looked confused, his eyes moving from one person to another. Then suddenly, he smiled up at her. "Momma. Momma!" he said again, as he put his arms around her neck.

Alima's eyes swelled with tears as she spoke into his ear. "Yes, my precious boy. I'm your momma. And this is your poppa." She raised her eyes to Balthazar, and rocked him. "His eyes are heavy, Balthazar. Can we go back? I want to see the girls before they fall asleep."

"Soon," said Balthazar. "First, we must tell Tariq's second man what's happened. Do you remember his name, Melchior?"

"Abdul. But I'd like to question Tariq's servants first."

"Go ahead," said Balthazar. "We should find out all we can before we call Abdul."

Melchior looked to the younger servant first. "Tell me boy, why did you take the girls to the pool tonight?"

The young boy's eyes darted around in a look of panic.

"It's all right, Abu. You can tell them," said the older one, putting his arms around the other. "The master is dead. He can't hurt you anymore."

Abu nodded. "Master say he give me a drachma if I take girls to the pool. He say there are mermaids in pool. That we can see if we hurry. So I tell girls, and they follow."

"Did you know what your master was doing while you were at the pool?"

Abu began to blink rapidly. He looked confused. "What master do? I don't understand. . ." he pounded his fists to his head. "I don't know. I don't know. I don't know . . ." he started to cry.

The older boy put his hand on the younger one's shoulder. "It's all right, I tell you. Don't cry. These men will not hurt you." He looked to Melchior. "Abu is my brother. He doesn't always understand things."

"The young one looks simple minded," said Melchior. "He probably had no idea what his master was planning."

"It would seem Tariq was just using him," said Balthazar.

Melchior looked to the older brother. "Where were you tonight, boy?"

"My master gave me some drachmas to buy him wine in the town."

"And did you?"

"Yes. I have it here." The boy held up a small pottery jug.

"Why did Tariq want the wine, boy?" asked Melchior.

"He said he was having a lady guest in his tent tonight. He wanted the wine for her."

Melchior nodded. "When you returned with the wine, did you see your master?"

"No. But I heard him arguing in the tent. He was swearing at that lady." The servant pointed to Alima.

"How do you know it was that lady? Did you look into the tent?"

"No, but my master pointed her out to me earlier in the day. He said she was the one who would visit him."

"Did you hear anything else he said?"

The servant nodded. "My master was very angry. He said he would not be laughed at. That he would have her even if he killed her first."

"Did the lady say anything?"

"She said she was promised. That he should keep his hands off her or he would be sorry."

"You didn't stick your head into the tent during the argument?"

"No, sir. I was afraid what my master would do if he caught me watching. I did it once, and he said he would make me a eunuch if he caught me watching him again. So I stayed outside the tent listening until I heard the lady crying. I peeked in then to see if she was all right, and saw my master dead. Then I ran to find my brother."

"You say you watched your master once before. How often has he done this kind of thing?"

"Once on every caravan. He would pick someone, usually a woman that he liked, but sometimes a boy or a girl."

"Did he use your brother in this way also?" asked Melchior.

Tears ran down the boy's face. "Yes. I wanted to stop him but he said he would kill Abu if I told anyone."

"Tariq was an evil man, boy. He did evil things and paid for it with his life. You and your brother are free now. There is no reason to fear him. But you must stay with us until Abdul comes. I want you to tell him what you told us, so he knows this lady was not at fault."

The older boy swallowed. "But I don't like Abdul! Must we stay?"

Melchior nodded. "Yes, we need you."

Tears continued to fall down his face as the boy bit his lip. "Can I retrieve my property from the master's tent now? Please?"

"Be patient, boy," said Melchior.

"I'll help him," said Balthazar moving toward the tent. "Asher, can you get Abdul? Tell him Tariq is dead, and he must determine what to do with the body. I think if he's smart, he'll leave it for the birds."

Balthazar accompanied the older servant into Tariq's tent. "What's your name, boy?"

"Fatin."

"That was my father's name," said Balthazar. "Where are you from?"

"From Khalan in the Hadramaut. It's . . ."

Balthazar looked dumbstruck and studied the boy. "I know where it is. Khalan was my town too. I don't remember you though. How did you come to be with Tariq?"

"When his tribe raided Khalan, they killed everyone except for my brother and me. They took us because they were angry with our father. They claimed he and another man cheated them. That they had lost many drachmas because of them."

"Do you remember the name of the other man?"

"I think they called him Sahl."

"Why did they take you?"

"They said Sahl had no sons but my father did. They wanted my father to know, before he died, that his youngest sons would be slaves to his enemies."

"How did your father cheat him, Fatin?"

"I don't think he did. My father was a good man. But I didn't know about Sahl. "

"What was your father's name?"

"His name was Jabir. He was a metal worker."

"I remember him. Did you have an older brother?"

"Yes. His name was Hakim."

"I knew him," said Balthazar. "I asked him to make a necklace for my sister once. He did very nice work."

"Yes. . . They were teaching me in the shop the day Tariq killed them. I hated him!" The boy kicked Tariq's body with all his strength.

Balthazar waited for his anger to subside. "What are you looking for? Tell me what Tariq took from you; maybe I can help you find it."

"My talisman. My father made one for me and one for Abu. We wore them on cords around our necks, but Tariq took them from us after our capture. He said slaves had no need of talismans."

"Let us look for them." As Balthazar helped the boy search Tariq's possessions, he came across a draw string pouch hidden with the man's clothing and dumped the contents onto the ground. "Could it be one of these, Fatin?"

The boy ran his hands through a variety of necklaces, bracelets, combs and chains. "I've found them!" he yelled in triumph. He scooped them up and ran from the tent.

Balthazar looked at the pile as he considered what Fatin had said. After all this time he finally knew. Sahl's cheating ways had provoked the Himyarites to destroy Khalan. He shook his head trying to take it in. Then something caught his eye in the pile of trinkets. Kneeling down he pulled up his sister's necklace, the very one Fatin's brother had crafted. What sweet justice it was to know that Alima had slain one of the killers of Khalan. Balthazar put the necklace in his tunic, returned the rest to the pouch and tossed it next to Tariq's body.

A short time later Asher returned with Abdul. "Where is she?" he asked angrily. "Is she the one?" Abdul advanced on Alima with frightening speed. "What have you done, woman?" he yelled, trying to pull her to her feet. "Why have you killed my friend?"

Alima recoiled, clutching Isaac.

With his free hand, Asher pulled Abdul back as Melchior jumped up to stand between Abdul and Alima. "What's wrong with you, man?" yelled Melchior. "That monster was your friend?" His face was red, and he could feel his blood pumping madly. "Tariq attacked her! She had no choice but to defend herself. Listen to the boy. He will tell the truth of it!'

Drawn by the shouts, Balthazar hurried from Tariq's tent. "What's going on?" he asked looking from one man to another.

"He doesn't understand!" shouted Melchior. "He's blaming Alima! It wasn't her fault!"

Balthazar stared at Abdul as he put his hand on Melchior's shoulder. "Calm down, my friend. We will work this out. Won't we, Abdul?"

Melchior's jaw was tight and he could feel his insides churning. He doubted very much if it would work out. Abdul didn't act like an agreeable man, and he was so very tired of waiting for men to be agreeable.

Balthazar frowned. "Melchior is right, Abdul. Go ahead! Ask the boy... Tariq attacked my wife. She did what anyone would to defend herself."

Abdul scowled at Fatin. "Tell me everything, boy!" he said gruffly. "You had better not lie or you will feel my wrath!"

Melchior put his face into Abdul's. "The boy has done nothing. Ask your questions with some respect."

Abdul snickered. "Respect? For these slaves! They're spoils of war, and they belong to me now that Tariq is dead."

"Why would you think that?" asked Melchior with a look of disbelief. "They should be free now that their master is dead."

"You are wrong! They belong to me because I helped catch them," said Abdul. "It was my idea to take them as slaves when my tribe conquered their village."

No, No! He thought. These boys cannot be slaves to this man! He felt a storm brewing inside himself, and when he looked again at the servant boy, it was Bina's face he saw. He had never given her freedom, but maybe he could redeem himself now. He felt inside his tunic, carefully palming the knife he'd taken from Tariq's body. If he could help it, Abdul would not enslave these boys or anyone else.

Balthazar looked to Fatin. "Is this true, boy? Was Abdul in Khalan on the day of the raid?"

"He was one of them."

"You scum, Himyarite!" Balthazar moved toward Abdul but Asher held him back with his free hand. He still held the torch high in the other.

With legs wide and chest high, Abdul laughed mockingly. "Yes, I'm a Himyarite. Our people will rule these lands one day because we know how to make people like you fear us. See how your friend holds you back? True warriors don't hold back. We know how to make people beg. We did it in Khalan, and we shall do it in Qana when the time is right."

Alima began to cry. And Isaac with her.

Melchior gripped the blade tighter. Just give me one reason, Abdul, he thought. One small show of aggression.

"Let me go, Asher!" yelled Balthazar. "This man will pay for what he did to my family!" Asher dropped his hand as Balthazar edged closer to Abdul. "You think you're great because you know how to make women and babies cry? You are a cur!"

Abdul jumped forward thrusting toward Balthazar, but Melchior struck first, driving the knife from his palm hard into the man's side. He pulled the blade out as Abdul fell back, a look of utter surprise on his face.

But Melchior could tell the man was not finished. "He has a knife!" yelled Melchior as Abdul regained his footing, and moved again toward Balthazar, who was now looking to protect Alima.

Breathing hard, Melchior pulled the weakened man toward him and plunged the dagger up and under the man's ribs. Abdul's face went slack.

Asher, Balthazar and Alima looked at Melchior in amazement as he wiped Abdul's blood from his hands. "What an ugly excuse for a man," he said solemnly as he looked at Balthazar. "I'm sorry if I robbed you of your vengeance. But I had to," said Melchior. "Look at his hand. I saw the glint of metal in the light of Asher's torch."

Balthazar bent down to examine Abdul's hand. "He's right. And it's a sharp blade. Thank you, Melchior. I owe you my life."

Melchior put his hand on Balthazar's shoulder. "You owe me nothing! The blade is yours. I took it from Tariq's body earlier. It seems right doesn't it? That the men who killed your family in Khalan should die from your blade? I wasn't going to allow that man to keep these boys." He shook his head. "I just couldn't!"

"I understand," said Balthazar nodding. "I think Bina would be proud of the way you protected them." He looked to Alima. "Are you all right, my love?"

"I am now." She squeezed Isaac tightly.

"What's to be done?" asked Asher. "Who will lead the caravan?"

"I can if I must . . . unless I can find another better suited," said Balthazar. "I'll assemble everyone tomorrow to explain what happened here, and see who is willing."

Melchior held his hand up. "But what if there are others from Tariq's tribe? They may not follow you so easily."

Balthazar looked to Fatin. "Can you tell us? Are there others in the camel train who rode with your master in Khalan?"

"I don't think so. Abdul was his only friend in the caravan. Those two were thick."

Balthazar nodded. "You see, Melchior. Anyway, I don't see another choice. We can't leave tonight, and everyone will know by morning that these two are dead."

Melchior nodded. "Then let us get a good night's sleep and hope for the best come morning."

CHAPTER 41
Celebration in Qana

§

EARLY THE NEXT MORNING BALTHAZAR and his companions made the rounds of the camel train calling out. "Important news! Come hear the news of the night!"

By twos and threes, men from all over the caravan gathered in an open space not far from Tariq's tent. Balthazar climbed onto a large rock and spoke to the assembled crowd. Some women and curious children also followed and waited behind the men to see what would be said.

"Fellow travelers! I have news of the night. It is not good, but it is understandable considering the nature of the caravan master. I speak of Tariq and his second man, Abdul. From the very start of this trek, Tariq threatened our women and girls with harm. So we did as any of you men would have done. We accompanied our women everywhere guarding them with care. Last night, however, Tariq, with the help of a simple-minded boy, drew my attention away. While I searched for my daughters, he stole my wife, and threw my baby son into the thorn bushes!"

Balthazar could hear that his words were having the desired effect, as words of sympathy and horror resounded to him from the crowd. "Yes! It was a terrible thing. I found my daughters unhurt, but my wife, Alima, was not so fortunate. Tariq tried to force himself on her . . . but she defended herself ably. He is dead now. Knifed by my wife as she fought to free herself."

Balthazar pointed to Gaspar and Asher who were dragging Tariq's stiff body in front of the crowd. "See before yourselves what his evil has wrought. I wish that were the end of the madness, but no! When we called Abdul to report the death, he pulled a knife on us and himself was slain." Gaspar and Melchior dragged Abdul's body next to Tariq's.

"I have assembled you here, to ask how we should dispose of them. And to seek your guidance on who shall lead us to Qana."

A young woman came forward from the back of the crowd. "Let the vultures have them!" She shouted. "I can vouch that these men were evil! They had no honor in life and deserve none in death."

"What is your name?" asked Balthazar.

"My name is Hadya. My husband is there in the front." She pointed to him. "I know from experience what you say is true. Tariq and Abdul were evil men."

"Did they do the same to you as they tried with my wife, Alima?"

The woman nodded. "They did. Tell me where your wife is, that I may thank her. She did what I could not."

"She is caring for our children, Hadya. But I'm sure she will want to meet you."

Suddenly, the woman's husband came forward. "Hadya, if this is true, why did you not tell me? We would not have stayed in the caravan."

"I was afraid of them . . . and I didn't want to dishonor you."

The man shook his head. "You could never dishonor me. You are my wife. I love you." He held his wife's hand then walked over to Balthazar. "My wife does not lie, so I add my voice to hers. Leave their bodies for the birds!"

Balthazar nodded. "Our wives were not Tariq's only victims. He abused his servants, and chose many others, even children from among the caravans they ran. So it shall be done! Their bodies will remain at the side of the road for the birds to pick. But what of this caravan? We must reach agreement on who shall lead us. Are there any among you who know the trail well enough?"

Two men came forward. "We're spice traders and have made this trek every year for the last five years from Qana to Najran and back. We know the trail well."

"Thank you." Balthazar looked to the crowd. "Are there any among you who would object to these men leading us? Anyone?" Balthazar waited but no-one called out.

"Well then. We have our new caravan masters! Tell us your names that we may address you properly."

"I am Hyder," said the one.

"I am Maalik," said the other.

"Thank you. When do you want to leave this place?"

"Now," said Maalik looking to his fellow trader. "Are you agreed?"

"I am. It is early yet. We can put many leagues behind us before the day is done."

"So be it," said Balthazar, and he jumped down from the rock.

Alima was grateful for the quiet days that followed Shabwa. Hyder and Maalik knew the trail well and by the week's end had led the caravan to the outskirts of Qana. "See girls! My home city is built along the shore of a big sea just like Caesarea."

"But I don't see any big buildings." said Miriam.

"That's because there aren't many," said Alima. "There's a big warehouse built into the cliffs and some others near the docks, but none like those in Caesarea. We are fortunate in other ways though. We don't have a bad king like Herod here," said Alima.

"Was King Herod a bad man?" asked Rebecca.

"That's what your poppa says and he should know because he met the king when he was in Jerusalem."

The girls looked in awe on Balthazar. "You met the king, poppa? What was he like?"

"When you are older, I will tell you. The king you should try to remember, is your little cousin, Jesus. If Melchior is right, Jesus will be a kinder and wiser king than any that has ruled Judea."

"Do you think so, too, momma?" asked Miriam.

"I do."

The caravan halted on the beach west of Qana. Those who had befriended each other during the long months of travel said their goodbyes. Alima made sure to speak with the woman Tariq had raped. "Thank you for coming forward last week, Hadya. Your testimony to the truth helped Balthazar greatly that day. If the crowd had turned on us, I don't know what would have happened."

Hadya hugged her. "I couldn't hold the knowledge inside me another moment. For many weeks, I struggled about what to do, what to say because of my fear. When I heard your husband's news, I had to speak up. I knew a dead man couldn't hurt me."

"Thank you for doing that. And thank you for taking Fatin and Abu into your household. I think they are good boys, but in need of a loving family."

"I would not be taking them if I didn't think so, too. They already get on well with my sons."

"That is good, "said Alima. "Peace be with you and your family."

"And with you."

From the beach where the caravan disbanded it was but a short distance to the docks and Alima's house.

"That's my mother's house!" said Alima to the girls as they got closer.

"Who are those men, momma?" asked Miriam.

"My brothers, Waled and Akram, whom you may call Uncle. They are the shipbuilders I told you about."

"I remember. They're very handsome, momma." whispered Miriam to Alima and Rebecca.

"It's nice that you think so, but don't tell them," said Alima with her finger to her lips. "They are proud enough already!"

The girls giggled.

The reunion was a whirlwind of introductions, explanations, exclamations and questions. Alima's mother, Jun, was more than a little confused trying to understand it all. "Who are these lovely girls? Your name is Gasfart? Oh, but my hearing is bad! My greetings to you Corinna. I hear the Greeks are wonderful cooks. You come from where, Melchior? You met who, Asher? The Messiah! Alima did her best to explain what she could when Balthazar and the others weren't doing it for her, and as she'd expected, her family welcomed everyone with great hospitality and happy hearts.

"No more mourning now!" said Jun. "I will plan you a glorious wedding!"

"I always thought he had an eye for you!" said Akram hugging his sister.

"But of course he did!" said Jun. "He paid a bride price, didn't he?"

Waled shook his head. "Yes, mother, but . . ."

"Don't bother to explain," said Balthazar laughing.

"Perhaps you are right," agreed Akram.

"So tell me again, where is Sameer?" asked Waled.

It was difficult for her to explain why Sameer wasn't with them and that they had no news of her father.

Waled shook his head. "All that way and you still don't know? Maybe it wasn't meant to be."

"Maybe not," said Alima.

Balthazar went on to explain what he knew of Captain Musa. "The crews of *The Baysan* and *The Serafina* haven't given up on Musa. You shouldn't give up on Sameer or your father."

"Speaking of missing men. You should know that cousin Umar left town soon after you set sail," said Akram. "He took what he could from Uncle Nibal and departed. We haven't heard from him since."

"How is Uncle doing?" asked Alima.

"Better than we thought. He doesn't worry so much now that Umar is gone. He's tends to his trees and walks the roads with his head high again."

Her family went on to speak of other things. Her mother, Jun, was especially happy to have children in the house. "I am a grandmother at last!" she said with pride. Alima smiled. "And I am a mother at last!" she said. "It feels so good."

Jun hugged her daughter. "And a very good mother you are from the looks of it. You have a good man in Balthazar and a lovely family. What a wedding celebration yours will be!"

Some weeks later, when the wedding was a day away, Waled and Akram announced they were taking Balthazar away. "As bridegroom you must collect your bride from afar, and we've arranged for you to do that from Uncle Nibal's."

Balthazar smiled. "Does Nibal know?"

"Of course," said Waled. "It was his idea. Surely you remember how he likes our traditions."

"And the others?" asked Balthazar looking to his companions.

"Welcome as well, though the accommodations are sparse, as you know."

Balthazar looked to Asher, Gaspar and Melchior. "Will you come with us, friends? We'll return tomorrow when the bride is ready."

"Will there be wine?" asked Gaspar.

"There will," said Akram.

"Even the king could not keep us away!" responded Gaspar.

"We shall have ourselves a special day, too," said Jun when the men were gone. As Alima sipped a cup of tea, her mother walked to the open doorway and clapped her hands loudly above her head. Soon, Alima heard cymbals and women's voices singing in the distance. The sounds came closer, and Alima laughed as a group of dancing women pranced their way into the house.

"What this?" asked Corinna looking on in surprise.

"It's our custom for friends of the bride and her mother to prepare for a wedding. I have known them all since childhood, so they are a part of our celebration.

"What will they do?"

"They will help me bathe and adorn me for my groom. Then we will celebrate together."

Alima bowed and greeted each woman with a hug and a kiss as they bobbed and bounced, danced and sang. Over fifteen neighbor women smiling and clapping their way into her memory. "Oh happy day! That makes the bride a beauty for her groom!" They circled round her then paraded outside pulling Alima along. On the sandy side of the house, opposite the dock, a special bath had been prepared for her in a large wooden tub. As some of the older women played with the children, the others made a human curtain around the tub. Alima disrobed as the aroma of scented oil rose from the warm water, and in no time she submerged herself to the accompaniment of claps and clanging cymbals.

She had almost forgotten what a luxury a heated bath was. The Arsinoe bath had been a delight quickly forgotten amid the threats of the caravan trek. Here the love of friends and family surrounded her quite literally; and thoughts of her groom made her as warm as the water that lapped her languid thighs. She closed her eyes as her mother washed her hair, her back, her legs and arms. Tomorrow night she would share the bridal chamber with her beloved, and she wanted to be perfect for him. The man she had traveled with, argued with, liked and loved for so many days. She had felt his kiss and his strong arms, but she had not surrendered to his caress nor the weight of his body. Not that she hadn't been tempted. Oh yes. Memories of his half-clad body on *The Baysan* were etched like a stone carving in her mind. But her wedding night would be different, and she awaited his touch like a dry wadi waited for rain.

"Arise, lovely one," said her mother interrupting her day dream. "It's time for your henna." Alima wrapped herself in the proffered towel and followed the still dancing women back to the house. There she donned a short tunic and reclined on a chaise that the women had decorated with vibrant colored cloth. She recognized three mehndi artists among the crowd and motioned the eldest to approach her. "Good day to you, Mira. Thank you for coming."

"How could I miss it? Your mother tells me your groom is a man of the highest stature. I am happy for you. Tell me what designs you have in mind."

"I want a mixture of flowers and stars. My beloved is a star gazer, so let's give him some new places to gaze at them!" The women around her giggled their understanding.

"Shall I hide his initials amongst the stars?"

"Yes, please. His initials are B K. Balthazar al-Khalan."

"I promise your henna will delight you both."

The artist began on Alima's feet and worked her way up. From her ankles to her outer calves, inner thighs, navel, lower back, shoulders, neck, arms and hands. It took many hours to apply the henna paste in the intricate designs that were Mira's specialty. Corinna and Jun brought cool drinks and a variety of foods while Alima reclined and visited with friends. Some of the other women entertained her with amusing stories of their men as they too were painted and compared designs. Since she had been married before, many of the older women were more open in their talk of what it took to please a man than they had been before her marriage to Sahl. She cried with laughter listening to their blunt language and ribald tales of how their men tried to pleasure them. There was a lot of mirth, rolling of eyes and shaking of heads as the day went on. The sisterhood of wives was alive and well in Qana and for a moment she was sorry to be moving to Parthia so soon.

When Alima's henna was done, Jun brought out more food, and the singing and dancing began again. Alima danced holding Isaac, Miriam danced with Jun and Rebecca with Corinna. As the sun set, the women drifted away to their homes and Jun's house became quiet once again.

Early the next morning, Alima was awakened when Miriam and Rebecca crawled into bed with her. "Momma, is this your special day?" asked Rebecca.

Alima rubbed her eyes and smiled. "Yes, Rebecca. This is my special day. Have you been to a wedding before?"

"No," said Miriam. "But momma Judith told us about them. She said the bride always wears a beautiful dress. Will you wear a beautiful dress?"

"I will. Because I want to look beautiful for Balthazar. Will you help me get ready later?"

"Oh yes!" shouted both girls at once.

"Good. Now it's time to get about our day."

Alima roused herself, put a shawl over her night dress and bent over Isaac. "Wake up sleepy one. The gulls are squawking and the sun is up.

So must you be!" Isaac opened his eyes and smiled at her. "Come on, Isaac. Let's get something to eat." She scooped him up and carried him out to the kitchen.

Miriam and Rebecca were sitting on the floor playing a yarn game with their fingers. "Did you enjoy your time with the neighbors yesterday?" asked Alima.

"Yes," said Miriam. "Look at the pretty painting on my hands!"

"It's beautiful!" said Alima. "How do you like your hands, Rebecca?"

"I like them, but Miriam has more flowers than I do."

"Let me see." Alima examined Rebecca's hands. "She may have more flowers, but you have more stars, and you know how much our family likes stars. I think your hands are very lovely."

"You do?"

"Yes! They are fit for a queen!"

"I love you, Alima," said Rebecca.

"I love you too, sweet girl. Now where is grandma Jun.?"

"I'm here on the dock." Jun's voice came from outside. "Enjoying this beautiful morning."

Alima prepared a tray with plates and cups, flat bread, hummus, yogurt, milk and tea and went out with the children to join Jun. Her mother helped herself as Alima served the children. As Alima sat down, Corinna joined them.

"I like," said Corinna pointing to Alima's henna designs.

"I like yours, too," said Alima. "Have you and Asher decided on a time for your wedding?"

Corinna smiled. "Asher want marry here. But I want wait. Meet his family. Marry in Parthia."

"I'm sure he understands," said Alima. "Having family around is important. Once he is back in Parthia, he will be happy that you waited."

"I hope," said Corinna. "What we do today?"

"We cook and make ready for the feast," said Jun. "Will you help us?"

"Yes, of course," said Corinna. "I happy help."

Alima's eyes wandered out to the sea as she finished eating. The gulf waters sparkled in the bright sunshine and the sea breezes brought back memories of Sameer and her father. Some small fishing boats dotted the water, but no merchant vessels like Musa's. At least none close to shore. There was a large ship off in the distance, some way west but . . . could it possibly be? No, that was wishful thinking. She rose and went inside, calling the children.

The rest of the morning, Alima and Corinna helped Jun with preparations for the wedding feast. Many of the neighbors would bring their own contributions of food and sweet breads, and the men would roast fish and meat in a pit on the sand. But her mother wanted to prepare some of her favorites. So Alima spent most of her time mixing and cutting, taking care not to wet her hands or ruin the fine efforts of the mehndi artist. By noon the work was done, and Alima took food to the children who were playing outside near the garden.

Miriam ran up to her excitedly. "Look momma! Look at the big ship that's nearing uncle's dock!"

Alima looked out toward the shipyard. "Mother! Come quickly!"

Alima grabbed Isaac up and ran with the girls toward the dock. Captain Musa waved from *The Baysan's* deck looking very thin but very much alive. "Hey there, Alima! We made it! And see, I brought your brother back!" Sameer stood next to him, smiling, and healthy as ever.

Alima jumped up and down like a gleeful child. "See children. Your uncle Sameer has come back to us! Wave, Isaac. That's it. Wave your welcome."

Jun and Corinna soon joined her. Together they watched as a sailor jumped wide to their dock, secured the ropes and laid Waled's gangplank to the ship. No sooner did it hit the deck than Sameer came strutting down to greet them.

"My son!" yelled Jun as she raced to embrace him. "You're back! Praise the Great One you're back!"

"I am!" Sameer hugged Jun tightly then turned toward Alima. "It's a relief to see you, sister. I debated long and hard whether to stay and look for you in Judea, but things are very bad there, and I figured Balthazar would watch out for you. Did he?"

Alima smiled. "The tale is a long one, but *Yes*! He cared for me very much. In fact, today we will be married! You've returned just in time."

"Your wedding day!" cried Sameer. "Musa, do you hear this? Alima and Balthazar will be wed today!"

Musa joined the group on the dock. "Well it's about time. Though I must say I'm surprised to see you here. I thought Balthazar would have you in Parthia by now."

"That is still the plan, Captain. But certain events required us to come home first."

"So where is the groom? I would greet him."

"He's preparing at Uncle Nibal's with my brothers and some friends. You must go home to rest, and bring your wife later to the feast. Then you can tell us about your journey."

Musa nodded. "Your sister is wise, Sameer. I shall drink to your happiness later. Will Waled be angry if I leave my ship at his dock? I'm too tired to move her."

"You have my permission," said Sameer. "What need have you for his?" The two men laughed as Musa went on his way.

"Come, Sameer," said Alima pulling him toward the house. "I want to know everything."

Balthazar scrutinized himself. He had bathed in a local cistern, dried himself with a Turkish towel from Melchior, and dressed in the finest clothes made in Qana.

"What do you think?" he asked Waled, seeking final approval. "Will she find me acceptable?"

"My sister is smitten. You could walk to her naked and she would approve you. Though you might have trouble fighting off the rest of Qana's women folk."

Balthazar laughed. "I wish I could be as confident as you."

Waled slapped him on the shoulder. "Be at peace, my brother-to-be. She is marrying you for your heart, not your body."

"So now you're saying I'm ugly. Which is it?"

"Both! Come call for your bride 'ere the sun sets. Let the bridal procession begin!"

Balthazar stepped out the door followed by Waled, Akram, Uncle Nibal, Asher, Gaspar and Melchior.

"Here is your camel," said Gaspar. "It will not do to have you sweat in your wedding attire."

Balthazar mounted the camel, which was also draped in brightly colored cloth and ribbons under the saddle. Gaspar held the reigns and walked forward. All of them were dressed in their finest, but Balthazar's tunic and cloak set him apart. His burgundy tunic was embroidered with dark blue stars. Silver threads trailed from each star like reams of light, encircling the sleeves, collar and hem of his garment. A white cloak trimmed in similar silver thread fell from his shoulders. If the night grew chill, he intended to wrap Alima in it, for a cold bride was not what he had in mind for tonight. He hoped she would like the way he looked. He had chosen the tunic from many others because he knew she liked this color, and tonight he wanted her eyes to himself.

"Slow that camel down!" yelled Nibal. "I'm not so young that I can pace the bridegroom's mount as I used to."

"Walk slower, Gaspar," said Balthazar. "My betrothed may not marry me if we kill her uncle on the way to the feast."

Gaspar laughed. "You may be right about that."

"Asher, I have a request for you," yelled Balthazar. "Will you and Corinna watch the children tonight? My plans demand no distractions."

"We can arrange that," said Asher smiling.

The procession made its way through the streets of Qana as fast as Nibal's legs allowed. As they drew closer, Asher played a tune on his flute, and the others clapped in time to the cadence of the melody. The sun was low to the horizon when they arrived at the front of Waled's house.

The neighbors had planted many torches in the sand to light their way from the road to the house. Many more surrounded the new terrace, which the brothers had built for the occasion. A moment later, Balthazar stood on Jun's doorstep calling out, "Alima, Alima my bride, Come out to me!"

Alima emerged covered in veils from her head to her feet. In the glow of the torchlight, she looked like a beautiful cocoon sprinkled with honey. He led her to the terrace where all their guests awaited, and ever so slowly unwrapped the veils from her body, then the veiled mantle from her face and bent to kiss her lips. She was a vision in blue, white and gold. He noticed first a sleeveless robe of sky-blue silk trimmed with gold embroidery. It crisscrossed her breasts, encircled her waist and fell from a twisted gather at the small of her back to her ankles. Beneath it, she wore a sleeveless white silk tunic. Numerous necklaces drew his eyes to her bodice, and a chin chain played with the contours of her mouth. Her sandaled feet sparkled with toe rings as did her fingers with rings in varying hues of blue. The flowers and stars of her henna paint dazzled him and complimented the simplicity of her dress. "Alima, you take my breath away."

"That is what I hoped to hear, my groom."

A small group of hired musicians played as friends and family mingled around the terrace. Balthazar struggled to take in the transformation. "Did your mother do all this?" he asked, looking at the long food table and pitchers of wine and water which awaited thirsty guests.

"No. We had a little help." Alima drew him over to a corner of the terrace and pointed to where Sameer sat talking with Musa and his wife.

Balthazar was stunned. "Sameer! Musa! I can't believe it! When did you come?"

Musa laughed. "Close your mouth, my boy, or your bride will be kissing naught but flies tonight."

Balthazar looked to Alima. "Would you fetch me some food so I may hear the story?"

Alima mocked a pout as she rose to leave. "So quickly the wife becomes a servant!"

Musa's wife stood up. "You stay, Alima. I will get the food. I've heard the tale twice already, and I'm sure not for the last time."

Balthazar made room for Alima next to him on a bench. "So tell me," said Balthazar to Sameer. "What happened after I left you at the shipyard?"

"I worked for weeks in the warehouse, looking for my father wherever I could. But I never saw him. I became convinced he was dead, and it brought me low, indeed, for I felt I was laboring in vain. But one day, a ship arrived in the bay, and *there he was* coming ashore!"

"You father is alive! Is he here?"

"Be patient." Said Sameer. "Within days I was assigned to work in a new bay . . . and with him! I waited to see if he recognized me, but for days he said nothing. I'm still not sure why. So I found a quiet time when we were alone to reveal myself. He looked at me as if for the first time, then sat back on his haunches and cried. I shall never forget it." Tears came to Sameer's eyes. Balthazar sipped his wine as he waited for Sameer to continue.

"We worked together for many weeks, and I eventually told him of Baysan's death, Alima's widowhood, and how you helped us search for him. I told him how much I liked you, Balthazar; that I hoped you would marry Alima someday. And see? I was right!"

Balthazar grasped Alima's hand. "Yes. You were."

"I knew it would comfort my father. He didn't look well but labored hard as ever for those Roman buggers. I began to devise a plan for our escape. I heard that when the ships were completed, the Romans would sail them into Caesarea harbor to show them off to Herod. I thought if we could hide on one of them we could get away in Caesarea when no one was looking."

"An ingenious plan. Did you follow through with it?"

"I did, but not with my father. He collapsed and died three days before the fleet sailed. I was desolate. To find him and lose him like that . . . I couldn't understand but I was grateful for my time with him. I watched from afar as the Romans buried him in a field near the barracks.

After that I couldn't wait to leave. The night before the fleet sailed I slipped out of the barracks and swam to the ship nearest shore. I had worked on it, so I knew a place to hide where I wouldn't be found."

"They didn't discover you were missing?"

"No. They had given us time off while we waited for more lumber so they weren't calling us to work. The fleet sailed early the next morning, and we made Caesarea harbor quickly. The pilots maneuvered the ships in a circle round the outer harbor as the king watched from the northern breakwater. Everyone had their eyes toward shore, so when our ship sailed near *The Serafina's* side of the harbor, I slipped off the back of it and swam underwater to the far side of Musa's ship."

"But how did you know Musa's ship would be there? He was supposed to sail many months earlier."

"I didn't know, but I hoped. If it was gone, I would have found another way home. The water was my only hope. Walking out of that shipyard would have been impossible."

"Did you go back to Judith's hut for Alima?"

"No. One of the sailors on *The Serafina* told me you had come by a week earlier looking for her. That worried me, but I figured if she wasn't at Judith's than I had no way of knowing where she was. And I thought by then the Romans might be looking for me, so I chose to stay where I was."

Balthazar looked around the terrace. It was bubbling with activity. Guests were talking, dancing, eating and drinking. He felt the urge to join them, but wanted to know the rest of the story. He whispered into Alima's ear. "Do you mind if I stay a bit longer? I don't want to ignore our guests but I must hear the rest of this. "

Alima kissed his cheek. "Don't worry, my love. I shall charm them in your stead. Enjoy your friends." Alima rose and went to join Waled and Akram.

Balthazar finished the last of his wine and turned to Musa. "It's so good to see you. I was worried when I saw your ship in Caesarea and heard you hadn't returned on time. What happened?"

"Who can say? One day I was fine and the next, sick as a dying dog. I was with a friend in the lower city, trying to conclude a deal with a silversmith when I collapsed. They carried me to the inn. I lay in bed for many weeks. Could hardly breathe or eat. My friend cared for me, and eventually took me to his house."

Balthazar raised his cup to Musa. "Here's to your health, my friend! When did you finally return to Caesarea?"

"My first mate found me and took me back soon after the Bethlehem massacre."

"Bethlehem massacre?" Balthazar began to feel sick, thinking of Joseph and his family.

"Did you not hear? Herod sent his soldiers to Bethlehem. They stopped at every house in the town, including my friend's, looking for boys under two years. Luckily, my friend's grandson was not there, or he would have been killed with all the others."

"Others? How *many* others?"

"I don't know for sure. Herod's men slaughtered every boy child in Bethlehem under two. There must have been many for never have I seen such sadness as in those days. I would have braved anything to come home after that."

Balthazar shook his head. "Our Isaac would have been slaughtered along with little Jesus."

"Perhaps I shouldn't have told you on your special day," said Musa, "but it seems you left Bethlehem just in time."

"Yes. The man in white made sure of that."

"Man in white?"

"A story for another time. Drink up, my friends! I must dance with my bride."

Balthazar put his arms around Alima and spun her to him. "May I dance with you, my bride?"

Alima smiled her consent as the people near her clapped and hooted. Together they moved to the sounds of the flutes and lyres, swaying and holding hands. For the rest of the night Balthazar did not leave her side.

He brought her food and wine, squeezed her hand, and visited with neighbors as they circled round the terrace. The feast would have continued into the small hours if not for a rain shower that extinguished the torches.

Balthazar took Alima's hand as they ran for the house. "Shall we find ourselves some privacy, my bride?"

Book Five

CHAPTER 42

The King Awaits

§

THREE MONTHS LATER IN SELEUCIA

GASPAR TRUDGED UP THE HILL toward Melchior's estate. His meeting with King Phraates had not gone well, and he must share the news, bleak as it was. The sky threatened rain, but it would be welcome. In fact, he hoped for a torrent. Nothing good had happened in the week since their return; the rain would at least be a respite from the unrelenting heat. Balthazar's wedding day was the last cool day he remembered. How sweetly the gulf breezes and sprightly music had serenaded his spirit. But the real balm had been Melchior's kind words at the wedding feast. The two friends had spoken very little since Bina's death, and he had wondered if the rift would ever heal. So it was with a glad heart that he accepted Melchior's apology as they paraded with Balthazar to Alima's house. "I am sorry, my friend. I was in the wrong about Bina." said Melchior. Very simple words but Gaspar could see in Melchior's expression how much he meant them. Gaspar kissed his friend on each cheek. All was right with the world again.

The rest of the day had been even better. Despite the news of her husband's death, Alima's mother had attended the celebration, and at Alima's request, Gaspar had entertained her. Surprisingly he had found Jun to be an enchanting woman, quick of wit and of lively intelligence. In the following days, his aging heart had awakened as he accompanied her in quiet walks along the sea. She said she would mourn aplenty when they departed, and he was not about to reproach her for taking some solace with him. How he had enjoyed those days, both the company and the weather. But the time to leave had come soon after, and with it the summer heat.

The first drops of rain spattered him as he entered Melchior's garden. Corinna met him at the door.

"Is he in?" asked Gaspar quickly.

"Yes. In his study."

Gaspar walked on. "Melchior! Where are you?"

"In here." Melchior stuck his head out of the room which had been his brother's counting room. "What brings you? I thought you had an appointment with King Phraates today."

"I did. That's why I've come."

"I know that face, Gaspar. It means nothing good."

"It's not. Phraates is sick, I heard whispers of poison from his servants, and the palace is in disarray."

"Poison? Who wants him dead?"

"It's hard to know. But from the looks of things I would say the queen. She attends him like a vulture circling its prey."

"She has played the part of a loving wife for some years now. Do you think the king suspects her?"

Gaspar shook his head. "His reason tells him he should, but I think his heart denies it. For years, he has lavished her with affection but she rebuffs him. And the more she rebuffs him the more he wants her. She sits by his bedside, but offers him no succor, no hand to hold nor kind words. She dangles herself like a plump worm on a line, but she knows the old fish has no energy to jump. And the worst of it is watching how she treats their son."

"What do you mean?" asked Melchior.

Gaspar grimaced. "She fawns on him . . . unnaturally. Touches him . . . not like a mother should. Something is not right between them, Melchior, and it disgusts me."

"In front of the king?"

"Mmm. She thinks the king is too ill to notice, but he does. I saw it in his eyes."

"Is there nothing to be done?"

"I think it may be too late. The king fears death, and his anger permeates the palace. He's lashing out at everyone. He asked me to predict when he will recover, and was furious when I shook my head. And then there was the news about Herod."

"What news?"

"Phraates got word that Herod is dead, and his kingdom has been divided between his three sons. Phraates asked if we met the sons at our audience in Jerusalem. When I told him no, he screamed in anger. "Not any of them? Not even one?" I thought he would slay me on the spot."

"Did you explain that we had no say in who would be there?"

"Of course I did, but he's not thinking clearly. He as much as told me that our journey was a waste of his gold. He is not happy with us, Melchior, and I fear what he may do before he dies. I think a promising report about the Messiah may be the only thing to give him some comfort."

Melchior shook his head. "I think it unlikely. Did he ask you about the child?"

"Yes, and I said you would give him a full account soon. That's why I've come. I thought we should discuss what you will tell him."

"I've thought of little else since we left Bethlehem, and I know I must tell him the truth! I may try to explain King David's humble beginnings, maybe draw some comparisons to help him understand. But I've grown tired of pretense. I know the truth of what happened in Bethlehem and I will tell him of it."

"What has come over you? No nuanced answers? No descriptions that skirt the edges of fact?" Gaspar gave him a probing look.

Melchior shrugged. "I think the reticent, careful astrologer you knew is changed."

"Because of what happened in Judea?" Asked Gaspar.

"Because of many things. My visit to the temple, the events in Bethlehem, and teaching Balthazar's children. Yes, especially the children ..."

"The children have changed you?"

"I've examined my life in light of what I teach them. I don't want them to discover me a fraud."

"Why would they think that, my friend?"

"Because, until I got to Judea, I lived as one. I've been afraid! Afraid to admit my ancestry, afraid to be known as a Jew. I don't want to be afraid anymore. It felt so good, so right when I told Joseph I was a Jew, and when I confronted Abdul. Now that I'm back in Parthia, I want to speak the truth. And I want the children to respect me. Did you know they call me, Grandfather? "

"No! But it's a fine thing. And I think I understand a little of what you say," said Gaspar. "What happened in Bethlehem changed me, too. But I'm still trying to figure out how." He paused. "I think it's admirable you want to be truthful with the king, as long as you're willing to deal with what happens after."

"I think I am."

"Then we need discuss this no further. I have only two requests."

"They would be?" asked Melchior.

"That you keep me informed."

"I will do so. And your second request?"

"Be careful, especially around the Queen. As King Herod once said, that one bears watching."

Balthazar leaned over Alima as she wretched into a pot. "Again, Alima? You've been retching all day. What can I do to help you?"

"Get me some water."

He stayed with her until she stopped heaving then went for the water. He ran back trying not to spill the bucket and dipped a cup into it. "Here."

Her hands shook as she raised the cup to her lips. "Thank you." She swished the water in her mouth, spit it out, took another sip and swallowed.

"Come inside," said Balthazar. "I don't want you working in the sun if you're not holding anything down." Grasping her by the hand, he pulled her to her feet and walked her inside to their bed. "What is wrong? For two weeks you have eaten nothing and still you wretch. You have me more than a little worried."

Alima smiled up at him.

Balthazar looked puzzled. "You retch for days and you can smile about it?"

"It is a blessing, my love. A true blessing." Alima looked down at her swollen breasts and patted her belly.

"You mean?"

"Yes. Your seed is fertile, Balthazar. You will be a father this year."

He knelt down in front of her, kissed her belly, her breasts and her mouth. "You are my blessing, Alima." He wanted to lay her down and make love to her here and now, but he could tell from the look of her that would have to wait. "I can hardly believe it. When did you know?"

"Before we got off Musa's ship. At first I thought it was sea sickness, but then my breasts became tender and my blood stopped coming. It was then I knew. Corinna knew too. She said I looked different. That she had come to know because she'd seen it in women at the brothel. She helped me in the first days when the nausea was very bad."

"Tell me, what must I do? I don't have any idea how to help you."

"Women have babies all the time, and I expect nothing different from you. Go ahead with your work at the school and help me with the children when you can. Everything else will take care of itself."

Balthazar kissed her again. "Will you tell the children?"

"Of course! But let us wait a while. Judith died while she was with child, and I don't want the girls to worry for me. Let's wait until I show."

"As you wish. I'm going to get the girls now, but I think Isaac is waking from his nap. Would you like me to take him along?"

"If you like."

Balthazar found Isaac talking to himself in his little hammock bed. "Come on, big boy! Let's go get your sisters." Balthazar carried him on his shoulders down the road. The small house they lived in was on the outskirts of Seleucia. It had belonged to a friend of Gaspar who died in the Great Death, and had been vacant since the man's death. It was a small place but suited them well.

Gaspar had given him a job at the school, maintaining and copying charts and records. Gaspar was teaching him astrology and allowing him to sit in on consultations with his wealthy clients. Balthazar didn't really like that part of the work, but he wanted to learn all he could from his mentor. And he knew well enough how the consultations helped pay for the school. They had learned that the king hadn't been sending his usual grants, and several teachers had gone without pay during Gaspar's absence. It was one of the things Gaspar wanted to address with the king, and Balthazar wondered how the meeting had gone.

Balthazar called the girls home and was returning with them when he spotted Gaspar down the road. He set Isaac down and waved to Gaspar. "Girls, take your brother into the house. And tell your momma Gaspar is here for a visit."

"Yes. Poppa," said Miriam.

"What brings you, Gaspar?" Asked Balthazar.

"I was visiting Melchior, and since your house is on my way home, I thought I would check on you. How is Alima? Is she doing any better?"

Balthazar laughed. "Yes and no. It seems her condition is something that may last a while, nine months to be exact."

"Is that so?" Gaspar clapped Balthazar on the shoulder. "I must congratulate you! This is the first good news I've heard since our return."

"I take it your meeting with the king did not go well?"

"You are correct. The king is ailing while the queen and her lover son await his death with smug effrontery. She neatly put off any discussion of the king's support for our school. I fear for the future."

"Is it that bad?"

"It could be. I am no fan of the queen's and she knows it. If her son becomes king, she will be a mighty influence on his decisions and then who knows. I hope you haven't come into a firestorm."

"Don't worry about me. I came here of my own will because I want to learn of the stars. One way or the other, I will do that."

"Your confidence is reassuring, Balthazar. Perhaps if I keep you near, it will flow into me."

"Don't belittle yourself. Your encouraging way is what drew me to you! I know you will rise above whatever obstacles the queen or her son present."

"I hope that is true."

"Will you join us for supper?"

"If Alima is up to it."

"Let us check on her together. After all the women's work we did on the caravan, a little more won't hurt us."

CHAPTER 43

Politics and Kingship

§

WHEN THE RAIN STOPPED, MELCHIOR went for a walk. He needed to think through what Gaspar had said, and tried to picture himself reporting to King Phraates as he roamed the date palm grove gazing toward Cistephon. What could he say to the man that would allow him to understand the Messiah? If the king was as sick as Gaspar said, the whole conversation might mean nothing soon enough. One of Phraates' sons would be crowned, and the Messiah's kingship soon forgotten. But what if the king lingered and his anger touched the school or his family? It was troublesome. It was true their journey had not improved Parthia's relationship with Judea in the short term, but it might help in the future should Jesus' kingship come to pass. That is what he must underscore with the king.

Melchior walked home. "Corinna, I'm going down to the city to call on my brother. I hope to be back for supper."

"Very good," said Corinna. "I have food ready for you."

An hour later Melchior pulled the bell cord to announce himself at the satrap's palace. "Please wait," said Mered's servant pointing to a marble bench in the entry hall. "I will tell him you're here."

An hour later, the servant returned. "Please follow me." Melchior was familiar with the palace, but trailed the servant in silence until the man showed him into the main hall. His brother sat on an ornate chair at the front of the high ceilinged chamber. A long beautifully woven rug ran the length of the room to Mered's throne, lending an added grandeur which he felt sure Mered coveted. "Greetings, brother!" said Melchior as he approached. "How are you and the family?"

"Never better! My sons ride in the king's regiments and represent our family well."

"You have reason to be proud. And your wife and daughters?"

"My daughters grow lovelier every day. And my wife? What shall I say? Dahab is Dahab." Mered squinted his eyes. "Surely you have come about more than my family?"

Melchior frowned. "Yes. I come to ask about the king. I hear from my fellow astrologers that all is not well at the palace."

"This is true. The king's health has been declining for months. Queen Thermusa wants Phraataces on the throne, and apparently she is not willing to wait for nature to take its course."

"Is she doing something to hasten his death?"

"Yes. My spies tell me she has been lacing the king's food with poison for some months. Just a bit more each day."

"Have you told him?"

"I tried when I first learned of it, but he chose not to believe me. He discovered who my informant was, and had the servant poisoned. The man died. The king said it was an appropriate punishment for one who accused the queen of the same. Then he threatened me."

"Threatened you how?"

"He said I would never eat again without fear if I persisted in 'my destructive tales of the queen.' So I have said nothing more."

"But surely as he gets sicker he must be questioning her loyalty?"

Mered shook his head. "If he does, he shows no sign of it. I don't understand it, but he remains smitten with the Roman slut and thinks he ails of a natural cause."

"And what of his son, Phraataces? Does he know of his mother's treachery?"

Mered snickered. "I'm told that he services her, so how can he not?" He wrinkled his nose. "They are a pair those two, and I dread the day I shall have to serve them."

Melchior pulled a chair onto the Persian rug and sat down in front of Mered. "If the king dies, will they keep you as satrap?"

"I can't be sure. I know this city as few others, and there are not many who will willingly serve them. The queen is widely hated because she was a gift from Augustus. Phraataces has Parthian blood but his actions make him worse than a slave to his mother. I hear from my sons that even the army derides him. How will he command their respect with such a repugnant reputation?"

"Is the young man right in his mind?"

Mered waved his hand through the air. "Who can tell? Anyway, what has all this to do with you, brother?"

"I must report to the king about my journey. And I want to know what awaits me."

"How clever of you! Why don't you tell me what you plan to say? Perhaps I can suggest an appropriate way to approach him."

"All right," said Melchior. "You know how the journey began, with that unusual star and the dreams. I should have known then, that our journey, and the Messiah himself, would not fit the usual expectations for a king."

"I don't remember hearing about any dreams, though I'm not surprised considering Gaspar's background. But what has that to do with expectations? You did meet with Herod didn't you? That's probably what Phraates is most concerned with."

"Yes. We met with Herod within days of getting to Jerusalem. Unfortunately, for reasons I won't go into, the Chief Priest and another young priest were there as well. It was an odd mix of men."

"Tell me more," said Mered.

"Herod greeted us with a great show of food and wine but we could feel the undercurrent of suspicion. He pretended to like the Chief Priest but openly mocked the young one, and the Chief Priest could do nothing about it. Such was Herod's way of showing who held the power. I did my best to represent us well throughout the evening, professing King Phraates' admiration on various grounds before presenting his gifts."

"How did Herod receive them?"

"With moderate appreciation."

"That is good. The fact that he did not reject you outright is excellent considering the history of our countries."

"I acknowledged the past rivalries, but managed to talk beyond it. I think I did as well as any man could with a man like Herod."

"Then why are you concerned about Phraates? It sounds like all went well."

"Hear me out, brother. Phraates told Gaspar that Herod is dead; his kingdom's been divided between his three sons. When Gaspar admitted that none of the sons had been at our audience Phraates became furious. He told Gaspar our journey was a waste."

"The king is over-reacting. Herod had many sons, and one never knew who was held in high regard and who was headed to the executioner's sword. Phraates will calm down eventually. Does something else worry you?"

"Yes. Both Herod and Joazar greeted the news of a Messiah with suspicion."

Mered rolled his eyes. "Melchior, Melchior! Once again you show your ignorance of politics! How else would a man like Herod view an upstart rival from a Jewish family? Why did you tell him of your Messiah search? You didn't honestly think he would be happy to hear of it?"

"I didn't want Herod to hear of it at all. But that idiot priest, Caiaphas, wouldn't answer my questions at the temple, and I had no recourse but to show him my commission. It was the only way I could get him to take my questions seriously. And once the Chief Priest heard I was seeking an audience with Herod, there was no chance to keep it quiet. "

Mered stroked his beard. "I see. So how did your discussion of the Messiah go?"

"The Chief Priest told us Bethlehem was the town where the Messiah was to be born. And Herod asked us to return after we found the child, so he could also pay him homage."

"Did you return as he asked?"

"No! Of course not. We were warned in a dream not to return so we didn't. We left during the night by way of Egypt and heard later that Herod sent soldiers into Bethlehem. They slaughtered every Jewish boy under two, hoping to kill the Messiah as well."

"Do you know what became of the child?"

"We think his parents escaped with him, but there is no way to be sure."

Mered clapped his hands. "Well done, my brother! You travelled all that way to find the Messiah and you don't even know if he still lives! Plus, you probably enraged King Herod when you did not return to him. But let us for a moment assume the Messiah escaped Herod's wrath. What kind of king will he make if he does? Can you tell that much at least?"

Melchior looked down. "He was not what I expected."

"Ah! So we are back again to expectations. You must explain yourself."

"It is difficult for I found both more and less than what I expected."

"You are no seer, brother. Stop speaking in riddles."

"I am no seer, but I wish I was for the child is a puzzle. He was born to poor parents in a cave in the Judean countryside, yet everything about him bespeaks power."

Mered shook his head. "There is no power in poverty."

"Not usually. But there was great power in that cave. Of that I am certain! The shepherds Asher met, the ones who were there on the night of the child's birth, attested to angelic visions. Asher himself swears he heard singing in the wind on the night he found the child. And on the day we left, Gaspar, who was very near death because of a rotting foot, was healed after holding the babe. I know it sounds unbelievable, but in all my years I have never seen such a miracle!"

"Unbelievable is the right word! Are you so desperate to impress our king that you would invent such a tale?"

"I am doing nothing of the sort! Everything I say is true."

Mered rolled his eyes. "No sane man will believe it! And even if you can convince Phraates, how will it matter? How can such a poor child grow to kingship? And how will it ever matter to Parthia?" Mered shook his head as he rose from his chair. "No. I think I was right last year when I said the Messiah had nothing to do with us. Now leave me before your tangled web of lies catches me as well."

Melchior went after his brother, shouting. "Mered! I swear. They are no lies!" But his words echoed back unheard as the door slammed shut before him.

Melchior took stock of his brother's reaction as he left the palace. Why had he expected anything like understanding from a man who had doubted the Messiah from the start? As far as the king was concerned, he could see two options before him. He could put off his report indefinitely hoping his journey would be forgotten in the tumult of a changing reign. Or he could give his report in a few days when the king's mood might be better. The problem was that he had no idea how long Phraates might last, nor how his anger might be stoked if he thought Melchior was purposely refusing to see him. Which option was preferable? Where lay the greater danger?

Three days later he rode to Cistephon.

He steeled himself for whatever might come as the guards escorted him to the king's bedside. The scene was much as Gaspar had described it. The king wore a deathly pallor, and his eyes darted from one person to another. The queen sat some paces away doing beadwork. It made for a domestic scene he knew was false. With a weak voice the king acknowledged Melchior's arrival. "I heard you were back. What took you so long to visit me?"

"Forgive me, my king. I was weary from my trek, and feared I could not attend you as I should. There is much to tell."

"Get on with it then."

"As you wish. It took us a little over three months to reach Jerusalem, your majesty. It was a long journey but our efforts were rewarded. We had no trouble securing our audience with King Herod and he received us with great cordiality."

"Is that so? I thought he might scoff when he saw my signature on your commission, but you had no trouble?"

"None your majesty."

"That is good. So tell me how the audience proceeded."

"Herod greeted us in the evening with much food and wine. We could sense he was suspicious at first, but I did the best I could to soothe over past rivalries. I told him how you admired the prosperity and peace he has achieved, and how you understood the difficulties of ruling when rebellion swirls from within." Melchior glanced briefly at the queen but she did not meet his eyes.

The king raised his head and his eyes grew piercing. "You were surely referring to the old times, were you not?"

"Yes, your majesty. Of course."

The king settled back on his pillow. "And peace in Judea? That was a pretty little lie, for I hear the place seethes with hatred from the Jews."

"You are quite right. The Jewish people had no great love for Herod."

"Will they like his sons any better?"

"I think not, your majesty. They are all considered Roman pawns. The people will never be happy until a true Jewish king rules them again."

"Which brings us to the Messiah. Tell me. Did you find him?"

"We think so, your majesty. Though as I told my brother, he was not what I expected."

"In what way?"

"I thought the child might be born to a wealthy Jewish family. Or at the least be the son of a rabbi, or a scribe in Jerusalem. How else would he learn the demands of government, and be ready to assume the seat of power when he's grown?"

"But that is not the child you found?"

"No, your majesty. The child is a descendant of King David, but like David he was born in Bethlehem and to a poor family, not a rich one."

"But David rose from obscurity to wield great power, did he not?"

"He did, your majesty. He was a great warrior and a great king, as was his son, Solomon, who followed him."

"Do you think such a kingship could happen again with this Messiah child?"

"It could, your majesty. And I believe it will. The child was born poor, but I felt great power in the cave where he lay."

The king closed his eyes for a moment before training them again on Melchior. "He was born in a cave? What kind of power can you mean?"

"The power of the Jewish God, your majesty. Unusual, one might even say supernatural events surrounded the child's birth. The star, our dreams, angelic visions all preceded him, and a miraculous healing occurred in the cave. The astrologer Gaspar, who was very near death from a festering foot, was healed. He was renewed to full health. Even now I have trouble understanding the meaning of what happened there."

The queen put her beads down and came to sit at the king's bedside. "Melchior sounds entranced, Phraates. Look at his eyes." The king looked at Melchior more closely. "Do you see how they glow when he speaks of the Jewish God's power? No god except Augustus and your god, my husband, wields power like that."

The king looked from his wife to Melchior. "My queen is right. You speak like you believe in this Jewish God. Are you a Jew?"

Melchior swallowed hard. Here was the test. What had he said to make them think him so? He thought of himself as he was in Jerusalem and Bethlehem. Happy to assert his ancestry. He wanted to say yes. But then what. Will they imprison me? Banish me from court? And what about Mered and his family? He began to sweat, and he felt his nerve deserting him along with his ideals. "No, your majesty! What would make you think such a thing? My family believes in the teachings of Zarathustra! My god is Ahura Mazda." As soon as he said the words, anger and anguish stirred together in his gut. I told Gaspar I am a changed man, but I lied! I don't want to be afraid, but I still am.

Queen Thermusa started to laugh. "Don't believe him, my husband. His mother was a Jewess. I have it on good authority that he sacrificed to the Jewish god more than once, and that he went to Jerusalem to bury his mother's bones. There is more to his search for the Messiah than he wants you to know. See how he sweats with the worry of being found out?"

How could she know? Wondered Melchior. Now the denial must continue. He looked from Thermusa to Phraates. "You know my family for many years, your majesty. My father was your satrap; he was no Jew. My brother serves as satrap now; he is no Jew. Like them I was born here, bred here. Would you brand me different on the word of this Roman concubine?"

The queen stood up, shaking in fury. "How dare you! Phraates, will you let him speak to me like this? I am no concubine! I am the Queen and mother of the future king!"

Melchior looked at her with hatred. Who was this woman? How had she managed to make him to deny his God? His very self? He lashed out with the first words that came to him. "You are a scheming harlot who pleasures her own son and poisons the king to steal his throne!"

The queen slapped him across the face.

"That is enough!" yelled the king with some effort. "I would not think it of you Melchior, but your mouth has sealed your doom." The king looked at his guards. "Take him away."

CHAPTER 44

Selling Spice

§

THE NEXT DAY BALTHAZAR AND Gaspar stood round a circular table in the school's chart room. "See," said Gaspar pointing to the papyri. "These observations are the basis for all our work. This first chart shows the arrangements of the visible fixed stars, the second concerns the positions of the sun, the moon and the five planets, the third indicates the conjunctions and phases of the sun and moon and this last one, their risings. In the months to come I will explain them all, and I trust you will study them well enough to cite them back to me."

"I will do my best," said Balthazar.

"I know you will." Gaspar drank some water from his flask. "By the way, have you seen Melchior today? He was supposed to meet me this morning and it is unlike him to miss a meeting."

"I have not. Would you like me to send a servant to his house?"

"Could you go yourself? I'm quite worried and if something is amiss you will handle it better than a servant."

"Gladly," said Balthazar. "If I'm late returning, it's because I stopped to check on Alima." Balthazar filled his water bladder and left immediately. Because the streets were quiet, he took the main route through the city center and was soon trudging up the hill toward Melchior's estate. When he got to the house he stopped to admire the view before continuing to the entrance. He knocked twice hard before calling out. "Melchior! Melchior are you in?"

Corinna came to the doorway just as he raised his hand to knock again. "Balthazar. I glad see you! Melchior no here. No come home last night. I worry."

"Melchior didn't come home? Where did he go?"

"Sorry but he not tell me."

"All right. Is anyone else home? Is Asher here or his father?"

"Asher no, but Amro work in vegetable garden. You want me get him?"

"I can find him. Is that the garden behind the house?"

"Yes."

Balthazar walked around the house. He could see Amro working a patch of land up the hill behind the stable. "Good day, Amro. I'm looking for Melchior. Corinna tells me he rode off yesterday but has no idea where he went. Do you know?"

Amro scratched his head. "I saddled his horse for him. He said he was going to call on King Phraates. Maybe he decided to spend the night in Cistephon. Have you cause for worry?"

"Yes. He didn't come home last night and missed a meeting this morning. Gaspar says it's not like him."

"He is right. Can I help you look for him?"

"Yes. Can you walk the grounds? Make sure something hasn't happened to him on the estate."

"I will. And when Asher returns, I'll enlist his help as well."

"Good. I'll look for him in Cistephon. Is there a horse or camel I may borrow?"

"I'll saddle a horse for you now."

An hour later, Balthazar had crossed the bridge at the Tigris and was making his way to the king's palace. He'd heard many teachers at the school speak of it with mixed emotions. They were proud to have such a beautiful edifice so near to Seleucia. They were not happy to have a Roman woman as their queen, nor to hear that she controlled the palace and its ailing king.

Balthazar pondered how he could find out what had happened to Melchior? His name meant nothing here, and simply asking would not get him into the palace. No, he must find another way. He decided to stop at the market for if there was one thing he was good at, it was selling spice. He examined the spices of a few different vendors, and after a little back and forth on the price, purchased a quantity of the highest quality he could find, enough to portray himself as a seller. He packed the spice in his saddle bag and rode on until he found a stable to keep his horse. With the spice tucked securely into his shoulder bag he walked until he came to a large tree just outside the palace grounds. There were guards at each door but no sentries patrolling the land so he started strolling as if he were a visitor. He walked slowly carefully scanning for any activity as he went. He saw some servants come and go from behind a low vine-covered wall. He was looking for an older woman. Someone who was confident in her manner, someone who had worked here for years.

It took almost an hour before he spotted the person he wanted. The older woman was dressed well and held her head high. He could tell she was used to serving someone in authority. He approached her respectfully and spoke in Arabic. "Pardon me, good lady. I am a spice trader from Arabia. Do you understand my language?"

The woman looked at him oddly before responding in his language. "Yes. I understand you. I am Arabian myself."

Balthazar bowed. "Then you know good spice when you see it. I am selling very good quality frankincense. I think the king will find it useful. I hear he is very sick."

"Unfortunately, that is true. The king suffers while the queen plays. But I think we have all the frankincense we need, young man."

"Not like this, good lady. Please let me show you." Balthazar started to open his shoulder bag.

The old woman put up a hand. "Please, young man! I'm in hurry, and must get to the market before the stalls close. If you can wait, you can show me your spice when I return."

"I will wait right here," said Balthazar.

Sometime later, the woman returned with a heavy sack. "You see, I have waited," said Balthazar. "You look tired as my mother at the end of a long day. Will you let me carry your sack as I do for her?"

The old woman smiled and handed him her sack. She led him behind the vine covered wall through a small courtyard, and down a few steps to a door also covered in vines. When the guards shot a questioning glance in his direction she said, "He's with me," and led him inside to the kitchen. She took her pack from his hands and set it on a table. "Thank you. Now show me what's so special about your spice."

Balthazar made conversation as he opened the pouches of frankincense. "You are Arabian but I can tell you have worked here for a long time. Am I right?"

"Yes. How do you know?"

"Because you walk with conviction as if you yourself should be the queen."

"Hush boy! Words like that could get us both whipped."

"Sorry, I mean no harm. I come from a long line of Arabian spice growers. And since you come from my country you must know it has many uses."

"I do. But I can tell from your tone you're going to teach me something new?"

"Maybe." Balthazar lowered his voice. "Do you know it can be an antidote for hemlock poisoning?"

"I didn't. But why should we need it for that?"

"Because. . ." Balthazar whispered. "It is whispered that the Roman queen is poisoning the king."

The old woman gasped. "Where did you hear that?"

"The truth has a way of making itself known."

The woman hung her head low. "It is a sad state of affairs. I have served the king well since I was no older than you. I watched him survive the Great Death only to succumb to the wiles of this wicked woman. I am no Parthian, but no man should suffer as he does."

"Then take this," said Balthazar. "Pulverize it as small as you can, and mix it in his food. If hemlock is what she uses, it should help him."

The woman took two bags of his spice. "I will use it. What do I owe you?"

"No drachmas. I would ask only for your help."

"My help?" The woman looked suddenly wary.

"I seek information about my friend, Melchior. He's an astrologer from Seleucia and came to see the king yesterday but never got home. Have you any knowledge of him?"

The woman nodded. "I heard there was a commotion in the king's chamber yesterday. That a man from Seleucia insulted the queen and was arrested. But I don't know his name."

"Could you find out? I can wait here or outside while you ask. Please?"

The woman wrinkled her nose at first then smiled. "You have a winning way about you. Promise me you will not budge?" She raised a finger to his nose.

"I promise."

"I'll be right back."

A little while later she returned clucking her tongue. "Your friend has quite a tongue on him. He was brave to speak to the queen as he did, and in front of the king!"

"So it was Melchior?"

"Yes. My husband works among the king's guards, and he said an astrologer named Melchior, a man the king knows well, called the queen a scheming harlot among other things."

"That doesn't sound like the mild mannered Melchior I know. He must have been very angry to say such things. Where is he now?"

"In prison, and likely to be for a long time."

Balthazar shook his head. "This is not what I hoped to hear, but thank you. . . I'm sorry, I never asked your name."

"I am Phaedra."

"Thank you, Phaedra. I am Balthazar. Good day to you. "

"And to you, Balthazar. I'll see you out." The woman walked him beyond the courtyard and waited until he was beyond the palace grounds before disappearing behind the vine covered wall.

Balthazar hurried home. There were many people who should be told, but he would leave that to Gaspar.

"Alima! Are you home?"

"We're in the garden." She sat weeding plants with Isaac at her side. Balthazar waved to the girls who were weeding at the other side of the garden.

He looked closely at Alima. "How are you feeling today? Any retching?"

"Thankfully, no. What's wrong? You look shaken."

"Can you come inside? I would speak to you alone."

Alima picked Isaac up and followed him into the house. "Is it something bad?'

"Yes. Melchior's been arrested."

"For what?"

"For insulting the queen. He met with the king yesterday in Cistephon and said some things that he shouldn't have. Now he sits in prison."

"Melchior? The man for whom silence comes so easily? How can it be?"

"I wondered the very same when I first heard. But there is no mistake. I must tell Gaspar." He kissed her hard on the lips. "I'll be back by supper."

He rode swiftly for the school, left the horse with a servant in the courtyard and ran to find Gaspar. "I have news of Melchior!" he yelled from the back of the room where Gaspar lectured to a group of young men.

"Excuse me," said Gaspar. "I must speak with Balthazar." Gaspar looked irritated. "Is the news so urgent that you had to interrupt me?"

"Yes. Amro told me Melchior went to see the king yesterday, but he never returned. So I went to Cistephon myself and managed to find a way into the palace."

"You are full of surprises my boy. Did you see him?"

"No, but I found out he's been arrested. At some point during his meeting Melchior insulted the queen so badly that he's been imprisoned."

Gaspar rapped his fist into the wall. "No, no, no! I was worried about such a thing. He is a different man since Judea. I first noticed it when he killed that swine Abdul. And when we spoke yesterday, he went on about needing to tell the truth. I warned him to be careful of the queen. Maybe I shouldn't have told him about her."

"What did you tell him?"

"What you've already heard. That she is slowly poisoning the king."

"Only that?"

"And that she's pleasuring her son."

"Ugh! No wonder the people here call her the Roman slut! But Melchior's a smart man . . . why would he throw that in the king's face?"

"I don't know. It's not something he would have done in the past, but he has been different of late. Haven't you noticed it? He speaks up more forcefully with the other teachers, defends his views more openly, and loses his temper more."

"Like he did with you in Arsinoe?" asked Balthazar.

"Yes. He used to be quiet, reserved; docile even. But there is a part of him, a deep pool of feeling that lurks beneath the surface, like a flying fish ready to jump. I think he is struggling with something, and hasn't found his peace with it."

"But he's a good man, Gaspar. Something else must have happened. Something that provoked his outburst."

Gaspar nodded. "Do you know what he said?"

"I know only that he called the queen a scheming harlot . . . among other things."

Gaspar frowned. "He said more? Oh, this is not good. Have you told Amro and the others?"

"No. I thought to leave that for you."

Gaspar sighed. "I will tell them, but first I must speak with Mered. Perhaps he can appeal to the king."

"What do you think they'll do to him?" asked Balthazar. But he received no reply for Gaspar was already out the door.

Gaspar hurried into the palace's main hall, and didn't bother to bow. "Have you heard about your brother?"

"Well it's nice to see you too, Gaspar. You're observing no niceties today? No small talk of the stars and their meanings?"

"Do not play with me, Mered. Not today. I know you have spies all over. Half the populace is probably on your dole. Where have they taken him?"

"Now, now. Take a deep breath and explain yourself."

Gaspar walked closer and looked into Mered's face. "Is it possible you really don't know?"

"The last I saw Melchior was five days ago when he came asking about the king. Though I admit I listened only briefly before walking out. His ignorance of politics can be quite tedious. But I've not seen or heard from him since. You talk as if you think something's happened."

"I don't think, I know! He was arrested yesterday at the palace."

Mered chuckled. "My brother? That submissive, naïve prick of a man! You must have him confused with someone else."

"I wish I did. He met with the king yesterday and somehow managed to insult the queen. The word is that he called her a scheming harlot, among other things."

"Melchior said that? Maybe he has the balls of a man after all."

"Enough with your brotherly barbs. We must find where they've taken him."

Mered pursed his lips. "I can probably find out. But then what?"

Gaspar glared. "He's your brother, you . . ." Gaspar stopped himself. It would do no good to lose his temper. He began again in a quieter tone. "You're the king's satrap. A well trusted accomplice in his government of spies. You must have some sway with him? Some thought for how to seek leniency?"

"You're almost as naïve as my brother, if you think I can convince him to ignore his wife and listen to me. As naïve as I was when I tried to warn him of her poison."

"You told the king?"

"Mmm. I told him she was lacing his food, but he didn't believe me. And what's worse, he told her. At her urging he discovered who my informant was and had him killed. My eyes and ears in the palace are gone now."

"So you really didn't know of Melchior's arrest?"

"No." Mered rose and started pacing.

"What's going on Mered? I've never known you to look . . . worried."

"Do you know how hard I worked to get this appointment? How many years I licked the king's boots and toadied to his family? And now his Roman queen turns him against me! She even threatened my family. 'How beautiful you daughters are! How ripe and luscious.' she said. 'They should be my guests at court.' She said. I don't want to give them over to her, but what can I do? I cannot lose this appointment. I cannot!"

Gaspar glowered. "You talk about Melchior's balls? Your brother is a far better man than you shall ever be. Don't you realize what will become of your daughters if the queen gets hold of them? And all you can do is worry about your position? Do you care so little for your own flesh and blood?" He thrust out his hands in frustration.

"I care for them, but what good will I be to them without power and position?"

Gaspar shook his head. "Power and position will not make them love you after you give them to that woman. And what of your brother? I understand your cowardice, but will you stand by and do nothing? You must help Melchior. We can't let him rot in prison."

Mered sat down again. "I'll find out where they've taken him, and try to buy off some of the guards. Maybe they will give him a better cell, decent food, an occasional walk in the sunlight. But beyond that I cannot promise. I will not go to the king on his behalf, for I know well enough what may come of it."

Gaspar sighed. "Tell me what you find out."

The sun was setting by the time Gaspar got to Melchior's house. Corinna met him at the door.

"You find Melchior?" she asked.

"Not exactly. Call Amro and Asher, will you? I will tell you all together."

When the men arrived, Gaspar explained what he'd learned. "I hope to know soon where they have taken him."

"Have they done this just to scare him or is it more serious?" asked Asher.

"I'm not sure. One thing I do know. The queen controls the king. Despite her treachery, he accedes to her every whim. Mered, who was always secure felt in the king's circle, now fears for his position and family. I think we must expect the worst."

"But Melchior's a Parthian noble. You don't think they'll execute him do you?" asked Amro nervously moving from foot to foot.

Gaspar sighed. "Anything is possible."

"What should we do?" asked Amro.

"Go about your business. I will pay your wages until we know more." He looked at Asher and Corinna. "I'm sorry about your wedding. I know Melchior was planning to hold it here, but that's not possible now. Would you consider gathering at my house instead?"

"Thank you for the offer," said Asher. "We will talk it over."

"Very well. If you don't mind I would like to sleep here tonight. It's been a long day."

"Of course," said Amro. "Corinna, can you fix a place for Gaspar in Mered and Dahab's old room?"

Gaspar rose early the next morning to the sound of horses outside the house. Who is visiting so early? He wondered. He had just finished dressing when Dahab barged into the room.

"What are you doing in my room?" asked Dahab.

"Your room? I thought your room was at the satrap's palace with your husband."

"Don't speak to me of that man. And get out of my way! I'm moving back here until I can make other arrangements." She dropped her bag of clothing on the floor and marched out before he could say more.

Gaspar gathered his things and went out to look for Corinna and Asher. He found them with Amro back near the stable. "What's going on? Dahab said she's moving back into the house?"

Amro spoke up. "Master Mered is angry as a hornet. He told me his wife said something to the queen that might cost him his job. He wants to divorce her."

Gaspar shook his head. "This doesn't make sense. Dahab's ambition for Mered was only surpassed by his own. Why would she say anything to threaten his position?"

"It's a puzzle," said Amro. "I was working in front of the house when they rode up. Mered's face was red, he said only what I told you, watched her dismount, threw her bags to the ground and galloped off. He had the look of a wild animal."

"Something is very wrong," said Gaspar. "Keep your eyes and ears open, and tell me if you learn anything more."

"We will," said Asher. "Must Corinna serve Dahab while she's here?"

"Unfortunately, yes. Mered still owns this estate. Until he divorces her or she moves away, all of you are here at their pleasure."

"But Master Melchior is the one who pays us," said Amro.

"That is true. You are free to leave if you wish. I cannot tell you what to do."

"I stay," said Corinna. "Serve her 'til marry Asher. Maybe learn what she know."

CHAPTER 45
Coming to Terms

§

ONE MONTH LATER

MELCHIOR COMPLETED HIS TENTH TURN around the cell. If he wasn't going to be let out to walk, he could at least do this. He shivered and kept going. He was hungry, cold, and guilty. Yes, guilty. He'd lost his temper with the queen and was paying for it. He looked up to the one high window in the cell. *I don't blame you for punishing me, Lord. For all my years I've been like a player in a Greek drama, but now my mask is gone.* He looked about his cell. It was dark and dank, but despite the gloom he could see himself for what he was. A liar. *I told the king I didn't believe in you, when I do. I am no better than the queen I accused.*

He sat down on a wooden stool and picked at the bits of hard bread his jailors had slipped between the iron bars. It was green with mold, hardly worth his effort, but his belly ached. He usually liked being a solitary man. Not now. His cell admitted little light, no birdsong, no music, no laughter; and except for his own occasional outbursts, no cries. If there were other prisoners, he could not hear them. The only voices that reached him belonged to the guards, and they had given him small comfort. "Ay. His brother gave me silver to feed him extra, but I'll not be risking my hide for that star gazer."

So, Mered did care about him. It was an unexpected piece of news. But no-one had come to see him, not Mered, Gaspar, or Balthazar, nor any teachers from the school. Surely they knew where he was by now?

Gaspar at least would try. Maybe they had all tried and been denied. There was no way to know, and when he tried to engage his jailors, to ask about visitors, they turned their backs. It was a lonely existence, and he was beginning to realize it might last a long time.

He set the bread aside, lay down on the dirt floor and closed his eyes. *Think about the journey. You were true to yourself and Me then. No playing the part, no lying. You walked through the land of your ancestors, as one of them. You made no denials at the temple, nor to Mary and Joseph. You told them all who you were and what I meant to you. You can learn to do that again. I will help.*

He opened his eyes and thought about those days after Bethlehem. He remembered being filled with confusion, but he realized now, the confusion had been of his own making. The Messiah had not been what he expected, but why should the Lord's chosen one conform to his ideas? After all, what was the child's poverty in the eyes of the Lord? Probably as meaningless as the color of his eyes, or hair. His mother had taught him the Mosaic stories, yet until now the essential truths had eluded him. The Lord of Moses was a God of infinite power and love. He could lay the powerful low and raise up the lowly whenever he chose. The Messiah's poverty would be no bar to kingship for such a God.

He could have said that to King Phraates and the Queen but he had not. He could have acknowledged his ancestry but he had not. He had denied himself and his family, and the rage that resulted from the Queen's truthful accusations had landed him here.

I'm not interested in revenge, Oh Lord. But how did Thermusa know? She said she had it on *good authority*. Who told her? All those years of hiding the truth, studying in secret, pretending to follow Zarathustra. I'm thankful the truth is out, but I can't help wondering. Who gained from telling my secret to the queen? And what of my brother and his family? Protect them Lord, please. Especially the children.

CHAPTER 46
Asher Shares a Secret

§

ASHER LOOKED OUT FROM GASPAR'S rooftop garden. "You have a nice view, Gaspar. Not as good as from my hills but nice."

"I like it. May I offer you some water?"

"No. I cannot stay. I've come to thank you."

"For what? I've done nothing."

"That's not true. You've been paying our wages since Melchior was imprisoned and you offered to host our wedding."

Gaspar smiled. "My offer still stands."

Asher looked down briefly. "You are most kind, but we've decided to be married in my home village. It will be easier for my family if they don't have to travel, and since my father is moving back . . ."

"Your father is leaving Melchior's estate?"

"Yes. He doesn't like working for Master Mered and says it not the same without Melchior around."

"I understand. I feel the same way at my school. How is Corinna? I suppose she's ready to get away from Dahab?"

Asher laughed. "She is. The woman orders her about from morning 'til night. But she does talk to Corinna now and again. Which is another reason I came."

"Have you something to share?"

"Yes. The other day while Corinna was helping Dahab bathe, Dahab talked about the queen. She said that she had gone to the palace some months back with the wives of other nobles. That the queen had invited them to bathe with her."

"I heard that Thermusa had Roman style baths built at the palace, but I've never seen them. Is there more to the story than that?"

"There is. Do remember the Arsinoe baths, Gaspar? How much we drank and what we were like after the hot water and wine? Corinna wasn't happy with me that night."

"I do indeed remember. Are you saying the queen plied all the wives with wine while they bathed?"

"Yes. Dahab described her delight to Corinna. She said the women laughed, and drank, and traded secrets as they scrubbed each other. The queen made a game of it, encouraging them with trinkets and gemstones. She offered the largest gems to whoever could tell the most telling secret about someone in their family. Dahab's said she chose to tell about her boring brother-in-law. She told the queen that Mered had never been as happy as he was with his Jewish brother gone."

"She must have been drunk indeed to admit Mered's brother was Jewish. Did Dahab say anything else?"

"Yes. She said the queen promised her a huge gem if she could provide more details. She won the gem by telling how Mered laughed when he heard Melchior was taking his mother's bones to Judea, and that he was glad no more sacrifices would take place on his land."

"Now I understand why Mered is divorcing her. He always worried that his ancestry might get in the way of his ambitions. If he discovered that Dahab told the queen of it, he would be furious. Now the secret is out, and I venture as soon as the king is dead, Mered will be out too. No wonder he was worried when I saw him."

"I thought you would want to know. Have you any word of Melchior?"

"He's being held in the palace dungeon in Cistephon. Mered passed some silver to the guards, but so far they won't let us see him."

"So, you don't know how he is?"

"No. . . . When are you leaving, Asher?"

"Tomorrow." Asher rose and put his hands on Gaspar's shoulders. "You have been a good friend to us, Gaspar. Corinna would still be at that brothel if not for you and Melchior. I thank you both. If you should see him again, please tell him we think of him."

"I will."

CHAPTER 47

A Roman Queen

§

THREE MONTHS LATER

BALTHAZAR RUSHED INTO THE CHART room. "Have you heard, Gaspar? King Phraates is dead! And Phraataces has been crowned king."

"What of Thermusa? She must have her hand in this somewhere."

"How did you know? She is marrying her own son. They will rule together!"

Gaspar stroked his beard. "The nobles will not like this. Not one bit."

"There is rumbling in the streets already. "What have we come to?" they ask. "A half-Roman king and his mother as his wife!" Everyone is shaking their heads.

"As well they should. With any luck the nobles will rise up and retrieve one of Phraates' older sons from Rome. It may be the only hope to restore a true Parthian kingship."

"Have you any word of Melchior?"

"No. They still won't let us see him, though Mered continues to hand silver to his guard. And now that Thermusa is ruling, I fear she may clean house in the prisons."

"Execute him?" Balthazar shook his head. "I have an idea. Do you remember how I discovered he was arrested?"

"You said you sold some spice to an old woman who works in the palace. How will that help us see Melchior?"

"She told me that her husband is a guard. She liked me, Gaspar. Perhaps I should go back and see if her husband will help us too."

"How can it hurt? Do you have the spice you need to sell her?"

"I do."

"Go then. I will pray for your success."

"What did you say?" Asked Balthazar.

"You heard me. I said I would pray."

"To Melchior's God?"

"I think of Him as the Messiah's God. He did cure me after all. How can it hurt?"

Balthazar made his way by foot to Cistephon. Two hours later he approached the vine covered wall where he had met the old woman four months earlier. This time he walked directly up to the palace door and spoke to the guard. "My name is Balthazar. Phaedra likes to buy her spice from me. Will you call her to the door?"

The guard looked him over from head to foot. "You want to see my wife?"

Balthazar stepped back. "Yes. Some months ago I sold her spice, hoping it might help the king. I was sorry to hear of his death."

"Phaedra told me about you. That you were from her country. Your spice helped the king for a time. But the queen started using a different potion and that was the end of him. I will get Phaedra . . . "

"Hold on!" said Balthazar quickly. "Phaedra told me you were in the king's guard. You sound like a loyal Parthian."

The guard whispered. "I am no friend of the queen if that's what you mean."

"It is. Like you, my friend Melchior is no friend of hers. He sits in her dungeon because he spoke up."

"He was brave for trying to warn the king, even if he did it in anger. You want my help for him?"

"If you have the heart for it. His brother has paid silver to one of Melchior's guards but after four months we still have no idea how he fares. The silver can be yours instead if you could get me in to see him."

"I must think of a way. Come back this time tomorrow and I'll see what I can do."

Balthazar bowed in acknowledgement and departed. The next day, he arrived on schedule at the same door, with a pouch of silver as well as his spice. A different guard was at the door, however. Balthazar decided to repeat yesterday's introduction to the guard. "My name is Balthazar. Phaedra likes to buy her spice from me. Will you call her to the door?"

"You know Phaedra?" asked the guard.

"Yes. I know her well. She and my mother were friends in Arabia."

The guard looked him over then said. "Wait here while I call her."

After a short wait Phaedra opened the door. "Balthazar! Come in my boy. Let us do our business inside."

This time he followed Phaedra past the kitchen down multiple sets of stone stairways into the depths below. They soon came to a wide hall-way at the end of which was an iron gate where Phaedra's husband stood guard. Phaedra bowed to Balthazar then turned in silence and made her way back from whence they'd come.

"Would you like your silver now or later?" asked Balthazar.

"Later will do," said Phaedra's husband. "You will have only a short time with him, but I can arrange for you to meet again, on a steady basis if you like. If the queen is away your next visit can be longer."

"That would be good," said Balthazar. "Can we arrange for my friend Gaspar to visit him as well?"

"It should be no problem. Just have him ask for me, Arsak."

They walked down a long tunnel and stopped at a cell where a man lay on the straw strewn floor. Arsak opened the iron door and Balthazar stepped inside. It was hard to believe this crumpled man was his friend. His clothing wreaked and he was very thin. Balthazar bent down to him. "Melchior? Melchior, it's me, Balthazar. Wake up."

Melchior opened his eyes. "Balthazar? Oh my God! Balthazar!" He looked dazed but sat up.

Balthazar sat down at his side. "How are you holding up?"

Melchior rubbed his hands up and down his arms. His clothes were dirty and smelled of urine and vomit. He did not raise his eyes to Balthazar nor did he answer.

Balthazar took off his cloak, put it around Melchior's shoulders and hugged him. "I'm sorry. Sorry it's taken me so long to come. Your brother was giving silver to one of the guards, but I can see it didn't help."

Melchior finally looked up. His cheeks were stained with tears and dirt. "I know. I heard the guards talking. I was surprised Mered would pay . . . to help me."

"What do you need, my friend? How can we help you most?"

"Can you get me out?"

Balthazar shook his head. "I don't think so. King Phraates is dead. Phraataces rules now with his wife Thermusa at his side."

Melchior blinked. "He married his mother? . . . They have no shame."

"They do not. He's taken the name Phraates V."

"What do the nobles think of them?"

"They are incensed. The streets of Seleucia and Cistephon roil with talk of rebellion. You can hear it in the markets, at the festivals, in the temple. Surprisingly, the king is trying to assert himself by threatening the Romans of all people. He wants control of Media and Armenia, and says he will wage war if he needs to."

Melchior's eyes looked suddenly animated. "The young king knows nothing of war. He has spent his whole life on his mother's couch, doted on and worshipped."

"Your nephews say as much. I met some of them at an archery tournament and they deride him as a fool. You must stay strong, my friend. If rebellion comes, you will break these chains and see the light of day again."

"When? How many years must I linger before it comes? I'm not young anymore. I haven't the stamina to survive forever."

"Not forever, Melchior. Just one day, then another, and another. I will come again, and so will Gaspar. We have made a friend among the guards. His name is Arsak. His wife Phaedra works in the kitchen. They do not like the queen or her son. They have promised to help us. We will get you better food and warmer clothes. You must not give up."

Arsak came suddenly to the cell door and rattled his keys. "It's time."

Balthazar hugged Melchior again and rose. "Keep my cloak as a reminder that you are not forgotten. Have faith. Pray to the Lord like Gaspar."

Melchior looked up at him. "Gaspar prays? To my God?"

Balthazar nodded. "Yes. And so do I."

CHAPTER 48

Duck for Dinner

§

SIX YEARS LATER – 4 A.D.

"COME MY DAUGHTERS. WE MUST make the house look good for Grandpa Melchior! Miriam, will you help the twins finish sweeping the court-yard? Rebecca, I need you to help me and Corinna in the kitchen."

"What are you making, mother?" asked Rebecca.

"Melchior's favorite has always been duck, so duck it shall be. Is your father home from his work yet?"

Balthazar walked into the house. "I'm here! They should be here soon. Is everything ready?"

"As near as I can make it."

"He will be so surprised to see you," said Balthazar as he put his arm around Asher. "Your family is getting so big! And I hear your farm is prosperous."

"Yes, praise God. I have increased my herds a hundred fold and am doing well with the farm. And look at your twins!" said Asher surveying the girls as they swept the floor. "They are getting so tall and beautiful. Who are they named for?"

"Chana is named for my sister and Baysan for Alima's. And strangely, they both resemble their namesakes. When Alima bore them she knew immediately what names they would take. How does Corinna like hav-ing three sons?"

"She enjoys them greatly. Her language skills are much improved because they're always teaching her new words. Not always the good ones, though!" Asher laughed as he shook his head.

"I have that problem with Isaac. He is a terror at times, the only boy among four sisters. He's hoping the new baby will be a boy."

"For his sake I hope so, too," said Asher cocking his head. "I think I hear horses. Come everyone!"

The families went outside in a rush. Four horses approached, with a wagon trailing slowly behind.

"Do you see him, children?" asked Alima."

"Is that grandfather in the wagon?" asked Isaac.

"That's him," said Alima. "You must all be very kind to him, and patient. He's been in prison a long time, and he can't see much anymore."

"Will he be able to see us momma?" asked Chana.

"I'm not sure. But if he asks, you can let him feel your face. That will help him to know what you look like."

"We're here, Melchior," said Gaspar reigning in his horse outside the garden wall.

Melchior smiled. "I can feel the sun of their smiles already."

"Welcome home!" said Balthazar as he put his arm on Melchior's shoulder. "Many of us have gathered to celebrate your homecoming, including your favorite shepherd and his family."

"Asher? Where are you boy?" asked Melchior.

"I'm here," said Asher patting Melchior's back.

Melchior reached out to touch his shoulder. "Oh my. You've grown even taller since our journey days."

"Yes. And I have three healthy sons with Corinna!"

"The Lord be praised!" said Melchior. Balthazar and Asher helped Melchior from the wagon, and twining their arms together under his, guided him into the garden.

"Would you prefer to sit in the house or the garden?" asked Alima as they entered the courtyard.

"The garden!" said Melchior emphatically. "For six and a half years I have yearned for the sun's heat and it feels glorious. Will someone fetch me a cup of water?"

"I will!" yelled Isaac as he ran inside.

Melchior smiled at the sound of the boy's voice. "Other than momma, those are the first words I've heard from him! . . . How you do you like being the lady of the house, Alima? Gaspar tells me you have done wonderful things with the estate since Mered's death."

"Balthazar has helped. There was no-one here for some years after Dahab left. The place began to look quite forsaken."

"So I heard. Gaspar tried to sell it for me, but no-one wanted to buy the place after they heard that Mered killed himself here. I was glad when you agreed to move in."

"It is a wonderful place, Melchior. I hope you will approve my work," said Alima.

"I can tell from its fragrance that the garden is beautiful. When I am stronger you must walk me round with your children. The summit of palm grove is one of my favorite places."

"It's one of mine, too," said Alima.

"Where are Phaedra and Arsak?" asked Melchior.

"We're here," said Phaedra coming closer. "What a lovely thing to have an adopted family like this, Melchior."

"Yes," said Melchior. "I am blessed to have them. And to have found you and Arsak. If you had not befriended Balthazar with his spice and helped me these past years, I would be long dead."

"You are a good man, Melchior," said Phaedra. "And now that we're together we must share a secret of our own. Balthazar was not the only reason we helped you. Did you ever guess that we shared your ancestry?"

"I wondered why you helped me and refused Balthazar's silver."

"Once Arsak told me your story, we couldn't stand by and do nothing. We wanted to help you escape years ago but could not."

"I understood," said Melchior. "You had to wait until the nobles rose up against the queen."

"We thought it the only way. Now that Thermusa and her son are dead, no-one will question your freedom. "

"Have the nobles chosen a new king?" asked Melchior.

"I hear they plan to offer the crown to Orodes. I only hope he rules better than his half-brother," said Gaspar.

"Come everyone, let us celebrate!" said Alima. "We have prepared a feast of ducks for you Melchior. We used one of Bina's old recipes. Would you like some?"

CHAPTER 49

Beyond a Doubt

§

TWENTY-NINE YEARS LATER – 33 A.D. IN SELEUCIA

"THAT WILL DO IT FOR today. You have made a good start." Balthazar bowed to his students as they left the lecture hall. The new class was smaller than in prior years, but the men were intelligent, inquisitive and devoted to their studies. Those were the qualities Gaspar had looked for, and in the ten years since his death Balthazar had tried to do the same. But he had also made changes. Astronomy for its own sake was more of a focus. He encouraged his teachers to share their ideas and observations not only to promote consistency in their predictions but to foster their studies. He was proud to see how many of them worked together and that their combined efforts had resulted in a more powerful lens with which to observe the heavens.

Balthazar closed the door to his chart room and threw his cloak over his shoulders.

"I'm going home, Isaac. See you in the morning."

"Wait father!" yelled Isaac from the next room. "There's a man here asking for Gaspar and Melchior. I told him you are in charge now. Will you see him?"

"Can he wait 'til morning? I'm too tired to hold a consultation now."

Isaac walked up to Balthazar. "That's not what he wants, father. He's come a long way. Will you see him, please?"

"Very well. Bring him to the courtyard." Balthazar walked to the courtyard to sit on his favorite stone bench, for if there was a breeze to be felt, this was the place. Ah yes! He closed his eyes for a moment and let the gentle wind wash over him. When he opened them, Isaac stood before him with a tall man at his side.

"Father, this is Thomas. He comes from the land of my poppa Noah."

Balthazar got to his feet and bowed. "Greetings, Thomas. My name is Balthazar. Is this true that you come from Judea?"

"I was born in Capernaum in Galilee. It's the country north of Judea."

"Isaac's birth mother was born in Nazareth in Galilee. Is Capernaum near there?"

"Not too far. Capernaum is a fishing village on the west shore of the sea."

"My wife, Alima, traveled through that country many years ago when she took Isaac and his sisters to Bethlehem. She said it is beautiful country, but a long way from Parthia. What brings you here?"

"A mutual friend sent me. Her name is Mary. She said our good news might be welcome here," said Thomas.

Balthazar's eyes widened. "Mary? The wife of Joseph and mother to Jesus?"

"The very same."

"By my stars! I often wondered how they fared, and now . . . after all these years! Did my son tell you that Gaspar died?"

"Yes. And he said Melchior lives with you and your family. "

"That's right. He's very old now and blind, but otherwise well. So tell me. What news is so momentous that Mary has sent you all this way?"

"It's a long story, and one which I would like to tell you and your family together. Mary bid me speak to you and to as many of your friends as I can find."

"I can arrange that. Will you come home with me? You will have all the time you need to share your news."

"I would like that very much."

Balthazar put his hand on Isaac's shoulder. "Run to Asher's house. Tell him and Corinna to come to our house as soon as they can, and to bring the family. Tell them it's important!"

Some hours later as the sun was setting, Balthazar reclined at table with Thomas, Melchior, Asher, and their families.

"You are a good cook, Alima," said Thomas. "Thank you for including me in your family meal."

"We are honored to have you!" said Alima. "Balthazar tells me Mary sent you, and any friend to Mary is a friend to us."

"She told me of your journey, and how you honored Jesus. She never forgot you, and when I told her I was coming east she told me to look for you in Seleucia."

"We never forgot her or her son, Jesus, who was the reason for our journey. What can you tell us of him?" asked Melchior.

"Jesus is the reason for my journey. I guess you could say he commissioned me to travel as your king once commissioned you."

"So Jesus is a king?" asked Balthazar. "I thought the Romans still control all of Galilee and Judea."

"They do. But the answer to your question is still yes. Jesus is a king! In fact, to steal a phrase from your Parthian kings, Jesus is the King of Kings, for his power goes far beyond any one country."

"I don't understand," said Balthazar.

"I didn't either at first. For three years I followed Jesus as he preached and I never fully understood the meaning of his kingship until after his death."

"No! No!" cried Asher. "How can he be dead?"

"He isn't dead. He lives," said Thomas smiling.

"How can both things be true? He died but he lives? Your words make no sense," said Balthazar.

"You are right. If Jesus had been a person like you and me, dying and living again would be impossible. But I tell you they are true. It is the good news Jesus bid me tell you, and as many others as my voice will reach."

"I am very confused," said Balthazar.

"Me too!" said Asher.

"And me!" said Melchior. The others who were gathered round the table murmured their agreement.

"It is confusing, but if I tell you of his life maybe it will become clear. Mary told me some of what happened in the early years. Balthazar, she said to tell you that your camel got them get safely to Egypt and that they stayed until they heard of Herod's death, then returned to Nazareth. Jesus grew up there and became a carpenter like Joseph. But after Jesus was baptized in the Jordan by a prophet called John, his life changed. He left Nazareth and traveled about the countryside teaching the people about God, his father."

"Did you say 'God his father'?" asked Melchior.

"Yes. Jesus claimed he was the Son of God. It was an astounding thing to say, and many thought him crazed and condemned him for it. But if you heard him speak and saw the things he did you would not scoff so easily."

"I understand what you say," said Asher. "I was in Bethlehem. I remember the night the shepherds brought me to the cave and I saw Gaspar's healing. Only the power of God could have done that."

"Mary told me of that healing, and of the strange circumstances surrounding her son's conception."

"What did she say?" asked Alima. "She never shared that with us."

"She said that Jesus was conceived before she had lain with Joseph. That an angel named Gabriel appeared to her when she was still a virgin. The angel told her she would conceive by the Holy Spirit; that her child would be Son of the Most High."

"No wonder she didn't laugh at us when we spoke of our men in white!" said Melchior. "Tell us more."

"Jesus roamed for three years through the countryside of Galilee and Judea. He taught in the synagogues, houses and fields, even from the shores of the Sea. He said the kingdom of God was at hand, and told many stories about it. He taught us what it means to love God and neighbor."

"What did he teach you?" asked Asher.

"So much. If we talked every day for years I would not be able to tell it all."

"Then tell us what you think is important," said Alima.

"He said: L*ove the Lord, your God, with all your heart, with all your being, with all your strength and with all your mind, and your neighbor as yourself.* He gave us a new commandment: *Love one another, as I have loved you.* He told us to love our enemies, do good to those who hate us, bless those who curse us, pray for those who mistreat us and be merciful. He said: *Stop judging and you will not be judged. Stop condemning and you will not be condemned. Forgive and you will be forgiven...*"

"They are not the words of any earthly king," said Melchior.

Thomas nodded. "No. He spoke with wisdom and authority. Unfortunately, the ruling powers resented him. And they were jealous because his actions attracted so many. He performed miracles every-where he went, curing the sick, the blind, the lame and the deaf. He commanded unclean spirits, forgave sins, calmed storms and walked upon the waters of the sea. He even raised people from the dead! Yet, many still doubted him - including me. "

"I understand that," said Melchior. "I saw Gaspar cured with my own eyes, yet I left Bethlehem wondering if Jesus was the Messiah. I doubted and even denied my God before our king. It was only in the dark solitude of prison that I understood what I had done, and how much I needed God. How did you doubt him, Thomas?"

"Bear with me. I will tell you in due course," said Thomas.

"How did Jesus die?" asked Balthazar.

"He was crucified by the Romans three years ago."

"Oh!" cried Alima. "What a terrible way to die. Did he foster insurrection?"

"No, but that didn't matter to those who plotted his end. His death was a conspiracy of sorts between the Jewish authorities, a fickle pop-ulace, and the Romans. Caiaphas, the Chief Priest, the Pharisees and other temple authorities resented Jesus' growing influence. They hated him because he reviled them as hypocrites."

"Did you say Caiaphas is the Chief Priest?" asked Melchior.

"Yes. He's been Chief Priest for seventeen years and heads the Sanhedrin which tried Jesus. Why?"

"Because he was the young priest I met at the Temple so many years ago when I asked about the Messiah prophecies. He was an arrogant man."

"And still is," said Thomas. "Caiaphas had many reasons to hate Jesus. I think he may have been jealous of Jesus' following, and because he was in charge of the temple treasury, he was greatly angered when Jesus drove the money changers and vendors from the temple. I don't know if it's true but some say he took a portion of the profits."

"I wouldn't be surprised," said Melchior. "I remember the Court of the Gentiles from years back. It was as much a marketplace as any in the city, and yet so near the Holy of Holies."

"That market had become accepted practice, and the people who made their livelihoods there didn't want it to change. Caiaphas and many others saw Jesus as a threat, so they found a way to kill him with the help of one of my companions."

Asher shook his head. "How could one of your own do such a thing?"

"We wondered that, too," said Thomas. "Jesus chose twelve of us to accompany him as he travelled. We shared his company and his love, we listened to him and helped him with the crowds, feeding them and ministering to them as he instructed us. We were a motley group. A carpenter, some fishermen, a tax collector, a Zealot, traders and farmers, but we became like family. All except for Judas, our group's money man. He took silver from the priests for the life of The Messiah." Thomas grimaced. "Money can do so much good, but it can also be the cause of pain and ruin. It was the ruin of Judas. Among my companions, his name shall always be remembered for shame and betrayal."

"From what you tell us, Jesus went about doing good. On what charge did they arrest him?" asked Balthazar.

"Because Jesus claimed he was the Son of God, Caiaphas accused him of blasphemy. It was a crime punishable by death, but the Sanhedrin didn't have the power to execute him, so they turned him over to the Romans to be crucified."

"You said you came to share good news. Where is the good news in this?" asked Alima.

"Be patient. You've not heard the end," said Thomas.

"Death is not the end?" asked Balthazar.

"Not at all. Let me explain. Jesus died on a Friday afternoon. None of us twelve except for John was there. He stood near the cross with Mary and some other women friends."

"Where were the rest of you?" asked Melchior.

"We were hiding in fear. It was sad, but we let fear overcome our love and loyalty."

"I know that feeling, when fear directs your actions and your words," said Melchior.

"It's not good," said Thomas. "Thankfully, John had the courage to stay with Mary. Even now he cares for her like a son. "

"Mary must have been shattered," said Alima. "How is she now?"

"She was distraught at first, but once she heard the good news that changed. Now she is joyful as we are."

"I still don't understand. How can she be joyful when her son was crucified?" asked Balthazar.

"After Jesus was taken from the cross, Mary and her friends anointed and wrapped him according to our tradition. Mary wanted me to tell you that she used some of the spice you gave so many years ago to anoint his body. They buried him in a new tomb in a nearby garden before going home in sorrow."

"Hurry up! Tell us the rest!" exclaimed Isaac.

Thomas smiled. "Early on Sunday morning, while it was still dark, one of Jesus' friends, also named Mary, went to the tomb. She found the large stone which had sealed the tomb was rolled away. Jesus' body was gone."

"Gone! Who would take his body?" asked Alima.

"Mary wondered that, too. She ran to tell some of my companions and returned with them to the tomb. They found the burial cloths in the tomb but no body. Jesus had told us on several occasions that he would be killed and rise in three days, but we never accepted his words. We didn't want him to die! We wanted him to be a great ruler and king! But he had died; and seeing the tomb empty brought back the memory of his predictions. My friends went home not knowing what to think, but Mary stayed by the tomb weeping. Then something wonderful happened. As she wept, she looked into the tomb and saw two angels in white sitting there.

"The men in white again?" asked Melchior.

"Yes. They asked her why she was weeping. She told them it was because she didn't know where Jesus's body had been taken. Then she turned around and saw a man who asked her the same thing."

"Another angel?" asked Balthazar.

"No. At first Mary thought he was the gardener, but when the man called her by name, and she heard his voice, she knew it was Jesus. He told her: '*Go to my brothers and tell them, I am going to my Father and your Father. To my God and your God.*' Mary left the tomb and came to tell us all that he had said."

"So he lives?" asked Melchior.

"He lives! Though I didn't believe it myself at first. That very evening Jesus appeared to my companions. But I wasn't there, so when they told me "We have seen the Lord!" I didn't believe them. I mean who believes such things? It is the talk of lunatics. I told them that unless I saw the mark of the nails in Jesus' hands and put my finger into the marks and my hand into his side I would not believe."

"A week later I was with my friends when suddenly Jesus stood among us. He said, 'Peace be with you.' Then he looked at me and said, 'Put your finger here and see my hands, put your hand into my side and do not be unbelieving, but believe.'"

"What did you do?" asked Asher.

"I fell to my knees and cried, 'My Lord and My God!' There he was, living, breathing, talking, even eating with us! Jesus said to me 'Have you come to believe because you have seen me? Blessed are those who have not seen and have believed.' That could be you, my friends! I declare, as surely as I stand here before you, the life of Jesus is no mere fantasy tale. No longer must you look to the heavens and wonder what the face of God looks like for it is his face. It is the face of compassion, love and goodness, even in the midst of evil and pain."

"Did you see him again after that? Does he still appear to you?" asked Melchior.

"He appeared several times to different groups of people in the days and weeks that followed. Then one day he led us to the town of Bethany, raised his hands and blessed us. And as he did so, he was taken up to heaven. We haven't seen him since, yet we have been filled with great joy. We no longer fear! We go often to the temple praising God and speaking in his name as I do now with you."

"Are the authorities in Judea still persecuting your companions?"

"Yes. They don't like to hear what we have to say. They thought Jesus' death would put an end to his ideas, to what he called the *new covenant*. The reverse has been true. More and more people join our ranks each day as we share the good news."

"And you're not afraid to speak out?" asked Asher.

"Not anymore. Since the Spirit came upon us one Sunday, my friends and I have begun to travel, giving testimony to the truth. What better news could we share my friends? In a world so torn with strife and death, we have his peace and love. I will never forget the feeling that came upon me when he said: *Peace be with you*. I pray I never do."

"What will you do now?" asked Balthazar.

"I will stay in Parthia for a while. I will travel and spread the news as far as I can. Then I will go east on the Royal Road. We met some Indian traders in Jerusalem on the day the Spirit came to us. I think India is the place I need to go next."

"You are welcome to stay with us as long as you like," said Balthazar.

"Thank you. That would be most kind," said Thomas. "There are a few things more I would say before I finish." Thomas looked at Melchior. "You said that you denied the Lord before your king, Melchior. In Jesus name, I forgive you. My friend Peter, the leader of our group in Jerusalem, himself denied Jesus three times on the night of his trial. Peter did it, as you probably did, out of fear. But the Lord forgave him. On the day he forgave Peter, Jesus said, 'If you love me, feed and tend my sheep.' The best way to show your love for the Lord is to take care of others."

Thomas looked at Asher. "Mary said you were but a young shepherd when you first saw Jesus in her arms. You know what it means to care for sheep. If you believe in Jesus as I do, share my good news and be a shepherd of men. Now, Balthazar, if you have some bread and wine, I would like to bless it in memory of Jesus, our friend."

Thomas remained with Balthazar for a month, during which time, he told Jesus' story to many of their friends around Seleucia. When he said goodbye, he was headed south into the hills where Asher had once herded sheep. They never heard from him again.

Some days after Thomas' departure, Balthazar, Alima and Melchior sat in the garden looking down at the Tigris. "What do you make of all Thomas had to say?" asked Balthazar.

"I believe him," said Melchior. "Asher said many years ago that the Messiah's kingship might not be what we expected. He was so right."

"I thought the same," said Balthazar. "It must not have been easy for Thomas to admit his doubt. But we are all doubters in our ways. Doubt is common when we talk of God, because there is a divide between men and God that seems almost impossible to bridge. We cannot see him and are not sure if he sees us. Until now. Jesus bridged the divide. He brought heaven to earth."

Alima smiled. "I wish Gaspar had been here to meet Thomas. He would have loved to hear about Jesus. And he would have loved hearing about all those other men in white!"

Melchior laughed. "Yes, he would have. Gaspar told me years ago that when he was scribing for my mother he asked what the word Messiah meant. She told him it meant 'God with us' and went on to explain how through time, the Jewish people always wanted to have God with us. First through our sacrifices, then in the Ark of the Covenant at the Temple. She thought maybe the Messiah was another way of having God with us. She understood what the prophecies really meant."

"I never knew your mother, Melchior. But she must have been a wise woman."

Melchior smiled. "Yes," he said. "She was right all along."

About the Author

§

S. M. McElligott has had a varied and interesting life. Holding a BA in history from St. Bonaventure University, she has also been a student of law, nursing, and human resources. Throughout it all, biblical history has held a special appeal for her.

An avid reader, chef, and traveler who recently celebrated her fortieth wedding anniversary, she is a proud wife, mother, and grandmother currently residing in Tennessee. This is her first novel.

Ahura Mazda - the chief deity of Zoroastrianism, is the creator of the world, the source of light and the embodiment of good[1]

Amidships – midway between the bow and the stern.[2]

Amphorae – Plural of amphora: a two-handled jar with a narrow neck, used by the ancient Greeks and Romans to carry wine or oil. Used in this story to carry spice.[1]

Aqueduct – a conduit designed to transport water from a remote source, usually by gravity; an elevated structure supporting a conduit or canal passing over a river or low ground.[2]

Arabic – The southwest Semitic language of the Arabs, now spoken in a variety of dialects chiefly in Arabia, Jordan, Syria, Iraq, Palestine, Egypt and parts of northern Africa.[1]

Aramaic – A northwestern Semitic language used as the commercial lingua franca for nearly all of southwestern Asia after about 300BC.[1]

Aristarchus of Samos – (born c. 310 BCE—died c. 230 BCE) an ancient Greek astronomer and mathematician who presented the first known model that placed the Sun at the center of the known universe with the Earth revolving around it.[3]

Ark (aka: Ark of the Covenant) - was a wooden chest clad with gold containing the two stone tablets of the Ten Commandments. In 587 BC, the Babylonians destroyed Jerusalem and Solomon's Temple. There is no record of what became of the Ark.[3]

Arsinoe – (aka: Arsinoites or Cleopatris), was an ancient Egyptian city at the northern extremity of the Heroopolite Gulf (Gulf of Suez), in the

Red Sea. The shortness of the road across the eastern desert and its position near the Royal canal were the principal advantages of Arsinoe as a staple of trade. But although it possessed a capacious bay, it was exposed to the south wind, and the difficulties which ships encountered from reefs in working up the gulf were considerable. Arsinoe, accordingly, was less eligibly situated for the Indian traffic than either Myos Hormos or Berenice.[3]

Astrology – the study of the positions and aspects of the heavenly bodies with a view to predicting their influence on the course of human affairs.[1]

Bab-el-Mandeb Strait - is a strait located between Yemen on the Arabian Peninsula, and Djibouti and Eritrea in the Horn of Africa. It connects the Red Sea to the Gulf of Aden. "Bab-el-Mandeb" means "Gateway of anguish", or "Gateway of tears"; the strait derives its name from the dangers attending its navigation.[3]

Babylon – The capital of ancient Babylonia situated in Mesopotamia on the Euphrates River.[1]

Bethlehem – A town in Israeli occupied Jordan, five miles south of Jerusalem, and the Palestinian village of Biblical times where David lived and Jesus was born.[1]

Berenike – (aka: Berenice **or** Berenike), city of ancient Egypt, on the Red Sea. Founded by Ptolemy II and named in his mother's honor, it commanded the trade with Arabia and India, flourishing from the 3d cent. B.C. to the 4th cent. Its harbor subsequently silted up.[4]

Berth – (nautical) A space at a wharf for a ship to dock or anchor.[1]

Betrothal – The act of becoming betrothed; a mutual promise to marry; an engagement.[1]

Bow – (nautical) the front section of a ship or boat.[1]

Brazier – is a container for fire, generally taking the form of an upright standing or hanging metal bowl or box. Used for burning solid fuel, braziers principally provide heat and light, but may also be used for cooking and cultural rituals. Braziers have been recovered from many early archaeological sites. [3]

Breakwater – An offshore structure (as a wall) protecting a harbor or beach from the force of waves.[2]

Bride-price - Bride price, also known as bride token, is an amount of money, property or other form of wealth paid by a groom or his family to the parents of the woman he has or is about to marry. The bride price agreed may or may not be intended to reflect the perceived value of the woman. The same culture may simultaneously practice both dowry (payment to the groom) and bride price. Many cultures practiced bride price prior to existing records.[3]

Caesar Augustus - the founder of the Roman Empire and its first Emperor, ruling from 27 BC until his death in 14 AD. The reign of Augustus initiated an era of relative peace known as the *Pax Romana* (*The Roman Peace*). Despite continuous wars of imperial expansion on the Empire's frontiers and one year-long civil war over the imperial succession, the Roman world was largely free from large-scale conflict for more than two centuries. Beyond the frontiers, he secured the Empire with a buffer region of client states, and made peace with the Parthian Empire through diplomacy.[3]

Caesarea Maritima - The ancient city and harbor was built by Herod the Great about 25–13 BC. The city had been populated through the late Roman and Byzantine era. Its ruins lie on the Mediterranean coast of Israel, about halfway between the cities of Tel Aviv and Haifa.[3]

Canteen – a flask for drinking water or other liquids** Ancient people would often cure animal bladders to make them strong enough to hold water to take on journeys.[5]

Caravan – A company of travelers on a journey through desert or hostile regions; a train of pack animals.[2]

Caravansary – an inn surrounding a court in eastern countries where caravans rest at night.[2]

Cartouches – In ancient hieroglyphics, an oval or oblong figure that encloses characters expressing the names or epithets of royal or divine personages. A scroll like tablet used either to provide space for an inscription or for ornamental purposes.[3]

Cinnabar – also called Dragon's blood, is a bright red resin that has been in continuous use since ancient times as varnish, medicine, incense, and dye. The dragon's blood known to the ancient Romans was mostly collected from *D. cinnabari*. Dragon's blood was used as a dye, painting pigment, and medicine (respiratory and gastrointestinal problems) in the Mediterranean basin, and was held by early Greeks, Romans, and Arabs to have medicinal properties.[3]

Concubine – a woman with whom a man cohabits without being married; one having a recognized social status in a household below that of a wife.[2]

Ctesiphon – was the capital city of the Parthian Empire from 224BC to 224 AD and one of the great cities of Mesopotamia. It was situated on the eastern bank of the Tigris across from where the Greek city of Seleucia stood and was northeast of ancient Babylon. Today the remains of the city lie approximately 22m. south of the city of Baghdad, Iraq.[3]

Denarii – the plural for the denarius in the Roman currency system, was a small silver coin first minted about 211 BC during the Second Punic War. It was often called a penny in translation.[3]

Dhows – an Arab boat that is low in the front, high in the back, and usually has one or two sails that are shaped like triangles. They were used in the Red Sea and Indian Ocean region.[6]

Drachmas – An ancient currency unit issued by many Greek city states, it was used extensively throughout the Greek world and thru the Hellenistic kingdoms in the Middle East, including Parthia.[3]

Eclipse – the partial or complete obscuring of one celestial body by another.[3]

Elephantegoi – Roman era ships built specifically to carry elephants trained to use in battle.[7]

Emmanuel – is a Hebrew word that signifies "God with us." And is the name of the child predicted in Isaiah 7:14: Behold a virgin shall conceive, and bear a son, and his name shall be called Emmanuel." [8]

Eudaemon – In the first century BCE, this Arabian city (usually identified with the port of Aden) was a transshipping port in the Red Sea trade. The city and surrounding country were the Latin Arabia Felix.[3]

Fatteh – meaning crushed or crumbs, this is a class of southern Levantine dishes consisting of fresh, toasted or stale flatbread covered with other ingredients such as yogurt, steamed chickpeas, eggplant or lamb.[3]

Frankincense – an aromatic gum resin obtained from African and Asian trees of the genus Boswellia and used chiefly as incense.[1]

Fodder – Feed for livestock, often consisting of coarsely chopped stalks and leaves of corn mixed with hay, straw, and other plants.[1]

Fore – Located at or near the front, the bow of a ship.[1]

Great Sea – as used in this novel refers to The Mediterranean Sea

Guardian – A short term for Guardian angels, spiritual beings who are given by God, one to each person, to guard them during life on earth.

Gypsum – A white mineral used in the manufacture of plaster of Paris, gypsum plaster and plaster-board, Portland cement, wallboards, and fertilizers.[1]

Haboob – an intense dust or sand storm carried on an atmospheric gravity current.[3]

Hadramaut – a coastal region occupying 58,000 sq. miles of Southern Arabia, on the Arabian Sea.[3]

Harem – The women occupying a harem, the wives and concubines of a polygamous man; a sacred forbidden place.[1]

Hebrew – The Semitic language of the ancient Hebrews, used in most of the Old Testament.[1]

Henbane – a poisonous plant, also known as stinking nightshade, native to the Mediterranean region, having an unpleasant odor, clammy leaves and funnel-shaped greenish-yellow flowers, and yielding a juice used medically.[1] It was historically used in combination with other plants such as mandrake as an anesthetic potion, as well as for its psychoactive properties in "magic brews."[3]

Himyarite – A member of an ancient tribe of southwestern Arabia.[1]

Himyarite Kingdom – also known as Himyar was established in 110BC, and took as its capital the modern city of Sana'a after the ancient city of Zafar. The kingdom conquered neighboring Saba in 25BC, Qataban in 200CE and Hadramaut in 300CE. It endured until it fell to Christian invaders in 525CE.[3]

House of David – another name for the royal Judean dynasty, this refers to the tracing of lineage to King David referred to in the Hebrew Bible and in the New Testament.

Hull – Nautical. The main body of a ship, exclusive of masts, sails, yards and rigging.[1]

Hieroglyphs – a picture or symbol used in hieroglyphic writing in ancient Egypt. Hieroglyphics was a system of writing in which figures or objects are used to represent words or sounds.[1]

Ibn 'Amm – is the father's brother's son. In many parts of the Middle East, cousin marriage is an allowed practice and a defining feature of the kinship system. In many cases there is not only a preference but a right to marry his father's brother's daughter, wherein if the girl's family wishes to marry her to anyone else, they must first get permission of the father's brother's son.[3]

Incarnation – Theology. 1) Any bodily manifestation of a supernatural being. 2) The embodiment of God in the human form of Jesus.[1]

Isaiah – was a Jewish prophet documented by the Biblical Book of Isaiah to have lived around the time of 8th century BCE.[3]

Isis – is a goddess from the polytheistic pantheon of Egypt. She was first worshipped in ancient Egypt, and later her worship spread throughout the Roman Empire and the greater Greco-Roman world.[3]

Jerusalem – the capital of ancient and modern Israel, regarded as holy by Jews, Christians and Moslems.[1]

Judea – The southern section of ancient Palestine, now comprising southern Israel and southwestern Jordan.[1]

Julius Caesar – (Gaius Julius Caesar 100-44BC) Roman statesman, general and historian, dictator (49-44BC); assassinated.[1]

Khalan – an imaginary village in the northern region of the Hadramaut Kingdom of Arabia (now Yemen).

King David - According to the Books of Samuel in the Hebrew Old Testament, David was the second king of the ancient kingdom of Israel (Judah) and according to the Gospels of Matthew and Luke, an ancestor of Jesus. His life is conventionally dated from 1040-970BC, his reign over Judah from 1010-970BC.[3]

King Herod the Great – (74/73BC – 4BC) also known as Herod I, was a Roman client king of Judea referred to as the Herodian kingdom. Vital details of his life are recorded in the works of the 1st century CE Roman-Jewish historian Josephus. He also appears in the Christian

New Testament as the ruler of Judea at the time of the birth of Jesus, who orders the Massacre of the Innocents. He is known for his colossal building projects throughout Judea, including his expansion of the Second Temple in Jerusalem, the construction of the port of Caesarea Maritima, the fortress at Masada and Herodium.[3]

King Phraates IV – King of Parthia reigned 37BC – 2BC, who murdered his father Orodes II and his brothers to secure the throne. After a battle with Mark Antony in 36, which Antony lost Phraates lost his throne in a revolt (for four years). He regained power in 30. The Roman Emperor Augustus made peace with Phraates and sent him a Roman concubine named Musa. On her advice Phraates sent four of his sons to Rome, where they remained as hostages of Augustus. Phraates was later poisoned by Musa, who then ruled jointly with her son Phraates V. [3]

King Phraates V – The son of Parthian King Phraates IV and his Roman mother Musa, he ruled Parthia from 2BC to 4CE. The historian Josephus alleges that Phraates V married his mother Musa and this being unacceptable to the Parthians, they rose up and overthrew him, offering the crown to Orodes II.[3]

Koosh – (or kush) is the word used for camels to command them to lie down.

Kulaf – a type of tall cone-shaped headgear worn by Parthian nobles. [9]

League – a unit of distance equal to three statute miles.[1]

Legion – The major unit of the Roman army consisting of 3,000 to 6,000 infantry troops and 100 to 200 cavalrymen.[1]

Legionnaires – any member of a Roman legion.[1]

Macedonian – A native or inhabitant of Macedonia, an ancient kingdom in the Balkan Peninsula, now a region in Northern Greece.[1]

Magi – The Zoroastrian priestly caste of the Medes and Persians; the "wise men of the East" who traveled to Bethlehem to pay homage to the infant Jesus.[1]

Media – An ancient country of southwestern Asia, now the northwestern region of Iran.[1]

Mesopotamia - The ancient country between the Tigris and Euphrates Rivers; also the name of the geographical region in the Tigris-Euphrates river system, corresponding to modern day Iraq, Kuwait, the northwestern section of Syria as well as parts of Southeastern Turkey and southwestern Iran.[3]

Messiah prophecies – a term referring to many prophecies found in the Old Testament of the Bible which refer to a Messiah who is to come.

Milky Circle - another name of for The Milky Way. The term "Milky Way" is a translation of the Latin via lacteal from the Greek galaxias kyklos (milky circle).[3]

Morning star – In astronomy. The most commonly used as a name for the planet Venus when it appears in the east before sunrise; may also be used to describe the first star seen before sunrise.[3]

Moses – The ancient Jewish lawgiver who led the Israelites out of Egypt. According to the Old Testament (Book of Exodus), he was a former Egyptian prince who later in life became a religious leader and to whom the authorship of the Torah (Ten Commandments) is traditionally attributed.[1]

Mount Carmel – is a coastal mountain range in northern Israel stretching from the Mediterranean Sea toward the south-east. Its elevation is 1,724 feet, it is 24 miles long and 5 miles wide.[3]

Myrrh – An aromatic gum resin obtained from several trees and shrubs of the genus Commiphora, of India, Arabia, and eastern Africa, It is used in incense and perfume, and was one of the gifts traditionally given by the Magi to the infant Jesus.[1]

Nabateans – A tribe on northwestern Arabia whose kingdom centered in Petra, and flourished from the fourth century BC to the first century AD.[1]

Nazareth – A town in northern Israel, traditionally the site of Jesus' childhood.[1]

Nisean horses – this horse breed which is now extinct, was once native to the town if Nisaia in ancient Persia. They were highly sought after in the ancient world.[3]

Ossuary – a container or receptacle, such as an urn or vault, for holding the bones of the dead.[1]

Papyrus – a kind of paper made from the pith or stems of this plant, used in antiquity as a writing material; a tall aquatic sedge, cyperus papyrus, of southern Europe and northern Africa.[1]

Parchment – The skin of a sheep or goat for writing or painting upon.[1]

Parthian Empire – also known as the Arsacid Empire, was a major Iranian political and cultural power in the ancient Near East. It was founded in the 3rd century BC by Arsaces I of Parthia, leader of the Parni tribe, when he captured the Parthia region, then a satrapy in rebellion against the Greek Seleucid Empire. At its height, the Parthian Empire stretched from the northern reaches of the Euphrates in what is now eastern Turkey to eastern Iran. The empire, located on the Silk Road trade route between the Roman Empire and the Han Dynasty in China, quickly became a center of trade and commerce. With the expansion of Arsacid power the seat of government shifted from Nisa, Turkmenistan to Ctesiphon along the Tigris (south of modern Bagdad, Iraq) although several other sites also served as capitals.[3]

Pelusium – was an important city in the eastern extremes of Egypt's Nile Delta 30 km. to the southeast of the modern Port Said.[3]

Pornai – is the ancient Greek word for prostitutes. In the classical era of ancient Greece, pornai were slaves of barbarian origin; starting in the Hellenistic era the case of young girls abandoned by their fathers can be added. They were considered to be slaves until proven otherwise. Pornai were usually employed in brothels.[3]

Praesidium – was the term for an ancient Roman fort, guard post or garrison.[3]

Qana – According to the Periplus, Qana was an ancient city on the South Arabian coast that was the chief port of the frankincense bearing land of the Hadramaut Kingdom. Qana was the port to where all the frankincense grown in the land was brought. Qana carried on an active trade with Roman Egypt, exchanging frankincense for many other products. Based on archaeological evidence it seems that Qana was founded sometime in the 1st century BC and that its foundation was directly connected with the establishment and expansion of the regular sea trade between Egypt and India.[10]

Red Sea – an elongated body of water, about 170,00 square miles in area, separating the Arabian peninsula from Africa; now connected with the Mediterranean Sea by the Suez Canal.[1]

Rome – as used in this story, Rome is both the city and the ancient Roman kingdom, republic and empire.

Royal Road – was an ancient highway reorganized and rebuilt by the Persian King Darius the Great in the 5th century BC. Darius built the road to facilitate rapid communication from Susa to Sardis. Mounted couriers could travel 1677 miles in seven days; the journey took ninety days on foot. Stretches of the Royal Road across the central plateau of Iran are coincident with the major trade route known as The Silk Road. The construction of the road as improved by Darius was of such quality that the road continued to be used until Roman times.[3]

Sand storms – a dust or sand storm is a meteorological phenomenon common in arid and semiarid regions. Drylands around North Africa and the Arabian Peninsula are the main terrestrial sources of airborne dust. The term sandstorm is used most often in the context of desert sandstorms, especially in the Sahara Desert, or places where sand is a more prevalent soil type than dirt or rock. Prolonged and unprotected exposure of the respiratory system in a dust storm can cause silicosis, an incurable condition that may lead to lung cancer. There is also danger of "dry eyes" which in severe cases can lead to blindness.[3]

Satrap – the name given to governors of the provinces of the ancient Median and Archaemenid Empires and in several of their successors. In the Parthian Empire, the king's power rested on the support of the noble families who ruled large estates, and supplied soldiers and tribute. City-states within the empire enjoyed a degree of self-government and paid tribute to the king. Parthian satrapies were smaller and less power-ful than the Archaemenid potentates that preceded them.[3]

Second Temple - was an important Jewish Holy Temple which stood on the Temple Mount in Jerusalem between 516 BCE and 70 CE. It replaced Solomon's Temple (the First Temple) which was destroyed by the Neo-Babylonian Empire in 586 BCE, when Jerusalem was conquered and a portion of the population of the Kingdom of Judah was taken into exile in Babylon.[3]

Seleucia on the Tigris – Eighteen miles south of modern Baghdad lies the site of Seleucia-on-the-Tigris, which rose, flourished and dwindled away between 307 BC and 215 AD. In the second and third centuries BC it was one of the great Hellenistic capitals comparable to Alexandria in Egypt and greater than Antioch in northern Syria. Lying at the confluence of the Tigris and a major canal from the Euphrates, Seleucia was in a position to receive traffic from both great waterways. As a vital trading center, she presided over the exchange of goods from Central Asia, India, Persia and Africa.[11]

Skiff – a flat-bottomed boat of shallow draft, having a pointed bow and a square stern and propelled by oars, sail or a motor.[1]

Storax - is a natural resin isolated from the wounded bark of Liquidambar orientalis.[3]

Temple of Serapis – An important religious structure in Berenike, probably founded in the late Ptolemaic period, was also dedicated to several Egyptian gods. The temple was built of gypsum blocks, a very soft material. Most of the temple decoration is early Roman.[7]

Tetarte – In Roman times, a 25% ad valorem [ta2x] levied on cargoes carried by vessels.[7]

Tunic – is a simple slip-on garment made with or without sleeves, usually knee length or longer, belted at the waist, and worn as an under or outer garment by men and women of ancient Greece and Rome.[2]

Toga – the loose outer garment worn in public by citizens of ancient Rome.[2]

Via Maris - is the modern name for an ancient trade route, dating from the early Bronze Age, linking Egypt with the northern empires of Syria, Anatolia and Mesopotamia — modern day Iran, Iraq, Israel, Turkey and Syria. In Latin, *Via Maris* means "way of the sea." It is a historic road that runs along the Palestine coast. It was the most important route from Egypt to Syria (the Fertile Crescent) which followed the coastal plain before crossing over into the plain of Jezreel and the Jordan valley.[3]

Yahweh – a name for God assumed by modern scholars to be a rendering of the pronunciation of the Tetragrammaton (the four Hebrew letters YHWH or JHVH used as a symbol or substitute for the ineffable name of God).[1]

Zoroastrianism – A Persian religion founded in the 6th century BC by the prophet Zoroaster (Aka: Zarathustra), promulgated by the Avesta, and characterized by worship of a supreme god Ahura Mazda who requires good deeds for help in his cosmic struggle against the evil spirit Ahriman.[2]

BIBLIOGRAPHY

1. American Heritage Dictionary, Houghton Mifflin Co., Boston, 1978

2. Merriam Webster's Collegiate Dictionary, tenth Ed., Merriam-Webster, Inc., Springfield, MA 1993

3. Wikipedia

4. Columbia Univ. electronic encyclopedia

5. Trails.com

6. Merriam-Webster Dictionary online

7. Berenike and the Ancient Maritime Spice Route; Steven E. Sidebotham, Univ. of CA Press, 2011; p.81-85, 219

8. Catholic Encyclopedia online

9. A History of the Jews in Babylonia; Jacob Neusner, Scholars Press, Atlanta, GA, May 2000

10. Food for the Gods: New Light on the Ancient Incense Trade; David Williams and A.C.S. Peacock, Oxbow Books, Oxford, UK, Feb. 2007

11. The Kelsey Museum of Archaeology Online – Univ. of Michigan 1998